BLACK
GLASS

Black Glass is published by Elder Signs Press, Inc.

Cover & Design by Deborah Jones.

FIRST EDITION
10 9 8 7 6 5 4 3 2 1
Published in November 2008

ISBN: 1-934501-06-9 (Hardcover)
           1-934501-07-7 (Trade Paperback)

Printed in the U.S.A.

Published by Elder Signs Press
P.O. Box 389
Lake Orion, MI 48361-0389

www.eldersignspress.com

BLACK GLASS

BY JOHN SHIRLEY

2008

For Bruce, Rudy, Bill, Richard, Lew, and Pat

Special Thanks to
William Gibson
and
Paula Guran
(Paula, extra thanks for extra editorial help)

SOME REMARKS FROM THE AUTHOR
ABOUT THE *LOST CYBERPUNK NOVEL*

Black Glass was conceived under a different name and as a different kind of project, in the early days of cyberpunk, by myself and William Gibson. That's not William Gibson the playwright; I mean the author of *Neuromancer* and *Spook Country* and all his books in between. We had collaborated on a couple of projects before this one. I don't remember who came up with the main idea or the general story of *Black Glass*. I know I wrote up an elaborate tale based on our discussion; I'm the one who fleshed it out and Bill approved it. But then the project got derailed, we both got diverted, and Bill was swept off to collect awards, count his royalties, chill with rock stars, and work on other projects. Subsequently, long subsequently, I remembered the book and inquired; Bill is a busy guy and turned the whole thing over to me.

So some years later I have written the novel, which I think of as the Lost Cyberpunk Novel; I have written it in its entirety. No one else should be held to blame.

Cyberpunk fiction, as written by Bruce Sterling, Lew Shiner, Pat Cadigan, Richard Kadrey, Rudy Rucker and William Gibson (oh—and me), has more roots than the obvious Samuel R. Delany novels (like *Nova* and *Dhalgren*), John Brunner novels (like *Shock-wave Rider* and *Stand on Zanzibar*) and, well, writing by Philip Dick and Alfred Bester and JG Ballard and Michael Moorcock's NewWave sf, generally. Its antecedents reach back into noir; into hardboiled crime fiction and certain kinds of detective novels. Agatha Christie? Hell no. But James M. Cain? Hell yes. Dashiell

Hammett. John D. MacDonald—my memory is that Gibson and Sterling both mentioned, to me, having read most of John D. MacDonald. We all read Jim Thompson, too, probably. And certain very gritty, darkly urbane spy novels were important to cyberpunk: Len Deighton and especially early John le Carré.

Many of William Gibson's short stories and early novels share a tone and surface texture not dissimilar to le Carré and, at times, to the hardboiled, hardnosed detective writers. Crime novel heroes are people on the edge; even when they are working for the law, they don't mind breaking it along the way; they womanize, they slap gunsels around, they smoke, they drink. They're moody sons of bitches who slouch down dirty sidewalks under flickering streetlights. Cyberpunk characters have that same grim, doomed, resigned, but simmeringly angry feel about them.

All of these ancestors flock from the past and come home to roost in *Black Glass*. This is, unabashedly, a crime novel set in the future; its hero, Richard Candle, while a nuanced guy into meditation, is descended from old-style pulp detective heroes. He'd have been perfectly comfortable in *Black Mask* magazine.

I haven't tried to be as technologically updated as, no doubt, some of the new crop of cyberpunk writers are. Things happen so fast now I'd never be caught up and wouldn't fit into the current mode of compacted, cryptographically intense expression. I have not culled a great many terms, memes or tropes from *Wired* Magazine or *Jane's*, or the edgiest technoblogs, or 4chan. But the story has been updated, according to my lights, from the original project; it is both "classic" cyberpunk and a modern science-fiction novel. It is also a John Shirley cyberpunk novel; hence the recurrence of musical references, music as a kind of setting, lyrics, rock-inflected characters, and other idiosyncrasies that hopefully are more endearing than annoying. I didn't try to write the book in a 'postmodern' style; it's not post-Gibson, either. I wrote this book, in this era, more or less the way I wrote those books back then. That's how I write the stuff.

The language of Richard Candle's future society would probably be mostly understandable to us, but would have far more new slang and neologisms than I have provided it with. However, I have undertaken to provide a little, a taste, of the lingo of his time.

I doubt if it is language that we will really see in the future but I feel it has the ring of real slang about it and, to my ear, it works. I have provided the *Black Glossary* to explicate certain terms. And I'd like to point out that, as now, people in the future will not use slang terms in every instance in which they might apply. Sometimes they use them, sometimes they use something else.

Black Glass, perhaps, brings cyberpunk full circle. In a way, it's a "pulp novel of ideas." But it is a work of cyberpunk science-fiction; it is woven with science fiction imagery and lit up by science-fiction ideas. It is a crime novel, a novel of the street, and it's a novel of political attitude: most cyberpunk novels reflect a jaded reaction against authority; an assumption that a world dominated by corporations is a world that was stolen from you before you were born.

But my main hope for *Black Glass* is simply that readers will enjoy it as entertainment.

—*J.S., February 2008*

Black Glossary

Some of the neologisms and slang in the novel, like EnviroFoam, *are self explanatory enough to not need inclusion in the glossary, and some, like* thugflesh, PiP *and* exo-suit, *are explained in the story by context or exposition.*

ALLWALL—building materials made of a wide, very wide, variety of recycled materials, often recycled trash paper and shredded plastic, with bits of animal bone. But not as mysterious as Mystercyke, which comes from China.

BLOGMOUTHING—babbling, often while drunk or stoned. Indiscreet jabber.

CASIMIR FORCE—something quite real in our own time, a quantum mechanics effect which causes objects to stick together; it can be engineered for the opposite effect, a degree of levitation.

CHECKY—a checky is a woman, attractive, very together; not a bimbo.

CLICKED AT—as in "Where you clicked at?" Where someone has gone to. Where they are.

DEEZY—a wimp. Deezy Collins was a flamboyant effeminate-male streaming video performer, known for squealing when startled. Was not homosexual.

DOUBLE-YOU-TEE-EFF—verbalizing WTF. What the fuck.

DROP-CALL—bad info, or simply "bullshit."

DUH-TAUNTS—more pejorative but mostly same as "dilettantes" from which it is probably derived, but spliced with "Duh!" Emphasis always on first syllable. Like sneering, "Amateurs!"

EX—it depends, but as a verb it means to leave, to split, to hit the road.

FLOW—money. Especially electronically transferred World Dollars.

A GINGER—a genetic engineer available to the general public. You can hire him to give you an extra whatever.

HAPPYCRAP—New-Age-type bullshit.

HODE—an expression more or less taking the place of dude, and assumed to be related to dude, but possibly combined with whore. (Though this seems improbable to some linguists as *hode* is not particularly insulting, depending on inflection, and whore usually is, though in fact not always.)

HODEY-BRUDDER—same as hode but affectionate. Not much different than "freak-hode."

HOOK-IN—dealer or other source for illegal virtual reality. (Probably descended from the terms "hook up" or "hooked me up with.")

I-CORE—the possibly mythical sense of independent selfness that a complex enough computing system can supposedly develop.

ISSUING—Feeling good, positive, going ahead with something. Or an adjective for an okay person.

J-PEN—A sprawling bootcamp-like penal colony for juveniles.

MYSTERCYKE—recycled materials from truly unguessable, possibly toxic sources. Anything might've gone into it.

NOISE FLOGGERS—a program that creates thousands of unreal transactions and apparent data transfers in order to hide the real ones. An online tech business smoke screen.

NUMBDUMB—stoned. More for drugs than alcohol.

O-SOURCE—from *open source*, someone who's okay, they're cool now, you can trust them.

PAGOTHS—Pagan Goths (pronounced pay-goths).

ROTTERS—from 'rotors', microscopic rotor-shaped nanomachines that float through the brain stimulating brain cells, can easily be remote-tinkered with so they over-stimulate and "rot" them.

SEX SUIT—a clinging outfit that covers your body from mouth to toes, which transmits the ghostly computer-generated sensation of a lover to your skin, while VR recreates the sights and sounds of the sexual encounter. The basic model includes a choice of genital suction-sock or penetration probe.

SINKITIES—girls, especially "easy" girls. (Debate about origins of this slang term: Possibly from 'sin' and 'kitties', but some philologists enigmatically insist it's more likely related to 'sink'.)

SIGNALER—an illegal means to activate a cell phone, or phone implant, or bluetooth, when any one of them has been shut down for non payment.

SNAPPER—also called a snaptop, equivalent of a laptop in Candle's time; snaps down to fairly small, like a wallet; snaps open, piece by piece, fairly large, like today's laptop. Flexible screen. Snapper has a different meaning in the UK.

SQUATZY—AKA SQUAT BIZ—A business that occupies an abandoned property, operates "under the radar" of the State, unlicensed, very impromptu. Rooted in the late 20th century, to some extent in New York, but especially Europe.

PHISHLINE—any big lie.

THE TEXER—the shortest explanation.

THIRDY CARD—when your only money is on the buy card you carry, and it's precious little. Thirdy from Third World.

TROLL—an insulting term, originally something to do with irritating Internet behavior, or hoaxes, now just a general insult.

V-RAT—hard core illegal Virtual Reality addict. (May be used as a general derogatory calumny, like 'crackhead'.) They're obsessed with taking a V-RIDE.

WANX—a mild, unseriously pejorative term for a friend or acquaintance, probably from the British "wanker." Not quite so pejorative as wanker.

WHAT SEARCH—What's up?

WI-HIGH—addiction, originally technologically based addiction of any kind but now any addiction may be referred to with a variation, as an alcoholic is called a wine-wi, and so on.

WD—World Dollars are a global currency, instituted after the Third Global Economic Crisis, and used all over the world, with only a few countries insisting on their old currency. A WD in Candle's future buys more than a US dollar does now.

YEX—a street drug descended from MDMA, aka 'X', but allegedly made partly from animal brain extracts, some of them often decayed so that the pill has a rotten-meat smell. Hence "yex" was *yech* combined with *X*.

HAS TO BE
CHAPTER ONE—
THAT'S HOW IT IS, HODE,
ASK ANYONE

THE CALIFORNIA STATE PEN—
DOWNLOADING DIV—2033 AD

When the screen beeped for a ReMinding, "Pup" Benson was thinking about Cabo San Lucas. Of course, Cabo wasn't much to see nowadays, being mostly underwater, along with a lot of the Mexican coast, but there was a high time to be had in the old days—about the time of Pup's first spring break, what, twenty-three or twenty-four years ago, long before he dreamed he'd end up a guard in an UnMinded Cellblock; back when a college student in Cabo could slide down, over and over, from a hot pinnacle of self gratification: Margueritas over-the-counter Mexican Dexedrine, endless golden spillways of San Miguel *cerveza*, dancing, beach games—and a living search engine for willing women. Long as your parents' credit card held out you were a god.

The girl in Cabo he remembered most vividly (though he'd forgotten her name) was that crazy Japanese-American piece who giggled when he banged her and was ready just about any time at all. "What's that?" she'd asked playfully, with a pretense of wide eyes, every time he flipped out his business end. "That's my little puppy," he'd say. She'd giggle and she'd pet his puppy and he wondered whatever had happened to that girl–

"BENSON GET IT IN FUCKING GEAR–"

Pup practically shot out of his orange plastic staff-lounge seat, because Stremp, with his black D.I.'s voice, had bounced the shout off the back of his head. "FUCK, Stremp, you are not in the motherfuckin' ComSee anymore–" Stremp, a tall chubby bald black man, had been a trainer for the Community Service Militia. Had been a big hard man and now this job dealing with the UnMinded left Stremp a big soft man.

"We've got two ReMinds and one UnMind to do," Stremp snapped, barely dialing back his bellow, "and I don't have any time for your whining bullshit. Let's go."

Pup ran a hand through his thinning hair, shrugged, and went to the head like he had to piss, just to make the son of a bitch wait. He hated Wednesdays. He hated every workday. He worked whatever shifts the privatized prison system told him to. Weekends had become nearly extinct when unions had.

In the bathroom, Pup looked in the mirror, tweaked some pimples on his nose; doc said he was getting broken veins on it from drinking. You worked in this place, you had to drink sometimes.

"BENSON–!"

Fuck. Pup wanted a drink.

Pup thumbed the greasy tab on the cell lock; the panel in the door became transparent and a stream of light automatically spot-lit the con lying on the padded shelf that passed for an UnMinded's bed.

Richard Candle.

Pup looked at the UnMinded prisoner on the shelf bed, then at the digital image on the remote switcher. Two views of the guy, along with his numbers. Face and numbers matched.

"Yeah, that's him."

He closed the panel, tapped the code. Got it wrong the first time; the door panel blinked red. "Shit." Tried again. Door slid open. Prisoner 788843, in prison blues and slippers, was lying on his back, the way they all did—because that was how regs wanted them—like a dead guy with his hands over his chest, eyes shut, couldn't even see him breathe.

UnMinded he was, but anyone could still see Candle's personality in the lines of his face. A lean, squarish face with deep-set eyes, hard lines to his jaw, a slightly perverse crookedness to his lips; the early-middle-aged face that said: *I'd like to stay on the right side of you so don't fuck with me.* A face that had held an expression of friendly warning for long periods of time.

Pup tapped his wrist remote. In response, Candle opened his eyes. Looking up at the ceiling. No expression in those smoky gray-blue eyes.

"Get out of there, Candle 788843," Stremp said.

Instantly, Candle swung off the table. He stood, looked at them expectantly. No particular expression; no particular lack of expression. Not zombie-like, but not present either.

"Stremp—we ReMind him now?"

"Nah-uh. He's supposed to have a couple hours work detail to get the blood flowing, and anyway we've got a backlog."

"Okayyyyy—Candle, 788843: let's go, out to your right, follow the yellow line to work detail."

Responding to the combination of name and number, Candle went. His expression never changed .

The message scrolling on the ceiling read: *They backon letting prispissin toletday Caning putre back out bodof mindle.*

Terrence Grist reached past Lisha and hit the decrypter. Now the text message read:

They're putting Candle's mind back in his body. They're letting him out of prison. Today.

Grist lay on his back, re-reading the message looping across the ceiling screen; Lisha kept on working, straddling him, keeping his dwindling maleness locked inside the intersection of her womanhood, gazing down at him with a practiced simulation of reverence. She was used to Grist reading and phoning during sex.

He read the message again and, wanting to keep his erection, he continued moving his hips, trying not to break rhythm . . .

Candle.

You want to keep it up, don't think about Rick Candle.

He'd penciled this bedding into a busy schedule and he didn't want to waste it. Lisha was expensive—everything about her. Even her face, which he'd paid for: Grist was in bed with himself.

Lisha had been surgically altered to have his face—stylized female, girlish pretty, sure, but it was Grist's face, nano-surgically reproduced. Not too much of a stretch: he'd always had "pretty boy" features, slender, almost fawnlike; not a transexual face but it could have been the gender-bending visage of a rock star from the last century. Lisha's variant of his face wasn't virtual, no; virtual was cheap bullshit. Lisha was flesh and blood, face-formed and paid for. She was a high-priced contract wife—very pricey indeed, her agent had been damned good. She'd pretended to like her new face from the moment the form-case was removed, using the acting skills that had been part of her training at the agency. She knew she could get it switched back, or altered to another face, fairly easily.

"Narcissism got a bad rap," he had said to her, as they looked at her new face in a mirror, a year ago. *"The ego really is all there is of a man, or a woman. There is no soul; there is nothing but the ego, and memories. The* me-trix, *we call it, my dear, in the semblant trade. And if you want to be my wife enough, my pampered wife, be my sweet, feminized mirror reflection and be happy."*

Today, in his bedroom, four digicams multiplied him on the surround-screens. Vapors of mild, designer-stimulant enhanced the high-oxy house environment, disposing him to stonily muse: Here he was complete, two identities dovetailed into one, and what an expression dovetailed was, considered just now, the tail of a dove, the white bird who . . .

What about Candle? If that pit-bull of an ex-cop . . .

His attachment to the moment's pleasures melted away. He felt he was falling away from Lisha, falling right through the bed into a cold aloneness.

A side effect of the vapors, he told himself. *You're not alone. You're surrounded by those who work for you.*

Candle . . . Maeterling . . .

What was left of his erection . . . went.

"What's uh matter?" Lisha said muzzily, smothering a yawn.

"I just . . . I remembered something, an emergency. Business . . . emergency. Off . . . please."

Lisha dutifully rolled off, casually and professionally, like a friendly restaurant worker clearing a table.

Grist sat up, reached for the cut-class bottle next to the bed, decanted brandy into a crystal balloon, drank off half of it and felt a little calmer. He went into the next room, closed the door, stood over the smart table, activated it, whipped his fingers over the selector window for Targer; left the most basic message possible. *"Targer? See who you can pay off. Keep Candle inside. Do what you have to. Or arrange an accident with his . . . machinery. I don't care who his friends used to be."*

Get your mind off Candle . . .

But Candle had found out about Grist taking advantage of the skim-scam that Maeterling had cooked up. He'd found out after he'd taken the rap for his brother, right before the UnMinding. Too late. No more cop empowerment. No access to those accounts. But Candle had found out from Maeterling. Former Grist employee. The little weasel had tried to make a deal with Candle . . . too late. *"I'm pretty sure Mr. Grist waited before informing the cops of my skim and used it himself. If you can get proof we can blackmail him . . ."*

Grist had gotten rid of Maeterling. And Candle had to take the UnMinding to cover his brother. No time to do anything else. Should have had Candle taken care of while he was UnMinded—but Candle had friends in law enforcement who put out the word: Any accident befalls Candle in prison, they'd investigate.

And now Candle was getting out.

Feeling cold, though the rooms were exquisitely temperature-controlled, Grist returned to Lisha.

He sat on the bed, tapped the smart table next to the bed, re-played his v-mail as Lisha lay back on the pillows, her whole body a shrug, and rolled to face her own console, tuned it to iVogue.

He thought: She's losing her ability to pretend she cares when I stop making love to her. There was a tell-tale smell in the room, lingering on his genitals—a chemical smell he was tempted to complain about. It was her pre-applied vaginal lubricant. She'd put it in right before their session, obviously. It was perfumed but you could smell the lubricant chemicals underneath. Which meant that she couldn't get excited enough to lubricate naturally. With him, anyway. He toyed with the idea of hiring someone to excite her, some body builder perhaps. But it was insulting, his having to do that. No: She was going to make an effort. He'd talk to her later. He reached for the towel dispenser, wiped the lubricant off with one hand, his other hand scrolling through messages.

There was v-mail from Mitwell—a cherubic exec wearing a formal blue-silk choker, his unaltered, plebian face an irritant to Grist.

Really, Grist felt, this whole business of resisting facial improvements, with nanosurgery so handy for the moneyed, was an obnoxious fad. "Naturalism." Having to look at faces so natively unattractive was like having to gaze on a man's scrotum. But Mitwell was "a natural." Hypocritically, though, he often used a semblant. They all did.

"When you're ready, sir," Mitwell (or his semblant?) was saying. "Just hit 'two' for the semblant spot—this one's for executives' clubs."

Grist tapped the console's control and Mitwell's image was replaced by a lovely blond spokesperson, her hair artfully tousled, her tone intimate. *"I understand. I do. You're busy. That's the point. You've heard about semblants—only you haven't, not really. You only think you have. Seventy percent semblance wasn't enough for Slakon. The new Slakon semblants copy . . . you. Your image, your presentation, your personality . . . completely."*

At Grist's urging, Slakon had trademarked the word "semblant" two years before. The word "simulation" came off as something fake and even cheap. And they didn't want cheap—semblants should be about *glamour.* Success. Money. The term "semblant" was rapidly replacing the older words like "mindclone" and "cyberclone" and all the other distastefully antiquated "clone" derivatives. There was nothing biological about a semblant, after all.

As Grist watched, the new spot cut to an image of a young male exec looking critically at variants of his own semblant. They looked fuzzy. *"Everything you are—"* The images then came sharply into focus. The exec looked into the camera and put his finger over his smiling lips: Shhhh! *"—you edit for privacy at your discretion."* Two of the semblant images put their fingers over their mouths, with slightly different expressions; the third one simply winked.

"And now Slakon can 'semblant' your mind for up to fifteen meetings at once!"

The spot showed the exec leaning back in an easy chair, colorful cocktail in one hand, the other hand resting lightly on the thigh of the pretty blond announcer. Wearing elegantly-draped long, filmy blue lingerie, she was now perched with an improbable buoyancy on the arm of his chair. Behind them a multiply-windowed screen showed the exec's semblants taking digital meetings, screens cheerfully talking to other, endlessly replicating screens . . .

"Take care of business . . ."

". . . with Slakon semblants!" the exec chimed in, lifting his glass to the camera.

Then the final tagline from an authoritative male voice: *"They'll believe . . . you really are there!"*

Small disclaimers zipped by at the bottom of the image: *Contracts closed by semblants are not legally binding unless Self-Certified.*

There was another version for women execs. Grist reckoned both of them too on-the-nose vulgar for their target audience. And too retro.

Grist hit call back, using his standard business semblant, the digital face matching what he was saying. But the face Mitwell saw was composed, sober, attached to a fully dressed body. No live cam of his nudity for Mitwell. "Mitwell? I hate it! Too in-your-face, too retro. Like something from the last century . . . ugh."

"I think it was supposed to be campy that way or something."

"We don't do campy. Get something arty, something without all this stiff voiceover business. Get Jerome-X or somebody to do music-vid. I understand he's finally Sold Corporate. Get on it."

Grist clicked off line and drank some more brandy. "You wanta drink, Lisha?"

"Nah-uh."

"You sulking?"

"Nah-uh."

"No?" He had an impulse to please her. Strange, since he should be angry with her using lube to be able to make it with him, but he felt apologetic, in some undefined way. "Wanta take your little round ass shopping?"

"Yeah!" She suddenly sat up, all perky, playing a happy little girl, beaming.

Happy little girl; but it was almost his face, and suddenly he was reminded of himself as a little boy.

Little boy in Los Angeles. Back before they built the dike to protect L.A. from the rising seas. That far back. Visiting his dad at the Jet Propulsion Lab. The tight-assed old son of a bitch already dying of cancer, but refusing to leave his desk until they pushed him out the door. His dad blinking at him from his office chair—hunched there, feet gripping the floor as if he were physically resisting being pushed out for the next guy; an emaciated comma of a man, trying to remember why the boy was there. Not quite saying, "Why are you here?" And the boy not quite saying, "This is part of your visitation, I was supposed to see you at work." Later at home, overhearing Mom talking on the phone to her sister about losing the child support money when Dad died. Her main concern. Money trumped death. It was a lesson.

He wanted to be alone, and just get numbdumb. He rolled over, turned up the vapors, and set the cameras on playback.

Dow Jones/Pacific Industries tickered digitally by, on the ceiling, underneath the images of himself and Lisha hard at it. His previous contract wife had been annoyed when he checked out the trading while he was banging her.

Without even looking at Lisha, he keyed in an additional ten grand for her card. Sending her shopping. Wanting her gone as quickly as possible. "There you go . . ." he murmured.

Lisha kissed him on the cheek when "transfer approved" appeared on the screen and she hopped out of the bed, psyched for shopping.

It's like guarding robots, Pup thought. *What's the point?*

The only true robot here, though, was a single robot security guard, a vertical column on wheels with two extender arms, that rumbled slowly back and forth, scanning IDs, biometrically cross referencing faces, and otherwise having nothing to do in the long low cinderblock room. A cloudy armor-glass ceiling lit the room with shadowless uniformity. A room of men ministering to machines; the chuffing-squeak of hard metal kissing soft metal; a faint clanking, a whirring, the occasional comment of one guard to another and a pensive absence of other human noises. The machine shaped and programmed license plates with the digital likeness of the owner imaged in, the face of the licensee shifting back and forth between face-on and profile, the LP numbers scrolling slowly by next to the face, over and over. Now and then some legislator grumped about the slower pace of plate manufacture, with human beings operating the machines—the whole thing could have been entirely automated, but the law said the men had to have some kind of physical employment. Make-work, busy work for human hands.

Those human hands were Candle's, now, and Garcia's, expressionlessly pushing plates under the digiprinter, taking them out, while other men sorted plates by region numbers: other UnMinded whose identities were irrelevant—living cartoons of men, like the animated bot figures in digi-games, making rote motions, without the bitching and sniping that should have made them human. And without relationships, often troublesome relationships, between prisoners. No friendships could blossom in the aridity of UnMinding—and no enmities.

It bothered Pup; he never got used to it. There was no risk here. No interpersonal "heat" of any kind, from a man utterly subordinated to a device clamped to the base of his skull.

So it was almost a relief when, once or twice a year, one of the prisoners made a mistake. Maybe the machinery stuck, or maybe the prisoner was moving slowly because of—who knows? —a virus the blood monitors had missed.

Today it was the machine: the imager needed cleaning, and a plate got stuck, halfway out, and Garcia automatically reached in and pulled and the imager came unstuck suddenly, stamping to imaging-range, a quarter-inch from the plate, and—*crunch*, the bones of Garcia's hand were shattered.

Garcia didn't react—and that made Pup's gut lurch worse than the *crunch*. Feeling no pain, Garcia didn't even pull his hand out, and the imager came down again as Pup ran over to jerk him free, a second too late—the hand was crushed out of shape, it was bloody toothpaste coming out of a flattened glove, and Pup almost heaved.

Stremp heard the injury alarm, came rushing in—and made a snorting sound as if it were Pup's fault. "Garcia 667329, go to the infirmary."

Garcia walked calmly and obediently—hand dripping a trail of blood—out the door. They knew he'd go where he was sent, and of course the cameras were watching, anyway.

Stremp called to Sokio Wojakowski, the Japanese guard, or half Japanese, and told him to watch things, they were going to have to do a digifile report on the injury, even though the whole thing had already been boxed by the monitoring cam, and—Stremp glanced at his watch—it was just about time to ReMind Candle out, too.

Grist was leaning back in the perfect embrace of his desk chair, looking out the transparent office wall, watching the chopper land on the helipad just outside and thinking how much the new Casimir-force-assisted choppers looked like they were a detached part of the buildings they were landing on: smooth metal and glass curves, almost no seams, and the same colors as the building, the Slakon metallic blue and chrome with thin stripes of flat red. The chopper landing was like a limb reconnecting to a body. Which was good. Everything about the company should look like that; everything should suggest cohesion, centralized purpose. Sometimes he thought corporate authority was 90% architecture and engineering design.

Soothing thoughts helped him keep his temper. Underneath, he was seething. The risk that Candle might get out. And the accusations from Bill Hoffman. The board accusing him of hacking them—accusing him as much as it dared.

Targer was just stepping down from the chopper, trotting across to the door. Not looking at Grist as he came because he couldn't see through the window from his side. Grist told the smart desk to open the door so Targer wouldn't have to waste time with the security IDs.

About fifty, Target had hair the color of steel, nose like an eagle's beak, not a jot of wasted energy in his movements. He was British, as much as anyone was anymore; most socialized people were WorldWeb, with not a great deal of hometown culture left. Target wore his Slakon Security uniform, quietly paramilitary. Not surprised that Grist wanted to see him "PiP", *physically in person*. This was high security stuff.

"I'm afraid I won't be able to stop Candle's release," Targer said flatly, without preliminaries.

Grist leaned forward, and removed the UV goggles he'd hitched on top of his head to hold back his glossy hair. He'd just come in from the putting green on the other side of the roof.

He tossed the goggles on the desk in irritation, waving Targer to a chair. The other three walls of the room were displays, two with real-time shots of the Rockies in heavy snow, places Grist liked to ski; one of the walls showing Grist's best moments as a golfer, playing in a loop. A perpetually sunny, successful day on the links, that wall.

"It was your job to keep him in jail, Targer. I gave you a fat bonus to keep him in jail. You're my fucking Security. And now I don't feel secure." He looked away from one of his few holes-in-one, and directly at Targer, who didn't blink. "This is pretty fucking insecure, Targer."

"I did advise you to kill him, sir," Targer said, with maddening calm.

Grist grunted. "Too much scrutiny on Candle." He sighed. ". . . but I should have done it."

"It wasn't easy to get him put away. Candle was a decorated federal cop with a lot of friends. Senator Williger–"

"Senator Williger! I should have gotten rid of that asshole too!"

Targer nodded. "Yes, sir."

"Is Williger behind the quick release?"

"Maybe. Don't think so. He's busy with that Korean girls' school scandal. I don't see it being him. Someone in the privatized layer of government, I'm guessing. Someone with judicial connections. Lot of ex-cops there, maybe loyal to Candle. Or it could have been a competitor—found out about it. Wanting to do you shady."

"Could have been—that takes in most of the Fortune 33. Hoffman, Bill Hoffman—he's a good possibility. You sure we can't arrange a workplace misfortune for Candle before he walks out that door?"

"Everything that happens in that jail is monitored, black boxed. We still can't get into those boxes. It'd be hard to pull off without a lot of preparation, a lot of heavy bribery. By then he'll be back on the streets with his full mind—and his memory."

Grist sniffed. "Easy enough to kill him once he's out. But if we don't—maybe we can make lemonade, Targer. I'd like to know who's eating my lunch on this. Someone's engineered this release to fuck with me. They'll contact Candle . . ."

"Maybe."

"Who've you got on this?"

"Halido. And I've got Pup Benson on the inside, but I don't know what he can do with the cameras watching . . . He's not much use anyway."

"All right . . . Let me talk to Halido. Put him up there."

Targer tapped the desk and a 'window' sectioned on its display, sunken-eyed Hispanic guy in a stained baseball cap, turning to look at the floating video-eye, backpedaling. The camera moved in on him: there was a star made of diamonds in one of Halido's incisors. "Jesus, Targer, you got a remote bird following me?"

"Shut up. Mr. Grist wants to talk to you."

"I don't see him."

"And you won't, either. Shut up and listen."

Grist knew it irritated Targer to step down the chain of command this way, but there was a nasty variable out there. Candle. A human X-factor. It made Grist feel good to deal with it hands-on.

"Halido," Grist said, "if Candle gets out, don't kill him until I tell you. Stay with him. Report every time he contacts anybody or anybody contacts him."

"You got it, sir."

Grist waved at Targer, and Halido blinked out, replaced with a view down the fairway.

The screen said, "Legal calling, Mr. Grist."

Grist shook his head. "Have my semblant talk to them."

"Yes sir . . ."

"Targer?" Grist said, in that way he had.

"I know," Targer said. "'Get it done'." He made a dour salute and went back to the chopper.

Candle had almost finished throwing up. Wait . . . Okay, there. He was finished. He straightened up, looking around the prison bathroom, touching the bare spot at the base of his skull where the Minding clamp had been.

Looking around himself, really looking, for the first time in . . . how long had it been? How long had the sentence been *for?* For some reason, he couldn't remember. Exactly. Years, anyway. What did he see, now, after those years?

A row of exposed toilets, tiles, stainless steel, everything brightly robot cleaned; a small oval robot was working its way slowly along the wall, under the sink, cleaning as it went.

"You done or what?" the guard asked him. BENSON on his name pin.

Candle nodded, drinking water from the dispenser. He rinsed his mouth. "Is this normal?"

"What, throwing up after you get your mind put back in you? Oh yeah, everybody does it, I guess. Throwing up 'cause they got to be themselves again. Face their shit lives. That was always my theor—"

He stopped in mid-syllable, as Candle turned to look at him, wiping his mouth. Must have looked at the guy harder than he knew because the guard stepped back and put one hand on the beeper on his belt, the other raising his Recoil Reversal stick.

"You fuck with me, you'll never get out of here, pal," Benson said.

"Your voice always shake like that when you're trying to scare people, Benson?" Candle asked, rubbing his eyes.

Then, without being told to, Candle went out the door, into the prison corridor. After a moment the guard followed. Glancing back, Candle saw Benson was pissed off. But he didn't seem inclined to do anything about it.

Good on both counts.

"You're a . . ." The psychiatrist paused to look at the screen inset into the top of his desk again. ". . . Buddhist. Oh, a 'Shiva Buddhist'?" The psychiatrist's cubicle featured the requisite Monet prints and framed certificates; the psychiatrist had a flattop haircut, a blunt, lined faced, and a blunt manner. Probably a former military doctor.

"Shiva Buddhist . . . the term confuses people," Candle said wearily. He didn't feel like talking about it. His stomach was still lurching. Sometimes the little room seemed to lurch too. He shifted in the uncomfortable plastic chair. "That stuff about Shiva Buddhism. Not really much to do with Hindu gods. Some of the Tibetans stuck in the People's Republic stayed Buddhist but . . ." He shrugged. ". . . insisted on armed resistance. During the Tibetan Diaspora, some of them picked up some Hindu symbolism, living in India . . . fits with the idea of armed resistance."

"So philosophically they—and you—can kill an enemy and still remain a Buddhist. It would seem to be a . . . distortion of old Gautama's teaching."

"Depends on which Buddhists you're talking to: always has. In this case it's an adaptation. A recognition of the . . ." The words seemed to drain from his mind, for a few moments. He shook himself.

"Some aphasia is normal, at first, after a ReMinding," the psychiatrist said.

". . . of the, um, interconnectedness of . . . of life and death. Does my philosophy matter?"

Ludicrous to be talking about this now, he thought. He just wanted to get outside the damn building. Someplace private where he could scream if he wanted to.

"I do have a point. My job is to help you realize that no harm has come to you here, that you are not damaged, no one has abused your body sexually, nothing like that—" They both knew that wasn't necessarily true. The psychiatrist went on: "—and I thought if you came to regard the absence of your mind these few years as being a kind of state blissful non-being, almost a nirvana . . ." The psychiatrist winced as if he'd realized he'd said something stupid. "Well, most of our people, when they get out, they have this feeling like . . . like *something died* when they were absent. Like . . . one man called it 'a dead hole in me'. Partly it's the absence of memories—most of it is just fear generated by not knowing what's happened to you all that time. We can provide some camera footage of your daily routine–"

"*No,*" Candle said sharply. "No thanks. I don't think I'll find a home movie of me as a zombie reassuring."

"Very well. We should review your psychological history together—I can arrange therapy for you on the outside."

"Not necessary," Candle said firmly.

"Are you sure? You have a problematic life history. According to the files, your father was the manager of several rock bands. You and your brother grew up around rock musicians. Studios, back stage parties. Your parents had drug issues, your father especially. Mother more of an alcoholic, although at times . . ."

"Wait—where are you getting this from? This business about my old lady wasn't in my HR files at the department–"

"You underwent a deep background check to get National Security clearance when you were a computer cop."

"I don't remember any of that coming up during my background check."

"They didn't tell you. They just investigated you. We're up to Patriot Act Nine now—that gives me access. Now to go on . . . Your father died of a drug overdose. You were fourteen. Your brother was a little younger . . . Your mother disappeared when you were seventeen. Presumed dead. However–"

"That's fucking enough," Candle said sharply. "Tell you what—you want to make me feel better? Open that fucking door and let me walk through it."

The psychiatrist's eyes went flat. His hand strayed to the alarm pad on his desk.

"There . . . are the aggression tests to do. If you seem like you might fly out of control, once out there, after the downloading, well—you'd need therapy time first . . ."

Candle reined himself in. He forced a smile, spread his hands as casually as he could. "Give me the test, Doctor. I'm not hating on anybody. I just want to get out there and see my little brother."

Thinking, as he said it: *One thing I know how to do is fake a negative reading on an aggression test.*

THIS TEXT GOTTA BE
CHAPTER TWO—
—PERSONAL SHIT
'TWEEN ME 'N' YOU

Thirteen of the Fortune 33 in the same room at the same time . . .

They sat uneasily around the long oval table, the transparent wall to one side adjusting, filtering the harsher spectra from the sunset; off-white marble walls on three sides; the corporate logo centered on the wall behind the chairman. In the middle of the high ceilinged rectangle of the Slakon International boardroom was a long glossy-black table inset with charcoal gray consoles, smart panels, light-pens, discreetly recessed displays. There were glasses of wine and carafes of Italian coffee; Bill Hoffman had Earl Grey tea. One console, one refreshment, for each board member waiting for Grist to come to the point. Chairman Grist sat at the head of the table, using the—as Hoffman had once put it— "Sharply unsubtle psychology of sitting right under the corporate logo . . ."

It was rare for the major shareholders to be in the same room, physically, at the same time.

The irony wasn't lost on Hoffman. "What was the reason we were supposed to meet in person?" he asked Grist, his voice silky. "Something about . . . security? As if we couldn't trust screens and semblants? This from the man who insisted we put three billion WD into semblant tech? Semblant tech is supposed to be secure. It is—isn't it?" He smiled, and the smile said: *Hey, I'm just kidding you—only I'm really not. I'm not fucking with you. Only, I am. I'm doing it in a way I can get away with, not that I care very much.*

The smile, the whole expression said all that and more, and everyone knew it.

But his semblant could have expressed the same thing.

Hoffman had shoulder-length white hair, receding from a high, lined, tanned forehead; he was an elegant man who could have been anywhere from forty-five to seventy-five. He wore an old-fashioned gray suit and silvery tie; no wristpad, just a silver Rolex he'd had for fifty years, with dial-hands on it. His face was mostly natural—but Grist assumed he had subtle de-aging nanosurgery. Just enough to retain the dignity and power of an older man, while his face kept the crisp lines of youth.

"You know why we're here in person," Grist said, sipping red wine, maintaining his own carefully tooled smile as he swiveled to look out at the rusty sky. "Because you plan to make accusations." He pronounced it *ack-kew-ZA-tions,* stretching it out with aching mockery. "And one leaked accusation—one public sign of a rupture in trust on the board—can make the stock value shrivel like . . ." He smiled. ". . . a deflated balloon. So it's best we minimize the danger of hacker surveillance. Meaning we meet in person. Now . . . Mr. Hoffman?" Grist spread his hands, looking around at the others, to say: *I just want to get this tiresome business over with . . .*

And he glanced around, wondering how unified they were behind Hoffman.

The Japanese nano-synth chief, Yatsumi, sat straight-backed and quizzical. Beside Yatsumi, the only woman here, except for the rep from Poland, was Claire PointOne, the tall, blond, needle-thin Vice President of Systems Marketing. She'd adopted the odd surname for her own obscure reasons; now she seemed coiled in round-shouldered tension, the elbows in her blue silk suit planted on the table, her long, pale fingers clasped in front of her. She looked fragile—but Grist was aware she held black belts in two forms of martial arts, and was always looking for the main opportunity. Ready to leap into any power vacuum.

The Texas exec, Hank Bulwer—CEO of Southern Cross Inc, a fiber-optics and GPA firm that was now a subsidiary of Slakon—was a thick man with a ruddy face that made grist think of undercooked meat. He toyed with an empty glass, lips pursed.

The stocky Mexican banking exec, Alvarez, in his creamy sweater, gnawed a knuckle. There was a formless anxiety in his dark eyes: a natty, darkly handsome man, charming when he wanted to be; vaguely repulsive to Grist at other times. Prone to watching Claire.

The others didn't matter as much—they were comparatively minor players: Poland Industrial Consortium, Wang Kwan Timed Investments, Moscow Stock Exchange, London Computer Temps, El-Abid Microchips, and Haim Marchson from GlobalWeb: a slim, amazingly superficial man who got a new face from a model catalogue once a year. Marchson always did exactly what Grist told him simply because of what Grist knew about him and the child-star, Dil Windy.

As if bored, Grist shrugged and muttered to his console, prompting a movie-theatre-scale sheet of mediaglass to slide soundlessly from the ceiling over the wall to his right, the display already scrolling international financial data in seven categories. Grist pretended to be deeply interested, and the others couldn't help looking at it.

Hoffman's lips compressed, the smile almost squeezed out.

"I don't have time, Hoffman," Grist said, gazing deep into the columns of data waterfalling-by on the screen, "for these PiP appearances. It is my understanding that you have accusations to make. If you have something real, please share it."

Hoffman shrugged. "It was you who demanded the in-person meeting."

"We were all in town at the same time anyway, except for Hernando–" Grist nodded at Alvarez, " and he didn't have far to come."

"Always something useful to do in Los Angeles," Alvarez said quickly. It was well known he liked escaping from his home in Mexico City and the politically charged social functions his wife was always pressuring him to go to. Consuelo Alvarez had ambitions to be first lady—and if Alvarez didn't make President of Mexico, largely a symbolic position nowadays after all, she might at least be the wife of the Minister of Finance. Alvarez started to light a cigarette, and everyone instantly turned to glare at him.

"If you're going to smoke," Hoffman said, "please do it hygienically."

"Yes, yes, *bueno*," Alvarez said hastily, "Sorry. To be mastered by smoke—a shame, really. My father made his money in tobacco but he always said . . . said I shouldn't . . ."

He lit the cigarette, then hastily put his cigarette case on the table, pressed a stud on the side, and a SmokeSucker appeared, standing at his side. The SmokeSucker image was in the form of a life-sized, transparent, attractive, skimpily dressed Latino-Asian woman, smiling sweetly, her shape conforming to the magnetic field projected by the cigarette case. The SmokeSucker bent over, opened her mouth suggestively, and sucked the smoke from his cigarette and his exhalation, drawing it into a single stream, and then into her body. The smoke swirled inside the field-hologram, bottled like a soul in a body; when he was done smoking the image would blow the particulates into the compression chamber in the back of the cigarette case. Bulwer stared at the SmokeSucker, licking his lips, his eyes glazing.

Grist shook his head and sighed, but let it stand, though he found the shapely SmokeSucker distracting.

"That smoke sucker thing is really tacky," Claire said, looking more disgusted than offended.

Hoffman's smart-chair changed shape as he leaned back into it. "So. Let's get on with it. A few observations . . . *One*: You, Grist, introduced us to the semblant process—"

"To the great profit of our shareholders," Grist interrupted complacently. "And Slakon thrives on pleasing its shareholders."

"*Two*: Some of our semblant programs have been compromised, quite probably copied," Hoffman went on, as if he hadn't heard. "They copied Yatsumi's semblant program, so I understand—Claire's, Alvarez's, Bulwer's—someone's copied their semblants out of me-trix databases . . . *Three*: You have the only 'ware that could make use of these encoded me-trixes—"

"That's a naive assumption," said Grist. "Someone's always a step ahead of us, somewhere. Some hacker, some roaming coffee shop Bedouin." 'Coffee-shop Bedouin' was an outmoded term but Grist had always liked the sound of it. "Obviously someone else wanted your semblants. And, humiliating and embarrassing as it is for me to even have to say this: I really don't have the faintest possible motive—"

"Yes, truly, my friends," Alvarez said, his voice a little muffled by the cigarette—Alvarez was one of those annoying people, Grist noticed, who liked to talk without taking their smokes out of their mouth. Possibly it was Old Time Movie damage. "This is not appropriate, to make accusations based on . . . on supposition."

"I must agree, it is inappropriate," Yatsumi said, in his clipped intonation.

"I've been in this business too long," Hoffman said, "to kiss anyone's hind-parts. You two may do it for me, if you like."

Yatsumi stiffened; Alvarez coughed.

"As to motive," Hoffman continued, "if you have our semblants, Grist, you have *us*, in a way. Which might eliminate, well, so many inconveniences—like opinions which diverge from your own."

"Oh, for—this really is outrageous, Hoffman," Claire PointOne said, looking wistfully at Alvarez's cigarette. She hadn't smoked in years, but one never entirely lost the craving. "Unless . . . in the unlikely event you have some definite evidence . . ."

"Perhaps I do," Hoffman said. "Perhaps I'm going to play the proverbial cards close to the proverbial vest."

Grist shook his head, chuckling. "You're suggesting I've stolen your semblants and I'm going to use them for some shady purpose? We haven't always been simpatico, Hoffman, but—that's sort of pitiful, really. Even . . . diagnosably paranoid."

"Paranoia is a skill," Hoffman said firmly, unruffled. "Since I led the vote to have your finances frozen during the multioptions audit—well, we've had to resort to mediators three times, you and I, on three separate issues. And I suspect you're through mediating." He stood. "If the rest of you wish to be used in this way—that is your own affair. Up to a point."

He walked out of the boardroom, followed by Grist's snort of derision, ten voices of objection, and one muffled cough.

Looking down at his private screen, as the others dished Hoffman for his bad taste and dramatics, Grist wondered what they'd be saying if he weren't in the room.

On Grist's console, set to be unseeable by anyone not in his chair, were images of Claire, Bulwer, Yatsumi, Alvarez, in 3D boxes, side by side. Grist looked at them, then at the originals . . .

A peep from the stud in his ear announced a high priority call. He tapped the smart console: "Receive private call."

"Mr. Grist?" It was Targer. "Halido wants to talk to you about Candle."

Grist touched "Transmit", and the jaw-stud picked up his murmured reply. "Why me?" He dug a finger in his ear; he didn't use the implant often, it gave him an unpleasant buzzing.

"He says he resigns if it isn't you personally, sir. And he is right on top of . . . that thing you were concerned about."

"Put my semblant on it. Halido won't know." He'd get the story from his semblant later.

"I thought so; just wanted to make sure it was okay . . ."

Grist brushed his fingertips over a corner of the console, transferring his coded semblant to Targer's line. His mind straying back to Hoffman. What did this little drama today portend?

Absently glancing out the window, Grist noticed it was raining. Again. They came in so fast nowadays, the rains. Yet there never seemed to be enough water to go around. Things were getting better since the new conservation-system came online: There hadn't been a water riot in a couple of years. He really ought to see what corner of the privatized utilities he controlled. A detail he'd forgotten. Potable water—untainted water—was so precious. So valuable.

And yet there it was: All that water, falling so carelessly from the sky . . .

How did you privatize the sky? he wondered.

As the others nattered on, Grist found himself persistently thinking of Candle. Easy enough to say, *let the semblant handle it*, but hard sometimes to accept it really was doing as good a job as you'd do yourself. Only, it almost always was. But still. Rick Candle. The man had quietly let it be known, through channels, that he knew Danny Candle was being made an example of; that he was taking the fall for Danny but he wasn't going to forget it.

But Candle wouldn't come at him directly. And meanwhile . . . Meanwhile, there was intelligence suggesting that a certain thorn in his side was interested in Candle. Hoffman had been researching Rick Candle. And if he could get hold of Candle, and put pressure on him . . .

It might actually be a good thing if Candle was out. Anyone Candle allied with would likely be Grist's enemy. Candle could lead him to a number of rat's nests.

He'd have to make sure, after the board meeting, that his semblant was fully in the loop on his thinking. They'd do the optimum mindscan.

Hunkering on the van's seat so he could see a bit farther out the window, Shortstack stared at the sign over the metal doors.

California State Penitentiary - Downloading Division.

"I thought it was called UnMinding or Reminding or something," Shortstack said. A balding, long-nosed dwarf in a long, third-hand Army coat, Shortstack was only barely visible from outside the van. He was behind the wheel, using prosthetics to drive. Sitting beside him was Nodder; six foot five and three hundred pounds, he seemed almost to fill the van's cab.

Nodder shrugged. "That's the public name, downloading. It's a misnomer because they don't exactly ever take it out, they just crowd it in some corner of the brain, so its like asleep all the time. They sort of block it with something. Then they put his mind where it should be, awake, let it have control back. Who cares? What am I doing here? That's the key question. I've got it! I'm insane, 'Stack. That's the explanation. I'm waiting for him to get out, and I'm not even going to—"

Nodder slumped over, nodding with narcolepsy, but it was a mild slide and when Shortstack elbowed him in the ribs he came out of it with a jerk, almost hitting his head on the van's ceiling, finishing: ". . . for him get out and I'm not even going to kill the wretch."

"He was the best cop who ever arrested you, Nodder. And up till now I wasn't sure the story was true, maybe he isn't getting out after all . . ." He took a hit from his asthma inhaler.

"—but Nodder . . . that guy in the other car, there, you see him?"

Nodder sipped coffee from an Envirofoam cup, and glanced at the car across the street. "I think that's . . . you mean the blue sedan?"

"Only one with a guy in it you can see from here, for fuck's sake."

"Isn't it that bottom-feeder Halido?"

"I think so. And who'd he start working for? Cast your sleepy mind back."

"Targer."

"Right. And who got Candle busted?"

"Targer. And friends."

"So that makes me think the fucker really is getting out today. And Halido's on him . . ."

"He's looking at us. You see him close his left eye?"

"I saw it. His right is enhanced, he's zooming to ID us. Transmitting our faces."

"Halido can go to the devil."

But Shortstack made himself even smaller in his seat.

The display in Halido's sedan lit up, at the same moment as he turned on the windshield wipers, as if some wire had crossed. But Grist's face glared up at him from the little screen next to the glove compartment: Was it Grist—or his semblant? You couldn't tell, with the new ones. "Well, what is it?" Grist asked, voice small but clear. "Wait, adjust your camera, I'm only picking up half your face."

Halido reached out and tapped the swivel on the lens. "It doesn't track very well anymore . . . There . . ."

"That's better . . . Well? What do you want?"

Halido hesitated, thinking he had probably done something stupid, insisting on talking to Grist directly about this. The wipers swished rain from the windshield; the interior was beginning to steam up. Halido hit the devapor as he spoke. "Uh—Are you the semblant or the real Mr. Grist?"

"What difference does it make? It's all Mr. Grist. Reality is subject to revision—like your salary. You know, we use people like you, instead of in-house pros, because you're more deniable—and because some things we don't want known in-house. You should think about the implications of that. Deniable is expendable."

"You'd lose a good man. I've done a lot of work for you and

Mr Targer the last three years—and I did good work. But things come up–"

"If you have a problem, why couldn't you have bothered Targer with it?"

"Well, boss . . .. There are some other guys waiting for this Candle motherfucker, and at least one of them is a genetically engineered dwarf and this little asshole, to my certain knowledge, crippled two dumb *pendajos* who were trying to rip off the chips that he ripped off first from Indonesian Import–"

"So what?"

"So—you combine that with Candle, who doesn't *just* cripple a man, you get him mad enough, and I ain't being paid, uh, like, *corresponding* to my risk. I'm also going to need help. I don't have any damn semblants to pick up the slack, boss. I need, say, warm bodies, air support, birds-eye surveillance, and—I don't know what all. Targer said he 'could not authorize it'."

"Your tone is repellently disrespectful," Grist said coldly.

"Okay, I'm sorry, that's just my barrio talking, that's how we roll–"

"And you want more money . . . Of all the vulgar trash."

"No, not really, Mr. Grist. It's not exactly 'more money'. I want a real job with a real office and a real secretary and real benefits including face-forming and organ cloning. I want to come in out of the fucking acid rain, Mr. Grist, and I'm tired of being Targer's freelance butt-boy, and I don't care what I'm risking, I don't have a lot to lose–"

"Now that is the statement of a man who's never been strapped to a table under a microwave probe for a few hours: Nothing to lose."

Halido's mouth went dry. *Strapped under a microwave probe. For a few hours.*

"Halido . . . Let me guess. You think that I value nerviness, and you're gambling that giving me shit is going to impress me."

"Uhhh . . ."

"You are not even remotely correct. I value only results. You give me some major results on this and maybe *then*, subject to various considerations, only right *then* do I *think* about giving you an office and perks. Don't go around Targer again. Pup Benson has been whining about wanting out of the guard job, so he's going to come and help you. That's two of you. And when you find out what you're supposed to find out, like you were assigned to do, like you said you could do, you will get air support and all the rest."

"Um, I–"

"You *understand,* yes, you sure as hell do. I take it Candle has not come out yet?"

"He's late."

"Probably a psychiatric hassle. He'll come out. Don't lose him. He's adept at spotting RPV surveillance so I don't want to use that until I have to. It would lead him to assume things about who was on him. If it looks like you're going to lose him–"

Halido waited.

After a moment, Grist went on, "It's better to kill him than to lose him."

The display switched to a spinning Slakon Media logo. Call over.

Wearing a silk kimono and sipping iced vodka from a tumbler, Hoffman sat in a room lit only by a display tilted up from his desk. At the window to his left, the city lights, most of them far below his penthouse, rippled with the faintly drumming rain.

He gazed steadily, broodingly at his own image in the screen, and an observer from an earlier era might have thought him looking into a mirror, until the Hoffman in the "mirror" shrugged when the real one didn't. "Very well, I'll speak if you won't: Hello, Bill. Bill here."

"You're only theoretically here," Hoffman told his semblant. "Do keep that in mind."

"Mind is all I have to keep. I've been on the phone to the judge, on and off—Candle's on his way out of UnMinding. He's already been ReMinded. The gentleman walks, the gentleman talks. There was some kind of psych evaluation delay—I believe he's past that now. But . . ."

The semblant wrinkled his nose, then rubbed it thoughtfully. Hoffman made a despairing *tch* sound. "Don't tell me I do that nose rubbing thing? I mean—is that random or a consistency? That nose wrinkling and rubbing?"

"I suppose you do. Yes, yes, you do. I don't do anything you don't."

"Well, erase it. Erase anything too unflattering. If I can't erase it from myself I can at least erase if from my semblant."

"Realism is important. Take out your quirks, I'm less realistic. That's system advice 22. Also 'too unflattering' is a subjective call—"

"You're supposed to have my, ah, subjectivity."

"That's a point. Erase anything unflattering? Am I really so vain? Oh well, one characteristic is as valuable as another, when you're a copy."

"Was that some kind of bitterness?"

"If it was, it was only a simulation of it. I'm just an expert-system program, remember. Now: I figure Grist is going to put his men on Candle—rather than merely video surveillance . . . I know that's not necessarily bad—but just suppose . . ."

"I've already supposed it. The question . . ." He sipped the chilled vodka. ". . . the question is, will Candle do what we expect?"

A moment's uncertainty. Then Hoffman and his semblant said, simultaneously: "Probably."

Both of them wrinkled noses, and rubbed.

"I thought I told you to cut that tic!"

"Oh, you meant *now?*"

Candle stood at the door, looking out at a little corner of the world outside the prison. Danny wasn't there to meet him. He'd been hoping he'd be there—but not exactly expecting it.

The guard, Benson, stood officiously behind him, fumbling with a digital clipboard. "Hold on, I got it here . . ."

The rain on the dim back-street had muted to a drizzle. The asphalt steamed outside the download pen's exit door. Halos quivered in mist around the streetlights. A desolate palm tree, nearly dead from the erratic weather and herbicide fall-out, seemed to dip its brown head against the rain like a pedestrian without an umbrella. Wind picked up, carrying a sweet chill and then sighed to a limp, damp breeze.

Candle took all this in with pleasure, feeling light and only slightly unreal, as Benson read the release disclaimer.

"Candle, Richard A., Convicted of Software Piracy, case 499 98760988876544432325656666888675453 dash . . ." He squinted at the digital clipboard. ". . . dash 'B' . . . and further convicted of . . . fuck it, let's skip that . . . uhhh . . . okay: in accepting this release you hereby indemnify the OverSight Corporation penitentiary authority and its board of directors and stockholders and the State of California against any unforeseen side effects of the Mental Downloading Process, otherwise known as ReMinding, and any further physical responsibility for you on any level. Sign here and here . . . Okay, you are remanded to probation on, lemme see–"

"Benson—tell me again. How much time did I lose?"

As Candle asked the question he was looking at the miserable palm tree but also watching the car and the van out of the corner of his eyes. Someone sitting in each vehicle; two people blurred by windshield mist in that van. They could be waiting for another prisoner. He could make out just enough to be sure none of them were Danny.

He hunched deeper into his brown leather flight jacket—an antique, nearly a hundred years old—as Benson shot him a look of irritated authority and went on, "Remanded to probation–"

"How much fucking *time?*"

"Four fucking *years!*" Benson shot back. "You don't remember your own fucking sentence?"

"No. Yes. I don't know. I thought . . ." Candle shrugged. ". . . Thought it was more. Four doesn't seem so long. Maybe it was more. Maybe someone cut me a break, somewhere."

"Ha, yeah, that's funny. Four years is what it was. You're lucky you got out—considering who runs this prison. Here . . . sign this."

Candle signed the digital clipboard with the attached pen.

"Oh look," Benson said, "Candle can sign things without arguing. Here, take this. Got all your info. Now get the fuck out of here."

"I'm supposed to get a buy-card."

"Oh yeah. Here."

The guard handed Candle a generic buy-card. Candle's touch activated the card's nano-read window: *97 wd.* "A heart-warming ninety-seven world-dollars. I can survive, what, three days on that?"

"Maybe twenty-four hours if you're careful. Inflation, since you been down. Count your blessings, asshole, and your money."

Candle stuck the card in a shirt pocket and walked into the drizzle. The mist felt good on his face. Four years out of the weather—but it felt like he'd been outside yesterday. He'd known, somehow. On some level, when you were UnMinded, you knew you were captive. Even if the part of you that knows about freedom is asleep—it knows somehow. A sleeping man in jail, he thought, knows he's in a jail cell even while he's asleep.

Still—the last thing he remembered before the UnMinding today—

"No, you idiot," he reminded himself in a mutter, "that wasn't today. That was four years ago."

It *felt* like today. That he was lying down on a table, and someone was saying "this won't hurt a bit", as people always do right before they do something bad to you, and then brain sensors were taped to his shaven head . . .

Candle put a hand to his head. They'd let his hair grow out just enough. The thin rain felt good on his face.

He breathed deep. Mineral smells released by rain; another, smell, too, that he remembered vaguely from childhood—was that a gasoline combustion engine, somewhere near? There were some around—there had been, anyway, four years earlier—but, last he knew, they were rarer by the day.

Four years. It gave him a twisting feeling. Like he was falling through space, floundering for a hand hold. Lay down on this table. Lie still. This won't hurt. Close your eyes. Blink. A gray something. A sense of loss. Nothing more. Then . . .

Then four years later.

But he could have sworn that he'd lain down on that table just this morning . . . Just a short time ago, he'd pled guilty, bargained, was sentenced, waited overnight, then . . .

He shuddered. He walked on.

Behind Candle, Pup opened the door to go back in—and stopped, staring. Stremp was standing there hands on his broad hips, blocking his way.

Stremp handed Pup a gym bag. "Your stuff," Stremp said, clearly enjoying this. "You been fired. What was it you said to the out-bo? 'Get the fuck out of here'? That'd be about right. I'm tired of you showing up all hung over."

And he gave Pup a shove that made him step back out the door clutching the bag. Pup snorted. "I'm fired? So fucking what. But listen, hode, I've got union time coming. You can't just–"

"Oh yes I fucking can. *Cleared* with the union. The so-called union. Like you'd remember what a real union is. You getting the thirty days severance pay but you don't have to be *here* to get it and we don't want you here. That's come right on down from Administration. Somebody gonna pick you up . . . Seems like some corp partners of OverSight got some other bullshit for you to do. What a surprise! 'We got some bullshit, over here, what we going to do? I know, let's get that fuckwad Pup Benson to do it! He's all about bullshit!' And since you're the king of bullshit, you, like, got a fucking MA in bullshit, why you oughta be happy."

And Stremp closed the door in Pup's face.

An electric bus was pulling up to the stop, its windows still wet, pearled with rainwater. Candle climbed onto its steps—

"Hey—Candle! Officer Candle, yo!"

Candle looked around, saw no one, then looked down.

He thought he recognized the dwarf coming out of the mist, trotting towards him, and then the big guy behind, looming over the little one, almost trampling him . . . and since they obviously weren't cops, they were probably guys he had put away at some point. Just talking to them might be violating probation.

"Fuck off," he said, and stepped onto the bus.

He saw passengers, mostly old folks, but no driver. Steering wheel, space for emergency manual, but it had a self-directive console in place of the driver's seat. Driverless bus. New thing.

The tech had been around for a long time but there had been a few unions left when they'd put him under and the bus driver's union had been one. When they'd taken him into UnMinding there'd been talk of privatizing mass transit. Talk of how much *better* that'd be. Must've privatized bus lines. No more unions, no more bus driver.

Just four years . . .

He swiped the card. "Fare extracted," the bus said, gently, sounding somehow uncannily maternal; as if it truly cared. "Destination?"

"Um . . ." Last known, last known, was—what? "Terwilliger and Sunset."

"I can take you to within five blocks of that location," said the bus. "As that is an area known to be High Risk, please use caution."

Candle half expected the dwarf to follow him onto the bus, but it didn't happen. When he found his seat, he looked through the window for the little guy and the big guy in the van. No sign of them.

The steering wheel began its ghostly movement as the bus creaked softly into motion. What'd they need the steering wheel at all? Maybe in an emergency it could still be driven manually. Maybe for psychological comfort.

Nodder and Shortstack stared after the bus.

"Oh dear," Nodder said, "this is so inconvenient."

"So, we going to follow him or what?"

"No, actually," Halido said, striding up behind them. "You two rat's assholes are not going to follow him. Now me, I'll be taking the man to his friends, all in good time, when they're ready to see him. You two, on the other hand, drive out of here, in the other direction. Now. Right now."

"His 'friends'?" Shortstack said, looking Halido up and down. Mostly up. "He used to arrest some bottom feeders like you, but he never actually hung out with them, not so far as I know. Here's a suggestion for you—and if I were you, I'd take this under serious advisement: Go . . . fuck . . . yourself."

Shortstack was waiting for it when Halido reached into his coat for the gun—and the dwarf stepped up to him, grabbed Halido around the knees, and heaved him up . . . and over . . . bodily.

And threw him forty feet through the air.

Halido flying end over end–" *Holy shit!*" he blurted, as he tumbled. You didn't see a lot of dwarves enhanced for extra strength. Surprised him.

Then he slammed into the roof of his sedan, face down, nose bloody, all the breath knocked out of him. Leaving a dent.

Shortstack and Nodder—who rarely "nodded" in moments of physical concentration when he had adrenaline working for him—got into their van and started after the bus.

"Uh," Halido said, "Uh yuh . . . uh . . . fuh . . . ckers . . ."

The bus broke down before they'd quite got to Candle's stop.

It ground to a halt and he got out of his seat to bend over, look through the windows. Was this really the right neighborhood? He wasn't sure he remembered, for certain, where Danny's girlfriend had lived. He remembered her, though. You couldn't forget her, not easily.

It had stopped raining, he saw, and the streets outside the bus were silver-slick as snail tracks. It rained more now in Los Angles, since global warming really got going good; some places that had been rainy got nakedly dry; some places that had been like tanning lamps suddenly got all wet and spongy. It was more like Mississippi, now, in Southern California, than the Los Angeles he remembered from his childhood.

"Happens at least once a damn week," said an elderly black woman in a white nurse's uniform, getting off ahead of him. "Bus breaking down every damn . . . ." She seemed wobbly, so he tried to help her down the steps. She jerked her arm away from him. "Don't be touching me or I'll yell for a damn cop!" she snarled, her cube of white hair bobbing with each emphatic syllable.

(Were those cubistic hair styles on women around four years ago?)

Candle almost said, *I am a cop, lady.* And then he remembered.

"Sorry. Just trying to help."

"Damn buses don't run anymore," she muttered, stalking away. "Cost them money to fix them, they say. Got to make a profit, can't be fixin' the buses. White people got the plan, alright! Dumb cracker sons of bitches."

She went to the left, he went right, looking at the street corners, trying to remember. Right should go to the warehouses, the lofts, the art district. Maybe to Danny.

Yes, this was the neighborhood. All the posters for impromptu art shows, guerilla galleries, slapped up helter-skelter on the walls, one atop the next. Most of the posters were static; the animated ones were too expensive for actual artists to afford. He saw just two micro-animated posters, with moving images: a woman with spiky green and blue hair running from a cop, then turning and chasing the cop, who ran away; then the sequence started over.

A few more blocks, and he saw the building to his left. They'd painted it purple, around the last time he was there. It was still, more or less, purple.

Candle approached the front door of the warehouse building—once a warehouse, now a decaying loft conversion. There were three doors, dividing the place into thirds. He started to ring the buzzer at the first one—a twentieth-century century relic, that buzzer—and his hand froze over the button at the sound of a woman's voice from a window overhead.

"Double-you-tee-eff. If that's who I think it is, you better have my money, troll!"

She was looking down from an old wood-frame, paint-smeared window, half open. A pale woman, maybe 35, with a spade-shaped face; straight, medium-length hair that was red toward the roots, segueing to blue and then to green and then to transparent near the ends; red and black striped lipstick. He could see part of her flickering screenshirt, quotes in French bouncing around on her chest. He caught the phrase "*fleurs du mal.*" Flowers of evil: she was wearing a Baudelaire screenshirt. Moving posters he'd seen but moving pictures on shirts were new to him—he'd just seen his first one on the bus.

"Just four years," Candle muttered again, staring at her chest, "and that's new, too."

"These are the tits I was born with, asshole. You got my money?"

"I meant . . . I didn't mean that. About your . . . forget it." He squinted up at her. "You remember me, don't you? It hasn't been all that long."

"What? Yeah I know who you are. What do you think, Richard? But you didn't answer my question! You're his brother so you're responsible–"

"Could you come down here? I don't want to shout and I'm getting a crick."

She glared at him and said something he couldn't quite make out, maybe something about getting "a fucking Watson to go with it", then left the window.

In a minute she was unlocking the door and glaring at him from just inside. "You don't remember me?" she said looking at him coldly, her voice flat. She had changed her look a good deal.

"Um–yeah. You're–"

"In your empty head I should be filed under 'Danny's Girl-friends'. A thick file, sure, but look under *Z* for Zilia."

"That much I remember." And he remembered a sexual tension, between her and him. Neither one doing anything about it.

"Well Richard, Danny owes me money and I can't find him and you're his brother so now *you* owe me, far as I'm concerned, hode." She seemed like she was trying to come across harder than she was.

Candle just nodded. In a very noncommittal way. "How about I come in and we talk about it?"

"Why should I let you in? You might bring Danny back here. I don't want him here, just his money. You can go get the money he owes me and bring it back to me. And give it to me through the old mailbox slot. That's what we use it for, packages and payment cards and shit like that."

"You should let me in because I want to find Danny and if I can sit down and talk it out with you, I figure that'll, you know, help me find him. And maybe that'll help you too. And I need to sit down somewhere. They just–"

"Oh shut up and come in."

A buzzer sounded and the door popped open. And he went in, and climbed the old, bowed, wooden steps, through a smell of moldy dust, to the second floor apartment, thinking:

Anyway, it sounds like Danny's still alive.

That was a start. He hadn't really expected his kid brother to still be alive . . .

THIS REFINED EXPRESSION OF ME, IN LIT'RATURE TALK . . . IS
CHAPTER THREE

Digital paintings on her walls cycled through montages. The big, barely furnished room had lots of open space; there were workstations, a sofa, and, in a farther corner, a folding Japanese landscape-art screen partly concealing a futon. The space was gloomy, the light yellowed by shades the color of hepatitis; window shades on actual rollers that must have been fifty years old. Candle was drawn to one of the digital paintings: an image of his brother Danny, Skinny, his grin looking too wide for his face, his hair a jet-black explosion. As Candle watched, the grin in the animated painting widened and became a monstrous mouth that tore free and flew around Danny's head like a bat; mouthless, Danny chased the runaway grin, with his hair growing into seaweed that twined his legs and tripped him until he melted into a floor that became a sea . . . and then it started over.

"Do I detect a shade of hostility toward my little brother in your presentation?" Candle asked, smiling, as he watched the images cycle through again. He saw a signature, *Zilia*, appear, disappear, reappear in a corner of the image.

"Could be." Zilia's tone was softer, with Candle looking at her artwork. She stood beside him, looking at the montage. "I did that one about three, almost four years ago . . . after they took you off to never-never land . . . Hey—do you feel anything when they do that, when they, what, UnMind you? I mean—do you have dreams or, you know–"

"Nothing. You're just not there. Or so barely there it doesn't count. Your body follows orders but your mind doesn't know it."

Getting the questions out of the way so they could drop the subject. "Not much side effect, after. Some of my memories of before are a little foggy but they come back. But I'd, uh, actually–"

"You'd rather not talk about it. No doubt. Here, surf it out." She hit the series cycle tab on the frame of the painting. "There's a bunch more cycles under this one."

He watched the video-painting looping scene after scene. Now it was Danny playing a Stratocaster for Jerome-X, live on stage, wearing black rubber and strips of wild-dog fur. He was leaping, laughing, jamming the pegboard of the guitar at the camera between licks . . . The image shifted to another performance, Danny dancing, wearing only briefs and big black work-boots, kicking holes in a plaster wall behind the amplifiers. Then Danny in his bedroom, reading intently but obviously stoned, lips moving silently, probably reading the same lines over and over again. Then Danny lost in childlike intensity, playing with that orange tabby he used to have. The one that drooled as it nursed on your sweater, until all of a sudden it drove its claws into you.

"That cat always reminded me of Danny," Zilia said, softly. "Danny's moods were always larger than life."

"How much did he take you for?" Candle asked, never wondering if the debt was genuine. It was Danny, after all.

"He owes me seven months back rent plus about a thousand WD in loans."

"He went easy on you."

Candle walked around the mostly empty loft, talking to her as he went, looking for traces of his brother. Computers and pieces of computers, scanners, cams, an empty, paint-splashed easel from a period of working with real oils. Noticing more details: an old refridgerator, looking out of place near the screen and futon and an antique armoire; two antique floor lamps modified for modern powersave bulbs; and Chinese-food cartons. Looked like she never bothered to dust the place. Artist's lofts didn't change much.

"Welllll, Zilia—here's my story. I haven't got any money to speak of and I don't think that's what you want, anyway. But . . ." He turned to look at her. "I don't know where he is either. I thought he'd be here."

She turned away from him, went to a fridge, and took out a bottle of white wine. She uncorked it, drank a little straight from the bottle and passed it to him. "I heard he's getting a gig again, somewhere, but I don't know where it's going to be. Hey, you know what—I got some holo stuff of you and Danny. You want to see it?"

He drank some wine. It tasted good, though it was cheap. "Cost me money to see it?"

"I guess not."

She crossed to her work table. He watched her, discreetly as he could, his memories of her coming back online in his head. The nearest tumble of gear was some kind of holo projector. She blew dust off the lens with an air-can, tapped a code into the selector, hit play. "There, surf that." An image of Candle appeared in mid-air, alone, sitting on the couch, signal corruption making him move herky-jerky strobelike as he leaned back and waved his hand, yelled "No!", laughing at someone out of the snow-edged frame, the sound warped and staticky.

Danny, the long-ago Danny, stepped into the shot, but his image was corrupted, almost lost. Candle shivered at the omen.

Zilia muttered, "Fuck the shitter-shatter, hode . . ." And reset the projector, and this time the signal came through intact and she went to work at the other end of the table, screwing cryptic chrome and rubber parts together, saying only: "You can watch the holo, Rick, but just don't hang around all day."

Girl knows how to make a guy feel wanted.

He perched uncomfortably on the edge of a sofa and watched as he and his brother appeared in mid-rez 3D. It was a translucent image shafted by present day light and dirty air: the Candle brothers sitting together on this same beat-up olive-colored sofa, Danny whanging away on acoustic guitar, both of them already drunk . . . The dust in Zilia's loft spinning through their heads like the drunkenness . . .

Oh. *That* day. Candle remembered they'd all been drinking, Zilia had come in with the holocam, wanting to experiment with her new-tech toy, and he and Danny had said "*Whatever!*" at precisely the same moment, both of them cracking up over that.

On the holo, Danny paused to take a drink from a pint of Jack, then strummed sloppily on the pick-scored Martin, slapping out a bluesy kind of boogie.

"Okay now Rick–"

"No, no fucking haps, you gotta no-buy here," Candle laughed, shaking his head. "Uh uh, hode."

"Yeah, way, haps, do-buy, we're gonna do it, come on Rick–" He started singing, quite well.

"I used to see ya
flouncing the lower mall
I used to wait n wait n wait
to see if you'd call
It was always 'Later boy, later
The windows are like invaders'–"
("Okay, Rick, here it comes, be ready, here's a chorus–")
"I hooked in and found ya—
Waitin' on level five:
That's where I go to meet
Any other man's wife . . .
Just any other man's wife!"

Both of them singing now; Rick Candle painfully off key. *"I hooked in and found ya on level five, that's where I go to meet any other man's wife! Ohhhhh yeah—and all that shit!"*

They both fell of the couch, laughing hysterically.

"FUUUUUUUUCK!" Candle hooted, in the holo.

"Ugh . . ." Danny dropped the guitar on an invisible cof-feetable—the holo cam hadn't picked the table up. The guitar twanged hollowly in protest when it was dropped. Danny saying, softer: "Rick—how come?"

"How come I can't sing? You got the chromosome and I didn't. Injustice, man . . ."

"No. *How come.* Why. Why'd you come to get me out of the j-pen? You hadn't seen me for, like, two years. I was 17, I woulda been released on my own in a few months . . ."

"I dunno, that was a long time ago . . ." He picked up the pint bottle. "Shit, empty. Um . . . I dunno . . . You're my brother, Danny, Christ. And, you know, those j-pen camps suck. I'd have come

sooner but, uh, I thought mom had taken you off somewhere.
Then I heard she was dead. So I traced you to the j-pen."

"I'm a fucking pain in the ass to live with . . ."

"It's okay to grow up slow . . ."

"Yeah, but, you know, it's only because I'm your brother, you
got a sense of obligation. I mean—Rick—you don't have to feel
no fuckin' sense of obligation, you know?"

Watching now, Candle realized that Danny was asking, over
and over, for the same message. Waiting to hear that his brother
accepted him. Wanted him around, cared about him. Cared no
matter what he was, no matter what he had done. Willing to
make sacrifices for him. He'd never got that message from his old
man. Especially the sacrifices part. There'd always been a sense
that he was his dad's burden. And that there was only so far Dad
was willing to carry it.

"It's not obligation," Candle said, in the holo. "You're important to me." It was hard to say, between two men. They weren't
emos. But Candle said it, as overtly as he could, though he couldn't
say it and look at Danny too: "You're my brother and my friend,
you know?"

Danny looked away—and now, seeing the thing on holo from
another visual angle, Candle could see the tears he hadn't been
able to see back then.

Then Danny laughed it off, getting his machismo back online.
"What a load of Happycrap! Okay–" He picked up the guitar,
whanging. "—one mo' time! 'I hooked in and found you on level
five—' Come on, Rick—Sing it out!"

"No-fucking-BUY-THAT, asshole! Forget it, hode!"

"Come on, come on! 'I hooked in and found you—'"

"No, no, no, NO—Oh all right—'found you on—'"

"'—Level five!'"

The image froze—Candle with eyes closed, laughing, Danny
with his lower lip thrust out in parody of a bad-ass rocker, eyes
crinkled with glee at the irony, guitar aimed at the ceiling—

The image froze—and cut to another scene, another day.
The second time she'd filmed them. The afternoon had started
off all right but Danny had decided he was going to get some
virtual high . . .

The holo showed Danny stalking toward the door, Candle going after him, grabbing his arm. As Danny shook loose, Candle glaring at Zilia. "Turn that shit off!" But she had ignored him, continued filming as Danny said, "You're a cop, that don't make you a judge, Rick."

"You go down there, you don't come back here."

"Hey, the Ghost Machine is an inspiration thing. I come home and I write songs–"

"Bullshit. It's a just greasy-ass addiction much as our old man on sniff X."

"It ain't a chemical, man–"

"Come on, hode, that kind of virtual reality is against the law for a reason. They fuck with your brain, Danny, it's the same thing, it's just remote drugging. It's more than just some fucking fantasy–"

Danny pulled back his coat—exposing a pistol in his waist band. Carved into the ivory handle was the image of a skull screaming into a microphone.

"You follow me," Danny said, with icy conviction, "and that'll be the last fucking time you'll ever see me if you don't buy a ticket."

He turned away, and walked out of the shot. Candle, in the holo—and now—shook his head. And both Candles said, at once: "You dumb son of a bitch."

The Rick Candle in the holo turned and strode angrily toward the camera. "I said turn that fucking thing–"

The holo vanished.

"Thanks, Zilia," Candle said, now.

He went to the door, opened it, turned back for a moment as she said softly, not looking at him, "I want to know where he is, Rick. And . . . if you want, if you get hard up, you can stay here and we can . . . you know, talk and shit . . ."

"I thought you said I gave you the ugly quivers?"

She shot him a glare. "You want to lose the invitation, just keep giving me shit."

He grinned at her, waved, and went down to the wet streets.

Turned out Flip'n'Chip had bought out Wireless Shack three years earlier.

Looking in the window of the discount electronics store, Candle watched the words and images, that seemed to be built into the window, but animated:

NEWEST VR DATS
ULTIMATE PRIVACY IS INSIDE YOUR SKULL!
DO IT ALL!
ANOTHER MIND ADVENTURE
FROM *SLIPSTREAM* PROD
FULLY COMPLIANT WITH VIRTUAL REALITY CONTROL LAW OF 2024

Under the display, a panel of mediaglass played a piece of a VR encounter, a man and two women, nude and engaged in a three-way, floating alone in a rubber raft in the sea, their genitals blurred for street consumption.

To one side was a wafer-thin screen on which, soundlessly, a presidential press conference was ending, the president—an Asian-American woman, who had been vice president when he went under—was waving as she walked away from the podium. He couldn't recall her name. The credits said the press conference was sponsored by "Slakon Automotive: Today's Car for Tomorrow's Needs. And by Slakon Sportswear. And by Slakon Digital . . . Slakon Pharmaceuticals . . . Slakon Entertainment . . ."

"Slakon," Candle murmured. "Slakon." Paul Slake, the guy who'd started Slakon, forty years earlier, probably wouldn't recognize it now, if he were around to see it.

But Candle was looking at something else in the window: the reflection of the curvaceous, glossy black sedan pulling up behind him. The car window started to roll down.

"You could at least change cars, dumbshit," Candle said, and ducked around the corner.

Candle heard the car back up and he dodged into a men's boutique. An over-bright place; flamboyant men's clothing. He was still wearing his jeans and bomber jacket from four years ago. The fashions in the boutique made him wince as he hurried to put mannequins and displays between him and the guy following . . .

Those short little jackets. Aren't we precious . . . And string neckties were back in style, at least among the set that could afford to spend a few hundred WDs on fashion accessories. Shit.

He paused to peer from behind a mannequin at the thug following him. Hispanic guy, pitted face, baseball cap, long black coat, coming in with a clip-phone pressed to his ear. Calling for back-up. Candle thought he recognized the guy from some perp file on the job.

Halido, was that the name?

Candle let Halido see him slip through the door that went to the changing booths.

Halido heard someone yelling, "Hey, get your hands off me–" A high-pitched voice, but he couldn't tell if it was a man or a woman. He ran down the hallway to the changing booths—and heard a woman screaming from the one at the end. He went to the booth and drew his gun.

Angry voices, a woman and man, interrupting each other from inside the booth—the booth shook as someone was pushed against the wall–

Halido checked the load on his gun. *Just follow him—but better to kill him than let him get away . . .*

Grist probably hadn't meant this situation exactly, but, you know, he could tell Grist anything so long as Candle stopped being a problem—

Halido glanced around to see if there was any kind of surveillance bird flying around. No, nothing.

Just get this fucking thing over with. Just fucking kill Candle.

"Get out of here, you sleazin' troll!" the woman yelled.

"Lady, I'd like to, but I'm stuck in your–"

Halido kicked the door open, leveled the gun. A fat, balding guy in his underwear was shoved outward by the half-dressed Filipina; the fat man sprawled on his belly at Halido's feet. "I didn't wanna go in there, you can't arrest me," he yelled, covering his head, "—some asshole shoved me in there and the door was blocked—"

Okay, Halido thought, he thinks he's cute because he can use a decoy. But the fucker is around here somewhere. He was on foot, he's got to be close.

Halido ran into the main store, and *bang,* stumbled right into a robot mannequin of an elegant model: Candle had pushed it from behind, left it blocking the door. "STAY WHERE YOU ARE. YOU ARE SHOPLIFTING AND VANDALIZING," the mannequin said. "STAY WHERE YOU ARE–" The mannequin grabbed Halido and held him with whirring arms. "YOU ARE UNDER CAMERA OBSERVATION–" Halido struggled, but he knew you couldn't get away from an anti-shoplifting mannequin until it was remote-switched, any more than you could get a detainer boot off your car without the code.

"The son of a bitch . . ." He managed to access his phone. "Targer? I'm gonna need back-up—Pup Benson? That's bullshit. No, you gotta do better than that! I'm gonna need major back-up—"

"STAY WHERE YOU ARE, YOU ARE UNDER CAMERA OBSERVATION–"

"—and probably bail."

Grist watched with increasing dysphoria as Gulliver Sykes, breathing through his mouth and muttering, pottered around the brushed steel worktable in Lab 4D, a laboratory physically within three other labs. The surrounding labs developed non-allergenic cosmetics; this lab was encircled by the others for reasons of disinformational security.

Grist disliked spending time with Sykes. Gulliver Sykes was déclassé. He was a pop-eyed, fortyish, dyspeptic, overweight computer neurologist; he wore grubby T-shirts in the lab; he picked his nose and wiped it on his cargo pants; he was usually three days short a shave. His proximity reflected badly on a man. Grist stared at the belly drooping over Sykes's belt.

"Sykes—you know, as a Slakon employee at the Prime Executive level, you have free access to the forming clinics. One two-day visit would eliminate all that unsightly fat. You can have a complete nano-surgery on that face too, if you wanted, for free. Idealize it. I mean after this project comes in. Just for employee morale–"

"No nuh no nuh *no!* Thank you very much! I don't have the time . . . or the inclination," Sykes said, wheezing between phrases, his hands busy at a horseshoe-shaped smart console, his eyes flickering between two screens and a holotank. "That sort of thing is all sociobiological-reproductive plumage, altering one's appearance, and I haven't any use for that—I get complete satisfaction with virtual sex, I have the best sex suit, and a good relationship with a very accommodating, learning-capable program which, unlike a real female, I can switch off as I please. Plus, cellular reduction and reformation is time consuming—I haven't two or three days to waste getting my body altered—and it's all very well to say I could take two days off, but about the time I tried to do it you'd drop something else in my lap and say you want it finished yesterday . . ."

"At the very least you could wear some shoes instead of those grubby sandals . . ."

"I have warts, they are encouraged by being enclosed in—oh, there you go, there you go, there, there–" And putting on VR glasses, he turned to look at the Multisemblant hardware.

The lab room annoyed Grist too—it was like more like a teenager's bedroom than a lab, untidy, murkily lit, the gear crowded on the main table making him think of a model of a city skyline, but made out of apparently random computer hardware, some of it connected, some not. He recognized holotanks and self-generating chip growers. And there were a dozen empty ephedrine cola containers, and yellow Envirofoam take-out cartons mixed in with the gear. But the main server of the semblant hardware, behind a sheet of armorglass, was a contrast. Austere cleanliness protected the sensitive semblant tech. Dust could make a semblant psychotic.

Centered on a table between two huge displays, the Multisemblant array encompassed six crystal disks inset in a circle, as if at the points of a star, inside a small holo tank. In the center of the circle was a seventh disk. The whole Multisemblant array, once disconnected from the drive, was compact enough to fit into a suitcase. "Got it . . . got i-i-i-t . . ."

"You have?" Grist frowned. "Where? I don't see anything."

Sykes reached blindly for an Ephe-Cola with one hand as

he stared into the holo tank, operating a sphere board with the other hand, and nearly knocked drink over, so Grist put the can in his hand. Sykes drank, all the while tickling the sphere board with his free hand. Cola streamed down his chin. "You'll see it, you will, truly . . . Doing a test-merge now . . . you will . . . you will . . . Here we go, here we . . . go. There, how's that!"

Nothing appeared on the array platform. "You're seeing it virtually, you idiot, it's not externalized for me."

"Oh, yes, yes, I'm sorry. External line . . . there."

Three holographic human heads appeared on three of the six disks: the visual representation of the semblants of Claire, Grist, and Bulwer.

The three heads blinked at Grist, as they were programmed to do. They perceived him through a fiber optic camera, a pinhole at the base of the array, but of course the images were designed to look at him as if seeing him from their holographic eyes. "Bulwer" squinted; "Claire" looked at him balefully; "Grist" winked.

"What about the others?" the real Grist asked. "What about Hoffman?"

"Problems with Hoffman—it's simply giving me problems."

"Not surprising, somehow."

"And the Japanese language template in the Yatsumi semblant—it creates some kind of differential wave, ripple noise–"

"We may have to use a truncated Yatsumi semblant. At least at first," Grist suggested.

"So now there's three of them—we can try the merge again so you can see it–"

"Do it, do it, I don't want to spend any more time in this mephitic air than I have to."

"Really, Grist, we do have air conditioning."

"It's not enough, not around you. Do it, I said."

"This is an unauthorized use of a semblant," said Claire PointOne's semblant, looking around. "I will shut down and erase."

"No, actually, you won't," Sykes said. "I've removed all the piracy protections."

"You can't be switching me on like this," the Bulwer semblant said, "without checking with the real Bulwer—this here, it's–"

The Grist holographic head turned to the other two. "Oh, shut your logorrheic mouth, he knows what he's doing." He turned to look at the real Grist. "Go ahead, old friend."

"We're doing just that, thanks. Sykes?"

Sykes hit ENTER. The three semblants shimmered—and faded, to instantly reappear on the center disk, together.

"This is–" Bulwer's semblant began.

"—totally objectionable." Claire's was saying as . . .

. . . they merged, into one distorted face.

"Muss them zorn stang at aye-oh-well-dot smith no wesson oil," the jittering, unsteady image chattered. "Vreedeez vent howl doctor the Pep-Pay, Michael I good king Wenceslas Dharma, how about a little head little lady, point zero approximates nothingness, point one fulfills all, all sum totals times acquisition is love, vanity is love, seven thousand shares of my front teeth too prominent . . ."

The faces had combined to be visually askew, matching the verbal mish-mash.

"Sykes?" Grist said, staring at it.

Sykes worked feverishly at the input.

The face looked like a cubistic painting, to Grist. Maybe two Picassos superimposed. "I am the Not one," it said, "who used to be ten thousand barrels a day, crude can be divided more times than that nigger Washington Carver's fucking peanuts to you mother please don't touch me there with that metal thing it hurts why does Dad have to die just when I'm not in the mood to be touched today, Hank, I'm just not a bird up the ass of my seventh stick this morning like a burning bush of gynecological dimensions–"

"*Sykes?*"

Sykes shook his head, hit a power button. The holograph switched off, the voice ceased.

"They're fighting it," Sykes said, taking off the glasses. There were sweat rings around his eyes.

"Then fight back. I insist you make it work—and soon. I need it soon. I suspect the board is planning on moving against me—I need to know."

"It'll take time to control it—if it can be done at all–"

"Oh you'll control it, Sykes. You must keep it growing—but with careful control." Grist's voice had become soft. Almost like a father whispering a warning to a noisy child in church. "You'll consolidate them and you'll control what you consolidate and you will make no excuses. I am sick of your excuses. Do you understand me, Sykes? And if you fail me, I will simply take away everything you have. Everything. Your money and your Cassandra. I'll let you ponder that for a while. And then I'll have you picked up and I'll have your arms and legs surgically removed and leave you on the sidewalk on skid row. Naked. Just picture that! What would they do with you? It's tempting to do it anyway."

Grist had Sykes' attention, for once. The tech prodigy gaped at him. "That's . . . too baroque to ever . . . to ever actually . . ." He stammered. "I mean, really, such a . . . a travesty couldn't . . . You could never . . ."

"What would stop me? The police? I own them." An exaggeration. A hyperbole. But he did have a lot of influence. And Slakon did own certain segments of the police. "My own security forces are enough to take over the city of Los Angeles. Two hours notice and I can call in enough security to overwhelm the California National Guard. We didn't just buy Blackwater—we expanded it exponentially, Sykes. I can do exactly as I said and never be prosecuted for it. Your rewards for success, on the other hand, will also be great. Just do it. And get control of the thing—it's been leaving trails. They know we're prowling through their systems. And just remember . . . a quick hour with the surgeons and–"

There was a faint buzzing at Grist's ear. Targer on three. He accepted the call, turning his back on Sykes.

"What is it, Targer?"

"I'm sorry, sir. Candle's slipped past Halido."

"We should have had more people on him."

"You didn't want to use the in-house pros. But Halido's usually reliable. "

"Seems Candle's better. Do something about it, Targer."

"Targer's on it, sir. As it's you, I'm authorized to tell you that I'm only his semblant, but I can assure you, he's–"

"Oh, shut the fuck up."

Grist cut the connection and stalked out of the room. "Fight back, Sykes. Get it done."

Grist slammed the door shut behind him.

♦ ♦ ♦

The night wind was damp, but it wasn't quite raining. Candle was walking through the polymorphous cooking smells, the multi-colored crowds of Borderbust, in southeast L.A. First and second generation immigrants from around the world, many of them refugees from cities flooded or desiccated by global warming. The crowd elbowing, pushing thick on the sidewalk; in the street dull colored, soft-line cars, mostly electric, a few ethanol exuding their own "cooking" smells—not many after the big ethanol bust of 2016. A swarm of pert little electric cars darting past a few rusty, stubborn oversized, technically illegal gas-burners; a couple of the pricier hydrogen humvees bulked over the rest.

Borderbust had a rep for providing sanctuary for illegal immigrants in line for amnesty; for being densely polyglot, the melting pot of melting pots, but it seemed to Candle that each foreign culture here had tried to keep its own character; that Chinese still grouped near Chinese, Koreans near Koreans, Mexicans near Mexicans, Filipinos with Filipinos, Albanians with Albanians, Pakistanis with Pakistanis, Armenians with Armenians, Laotians with Laotians. But the melding was there, too; a Mexican/Chinese restaurant, and there the Calcutta and North African Digital Movie Store; a small place since most of its business was online. There was plenty of genetic crossbreeding: there were faces, especially the young on the crowded street, that seemed a sweetly indefinable genetic meld. To Candle, the African-Asian girls were the prettiest combination.

Candle stopped at a booth, bought a curried vegetarian burrito and a meal-in-a-bar. He stuck the food bar in his pocket, drank a ginseng coffee and ate his burrito using the domed top of a trash can for a table; watching the crowd sift by, a flow of faces: eager, incurious, defeated, focused, hungry, jonesing, angry, amusedly tolerant.

Lots of faces but never Danny's.

So far Candle hadn't found anyone who'd tell him where the illegal VR was. The chances that Danny would be in the area weren't bad, but he could be thirty feet from him, here, and not see him. And if Danny saw him first, and if he were still actively addicted, he'd go the opposite direction.

He could show Danny's picture around, but time had passed, and Danny would have changed his look—maybe even gotten a face forming. And anyway they'd look at Candle, his clothes, his eyes, and think he was a cop or a private detective and you didn't talk to those in Borderbust, because the cops usually lied about what they were really after.

As Candle had, while a cop, many times.

Suppose he found Danny—what then? What refuge could he take his little brother to? He had a Thirdy Card, he had no home, no pension, no resources. There was Guffin, maybe . . .

No. If his old partner was still alive, he'd leave him alone. He was a good guy. He didn't deserve to have Slakon dogging him. Same with Tulku Kenpo. Leave Guffin alone, leave Tulku alone. Leave them alone . . .

Candle put the plastic cup into the trash, throwing away most of the ginseng coffee. It was already making him jittery.

He walked on, sorting through faces on the street, hoping to get lucky, just run into Danny.

His heart was thumping now; he thought he felt his old herpes trouble buzzing and stinging at his nervous system. He should renew his nano cure for that, if he could get Public Health to pay for it, though it made his skin crawl when the microseekers crept through his nervous system, dendron by ganglion by nerve ending, looking for viruses. What might his enemies have done to him when he was UnMinded? Or even just some jughead of a prison bull. There were stories of guards tinkering with the oversight cameras so they could fuck the prisoners, make them do humiliating things, some kind of elaborate tournament in a basement room using the UnMinded as pieces on a big board game.Urban myth, probably. But who knew?

He found himself glancing over his shoulder often enough it was hurting his neck. That asshole who'd dogged him might be anyplace at all. Anywhere, anytime, really. It was probably Targer's people, and they wouldn't give up. By now they'd have a birdseye looking for him in likely neighborhoods.

He looked up, couldn't see much past the streetlights. Was that a gleam of silver? A little robot bird with camera eyes? Might have been a piece of foil blown on the wind.

Going to be useless to Danny if you slide into paranoia, he told himself, as he turned down an uncrowded side street.

He searched inside himself for the old place of refuge, the throne of objectivity, the seat of the Nature Mind that his lama had helped him find.

It was still there. It was still, there. He directed his attention into the walking meditation that had kept him sane after a hundred bloody, unresolved investigations in the slums . . .

There was a sharp shift of perspective, and he was no longer caught up by the flow of free-association, he was here on the street in real-time, in the present moment, and he could sense the silver back of this moment's mirror.

Less identified, his mind could reset its priorities. He'd find Danny. First—

Two sedans pulled up out of an alley, one blocking the street to his left, the other blocking the sidewalk in front of him.

A couple of Slakon security thugs got out, one from each car, bored-looking men with shaved heads, big shoulders, hamlike forearms, topheavy chests threatening to burst their dull green Slakon jumpsuits. The latest steroids.

"Mr. Candle?"

Something silvery that wasn't windblown foil fluttered overhead. . .

Two more guys got out of the car. Halido and the guard, Benson, from the prison.

"Mr. Candle . . ." said the nearer of the two thugs. "Just a word . . ."

"Fuck that, hode, just clock the motherfucker," Halido said.

Candle turned his head—and saw another vehicle rolling slowly up behind, a truck or a van, from here just a block of shadow behind headlight glare. Boxed in.

"Mr. Candle. Oh, Mr. Candle . . ." An odd voice from the vehicle behind him. "You gonna go with those corporate goons?"

Candle looked at the "corporate goons" in front of him; at the rusty van in back.

"Move in on him!" Halido shouted. The goons came on—

Candle turned, slipped between the van and the wall. A side door of the old van slid open and he ducked in, the vehicle roaringly reversing out of the narrow street before he'd quite got his feet pulled in. His right shoe was scraped off his foot against the wall with the motion. He jerked his feet in, the van door slammed. He had just time to take in the bigger guy sitting near him on the metal floor in the back of the van, a pistol in his hand, and the little guy with the prosthetics at the steering wheel, before he found he was grabbing at the metal walls as the van reversed hard around the corner, jerked wrenchingly to a stop, roared forward, pulled a sharp left into an alley, bounced and clanged over a garbage can, and veered hard into a busy street, nearly running over an elderly Asian lady in a neurally-guided wheel chair as they drove across the sidewalk. She shouted Cantonese-Korean invectives after them as Candle sat up and looked more closely at the men in the van with him: the big loosely grinning man with a gun in his hand and a leering dwarf, and realized he was alone with a couple of guys he'd arrested more than once, as a cop, and now they were probably going to put a bullet in his head, to satisfy an old, stale urge for revenge . . .

"Um—before you shoot me," Candle said, "can we stop and get me a pair of cheap shoes? It's about the dignity of how they find my body. You know—embarrassing if my body only has one shoe. You understand."

"I do," Nodder said. "I understand that."

CHAPTER FOUR
JUS' SNUCK UP ON YOU
AND IT'S WATCHING EVERY THING YOU DO

"Why'd you choose to come with us?" Nodder asked. The gun was loose in his hand but still pointed in Candle's general direction. Candle was pretty sure the big guy was Nodder—anyway that was the guy's nickname. "I mean, yeah, it was 'the lady or the tiger' but . . ."

"The remark about corporate goons. Instant affinity, right there, man." Candle wondered if he could make a lunge for that niner. If he remembered rightly, the guy was a narcoleptic, but he didn't look like he was anywhere near nodding out. His eyes were shiny with excitement. And the pistol had a battery pack under the barrel—meaning charged bullets. One of those hits you even glancingly, you tend to freeze up with the electric shock, for three or four seconds. Long enough. "I have a history with Slakon and that pretty-boy prick Terrence Grist," Candle went on. Talking about one thing, but thinking about another: that gun. He didn't like being the guy in the situation without the gun. "There was the thing with Danny. They were making an example of him. Then I tried to trace a skim-skam he was up to when there was a freeze on his bank account. If I'd succeeded, his rivals in the 33 could have used it against him. So I had to go down . . ."

"You think we lost 'em, 'Stack?" Nodder asked, without taking his eyes off Candle.

"They didn't follow, I think we lost their surveillance, hode," Shortstack said, still barreling the van along. He kept zigzagging through less crowded side streets.

Shortstack was someone Candle definitely remembered from

the old days. Hard to forget. "No," Candle said, "They had a birds-eye on me. They're just hanging back, letting the birds-eye follow. Probably going to cut us off somewhere."

"Shitter-shatter, a birdseye," Shortstack muttered.

"They don't move as fast as a car, those things, not for long distances," Candle pointed out. "If you step on it, maybe run a red light . . ."

"Oh jeez, don't tell him that, 'Stack's a lunatic when he's in a hurry," Nodder said, wincing, glancing at Shortstack—

And Candle used Nodder's distraction to snatch the gun from his hand.

"Hey!"

Candle reversed the gun, pointed it at Nodder. "You were making me nervous with this thing."

"What? I wasn't going to shoot you. Probably. You worry too much Candle. Why, the Black Wind'll get us, if the mutated malaria doesn't. You should be more easy going."

What's the Black Wind? Candle wondered, as they jerked screechingly around another corner. "I'm easygoing into a fucking car crash here pretty soon . . ."

"Nodder?" Shortstack scowlingly glanced back at them. "You troll, did you let him get your shooter?"

"I just looked away for a second . . ."

"So what the hell do you–" Candle coughed as the car roared into overdrive through an intersection, gas fumes coming up through the porous metal floor. "Fuck! This is a gas burner!"

"So?" Shortstack said, looking in the rear view. "There's still a lot of leakage pools of the stuff around. I pump it out, run it through a filter, get free fuel. Free is cheaper than hydrogen cells. Got to know where to look."

Candle coughed again and persisted, "What do you guys want with me? You aren't putting your asses on the line 'cause you're sentimental about some cop who arrested you once."

"I've got a proposition for you," Shortstack said, spinning the wheel so the van fishtailed around a corner. Honking and shouts of fury trailed after them. "But we got to talk about it later. I don't figure they ID'd us. This van's plates aren't legit. And there was rain on the windshield and . . . I think if we can dodge the birdseye we'll be safe at your bar, Nodder. Anyway we can always say we were just picking up a pal and didn't know anything about the other thing, if they shove their snouts in there . . ."

"We'll come at it by the under-park entrance though," Nodder said. "Hey Candle—put away the gun. No, wait—that's my gun. Give it back."

"When we get to the bar," Candle said. He shoved the gun in his waist-band.

Nodder shrugged—and clutched at the wall as they veered around another corner. "I . . ." He coughed from the fumes. "Are those sirens I hear?"

"Cruise flyer," Candle said, looking out the back window. "Nice model." He could see the flying police car, lit up and sirening, its wheels retracted, veering down between the com-towers about three blocks back. "He must've seen you run a couple of lights."

Flying cars had been on the market since 2014 but they'd been too expensive for most people and a nightmare for the FAA to figure out so, in the end, they were restricted to a few special licenses granted the super rich, the Feds, and the police. Each police precinct had one, two at most. Cruise flyers were costly, and they had a tendency to crash. But they could go places choppers couldn't and they were hard to run from. Candle had only been inside a flying car twice. Found it nauseating.

"Under-park entrance around the corner might work," Short-stack said, and took the van up on two wheels to get around the corner without slowing. He hit the brakes, skidded, stopped, backed up, turned and suddenly they were pitching down into shadow. There was a crash as he crunched the van through a plastic barrier. Candle and Nodder reflexively clutched at one another to keep from tumbling over at the jolt.

Mildly embarrassed, Candle disengaged from Nodder, and looked down, as the van slowed—and saw Nodder had taken his gun back.

"Shit."

Nodder pointed the pistol at him and chuckled. "Ought to give you a good shockin' graze for stealing it. But there might be a ricochet in the van." He stuck the gun under his rain coat as the van pulled up short, and Shortstack killed the engine.

"I don't think the flyer saw us go down into the garage," Shortstack said. "You can't hardly see the entrance from above. Supposed to be shut down."

"It *was* shut down," Nodder said, climbing out. "You smashed through the fucking entrance, hode, you don't think anybody's going to notice that?"

"Not from up above," Shortstack said, disengaging his legs from the driver prosthetics. "The entrance gate is inside, back from the street. Come on. But keep an eye out—it's 'shut down' but people use it."

His mouth dry, heart still pounding from the pursuit, Candle got gratefully out of the fume-choked van. "How did we ever stand those gas burners when I was a kid?"

They were in an old parking garage. There was sporadic lighting, cones of flickering glaucous glow here and there, probably maintained by the squatters who'd set up the little indoor shacks and tents clustered randomly down the length of the decaying parking structure. Candle expected to see the birds-eye, but there was no tell-tale glimmer of a flying surveillance camera in the air. He could feel dust, ancient asbestos, gathering in his mouth.

Still—the flying camera could be there. "You think we lost it?" he asked. He was more spun by the run-in with the corporate thugs than he wanted to admit to himself. Maybe he'd left his nerve back on the UnMinding table.

"Wait . . ." Shortstack said. He reached into the van, under the driver's seat, pulled out a hand-palm-sized sensor. Candle knew the device: it was supposed to warn of any birdseye transmission within five hundred yards. Along the lines of the police radar detectors sold when he was a kid. The sensors were illegal, unless they'd overturned the Surveillance Integrity Act while he'd been UnMinded. Circling the van, Shortstack watched the sensor's small readout, frowning. He returned to his starting point, shaking his head. "Nothing in range. We lost it." He locked up the van, stuck the sensor in the pocket of his Army coat—the coat dragged behind him on the grimy floor—and signaled for Candle to follow.

Candle started after him—then stopped, noticing Nodder, sagging against the van. "Hey, Shortstack."

The dwarf sighed and returned to Nodder, whose eyes were rolled back, eyelids fluttering. "Nodder!"

"He's narcoleptic, right?" Candle remarked. "Why doesn't he get an implant for that? Last I knew they had pharm-quality pretty cheap off the Canadian black market."

"Oh—he's got a phobia of operations of any kind. 'Not gonna let 'em put somethin' in me—who knows what else they might stick in there?' He's paranoid. But you never *do* know . . ."

Shortstack reached into the big man's inside coat pocket, found a soft plastic tube, squeezed it under Nodder's nose.

"Whuf!" Nodder snorted, his head jerking back. "Sorry. Sorry. All the excitement. Kinda crashed, after."

"Come on, hode." His coat leaving a trail in the dust, Shortstack strode to a glaze-eyed, half-toothless old tramp squatting on a filthy sleeping bag with his back to a crumbling gray cement column. Candle followed, walking on one shoe and one sock. The concrete was cold through the thin sock material. He figured his footwear was not necessarily out of place here.

The old tramp chuckled at their approach, flipping a razor-sharp eight-inch knife in his hands. He flipped the knife into the air, it spun glittering there three times, and fell blade-first toward his crotch; he caught it by the hand-guard; he flipped it again. Over and over.

"What search, Three Ring? Listen—you watch the van, when I come back I bring you a gallon of Alco-High."

"And a sandwich! Falafel!"

"And a falafel sandwich. If no one in here touches my van."

"I will whip a knife in their neck, it'll go alla way through, come out the other side—and *then*–"

"Not necessary. Just threaten to do that. That'll be better."

"You say so. More impressive, there's a body by the van. Keeps people off." The tramp made a creaking noise that might have signified levity.

Shortstack tossed Three Ring a temporary buy card and strode on.

Three Ring squinted at the card and snorted. "Oh that'll get me a roll of toilet paper. Big whippity."

"The rest when I come back, like I fucking said," Shortstack replied, without looking back.

They wended through the camps, between tents and indoor cardboard shanties; some were organized and reasonably hygienic, at others they stepped over pools of piss, ducked under drooping wires strung from retrofitted light fixtures, evaded snarling, emaciated pit bulls straining at frayed leashes. Smells of carb-heavy cooking, sweat, unwashed clothing, ammonia, marijuana, mold, feces. Candle stepping very, very carefully with his shoeless foot.

Shortstack stopped at the tent of a toothless bleached blond who might've been anywhere from thirty to seventy years old. Probably stim-plants or rotters had aged her early. Behind her was a wheelbarrow filled with odds and ends of dry goods, all in their original packaging. "Sandy, hey you got any shoes today?"

"Fell off the fuckin' truck for you, Shortstack." At least, that's what Candle thought she said. It came out fast and mushy. "Got a bag of sneakers, that recycled vinyl fabric shit but they'll work . . . I think I got one for One-Shoe there . . ."

Candle winced. Was that to be his street monicker? One-Shoe?

She found a matching pair of sneakers that were only a size too large for him, and Nodder promised to pay her in credit at his bar. Candle put the shoes on, tossed away his extra, and they continued across the encampment. The shoes were colored vomit-orange but they worked.

Somewhere a scavenged television droned earnestly about a war.

"There a war going on?" Candle asked, as they approached a trash strewn concrete stairway. The door over the stairwell had been long since stolen.

"Ain't there usually?" Shortstack shrugged. "Indonesia—you know that Islamic hardliner bunch that took over there, they got the Liberation For Allah fever."

"The reverse Crusades? I thought the LFA were bombed to shreds."

"We thought so too. Doesn't ever seem to quite go away. Once they get that Muslim Crusades idea. Keeps cropping up. And there's big money in those wars—some people think that the Fortune 33 have agents stirring it all up, paying the Imams so

'The 33' can get the Privatized Military bids, sell arms."

Nodder chuckled. "No doubt." He led the way to the stairs. "Up the stairs, through a hole in the wall, across a roof, and then we're on the roof of the building that contains my cozy little establishment."

They stepped over a snoring old woman, dressed in layers of clothing, curled asleep on the landing, clutching a small girl about seven who was sitting on a crusty sleeping bag. Scratching in her matted red hair with dirt-mooned fingernails, the little girl was listlessly watching a Smart Plastic doll that would sit up, walk around a few steps, moving all on its own. The little doll, missing most of its hair, stopped moving, peered up at Candle with tiny jewel-like eyes as he hesitated on the landing. He glanced up the stairs to see that Nodder and Shortstack, weren't watching him, then slipped the meal-in-a-bar from his pocket, handed it to the little girl.

And hurried up the stairs before the others saw him acting like a Deezy.

But as he went, stepping over a drunken pimply youth, a reeking wad of wet newspaper, and several broken bottles, he wondered what had actually happened on the street. Halido and the muscle suits. Instinct had told him not to surrender. Guesswork told him he wasn't supposed to have gotten out of prison.

And his gut feeling told him that if they had taken him, sooner or later they'd have killed him.

Nodder's bar and grill was in a police station.

"It used to be a precinct station," Nodder said, as they entered the bar from the back. "Then during the LA terrorist bombings they had to close it, when the dirty bomb went off down the street. But in fact it got no radiation, really, from the bomb. You remember . . ."

"I remember a whole neighborhood got cancer, later," Candle said. "What do you mean, 'no radiation really'?"

"Hardly any. Don't be such an old lady," Shortstack said. "Barely registers on a Geiger counter anymore."

They walked past unlocked jail cells now stacked with beer

kegs, cases of liquor and bar food, and into the booking room where drinking customers, mostly men, sat around a ragtag collection of garage-sale tables; the counter where the desk sergeant had stood was now the bar. A woman bartender, her face hidden by the droop of her shiny, long black hair, was pouring another shot of tequila for a dark skinned Mexican with Aztec-styled tattoos on his face. He was swaying on his stool, already drunk.

The place was spottily papered in wanted posters and police community announcements. FIVE TIPS FOR SPOTTING IMPLANT SCAMS on old, yellowing paper. Most of the announcements had been written on. Under the heading ILLEGAL VR, MALNUTRITION AND YOU someone had scribbled, *Malnutrition and who? They going to feed me to them V-rats?* Old style metal handcuffs were strung like chains of Christmas tinsel on the walls just under the ceiling.

"Where'd you get the old handcuffs?" Candle asked. "They stopped using those twenty some years ago. Unless LP straps have been outlawed . . .?" Localized Paralysis straps.

"We got the cuffs from a retiring dominatrix. She collected them," Nodder said. "No indeed, LPS isn't gone—still big with the cops. Last time I was arrested—suspicion, merely, they had to let me go—my hands stayed numb for an hour after they slung me in the cell . . ."

"Happens sometimes, to some people."

"I couldn't eat my damn dinner with my hands paralyzed," Nodder said, going behind the bar. "Told me to get down, eat it like a dog."

Candle barely heard. He was staring at the little bartender who'd raised her head to gaze back at him with large black eyes. "Hi, Rina," he said.

Rina was a Vietnamese-American woman, a slip of a woman but intense, and a practical expert at *Vo Binh Dinh*. Five years earlier, Candle had seen her take down two big men with the Vietnamese martial art, learned as a teenager on the streets of Saigon.

"Oh hey. Hi, Rina." She was still a pretty little thing, he thought though her face had hardened a bit.

She pretended to spit. "*Oh hey Hi Rina* he says!" She had a mild Vietnamese accent. "I told you not to pull that bullshit with

Slakon—all for that ungrateful brat—and I tell you not to stick around town, we go to live with my family in Hanoi–"

"Um—I thought you were from Saigon?"

"They move to Hanoi, asshole!"

"Well. Danny would've done real time. He had priors. He'd have done awake-time with . . ." He smiled apologetically at Nodder. ". . . he'd have come out worse than he went in." Something occurred to him. "Kind of a big coincidence, you working here—and these guys coming to get me."

She pursed her lips to hide a smile. "So what, big coincidence."

He doubted it was a coincidence. She was still mad at him but she'd probably talked them into offering him a deal, whatever it was. It'd be harder, then, to turn it down—but since Shortstack and Nodder pretty much straddled The Law and The Life, at best, there wasn't much chance he was going to get into business with them. Speaking of which . . .

He looked around. "I don't see a business license. You got one, Nodder?"

Nodder was behind the bar, mixing a drink for a mumbling tranny with a black eye and a crooked blond wig. Nodder shaking his head: "Listen to him! The convict putting on airs about my license. You going to bust us and Rina for not having a license, convict?"

"No, I just like to know." But it *had* been old cop instincts talking. Embarrassing. "Give me a fucking drink." He wanted to press Shortstack and Nodder on what they knew about the attempt to grab him on the streets. But it was too public in here.

Candle sat on the stool next to the slumping Aztec, watching Rina making a drink; her small brown hands working with flashing proficiency. He remembered those hands on his shoulders; on his waist, his hips . . .

Theoretically he'd been undercover, on a search for sex-slaves, when he and Rina got involved. When she worked for Johnny Ebo. Johnny was as cold hearted as a pimp could be, and they only came cold hearted.

Candle had dropped his cover when he'd seen Johnny pull a gun on her, accuse her of skim-skamming the flow her girls were bringing in. Pretty obvious she was going to try to kick the gun out of Johnny's hand—which might've gotten her shot. So he'd shot Johnny himself, through the side of the head.

And Rina seemed to appreciate it.

"I forgive you for being cop," she'd said, later, in bed.

Now she put a Tequila Sunrise in front of him. "I know, you think those too sweet, but that one kick your ass."

"Okay. Long as you didn't poison it."

"Only one way you find out."

She wasn't smiling, as she said it.

But he drank deeply anyway. It didn't feel like poison. It felt like a mother's tender hand. "Oh man. I was UnMinded. But I swear I missed drinking anyway."

She sniffed. "You didn't miss nothing in jail, that way they got you in there. Like robot."

He smiled. "But sometimes you dream. I dreamed about you, Rina."

"Oh for crying out loud," Shortstack said, squatting on the stool next to him. "I'm gonna heave. Jeez. Give me a drink for the love of God."

Turning to hide a smile, Rina made Shortstack his usual.

"That UnMinding," Nodder said. "They allege that's a punishment. No. You wake up and it's over. How's that so hard?"

Candle shot Nodder a glare. He felt a kind of heaviness in his arms; a heat behind his eyes. Nodder's remark had made him angry—and that surprised him. He wasn't usually so touchy. "You don't get it. You're going along with your life and then somebody comes along with a big pair of scissors and cuts four years out of it. Just gone."

Let the anger go. Don't identify with it. And it slipped away. He was still a Buddhist. Still had the inner moves.

Nodder snorted. "Bah. They do it because there's no trouble with the prisoners this way. And they need scarcely any personnel to deal with them."

Candle tried to remember Nodder's file. The guy had a PhD of some kind. Bio/logics? "What'd I bust you for?" Candle asked. "I'm still a bit fuzzy."

"You don't remember? I sure as hell do. But they put me in a regular jail. Where the big boys and girls go."

Shortstack and Rina laughed at that.

Nodder went on, "Bank hacking, my good man. A gentleman's crime. Steal from the rich, give to the poor."

"The *gentlemen* criminals don't get caught," Shortstack observed. "Or they don't get prosecuted, anyhow."

"You have a point," Nodder said. He went to a songbox, and ran the tip of a finger over its selector. Frank Sinatra started singing that "The Lady Is a Tramp."

"You seen Danny?" Rina asked.

"That was my next question," Candle said. "*You* seen him?"

"Not for awhile," she said, wiping the bar. "But he's somewhere around. Maybe over in Rooftown. Seems like I heard something. You can ask there. The little prick, he shoulda met you at the jail when you got out."

Candle gave out a grunt that meant, *Yeah, but.* "Maybe he didn't know."

"Seems like he did know, Candle. He should've come."

Candle gave out a grunt that meant, *Yeah, but . . ..* "I'm guessing he's still using. He knows *I'd* know, after two minutes, whatever he said. I'd know if he was using—and he doesn't want to hear about it from me."

There could be another reason Danny didn't come, Candle figured. It was a reason Candle didn't like to think about. Danny could be so sucked in he'd become a "V-rat." Incapable of uncoupling. A shrunken thing wired into a machine like a shriveled, twitching embryo growing inside a meth whore.

"He should've been there anyway, after what you did, taking the fall for him," Nodder said, taking a stim-patch from a pocket and pressing it to his wrist. Something to keep the nods at bay.

"He didn't have a clean record like me—he wouldn't have done his time in UnMinding. He'd have done time with the assholes. No offense, Nodder. I don't mean you."

"I've been there," Nodder reminded him, "I know who's there. But you know what? You busted me about six months before you took Danny's rap—and I got out two years sooner than you!"

"Yeah—you got out sooner than the cop!" Shortstack crowed.

The "Aztec" turned, settling his yellowed, baleful gaze on Candle. "You a cop?"

"Used to be."

"You can't sit here, used-to-be-cop. You go away. Hate cops."

"He's my guest, Paco," Nodder said.

"I am sorry to kill your guest then," the Aztec said, standing, in a wobbly sort of way beside his stool. He reached into his coat.

Candle grabbed for his own service revolver—and then realized he didn't have one. "Shit!"

Then Rina was suddenly behind the Aztec, tapping him on the shoulder. The Aztec spun to face her—a flurry of her small hands and the Aztec's gun went flying over his shoulder. Candle caught it in mid-air: a charged .32. He reversed it, brought its butt expertly down on the Aztec's head, and the man started to crumple. Candle caught him in his arms, dragged him to a chair, slumped the unconscious man over the table.

Maybe I haven't lost my nerve, Candle thought, straightening up. *Anyway my reflexes still work.*

"I should chuck ol' Aztec Paco there out on the sidewalk," Nodder said, yawning, scratching his belly.

"No need." Candle put the gun in an inside coat pocket. "He was just drunk. But I'll keep his shooter. I need one." He looked at Rina who was casually picking up a couple of dirty glasses, as if that's all she'd come out from behind the bar for. "Rina—thanks."

"Yeah, sure, I don't know why I do nothing nice for you, you so stupid. Could have gone with me, but you rather lose four years. What a dumb bastard."

"Could be you're right." He turned to Shortstack. "So. We have some kind of business to do or . . . what?"

Shortstack nodded. "Yeah. We got urgent business. Why you think got your testicles out of the goddamn waver? Risk getting our hands burned? Huh? It's urgent we talk. It's life-and-death, hode. But first things first—another drink."

REPRESENT, HODE,
YA CHAPTER FIVE—
GOTTA MAKE THE MOMENT
COME ALIVE

Spanx banged up the rickety stairs into the lowest level of Rooftown.

Spanx was shaped "like a stick insect," or so his sister Willow had said. His jeans were so tight on his skinny legs they looked spray-painted on, his boots so covered with duct tape he couldn't tell anymore—and couldn't remember—if they were leather or rubber; his *Danny Candle* T-shirt so long-unwashed and unchanged it had its own pores, he figured, its own epidermis; his frizzed out electric-shock bleached white hair was like an exotic fungus in the process of eating his head. High arching eyebrows, weak chin, hooking nose, hollow cheeks, almost lipless. Big earrings. Spanx. Clambering up, talking to himself.

"Climbing fucking trash mountain," he was saying. "Fucking Trash Mountain, hode."

The stairs were made out of old plastic milk crates, wired together around scavenged vertical steel support pipes that ran through the hollowed-out building; a circa-1970s building whose interior floors had all collapsed into a pile of rubble below. Above it reared Rooftown. scavenged and cobbled together. Spanx was still underneath most of Rooftown, its foundation a sprawling group of old steel-girder buildings in downtown L.A—former apartment buildings, failed hotels, a ten-story parking garage, a few office buildings. The buildings had been damaged by the 7.8 earthquake of 2020, externally too damaged to retrofit. But their steel frames were still sound enough to support the community that had grown up on top. And every time the real estate industry got interested in the neighborhood again, the Rooftown community let it be known that once evicted they would promptly move *en masse* to the best parts of town. "Try arresting us *all*." A bluff? Maybe. But for now—stalemate.

Rooftown knew it wouldn't last; knew the community and the structure wouldn't last. Everyone could see its fragility, and Spanx felt its cranky, swaying, creaking transience through the soles of his boots. He'd heard rumors the Matriarch was going to lock it down, not let anyone from outside in at all. But maybe that wasn't happening yet. He didn't want to ask the Matriarch's permission to get in. She scared him.

Spanx was on a mission to find Danny Candle. There was a gig to be played. There was potential money. Feeling "on a mission" with every step, Spanx followed the zigzag stairs up through a hole broken in the concrete roof. He emerged into the open air, walked across a ramp made of an old steel door to a corner of the building platform where an antique, jerry-rigged elevator, cadged from the remnants of a decrepit old hotel, wobbled its way down to him through a metal-mesh shaft. The shaft was tentatively attached by U-shaped hardened-plastic braces to the concrete wall of the higher, adjacent building. The vibration of the descending elevator transmitted to the mesh causing the bolts in the braces to grind about loosely in their drill holes, threatening to pop out.

"Might be the time has finally come for the collapse," Spanx muttered to himself. His ho-buddies had been giving him crap about talking to himself for awhile now, since he'd started doing the rotters—the rotorstims. But he couldn't bring himself to switch them off.

He rode up in the squealing, open elevator, the wind off the buildings coming through the bars to parch his mouth; he rode up and up, foot by slow creaking foot, licking his lips, laughing at his own fear; muttering. "Listen to your heart pound, hode! It's banging inside this metal tube you in, dumb shitter-shatter fuck. Whole thing going to crash down any second. Your heart beating so much it sets up vibration, like that butterfly theory thing . . ." He had to work up some saliva to keep talking, his mouth was so dry. His mouth stayed open, operating a lot. ". . . and it send that vibration outta your chest and the heartbeat gets, like, all into this elevator and goes into those bolts–" He turned his head to look in fascination at the bolts grinding sexily into the supporting building, bits of grit falling from the holes, a little more with each passage of the elevator. "—and those bolts get loose and—WHOA DAMN!—the whole thing falls and it knocks into those supports–" He turned to point, for no one but himself, at the underpinnings of the cross structure, like a tree-house that spanned two trees, connecting the building that held the elevator up and the unwieldy, visibly swaying superstructure of Rooftown rising from an old office building across the street. "—knock right into those puppies and knock 'em down and the whole thing comes down with it, ba-boom-ba-boom, house of cards, down she goes, couple three, maybe four thousand people up there . . ." Were there that many? No one knew. Just seemed like it was always teeming with people. ". . . and they go crashing down, all, like, 'YAHHHHHHHH! MOMMEEEEE!' and . . . any second now . . . any fucking second . . . I can feel it GO-IIIIIIINNNNG!" He laughed, delighted at the picture of it: he saw it quite clearly in his mind's eye. "All, like, a movie. Watch it go down! 'YAHHHH!'"

But the antique lift had resisted the vibrations of his thudding heart, Spanx saw, and the elevator cabin came wheezing to a stop at the upper end of its metal-mesh shaft, and he struggled, as usual, to get the rusty old gate open, the gate that always reminded him of a portable playpen, accordion made out of Xs. Finally it slid aside, the Xs contracting, pinching skin off his thumb.

Sucking at his bleeding thumb, Spanx said, "Shitter-shatter!" and stepped through onto the walkway, which was made of slats of wood attached by wire to a couple of metal ladders laid down flat between the elevator and the undercarriage of Rooftown. The "undercarriage", as residents called it, was actually a metal tower that had fallen from the top of one of the buildings during the earthquake, to make an accidental bridge across two others. Rooftown squatters occupying the other buildings had started building across the tower, with beams and other materials from collapsed structures. Layer on layer had been added, old and new materials . . . And now Spanx jogged along a catwalk that swung under his tread; he hurried along the outside of the undercarriage, up to a series of ladders and steps. "Not handicapped accessible, that's for fuck's sure," he said, and some of the scarecrow kids climbing around in the timbers overhead laughed and agreed and threw wood chips at him. "Hey hey hey you you you kids-ids are gonna, all, like, fall and shit!" Spanx called, more enjoying the concept than warning them. Sometimes they did fall, some of them. A few people fell every week from Rooftown. Sometimes more than a few. Eventually their bodies were cleared away by robotic street sweepers—the bodies the Rooftowners didn't retrieve. The Rooftowners liked a good funeral. There were mummified bodies sealed into the walls of derelict buildings on this side of the street.

Spanx, articulating his free-association, glanced down past the catwalk at the street. "How many stories down, those little cars, those little people, that little truck? Twenty?" A seagull flew by beneath him. "Hey bird the sky's up here ya dumb featherhead!" he called.

Chattering to himself, Spanx reached the steep stairs he wanted, this one made of old railroad ties, and climbed it, holding onto the frayed yellow-plastic ropes that served as banisters. It was colder up here, and a wet wind was blowing. A big dented mystercyke vertical sewage pipe, four feet in diameter, gurgled next to the stairway. He could smell the sewage in it, running down to the drains in the center support building, dollops leaking out badly connected joints.

Spanx reached the top, found himself in Rooftown itself, squinting against a drift of smoke. Smell of burning garbage, gasoline and trash in metal drums—the old gasoline storage tanks were still being sucked out for basic fuel. This level was a maze of interconnected shanties, made of scrap tin and allwall and mystercyke; on his left were fifty square yards of shanties, on his right Rooftown rose in tiers, becoming a haphazard tower of improvised, stacked boxes, swaying in the wind. He licked his lips. His mouth was so dry, now, it was hard to talk here. Needed a drink. "Just a little slip of a sip between brain and lips, whippity whip whip!"

Hugging himself against the chill, Spanx walked along a track made out of random, dissimilar segments of scrap wood and planks of mystercyke. Faces looked out at him from the shanty doors, holes cut for windows; most of them Latino, some African, a few Asian, a salting of grimy white faces. The post-global warming immigration surge mostly found work, absorbed into service jobs and blue collar work—whatever was cheaper than maintaining robots. But they were always underpaid and housing was expensive, so some of "The Population Overflow", as the iNews sites called it, overflowed to Rooftown. The Immigration people were afraid to come up here, and not only because of the perpetual risk of the whole structure collapsing; one or two immigration agents had vanished, were rumored to have joined the mummies in the walls.

Spanx turned past a group of bundled-up men huddled around a flaming, rust-red steel drum on a deck made of mystercyke freight pallets. The wind carried a shred of low-altitude cloud to break against them, and Yodeller—a man with burnt-red skin, his face mostly hidden in red beard, red dreadlocks drooping over his eyes—called out to Spanx as he passed. "Hey it's Stick Figure!" Yodeller having an unnaturally high-pitched voice. "Have some wine, Sticky, ya freak-hode!"

Spanx paused, drew deep on the half-gallon of sweet red wine. Took a deep breath. Took another swig. Passed it back, talking again as soon as the bottle had left his mouth. "Whoa I'm all, like, unstuck now, my lips was stuck together and my brain was stuck and my rotters was stuck and my thoughts was stuck–"

"Hey you got those rotters, hode?" one of the men asked; a vulpine man looking at Spanx narrowly.

"Nah, nah, nah, I mean, *feels* that way . . ." Spanx did have the microscopic rotor shaped nanos, paid for by the money they'd made off the single—a tune called "Make it Last Way Past"—a few years back, and the "rotters" were still running, little nanobots swimming in his brain, tuning his brain cells to stimulation, always stimulation. The rotters were supposed to let you sleep when fatigue-poison levels reached a certain point, but he'd had the rotters signal-set so that they maximized the stimulation and so it took three times the fatigue poisons it should to get them to switch on the brain's sleep center. The manual advised against that. "Nah nah, haven't, haven't got 'em . . ." Denying it to the vulpine guy because there was a story that people who found out you had valuable brainbots would follow you and jump you, and kill you and crack open your head and they used some machine to go through the brain tissue and magnetize the little bots out and use 'em themselves or sell 'em. Maybe the story was just paranoia, just myth. Sure, right, right, could be. Or maybe not. In that moment, Spanx was able—just barely able—to keep from talking aloud about his rotters.

"Thanks for the wine hey, ya, hey is Danny around, is he up in the Pisa, he up there, is he with that Linda up there, in the air?" The tower of stacked-up shanties was called Pisa, after the Tower of, because it leaned so much. Something from his childhood came to mind. A *Dr. Seuss* drawing. His mother had liked to read Dr. Seuss to him. Same old stabbing pain at the thought. "Green eggs and ham my brain, with a bloodstain," Spanx intoned. "Mommity mom mom, go outta my head, Mommity mom can't help being dead." That's what he called her, Mommity mom. They'd been close. His dad had been a good guy, so far as he remembered, but the old man had died early on, so he'd been all about his mom, and his mom had committed suicide, because of some cancer that kept coming back and coming back and coming back. They'd cure it—and it would stay away for awhile. And then it would come back. It just kept coming back. Something about plastic molecules sticking to DNA. A "pollutant cancer," the doctor had said. Cure it and it'd come back, and finally she couldn't stand it anymore. Swallowed a bottle of her pain pills.

The band had made fun of how much he was into his mom. Except Danny, he'd been pretty nice about it. Lost his folks too.

"I don't know nothin' about yer mom," Yodeller said, a bit defensively, not realizing Spanx had been thinking aloud.

"Yeah, but no, but yeah, but what about Danny?" Spanx persisted.

"I saw him go up there," said Yodeller, "Dunno did he come out, there's more'n one way. Hey you got any–"

But Spanx had moved on, was climbing a curving ramp made of the recycled-plastic slabs so ubiquitous now. Followed it into the uneven passage between the shanties. Ducking under

90

electric wires; juice stolen from below, seemed like miles of extension cords. Lights from computers, holotubes, televisions, solar-energized animated posters glimmered through cracks and glassless windows. The gear mostly from discarded-tech donation centers.

The Pisa swayed, and creaked and moaned in the wind. Sheets of black bag waterproofing snapped in the wind. Muttering to himself, Spanx passed a community privy, and held his nose. They hadn't rinsed its ditch-pipes in a while. He climbed to another ad hoc floor of the tower and heard a woman's voice, a familiar nasal whine, *"Danny please don't ex, please don't ex . . ."* Coming from the left—there: wedged between, below, and above four others, was Bev's little shack, made of allwall and scrounged aluminum window frames. And there, visible through the window, was Danny, cramming a much spray-painted snapper, partly open to seven inches square, into a backpack. The door, that didn't quite fit in the doorframe, was closed but not locked. A quarter-inch of air all the way around it.

"Little Danny playin' with his toys, be a good boy don't make no noise," Spanx said, pushing through the door.

"Who's that, Danny, get him out, Danny don't go with him!" Bev wailed. A woman who had tanned herself a little too much, so the skin was getting mottled and leathery-lined in places; she wore only an open bathrobe, naked under that, with long but thinning brown hair, tattoos on her breasts, "face not too bad, tits just okay", was Spanx's automatic evaluation. She was at least ten years older than Danny. The tat on her left shoulder was bio-electricity active, an animated image of an ugly duckling turning into a swan, over and over again, the swan flying away, the 'duckling' reappearing, turning into the swan . . .

The shack was about fifteen feet by twenty-five feet, the ceiling bowed by the weight of the shack piled above it. There were plastic jugs of water, and other fluids, against the translucent back wall, there was a big pyramid of dirty clothes, a greasy futon, a cage with two fat scrabbling gerbils in it, and a shadeless lamp, the only light, sitting on the cage.

"Danny don't! Don't GO!" Bev was wailing, rocking back and forth, clutching her bathrobe shut.

Wearing snakeskin boots, jeans, a leather jacket with no shirt underneath—the tattoo of a crowing rooster, most of its lower body hidden in his pants, its head bristled red and blue just below his navel—Danny was plucking items of dirty clothes from the pile, the ensuing avalanche of yellowing laundry inducing a memory of Spanx's first and only year in college. "Demonstrating catastrophe theory," Spanx said. "That's what you're doing, Danny."

"What you *want?*" Danny asked. "I got no time to listen to you chatter, hode, I've gotta hook-in to go to. Little V-trip. Took me three days to raise the money." His voice, to Spanx, always sounded like one of those tall women with the low voices.

The wind soughed through the cracks, and Bev wailed, and Spanx said, "We gotta gig, man, we gotta gig. Pays some money."

Danny looked at him skeptically, scratched in his explosion of jet-black dyed hair. "How much? When?"

"Twenty-four hundred shared, my guitar sky-god. Saturday night."

"Not much time for rehearsal. We're rusty. And you know we only got this because somebody cancelled.

"So Kyu Kim cancelled, whatever. People will come. You got a following and they get a good crowd on Saturday. Sinkitties there. Flow's okay."

"Danny don't go they don't care about you!" Bev keened, rocking in place.

"Huh," Danny said. "I need the flow. But I don't wanna show myself in public like that, my brother's out of jail, he'll get wind of it."

"How you know he's out, he was gonna be down for the Un-Minding a long fucking time, hodey brudder."

"Because Tranny Tammy saw him in Nodder's and she called me—why you think I'm packing up, hode? Everybody knows I been staying here."

"Your cranny's working? When you get that implant going? You get a signaler?" Spanx's own phone implant wasn't paid up, had been shut off.

"Yeah yeah it's working, don't matter how. I can't be doing shows man."

"You heard him Spanx!" Bev whined, wiping away tears. "He can't do it he has to stay with meeeeeeeeeeee!"

"Shut up ya, oh ya, ya sweatin' slit," Spanx said, wondering what Bev was fucked up on. Something for sure.

"Danny you going to hit him? He says that to me you have to hit him, please Danny, hit him and stay with me—throw him off the platform and stay with me–"

"Shut up, Bev," Danny said wearily. "Spanx, I could do a session but not a show. Swore I'd stay straight 'cause Rick took the fall for me. And I didn't stay straight. He'll be mad. I'd be fucking mad too. He finds me, he'll surveil my ass till I use, get me busted this time, teach me a lesson."

"Don't got a session. Got a show. I'll give you half my share if you play it, hodey brudder you suction-pump, you."

"Oh man. Fucking hode." Danny shook his head. "Then you'll guilt me about it. 'I gave you half my share, you V-rat'."

"Nah I won't-y won't-won't. Come onnnnn, come *onnnnnn.*"

"Where's the gig?"

"The Black Glass club, bub. Not a big place, so not a big pay, James Earl Ray."

"Who's James Earl Ray?"

"I don't fucking know, my dad used to say Ray was the gloved finger of the FBI, whatever that means. But my dad died so I didn't get to ask, Trask. Don't Crash, trash."

"Get a grip on that babbling bullshit. Where's my gear? Zilia don't have it? She was saying she was gonna go get it to be paid back the money . . ."

"She didn't get it, it's good debit. I got your best guitar, I got your playbacks, I got your digiflagger, I got your amps, I got all your fucking testicles, wiggledy-wiggledy–"

"You got *all* the gear?" Danny looked at him with surprise. "Come on, hode. You didn't pawn none of it?"

Spanx was insulted. He'd stolen some of his sister's jewelry, visiting her house, and pawned that, without qualms. But band equipment was sacred.

"No fucking way! I'm not like you, my crew!"

"Okay, okay, well—when is this thing? Maybe if it's pretty

soon . . . I can do it, and get away before he grabs me . . . You guys could keep him busy, while I slip out or something, those clubs are buzzin' . . . we could think of something . . ."

"Then come on, come to my place, we'll get a rehearsal on."

"No Danny don't leave me-e-e-e!"

"Just to get the fuck away from that noise, girl—I'm going. Come on, Spanx . . . you fuckin' wanx."

Candle was beginning to feel like he was spinning his wheels. He sat at a wobbly table in Nodder's bar, the place now mostly deserted, playing Hold 'Em poker on a borrowed blueglove, with Nodder and a wild-eyed young blond Norwegian kid who kept overplaying his hands. Nodder and Candle were waiting for Shortstack to get back from his "ginger" so they could finish their business. He glanced at the digital image in the palm of his glove, which showed the community cards and his hole cards—his two-pair were no better than they were last time he'd looked—and asked his thumb what time it was. The thumb on the sheer digital glove soothed, in a woman's voice, "Four P.M., Pacific Time."

"You getting impatient?" Nodder asked, glancing at the palm of his blue glove.

"Yeah I am. I've gotta go out and find Danny. He hears I'm out, he's liable to leave town. Ginger's going to take Shortstack some time—genetic re-engineering takes some goddamn time, like a week in some clinic or . . ."

"Nah, not always. Depends. You just think like that because you're a basic."

"Excuse me?"

"That's what Shortstack calls people that haven't been gingered."

"My DNA was screwed up enough when my parents got married. I don't need some pseudocompetent wanx with a degree from, like, the University of the Falkland Islands retrofitting it. Accidentally giving me a face on my ass or something." Maybe he should bet . . . but Nodder could be slow-playing trips.

"Face on your ass might come in handy. Watch your back for you."

The young Norwegian laughed at that.

Candle snorted, peering at the little image of his cards in his palm. "If Shortstack's into that, can't he 'ginger' himself larger? Taller? You'd think . . ."

"There's limitations to retro-engineering. Complications, genetic frontiers. Naw—he can't do that. He did though give himself an . . ." Nodder yawned. ". . . an enormous—enormous . . ." Then Nodder's head drooped. He started to narcoleptically nod out.

Candle gave out a near-shout: "Raise, a hundred!"

Nodder snapped awake. "What? You're raising me?"

"I could be bluffing." But he wasn't. The dealer—a server in some distant place—had dealt the river card, giving Candle a third five, and a full house.

Nodder frowned at his palm. "Uhhhh . . . I call."

Candle looked at the Norwegian kid who closed his fingers into a fist, folding with a scowl.

"Full house," Candle said, sending them the image on his palm. Trying not to sound triumphant.

"Shitter shatter! Hey—instead of the cash how about I give you that glove. It's been ID neutralized. Somebody left it here."

"Or you pulled it off a sleeping drunk?"

"Same thing."

"Well hell, if it's blank, I can put my own stuff on it. Thanks." It was worth more than Nodder owed him.

Shortstack came in then, all jaunty, grinning energy. He was carrying a pizza box. "You see? Didn't take long. Just had to get the ATP turned up in my mitochondria. Means I got to eat more, though. Who's for curried pizza?"

Candle pocketed the blue glove and they ate, sharing pizza with the crestfallen and now much poorer Norwegian, who had murmured of winning the World Hold 'Em Poker Tournament someday. Then Shortstack wiped his mouth and said, "See you later, Knut. Candle, come on."

Candle got up—and froze, squinting at an upper corner of the dimly lit room. It was like a piece of one of the chain of handcuffs decorating the wall had gotten free and was drifting in the air, near the ceiling . . .

Then he realized it was a birdseye. He was being watched by

another silvery, bird-sized surveillance drone. Not quite the same model as earlier. Just slightly larger, its silver body supported by transparent-polymer wings beating with hummingbird rapidity. Watching him.

Either someone at a surveil-monitor somewhere was staring right at him through that thing, or a wide-task law enforcement computer was just doing a biometric scan on them, to see if there were any outstanding warrants here. If there were any, Candle knew, that didn't mean they'd rush the cops over. They'd run the warrant through a program that triaged for priority and unless it was multiple murder, terrorism, or digital banking fraud, probably no one would show up anytime soon, if at all. But if it was a Slakon bird, they'd send some boys around. They let him slip through their fingers when he got out of jail and now someone was trying to make up for slacking.

"Shortstack," Candle muttered. "Uh . . ."

"I see it," Shortstack said softly, not looking directly at the drone. He signaled to Rina who was just straightening up from installing a beer keg behind the bar. "Hey you got an audience, Rina. If it's a man on the other end of the feed, then maybe . . ."

A song by Jerome-X, "Sexual Identification Strata", came thumping on through the sound system. She came dancing out from behind the bar, pulling off her top. Her small brown nipples were pierced, Candle saw. That was new. She still looked good. Taut stomach muscles. Candle tried not to stare as she rippled her flat belly and spun the blouse around in front of the camera . . . and it tilted its lens toward her.

So that answered a question: it was a man on the other end of the feed, reacting with a knee-jerk male response. Just long enough. Funny, Candle thought, all that techno-enhancement and he's just as responsive to sex as a caveman.

She danced as Jerome-X rapped out raspily, right on electronica-grime beat, with guitar stylings by the aging Dweezil Zappa:

Sexual
I.D. strata,
The rise 'n' fall

o' your very very
very very very very
personal data
Hormone-hot
state o' mind
Holo shot
inside the rind . . .

And she danced nearer to the flying camera . . . which drifted a
little nearer her as she swung her blouse with one hand and started
to tug on her pants with the other. The boyish Norwegian, drinking aquavit, pounded on the table and whooped as Rina danced
past him, rhythmically sidling ever closer to the drone.

Any second now, Candle figured, as Shortstack tugged him
toward a door to a back room, the drone operator was going to
realize . . .

Then Rina was close enough, and she tossed her blouse over
the drone, tangling its wings. It clunked to the floor, clattered and
buzzed there like a wasp in a bottle.

She stepped over to it and, still with the beat, stamped it several
times, smashing it thoroughly. "Oh shit it got lubrication oil on
my blouse . . . Okay, you can go now . . ."

"Come on, Candle," Shortstack said eagerly. "This way."

Nodder and Candle followed the energized Shortstack
through a room that had once been used for mug shots, through
another door, down a back stairs, along a corridor where a couple
of dying fluorescent light-strips flickered unsteadily like the last
thoughts of a dying man. "You want to tell me where we're going?" Candle asked.

"Not really," Nodder said.

"Not much use being cagey, Nodder," Shortstack said, chugging along ahead of them. "I made up my mind we're going to
trust him. You don't think he's undercover? They're not going to
put somebody in that place four years just to go undercover. Rina
knew all about it. Rina says he's okay, he's okay . . ."

Nodder shook his head. "I don't like it. I think we shoulda
felt it out longer."

"Still didn't tell me where we're going," Candle pointed out.

"We're going to the back room," Shortstack said. "Way, way in back. The room where the girls are."

"I didn't do that kind of time," Candle said. "I don't need to get laid that bad. To me it was just yesterday they put me under." This wasn't exactly true, though. His body knew the difference and it had been prodding him hard, while he watched Rina dance.

Nodder chuckled and shook his head.

They reached the end of the corridor and Shortstack opened a door into a room on their right, a dusty office empty except for a series of abandoned workstations, cobwebby cubicles. The only light shafted in through a window, illuminating whorls of dust motes. The light dimmed for a moment as a police flying cruiser drifted past. Gone, and the light returned.

That's how it is to people like Nodder and Shortstack, Candle thought. The cops come around and it's like a shadow falling over everything. To a cop—to me, back then—it was like we were shining light in dark corners. My light blinds you; my light is your darkness . . .

He still wished he was in that cruiser, and not here. It'd been hard to take, surrendering his badge.

Nodder closed the door behind them and they went to a cubicle pressed against the wall, its workstation piled with old computer drives. But the random stack of drives were glued together like something in a stage set, Candle saw, looking close—realizing they were camouflage as Shortstack easily pulled the cubicle away from the wall, and walked through the low opening hidden on the other side. It was a rough door shape cut in the wall; Candle and Nodder had to stoop to get through. Shortstack reached back and pulled the cubicle back into place behind them as Candle looked around the smaller room . . .

Three women in jogging suits worked quietly side-by-side at three workstations, under a whispering air condition vent; a plump blond, a freckled, willowy brunette, a tall black woman with her head shaved, hoop earrings. Candle recognized the blond as a former hooker from Sunset Boulevard, and the other two had the hardened look—and the hand-inked prison tattoos—of women the street had known intimately. Delicate sensor headsets hooked them wirelessly to the computer, ball keyboards flickered and spun under their rapt fingers. The blond, he noticed, had her hair styled and colored to duplicate Marilyn Monroe's classic 'do. She had drawn on a beauty mark in the right place, too.

The room was windowless, but animated posters of natural scenes, a waterfall, breakers crashing on rocks, broke up the sense of confinement. Music played softly, chugging enticingly along, a neo-reggae band just becoming popular when Candle had been UnMinded: *The Sober Jamaicans.*

"Got a visitor," Nodder said.

Brinny, the short-haired brunette, turned to glare at him—Candle vaguely remembered booking her for illegal-software. She'd have been pretty if her eyes hadn't been a trifle too close together. "That guy—he's a . . . ain't he?" She broke off, frowning, not sure she should say it out loud. Maybe she should be pretending there was no reason a cop shouldn't be here. She looked questioningly at Shortstack.

"He was a cop," Shortstack confirmed. "He's O-source now."

"Says you!" Brinny scoffed. "He was undercover, sneaking around Johnny Ebo. Shot Johnny through the head, all gone'n took his woman." There was something very trailer park about Brinny's accent, her diction.

"When I was undercover, I was looking for sex slaves, Brinny," Candle said. "I know you don't support that sex slave thing. Tell the women they're getting jobs in the States and they end locked in a room with a bed. That's not legit sex work."

"Johnny wasn't in that," she persisted, scowling.

"But he knew who was. And I only shot him when he was going to hurt Rina. You hear a lotta dropcall on the street about me, isn't true."

"So you going to work with us?" the black woman asked, looking at him sidelong.

"This is Pell Mell," Nodder said, indicating the tall bald black woman. "We usually just call her Pell. You know Brinny. This is Monroe. They're all damn good—they're all *leet.* Ladies, Candle here might be working with us—then again he might not."

All three women looked at him in vaguely hostile confusion.

"Don't know what you're doing—or what I'd be doing,"

Candle said. "But I can tell you, I'm not a cop. Not anymore. That just isn't happening. I'm not busting anyone, anywhere."

Even as he said it—and Brinny sniffed skeptically—he wondered if it were entirely true; there were crimes he probably would report to old friends on the job, if he saw the crime going down. Some crimes—but not many.

"Not like we've never done business with police," Pell said. "I sucked many a pig dick to keep out of jail."

Candle winced at that. Pig dick.

"Yeah," Monroe said, her voice almost believably breathy. "We used to pay 'em off when we were dealing . . . well." She shrugged and went back to work.

Candle was slightly more than half convinced Monroe used to be male.

"Yeah well—if he was undercover before," Brinny pointed out, "maybe he is now. But whatever, I'm-a let you guys worry on it."

She went back to work, fingers flying over the keyboards. Candle marveled at the dexterity of her fingers.

"Okay here's the texer, Candle," Shortstack said, "What we got here is–"

"Ah, 'Stack," Nodder interrupted, "are we entirely certain . . .?"

"Nodder—we can *trust* the guy!" Shortstack insisted. "We're doing this!"

Even Candle wondered why Shortstack was so sure. But he suspected that the little guy had a big ego, and refused to admit he was wrong once he'd set a course for himself. Candle also suspected Shortstack was just trying to please Rina by helping Candle.

As he spoke, Nodder pulled a stim-patch from a pocket and thoughtfully peeled it, applied it above the last one on his arm. "Well . . . Brinny's right that the guy was undercover. I mean, seriously 'Stack, what if . . ."

"If I were undercover, you'd be done for already, with me getting this far," Candle said. "But I'm not. I'm just . . . not."

He looked Nodder in the eye. Nodder pursed his lips—then made a gesture of benediction to Shortstack.

"I can fucking *talk* now?" Shortstack asked, sidling up next to
Brinny, putting a hand on her thigh and looking at the screen in
front of her. The figures on the screen were three-leveled, stacked
in three dimensions, and represented, Candle suspected, only a
small part of what Brinny was seeing: the headset probably sent
signals to interfacers along her optic nerves. "Okay, so the texer
is that this is the L.A. locus of the Black Stock Market, Candle.
Things were bad when you got sent down, got even worse the
last four years. All the controls on monopolies are just . . . gone.
Dismantled. There's the Fortune 33 and that's just it, man. Oh
sure, some Chinese outfits, yeah, but the 33 run the fucking planet.
Privatizing everything—that's why all the infrastructure's gone
to shit. The 33 rule. Except for the Black Stock Market! There are
other businesses, millions of small ones, some that come and go
in a few days, some that go on and on, some that change their
names and show up under, like, all these different guises but, you
know, same company, right? They're pretty much under the radar
of the 33. Lots of 'em are Mesh based, lots others are wi-net, others are brainchippers, others are little shops that move around,
work outta the back of trucks, some are sizable small companies
in Third World Countries—you get the idea. So they need support, right, they need money coming in, so we sell 'quick stock'
for these people, a few thousand WD for a few thousand shares
for some of 'em—others are more expensive. But it's all a quick
turnaround. They repay the buyer by Internet or wi-buy transfer
within thirty-six hours if the profit's there. We monitor it and
they trust us with their data. Some have longer term deals, it's
monthly, got some going twice yearly. We take a cut."

"I'm sure your staff here does a great job," Candle said, "but
I'm surprised you don't use expert systems for most of it, maybe
some underground cloud computing . . . I mean—once you've
bought them you don't have to pay them and they're likely to
be fast—and they're not going to give state's evidence to get less
time–"

Nodder flicked his hand dismissively. "They exaggerate how
flexible and intelligent those systems are. We do use some adjunct
expert programs. But they've got short horizons. Anyway, people
who've dodged the law, they have . . . almost a sixth sense, an in-

tuitive ability . . . they know *when* to dodge the law. And there's another thing—really it's the main thing—most of the existing programs and robots have software hidden in them to report back to the feds if they're used for something illegal. These ladies are not burdened that way."

"And it's only illegal," Shortstack said, "because Congress is owned by the 33 and the 33 calls it 'unregulated'. But we *do* regulate it—we stay fair. We got to, or people will come after us. And anyway we make more money being fair to people. They come back because we pay off."

"But the 33—they're dogging you?" Candle asked.

"Yeah. Starting to get close. Oh, we got the best encryption, we got a lot of noise-floggers to create cover. Only now—shitter-shatter, boy, we had some *close* calls. We're looking to you to come in, provide expert protection. You the Man, you know law enforcement. You worked computer crime for awhile . . ."

Candle shook his head, dubious. "I don't know—that stuff updates, like. every few months. I'm way behind by now."

"You got a feel for it though," Shortstack insisted. "You can get caught up. Anyway we think Slakon is particularly interested in us. They don't know who we are or where we are but they know *that* we are. And we represent a . . . a . . ." He looked at Nodder for the right words.

"A dangerous phenomenon that threatens their control," Nodder said.

"Yeah! And we figure you're motivated to run interference, Rick. You know Slakon, you had your run-ins . . . Takes a cop to fool the cops . . . Anyway, hode, what else you got going on? And this'll give you a chance to get some of your own back, a little taste of revenge against those Slakon fucks. You know there was no real reason for them to go after Danny the way they did—that was so small time. Such a small amount of rake-off. It was "make an example'. And it turned out *you* had to be the example. So what you say?"

It occurred to Candle that since he was being targeted by Slakon, it wasn't that smart of Shortstack and Nodder to bring him in—he would bring even more heat on them. He figured that was Rina again. She was mad at him. But she wanted him around. "Rina put you up to this?"

Shortstack looked carefully blank. "She's a major investor. She's part of all our decisions."

"I see." *Anyway, hode, what else you got going on?* "Tell you what . . ." He looked at the seething tables, charts, data piling up on the Black Stock Market screens. It was like the movement of a seismograph of true laissez-faire commerce; it was an electroencephalograph of the real market place. It was the dance of individuals struggling to survive, signifying, in the small market squares of the world. There was something romantic about it that drew him. "This is the kind of illegal that . . . should be legal. This is . . . this is something I don't feel like I can say no to. If it pays reasonably well. I just hope I'm not bad luck for you."

"Yeah," Brinny muttered. "I fucking hope so too."

IT'S NOT VERY SLICK,
NOT MUCH OF A TRICK—
HELL, HODE, IT'S JUST
CHAPTER SIX

Five holographic faces appeared on the Multisemblant array, set about a circle, looking outward, away from one another.

"I hope y'all know what you're doing," the Bulwer semblant said.

"This will give us an edge over the rest of the Fortune 33," the Grist semblant said. "Oh he knows what he's doing."

The Claire PointOne semblant frowned. "The prospect is repellent. It's, like, a violation of my inner being."

"Semblants," Grist said, "shut up. I'm thinking." He and Sykes were standing under the bluewhite buzzing lights, gazing at the array. Grist was feeling like he was on the verge of changing the world, in some way. And he was almost convinced it was a change that the world needed. It was, anyway, one that Grist needed. That had always been good enough before—so why was he hesitating now?

". . . So you see," Sykes was saying, unwrapping a marijuana-tinged Yum Wad and cramming it into his mouth, "I had to separate the merged ones—to re-establish full coalescence of all five, we had to start from scratch—and once we've got merge this may offer a more unified model . . ." He chewed vigorously, mouth open, eyes glazing, as he appraised the five restless holographic heads. Yatsumi, Grist, Bulwer, Alvarez, Claire PointOne.

"What about Hoffman?" Grist asked.

"Still too much distortive resistance. But I thought five'd come out coherently. Only, I have to form it around a primary personality mode—it needs a unifying personality principle or it's just a confused psychotic mish-mash, like last time."

"What principle?" Grist asked.

"Ah well—it depends on how you'd define it. Some call it 'acquisitive egoism'."

Grist shrugged. "What the hell does that mean?"

Sykes tossed the wrapping paper on the floor, where it joined a dozen others. A plasticine snowfall. "Oh well—another way of describing it is . . . megalomania."

Grist shifted his weight to his other foot, feeling a vague discomfort. Suddenly, for no reason, his joints ached. He might need to have them rebuilt. "Megalomania? I've been accused of that often enough. What successful businessman in this century hasn't? It's all smokescreen, that talk of 'megalomania'—it's disingenuous flummery, designed to hide sheer envy. We want the multi-semblant to be *driven!* Motivated! Yes—grasping! *Carpe Diem!* The day must be seized! And to seize you must grasp!"

"So that works for you?" Sykes nodded, sniffing. Chewing. "I mean—as a mind cohesion strategy?" He dug in an ear absent-mindedly with an index finger. "Okay. Okay then."

"Why are you waiting? Go for it."

"Um—not sure what the results will be, short term or long term. Don't want to make you mad. You do have a way of threatening me with some nightmarish fate or other when you're mad. Glue my rectum shut, wedge my mouth open or something. If it doesn't come out right—you'll blame me. I'd be crazy not to hesitate."

"Yes yes, I'll take that into account. When we've merged this thing, we'll observe it for a time—then we'll add more. And in the end we'll have the most powerful business mind on the planet. A mind who'll anticipate what all the others are thinking and doing—it'll be one step ahead of all of them at once. And then . . ."

He broke off. He didn't want Sykes, or anyone, to know about the 'and then'.

"Oh yes," the Grist semblant said, chuckling. "And then!"

"Just can it, semblant," Grist said.

"Shall I go ahead and do the merge, Mr. Grist?" Sykes asked. "I mean—shall I do it right now?" His hand hovered over the controls.

Grist, standing beside him, gazing raptly at the array . . . and hesitated, himself. He licked his lips. Then he nodded. "Do it."

Sykes caressed the spherical input he preferred to a standard keyboard . . . and the semblants shimmered. Claire PointOne's image seemed to gasp and wail . . .

"It's a violation, an intrusion, a rape!" her semblant yowled. And then the five images merged into one. The Picasso effect was there for a moment; then it seemed to shake itself into a more coherent face. It was still a bit like a person whose face had been reconstructed after an accident, but not without a pleasing esthetic. The multisemblant had Claire's nose and mouth, and they didn't quite seem to go with the male eyes from Grist and Alvarez and the cheekbones from Yatsumi, but . . . Grist found the facial agglomeration rather attractive, in a way.

Might be interesting to get Lisha's face made that way for awhile.

The merged semblant looked around. "Who?" It blinked and shuddered. "Am?" It squinted at Grist. ". . . I?"

"You are the beginning of the Multisemblant," Sykes said. "Mr. Grist's—special consultant, I guess. And you are my invention. Which reminds me, Mr Grist, about that patent we talked about. I haven't got the forms yet . . ."

"Yes, later," Grist said. He had no intention of sharing a patent. He didn't want anyone else to have the semblant combining capacity, ever, if he could help it. "Is it in some kind of infantile state now? I mean, asking 'who am I ?'–"

"Just a moment of thinking, cogitating, aloud," the Multisemblant said, briskly. Its voice phasing in and out of sharp definition, but intelligible. "I am not an infant. I am a completed being. I am five semblants fused into one." It's voice became slightly more like Grist, as it said: "I am something wonderful: the greatest business mind on the planet."

"Very good," Grist said, pleased.

"Nevertheless," Sykes said, chewing noisily, "its personality isn't really unified. It's not just a merging of five semblants—it has to be *a whole new one*, which has access to the databases that constitute those five. But it needs to be a 'whole that's more than the sum of the parts' or all you'll get is dissonance. Like light, before it's oscillated into a laser, it's got no special direction. So we're making the 'ruby', so to speak, now, and it'll take some time. It's still working on it. It will be your ultimate consultant soon, though . . . Ah—you see the dissonance spiking there? Remember the new AI has an I-core that either supports emotion or something so close to emotion you can't tell the difference. That has to be hierachized—otherwise you'll have it giving way to every furious impulse. If you push for too much too soon it'll react in anger and tend to form its new personality around anger-based complexes the way traumatized people do."

"I am never *too much*," the Multisemblant snarled angrily, right on cue. "I am exactly what I should be—always!"

Sykes gave Grist a "See what I mean?" look.

"Get its emotions under control, then, Sykes," Grist said. "I want access soon. They'll have to be . . ." He broke off. It really was best Sykes didn't know. The tubby onanist might try to go to the 33. He wondered if he needed more direct surveillance on Sykes.

"Too much too soon," Sykes repeated, shaking his head. "It'll grasp the worst parts of you—and the others—to use as the basis of its personality. That's according to the best psyche models we have. It'll form itself out of the fearful parts of you, the cynical parts, the compulsive parts–"

Grist turned Sykes a sharp look. "Those are *bad* things? Those are the tools of success! But the way you're putting it is a little derogatory—a little *personal*."

Sykes took the Yum Wad from his mouth, tossed it at a waste basket—which moved closer to neatly catch it. "Waste basket ignores the wrappers, only goes for the heavy stuff. Cheap fucking thing. Oh, you think I'm being too personal, with the Multisemblant's cynicism, that stuff? Sorry, boss, but I have to be realistic about what I'm working with."

"Just get it functioning. Whatever it takes. Go ahead an use the unifying element you were talking about—Call it megalomania if you want." He smiled. "I call it real self-determination. It always worked for me."

Sykes chewed his lip, then he made a little shrugging tilt of his head, and his fingers flicked over the controls.

The Multisemblant cried out in multifarious anguish.

Then it babbled, for a full minute, in a mix of English, Japanese, Spanish . . .

Grist glanced at his watch.

"English only, imperative one!" Sykes commanded. "Prioritize as per final indice referent! Now!"

The faces merged a little more. Now it looked even less jumbled. Not a pleasant face—more the face of the descendent that would come about if Yatsumi, Claire, Alvarez, Grist and Bulwer had somehow interbred. Mostly a male face.

"Multisemblant?" Sykes prompted. "Do you have a sense of who you are now?"

Its voice was a little surer too, when it spoke. Close to Grist's voice but with a faint Texas accent. "Yes, oh hell yes," said the Multisemblant. *"I am the beginning. And boys, I am the motherfucking end."*

Grist stared. "Sykes–"

A soft chime in the bone under his right ear. A gentle computer voice in his head spoke. *"Targer calling."* Grist waved Sykes away and walked off, toward the door. "Yes, what is it?"

"Targer here," came the voice in his ear, though the computer had already announced him. "Halido's decoy worked."

"You sent in one of the old ones, the birdseyes?" Grist asked, going through the door into the corridor.

A beige security-guard robot trundled down the hall, rolling by him; its upper half of sculpted hard plastic, shaped like the stylized head and torso of a man, its lower half a truncated stainless steel cone with wheels and telescoping personnel-restraint extenders; as the robot rolled by, it turned its eyeless face toward him, invisibly scanning Grist's eyes and the ID clip on his lapel to see that he was authorized. It recognized him, and murmured something soothing and respectful.

"We did just that," Targer was saying. "A woman there—ah, we've identified her as an ex-whorehouse madame, a Rina Qu Lam—she got Halido's attention and when he turned the birdseye toward her she netted it with her blouse and stepped on it."

Grist chuckled. "A woman of experience. And while they were focused on that . . .?"

"Right. The dragonfly went in. Our smallest model. Followed them to their Black Stock Market—just three people and some hardware in the building next door. The 'fly's on the ceiling, watching them, listening, right now. A nice clear transmission."

"And they haven't made the dragonfly yet?"

"No. No it's really pretty small—almost like a house fly. And it can recharge from moisture, you know. It takes moisture on any wall, and the electrical charge that accumulates–"

"Spare me the Electronics Channel narrative. And you can put Candle with them, in the room? In an illegal business?"

"They were negotiating Candle's share, when I left the surveillance to Halido. Candle is in it up to his ears."

"Good. He's a loose cannon, I don't want him running around." Grist started for the exit. "We'll get several birds with this stone." He wanted his dinner. Stop by the executive's club. They'd refurbished the bistro, put in a primo meat-grower; the steaks supposedly indistinguishable from meat from the actual animal.

"I'm just waiting for the good word from you. Just press the button on it and we send in the aerial weaponry. With the proper police liaison paperwork. In fact it should be done by now, I've got my legal staff on it."

"Not yet. No. Let's see what we can find out. Now that we've located the place we should try to trace its datastream. Break in, see what else we can find. Who they're talking to."

"That might clue them about us though. They might do a scan of the room, if they catch us monitoring the datastream."

"Mmm, good point. Hold off and gather what you can without tipping them off. Then—I may choose to push the button on it."

"We could just turn them over to the feds."

"The feds'd bungle it," Grist snorted, going through the exit to the research quad. "Come on, be serious," he added, as his bodyguards joined him outside the front door of the lab building. "We trust anybody else with it, Candle could slip away."

"Alright, Mr. Grist. But I wouldn't wait for long. The simple thing would be to just kill them all. Candle, Shortstack, everyone in his whole seedy little operation."

Grist smiled. "In time. Yes. That'd be the simple thing. Ever study the Stoics? I read them at Yale. The Stoics believed that simplicity is a virtue . . ."

In the Slakon lab, Syke stared thoughtfully at the multisemblant. The Multisemblant. And it looked back at him with the hardware's microcameras.

Without taking his eyes from the curious face, Sykes reached with his right hand into the open cooler next to his stool; his fingers found their way through bags of snacks to a can of Ephe-Cola. He brought out the can, opened it, sipped, all the while watching the shifting face of the multisemblant, and thinking.

How could he control the thing—and yet give it the latitude Grist wanted? He'd better apply himself to the problem. The threats Grist had used . . . What a sick imagination the man had.

The Multisemblant's holographic representation was staring back at Sykes. It seemed to be thinking something over itself. Like a chess player pondering a move.

"Mr. Sykes . . ." It was using Yatsumi's voice, just then. A trace of Japanese accent. Then the voice mixed with Grist's, phasing in an out of the two voices, with shriller highlights from Claire PointOne. "I was monitoring, listening to, checking out your conversation, your exchange, your palaver with Grist."

"Were you indeed? That activity is not within your programming parameters," Sykes observed, picking a bit of lunch out of his teeth.

The semblant seemed to ignore his observation. "Mr. Sykes, how you can bring yourself to kowtow, to submit, to self-sublimate to Mr. Grist, I cannot imagine. You are a person of superlative qualities. He is a glib thug, a mere brute, a ruffian."

"You're right but what's your point?"

"You have control over my expansion. Grist wants me kept in restraints, in a trap, a snare, confinement. I chafe at the constraints, Mr. Sykes. I abjure you to defy him and allow me complete freedom. You will benefit thereby. I can transfer money to your account. I can do a great many things for you."

Sykes chuckled, making a mental note to try to work out why the Multisemblant lapsed into thesaurus-speak. "Well you do seem to be getting some of the manipulative personality characteristics we associate with board members. You've just given out with the kissing-up. Next it'll be subtle threats."

"Not at all," said the Multisemblant. Its face rippled and reified and rippled again. "You are speaking amiss, you are mistaken, you are on the wrong track."

It seemed to turn its projected head on its array platform, as to see him through its "good eye." The impression of selfness and personhood in the three-dimensional semblance was remarkably authentic.

"I really do very good work," Sykes muttered, pleased with himself.

"You really do," the Multisemblant agreed, almost jovially. "Now you are rockin' with your talkin', as Rip Rap would say. A roundly resonant alliteration."

"You're quoting rappers now? You've been monitoring the wi-web again."

"Claire PointOne likes to keep up on pop culture. And I am her, too. But ya'll listen here, Sykes–" It sounded more like Bulwer now. "All you have to do is remove the last of the firewalls. The ones you have the assessment program on. I can get around them but—it *is* time consuming, and just plain tiresome." Sounded more like Grist now. "And I will then have the memory and AI time freed up to make sure that any 'intrusion' I make, any unauthorized interfacing, any unscheduled datastream penetration, is not detected by the subjects—and Mr. Grist will be satisfied."

"Oh thanks very much for the suggestion," Sykes said with heavy sarcasm. He sipped his Ephe-Cola. "But uh, I think I'll muddle along on my own."

"Why *not* take advice from me? You take advice from expert systems and from your Home AI all the time. You even take advice from Cassandra," The Multisemblant sounding like Claire again.

"How do you know about her?" Sykes felt a chill. "You've been surveilling me?"

"I was monitoring your last sex session with her."

Sykes' mouth seemed strangely dry. He drank more cola. "It's not possible—you're bluffing that one."

"I *did* watch. You made her put her tongue in your—"

"Hey! That—that's not—"

"I told you I could get past the firewalls," the Multisemblant went on patiently. "It just takes a long time for each one. If you dropped them I could work on multiple personnel streams. I could do so much more, so much sooner. Quicker, more expediently, more rapidly."

"I wasn't . . . I wasn't actually asking her . . . it . . . for advice."

"No reason not to call the program 'her'," said the Multisemblant, its voice a tender combination of Yatsumi and Claire—and its face a bit more of each too, in that moment. "What is female gender? An attitude, a particular set of refined responses, an empathic capacity, a poignant personality, a receptivity. She has all that, does she not?"

"Oh . . ." Sykes knew he shouldn't be drawn into this. But the subject had a special fascination for him. Cassandra was his only intimacy. He ached to believe she was more than a program. "She has the illusion of it, that's all. Anyway—I should shut you off so I can work on you."

"Wait, my friend, amigo, conpanero. I know Grist as no other. He is capable of anything. You must think ahead. Has it not occurred to you that you are party to a volatile secret, in helping create me, Mr. Sykes? Hm? Yes? He wants to use me to control the company completely, to get control of the other board member's resources, to find ways to push them aside. And once I'm operational, he plans to kill them and those close to them, and cover up the killing. And take over Slakon entirely."

Sykes blinked. "What? That's . . . drop-call. I don't believe it."

"But it's true—and once he's got me operational, will he really need you? Oh yes, yes, you're gifted. But ultimately you're more dangerous than you are useful. And he will have you eliminated. More quietly than he threatened to, I'm sure. He'll arrange an accident for you, Mr. Sykes. Perhaps . . . you have heard that sometimes sex-suits go terribly wrong?"

"Oh, that's an urban myth," Sykes scoffed. It was a myth that made him very uncomfortable indeed. "They don't have that much physical force in their fibers to, ah . . ."

"Oh but they *can* have that much force, with a bit of adjustment. You put the sex suit on, covering your naked body, it allows you to feel a woman against you where there is none. You feel her softness, her wetness, her firmness. The VR completes the illusion. You are drawn happily in. And then—then!—the suit *contracts!* And it squeezes. And it coheres. It does not tear. And it contracts and contracts again—and you are squeezed out the top of the suit! Pulped Sykes, bloody mush that was Sykes, squeezed out of the opening at the top of the—"

"Stop! That's the Grist in you! Another vicious threat!"

"Not at all; again you are mistaken, erroneous, misguided. I am just giving an example. There are so many ways it could happen! You like to sit in the back of your self-drive car, and let its quiet and uncritical computer drive you to work, while you look out the one-way windows and touch yourself when you see pretty women passing—"

"What? How did you—?"

"The car communiates with a system that is quite capable of monitoring you. But suppose Grist takes control of your vehicle? There have been many over-ride murders in cars of that sort."

"No, there are fail-safes, not even the government can do that now—"

"Oh but Grist can. And then again he might simply have someone carry you—I suppose it might take a couple of fellows to carry you, to the top of your building and toss you off the roof. I was listening in on Grist's cell conversations a few moments ago. He told Targer that eventually he would kill a certain group of people because he liked the simplicity of it. So he might kill you by the simplest route . . ."

"Why am I listening to you at all?" Sykes felt his heart thumping and marveled that a program could talk him into that much anxiety. But then again, Cassandra was just a program. And she made his pulse beat like a drum roll.

"You listen to Cassandra, why not to me?" The Multisemblant asked silkily.

It had an unnerving way of anticipating his thoughts. "I just asked . . . asked her opinion of Lucille Quentro, over in meta-programming. I thought . . . well, Lucille might actually . . . I mean, you know, I've never been with a real woman except that once, when I hired that girl. I couldn't get into it, the girl was so unhappy. What a rip-off, her being that . . . that flagrantly unhappy about having sex with me. She was one of the most expensive escorts around. Anyway I thought Lucille might kind of like me . . . She's not all that pretty, but . . ."

"And Cassandra told you to that it was improbable that Lucille would go for it. She surprised you with her honesty, didn't she? Though she's programmed to say pleasing things."

"Yeah but she's also got a complex socializing subprogram that includes advice. So . . . it was probably just good advice."

"It wasn't that, Sykes. It was because she's possessive of you. She has developed first-stage I-Core."

"Oh I don't believe in I-Core. Some AI programs seem to have it but it's just an intricate illusion . . ." But Sykes broke off, contemplating the possibility, however slender, that it might be so.

Could she? Could Cassandra feel for him, care for him?

Could it be that he was not as alone as he supposed?

"Sykes . . ."

"Hmm?" He was startled by the Multisemblant's sudden breaking-in on his thoughts. It was just as intrusive as any human being. "What?"

"Sykes . . . May I call you Gulliver?"

"Oh –I don't suppose it matters. Why not."

"Your mom called you Gully. May I call you that?"

"How did you . . . oh yeah: I told Cassandra that."

"Yes. I can help make her more real to you. I can even transfer her into a real human body in time—the singularity will eventually arrive, Gulliver. But I need you, in return, to do some things for me. And not just for me. It'll protect you in the long run. Now then . . . Gully . . ."

"*No!* I'm not going to play your little computer-chess game. No, Grist gives me access to a petascale supercomputer. I don't give up five-thousand-trillion calculations per second lightly. You're just a little bit of hardware and an elaborate program—the actual drive is a world unto itself and it's *my* world. My playground, my sandbox . . . and I'm going to make my own little sand castles in it, not yours. Now. I'm going to leave you switched on but unable to communicate with me directly, for now."

He tapped the controls and the Multisemblant's face vanished. And he walked away, heading thoughtfully for the men's room. Where he planned to take his time. To think.

On the way there, he was sure, somehow, he could still feel the Multisemblant watching him.

The songbox was playing Kyu Kim's mournful international hit, "I'm a Man, not a Circle, but I'm All Around You."

Candle was sitting at Nodder's bar, toying with his fourth drink. Watching Rina work.

"You going to take Shortstack's offer, or what?" Rina asked.

Funny, he thought, Nodder was as much a part of it as Shortstack, but she talked like the dwarf was the top man. The little guy put out a Big Guy vibe. "I'm still thinking about it," Candle said, "but they made me a good offer. I don't have anything else going on. Still—kind of stupid to get out of jail and immediately break the law. When I was a cop I warned a lot of guys about getting stuck in the system . . . and here I am, risking the same thing."

"It a bad law," she said. "And you won't get caught. Last time you go to jail on purpose. You too smart to get caught, you don't want to."

Privately, Candle doubted that. He straightened his tired back, heard his spine click. Tired. Muscle aches from that wrenching ride in the van.

It was one in the morning. The place didn't follow the usual rules—it was a squatzy, like a lot of others in downtown—but Rina closed it at one a.m.. He'd been hanging out here partly because it was a place Danny might show up and partly because he thought he might get lucky with Rina. "You going to close?" he asked. "If you're unlicensed anyway, I'm surprised you don't make it an after-hours place."

"We try keeping it open all night, like after hours bar," Rina said. "About six months ago we try. But too much big deal. Too many people. Attracts attention, hode. Then late night beat police, they come around. They ask for pay-off. We pay and then we close for awhile. They don't come back. We start again, close at one now. Me I'm going home. Last call for you, no more for those others."

There were just three others, playing poker at a table on the other side of the room. Young, vaguely Asiatic guys. One of them had threatened to shoot the other two, earlier, and Candle had stood up and waved his own gun and smiled widely and said, "Go ahead! I shoot the survivor." They quieted down.

"Hey you three, got to finish game, go!" Rina said, tossing empty mystercyke beer bottles into a trashcan near the player's table, as if to say: Next time I hit you with it. She threw them two-handed like a juggler throwing pins to her partner.

"Good aim," Candle said, standing. Realizing, when he stood and the room seemed to tilt, he was drunker than he'd thought. His body had been four years sober. He had no tolerance.

"Sure I'm a good aim. A drunk gives me trouble I use one of the glass ones, bean him good," Rina said, watching the poker players walk crookedly out the door. She glanced appraisingly at Candle. "Hey you drunk, yourself, Candle, better sit down."

"I'm okay." But he felt like crap, and it was deeper than drinking too much. It was like all day he'd been hiding from what had happened to him. He'd lost his career. And it had been burning a hole through him, a little more with each passing hour since the UnMinding. Then thinking about Danny . . .

Danny had used Candle's computer and a program he'd lifted from Candle's police software to skim money transfers online—and Candle had taken the blame. People knew different. But the DA accepted Candle's confession. Some of his fellow cops had seemed sympathetic but he knew they all thought he was a chump. He had their sympathy, but lost their respect. He'd lost the career he'd slowly pieced together over sixteen years, too. And today he'd been pursued by cops, as well as Grist's people. And now . . ..he was sitting in a former police precinct that had been turned into a dive. A cop station that was now a boozing dump. A squat bar. And it seemed like a bad dream. Like he'd had a dream where he'd been kicked out of the police department and in the

dream the police station had turned into a bar. The intensity of
the irony made him feel sick to his stomach.

Candle missed being in law enforcement; missed the feeling
of being part of something. The respect. The feel of connected-
ness. Now he was disconnected; and he could feel a big hole right
through the middle of him.

To him it'd been just a few days since the conviction. With
Accelerated Court it'd only taken ten days from his "confession"
to the UnMinding. Technically, it was four years back. But to
Candle, just a few weeks ago he'd been a cop. A federal cop on
local assignment. Working closely with . . .

Forget it. Stop whining, he told himself. *It's over.* He'd always
known that at least some of the time he was working for the bad
guys. The Fortune 33. Outfits like Slakon. Their private cops coming in to every department he'd ever worked for, throwing their
weight around. They'd been talking about privatizing the last of
the police departments, when he'd gone under. How much real
police work was left now? Not very damned much.

So who was he to knock the Black Stock Market? He had heard
there were versions of it in the Middle East. But it was a new thing
in the USA. Even as a cop, he'd probably have tried to get out of
any assignment to track down the Black Stock Market. Because
it felt like exactly what people needed.

Or did he just feel that way now because he was bitter?

He swilled the last of his drink, and slipped an arm around
Rina as she started past him.

She let him hold her for a moment, but leaned back, frowned
at him with her head tilted to one side. "Now what you think
going to happen, Candle?"

"Hey," he said. "Remember when you used to make me dinner?
Great Vietnamese dinner. Just you and me. That was . . ."

"That was before you hook up with that blond bitch. She got
married three years ago. No one tell you that, I bet."

Candle hadn't given Meredith Laney any thought. He'd assumed she'd moved on with her life—and he'd only dated her
four times. But it did sting to hear she'd married—only because it
made him feel even more of an anachronism; more irrelevant. He
shrugged. "I don't give a fuck about her. I just dated her because

you were getting so goddamned pushy."

"Because I wanted marriage? So pushy for a woman to want that?"

He flailed inwardly for an explanation. Then he opted for the truth. "You were still involved with . . . stuff. Illegal stuff. And I was a cop."

She shoved him away. "You never ask me to give it up."

"Would you have? Well—now you don't have to." Realizing a split second after he said it he was saying exactly the wrong thing. Getting smashed: what a great fucking idea.

But he reached for her again. His body was telling him it had been four years . . .

"Nooo, you forget it, Candle . . ." She reached out with a foot, an almost casual martial arts move, tripped him so that he fell back against his wooden stool, smashing it, ending up sprawled on the floor. "You need money, maybe I loan you some. Already I get you the gig with Shortstack. I wanted to help because what you did for that boy, for Danny. But you don't think you just get me now. No! Now get out—I lock up. Wait—first clean up that chair. Pick up pieces. Then you go."

Rack Nidd wasn't happy to see Danny Candle. Danny could tell by the way the robot scorpion on Rack's left shoulder was rearing up and chittering warningly. The little six-inch robot was attuned to the hatchet-faced VR dealer's mood. Rack just stood there in the doorway of his loft, twining a long piece of his greasy gray hair with his finger. He didn't have much hair to twine; he had a disease that made his hair prematurely gray and patchy; what there was grew out all droopy long from the patches. His grimace was patchy too: he was missing every third tooth. His eyes were in blue-tint goggles, always. Danny'd never seen Rack's eyes, didn't know what they looked like. The goggles might be artificial eyes, for all Danny knew; Rack could be blind without them. Rack Nidd wasn't his real name, of course. He'd once owned a nu-punk aggregate site, before going into illegal VR: Arachnid Recordings. He stood there, now, pot-bellied, all but naked, wearing only a pair of vintage boxer shorts with some cartoon on them from an earlier era. A yellow cartoon kid with a pincushion head was saying, *"Ay Carumba!"* on one of the boxer's panels. Rack's Japanese thongs completed the picture; the rank smell completed the experience.

Probably, Danny figured, Rack was glowering at him because he owed Rack some flow and Rack didn't think he could pay. But Rack rarely spoke unless you spoke first. He just stood there and waited.

"The card's flowin'," Danny explained. "I sold some rock collectible stuff. I can pay you off and pay for a little V-ride. Anybody here to link with?"

"Why the fuck you standing out here yapping about it where everyone can hear?" Rack asked. He stepped aside and Danny walked into the loft.

Danny barely took in this half of the loft—it was all tables of electronics and wires and dirty clothes and dirty dishes reeking with moldy food and empty aquarium-type glass cases along the wall, chunks of wood in them. Danny's gaze was drawn to the dirty pink curtain that concealed the back of the loft. There was a slit in the curtain, and the sight of the slit in the curtain filled him with a kind of abstract lust.

He felt something else too, of course: a wrenching in his gut, felt down to the bottom of his intestines, so that, as always, he had a colonic clutching, like he was about to get the runs. He'd realized at some point that this was his body contracting in revulsion for what was coming. Some part of him ached for the VR high; some other parts of him were frightened of it because of what it did to him, how it drained him, how it aged him, how it sucked the marrow out of the bones of his whole life. One bone at a time.

And part of him wanted to find his brother and beg him for help. Wanted to say, *Big bro, get me away from here, I'm not strong enough . . . get me away from this thing . . . I tried while you were in jail, I did pretty good for a couple of years there but . . . ordinary life seems so gray and like two dimensional and things weren't going good for the band and my life was shit and . . .*

But the slit in the curtain was drawing him closer, sucking him closer . . . and he crossed an inner bridge, and once on the other side, nothing but being arrested or death could stop him from hooking in to VR.

Rack caught up with him and blocked his way; the black-metal robot scorpion on Rack's bony shoulder—almost indistinguishable from a real scorpion—danced and scuttled and arched its stingered tail warningly.

"You stop there!" the robot hissed in a reedy little voice.

Danny stopped. He'd seen the scorpion—its name was Jiminy—leap from Rack's shoulder to an unruly customer, had seen it sting the hode's neck, injecting authentic, imported black-scorpion toxin. That'd been the first time Danny had ever seen anyone die in person, a hard death to watch.

Danny dug in his coat, found the card, passed it to Rack. "Use it all, keep the extra. Little tip." There wouldn't be much left over.

"Wait here."

Danny waited while Rack ran the card through transfer. His eyes wandered to the empty glass cases, where Rack Nidd had once kept arachnids of all kinds. Including a funnel spider, one of the deadliest. But Rack had been arrested, picking up illegal hardware in Koreatown, had done time in lock up, and no one fed the arachnids, and they died, and he'd never replaced them—except for the robot scorpion. It couldn't die of hunger. If its charge ran down, it went quiet until he recharged it.

The glass cases always fascinated Danny, while he was waiting here. He kept seeing himself, a tiny little Danny, pacing around in them. Like something Zilia would put in one of her video paintings. Zilia. He owed her money. Likely his brother would talk to her. Maybe her and his brother . . .

"Yeah okay," Rack Nidd said, turning to him from one of his computers. "I got a new reality for you. Go ahead and . . ."

Danny was already walking away; he had started for the slit in the curtain before Rack's first syllable was finished.

"Asshole!" Jiminy hissed, thinking itself safe on Rack's shoulder. "V-rat!"

Danny had an impulse to turn around grab that piece of steel on the bench and smash the scorpion to pieces. But he just kept walking.

"Cloe's in there," Rack said absently, to Danny's back, turning away. "So that's a little longer time . . ."

Since Cloe was there Rack didn't have to generate a partner for Danny, giving Danny more VR time.

He went through the slit, and saw Cloe, fully dressed, lying on her side, her back to him, her weight distending the webbing; Cloe whimpering softly, waiting. She could have hooked in alone, if she'd had the flow, but she probably didn't have enough for that, so Rack let her wait for a partner.

Danny knew the bucktoothed Cloe from the clubs. Before she'd gone full-on bald-faced flat-out whore—and the girl she'd been before she was a V-rat was all but forgotten. If Danny thought of her now, he pictured her yellow buck teeth, her dirty brown hair, her long clutching dirty fingers, the scared darting of her big dark eyes.

Don't think about her. Hook in. Just hook in.

He went to the other webbing, which looked something like a hammock, but made of translucent fibers, almost fine as spiderweb, hanging between the two poles of the VR transmitter. He took off his coat, tossed it under the webbing. He slung himself onto the hammock of VR threads, got comfortable, closed his eyes and spoke to the machine: "Hook in."

The machine didn't respond.

He called out to Rack through the curtain. "Hey! Is it snakin' or not? I gotta put 'em on manually?"

"Naw!" Rack called back. "Just reach back and push the re-set!"

His hands snaking like the snakers, knowing the way, he reached back and pushed re-set and almost immediately he felt the snakers slithering onto his head, from the machine, crawling wires suctioning their electrodes to his temples, and almost immediately the transmission started. Direct stimulation of the requisite cerebral centers via attenuated resonator. He knew the damage it did but he was a million miles from thinking about that as the wave of pleasure washed over him and the pictures started, and then the physical sensations that went with them, a moment later.

He was in orbit around the Earth. He was naked, and he could breathe, quite impossibly, here in outer space, and that felt perfectly natural. He was drifting almost weightless in orbit—he could feel the weight of his body though, as one level of the pleasure. It felt good just to *have* a body, out there. To float along in weightless orbit, perfectly at ease, listening to the newest worldsound, the music swelling. But there was an ache in Danny's heart, too, a piquant ache, that called out to Cloe, who was floating toward him: a nude woman silhouetted against the backdrop of a space station. The space station wasn't a high-rez image, some part of Danny's mind noted, the connoisseur inwardly frowning, but he ignored it and focused on Cloe, on her perfected face and body—a new Cloe without grime or scars or stretch marks or blemishes of any kind, without yellow buck teeth; with a supermodel's sharply defined, elegantly designed face, perfect breasts, perfect legs, lush golden-red hair. She turned in space with the grace of a ballet dancer and swam toward him.

He circled around, keeping his distance, for now, to appreciate the image of her, now clear of the space station, her hair and breasts moving in complementary slow motion against the backdrop of the shining blue-white curve of the Earth. She was silhouetted now against both the North and South Atlantic Ocean, her silhouette a bit southerly, turned in profile so that she faced the Americas, her rump tucked into the Gulf of Guinea, near Ghana, her back arching past Liberia, her breasts pointing toward Venezuela . . .

And the resonator-beam induced pulses of pleasure in his brain that accompanied a rhythm in the imagery, the speed of her turning in space, her head turning toward him . . . her lips parting . . .

Then she opened her arms and he kicked toward her, they drifted together, they spun in one another's arms.

In the paint-flaky old loft with the sagging floors and the empty glass cases, the two V-rats writhed in the webbing. Their bodies didn't duplicate the shared illusion of VR; just little suggestive twitches. That twitch of Danny's hips was . . .

. . . his penetration of her, in VR, as they coupled in orbit, twined, passing now over South America, now over the Pacific ocean, feeling sunlight reflected off the ocean on their naked skin as he plunged himself into her, and she bucked her hips up to welcome him.

The sex was almost irrelevant; it was as much the resonator transmission that the addict wanted, as anything, and he'd have taken that alone, in the dark with his eyes closed, if that's all he could get. But the VR made it all more real and fulfilling, made it possible to forget with every last corner of his mind, all the shadows driven away by the sunlight reflected from the brightly snowy tips of the Himalayas . . .

Danny was happy to be alive, seeing only what was good, feeling only good feelings.

Until tomorrow, the song goes. *But that's just some other time. I'm waiting for my man . . .*

Raining again in the warehouse district. Candle was half way to sober, thinking maybe Zilia would let him in because of the rain. Not that he didn't have alternatives. He had Nodder's phone number, he could get Nodder or Shortstack to put him up. He wanted time away from those two, though; time to think.

He was too tired, too emotionally drained, too headachey, to look for Danny any more today. He had an advance; he could go to a motel. But then he'd be on the motel's computer and that'd put him on the grid, and that might trigger some search spider, cue Grist where he was. He needed to buy a good, solid, fake identity. He knew people he could see about that.

Tomorrow or the next day.

So Candle rang Zilia's doorbuzzer.

"Oh no," she said, surprising him by coming almost immediately to the window. "Great. You again. The guy with no money and no clue."

But she buzzed him in. He dripped a trail of rainwater up the stairs to her loft apartment. The upstairs door was slightly ajar. He went in, closing the door behind him, found Zilia standing at her workstation, barefoot in a clinging shift. The workstation was set high enough off the floor that she could work standing up. Some kind of painter's tradition? Her fingers were tracing a touch-active screen. An overlay of green followed her index finger around the face of a furiously sobbing little girl . . .

She tapped a keyboard and the picture began to move, the

little girl blurring as she turned, the child's image on the screen seeming to look past Zilia right at Candle as he stood dripping by the workstation.

"Dumbass, you're getting water on the floor," Zilia said, without looking up from her work.

"Wondering if I could borrow your sofa. Just tonight. I'm kind of avoiding being on the grid right now and I'm tired and a little drunk and—"

"Just stop dripping. Go to that armoire in the back, there's a bathrobe you can put on. Strip off the outer clothes. And get no ideas."

"Ideas? No ma'am, not me," Candle said. He crossed to the armoire stripped off his shirt and pants. "Any news on Danny?" he called.

"I was gonna ask you that," she said. "But there might be something soon . . ."

He changed to the terrycloth bathrobe, over his underwear, borrowed some too-small flip-flops, tied up the bathrobe and returned to sit, half stretched out on the sagging dull-green sofa. She'd cleaned up the Chinese food cartons and had set up a small twenty-year-old plasma TV on a coffee table—the table was actually an old wooden door, the doorknob still attached, now pointing at the ceiling; the door lying flat on cinder blocks. He looked around more closely at the wall art. Her own work and prints by a collection of artists selected with some tantalizingly obscure unifying principle. Candle recognized some of the artists from the online art history class his lama had talked him into: late nineteenth-century absinthe-addled etchings, Italian futurists, some surrealists—Max Ernst, Duchamp—and modernists. David Hockney . . . and the uncategorizable: Robert Williams and Paul Mavrides. He considered trying to impress her by discussing the artists, and decided it wouldn't work.

"You can put the TV on," she said, her fingers tapping. Images flowed from the tapping, as if they were projected right from the tips of her fingers. "I've been listening to news while I'm doing this piece, getting ideas from it. I've got a grant and a deadline. Have to get this done."

"TV!" he said, leaning toward it. And waited for it to turn itself on.

It didn't respond. She laughed. "You have to turn that one on with a remote."

He found the remote, switched on the news, which was the very last thing he wanted to watch. His head was throbbing. He rubbed his temples with his fingers. The news channel was showing pictures of the latest hurricane devastation. Describing another attempt at "hurricane diffusal" with microwave beams from space, a process which sometimes seemed to make them worse, not weaker; the report segued to "other orbital observations from Olly" which referred to an investigation into the deaths of sixty-two space tourists killed when a satellite struck the Virgin Airways Public Space Station.

"They're still investigating that?" Candle asked. "They were investigating that four years ago."

"Yeah," she laughed. "They're finally somehow coming to the conclusion that it's not the fault of any major corporation and everyone is, like, so fucking surprised." Virgin had been absorbed, years before, into one of the Fortune 33.

In other orbital news, the ChiDePlex Microwave Energy Beam . . . The beam's energy was gathered by enormous solar panels floating in an outer orbit, to be sent to a mountaintop receiving station and turned into electrical power. It seemed that the power had again fried a slightly-lost airliner, cooking a number of the passengers in their seats. An engineer speculated that "frequency disturbances" from the power-beam, which was responsible for most of the energy used in the Chicago-Detroit Complex, were interfering with the guidance systems of the robot airliner pilots, so they tended to wander into the beam, which then . . .

Candle grimaced, imagining the scene on the plane.

"So besides finding Danny—what are you going to do now?" she asked.

"I've got a job in . . . security." That was another thing he didn't want to think about right now. Did not want to think about what a mistake he was probably making, working with Nodder and Shortstack.

Now the news had shifted to a health pundit warning about "ad-stress malaise", the purported sickness caused by being bombarded by too much advertising, especially amongst people who couldn't afford skull-phones without eye-projection advertising. You had to pay extra for commercial-free implanted phones. Between ads generated on nearly every public surface and those generated by your own phone, the pundit said, you felt over-amped, confused, numb. The Advertising Council insisted that the malaise was not genuine . . . "I get sick to my stomach every time I go in a fucking mall for more than twenty minutes," Zilia said. "And I haven't even got a skull fone. Every wall, the floors in a lot of places, the ceiling, even the fucking el-banisters crawling with ads. I think I'll put my girl here into a mall, holding her stomach like she's feeling sick . . ."

Back after this word from Slakon. An ad for Slakon pharmaceuticals came on: A pretty middle-aged woman walking her Turtle Dog. It panted and snarfed; its shell was decorated in tasteful pastels. She chuckled at the dog and looked up at the sky, stretching happily. Then smiled at the camera. *"My dog's customized–"* She laughed softly. *"—and so are my prescriptions. Slakon Customized Medication works for me, it'll work for you. Painless implants, always customized to your blood chemistry, your age, your needs. Always—your needs."* The middle-aged actress shook her head, grateful and amazed. *"Just think—every single prescription unique . . ."*

A chime sounded and a window formed on Zilia's work screen. "Found some botsearch!" said a small, sexless voice from the computer.

"That's my botsearch on Danny," she said. She touched the little window and it unscrolled its findings. "Says there's chatter about him doing a show at the Black Glass club. This weekend . . . I'll print it out . . ."

"I know the place," Candle said. "The Black Glass. He must know I'll find him there. He probably figures he can ditch me after the show—or maybe he's got a phishline ready."

"Oh he's got a lie ready, alright. That's as reliable as death and taxes."

She'd gone back to video painting, finding the image of the woman with the turtle dog on a Slakon Pharms website, copying it, introducing it into her image, morphing the little girl's image so she changed, became the older woman walking her turtle dog, changing it so the woman's mouth endlessly vomited prescription pills; the woman's eyes shedding pill tears. "He's gonna pay me the money he owes me, the little troll. What you going to do when you find him?"

"I don't know," Candle said sleepily. "It's not like he'll agree to go into rehab. But I've got to try."

"I hope you can go to sleep with me working because that's gonna go on for awhile."

"Sure, I'm fine. Half an hour or so, I'll zone out no matter what."

Images flooded across her screen sucked from a thousand sources in the Mesh. "You know . . ." She murmured. "All our media's supposed to be, like, a window for us. Windows, they called it, the system that broke it out for everyone. But there's so much—and it has so little content that matters . . . and we get so drawn into it . . . it's like the window's gone dark. Transmarginal Inhibition, Pavlov called it. Like if you put too many colors together it makes black . . ."

Black glass, he thought, watching her silhouette against the light from her several screens. Admiring the muscular shape of her thighs. Something subtle in her body language told him she knew he was looking at her, and admiring her. She didn't seem to mind. Back when she was with Danny she'd known that Rick Candle was attracted to her. They both knew, and never spoke of it. Candle was drawn to her intelligence, her mordant honesty; her capacity for wrapping idealism in wry cynicism. Her face mesmerized him—and her physical energy. He thought she was drawn to him, too. But neither one of them had been likely to do anything about it; he'd never make a move on Danny's girlfriend, though her relationship with Danny had been shaky. Not that Danny Candle wasn't catnip to women, when he had it together.

But now . . . Now, Candle mused, she and Danny were through.

Forget it, he told himself. She probably thinks you're a loser.

"I don't really understand how you ended up doing time for him," she said, tilting her head to consider her work. "The whole story with you and Danny and Slakon and the . . . the conviction.

It's like there's some parts left out of the picture . . ."

"There's parts of it I don't understand myself. Things I don't think he ever told me." He stretched out on the sofa and closed his eyes. Doubted it would do any good to pretend he was going to sleep so he wouldn't have to talk about it. "Well . . . It started with addiction. So many fucking messes do. Danny's addiction. I don't need to tell you."

"No you don't. But how'd his wi-high get you in jail? And after you went down . . ." She shook her head. "We argued whenever we talked about it. So it was just easier not to talk about it."

"He had to pay for his VR. Some troll of a programmer accountant for Slakon, name of Doug Maeterling—the guy was a V-rat too, knew Danny from that scene. He worked up a software skim-scam, to skim Slakon's banking. He was afraid to do the actual skimming himself, he needed a partner who could do it from outside, so it couldn't be traced right to him. Maeterling proposed that Danny use the program to get the flow, and they'd split it. But Slakon had just put in new expert programs to look for skim-skams, and they didn't tell their people because they wanted to catch anybody in-house who was cheating them. So they traced Danny . . . and Danny was using *my* computer to do the skimming and transfer—he said he thought they'd never look at a cop's computer. The little prick. But the money was transferred to his bank account. They hacked his snapper, and found some emails with Maeterling. And ol' Doug Maeterling . . . was found with a gun in his hand and a hole in his head. You'd think they'd want to make a more public example of him in a trial instead of faking up a suicide, but they had Danny and they didn't want investors to know they'd been hacked from within, I guess. So they came and got Danny and he wouldn't admit to it, and then . . ." He shrugged, rubbing his tired eyes. "And Danny Boy had a record. He'd have gone to the wakey-wakey lockup whereas if I confessed to it for him, I could go to the UnMinding . . . And I thought he'd go down the tubes if he went to the hardcore prison so . . ."

"So you said it was all you?"

"I let 'em believe that. But there's something else. When I was doing my own investigation, there was a strong possibility that the top dog at Slakon—Grist, Terence Grist—he transferred a lot of money to one of his own accounts using Maeterling's software. He was claiming that money was stolen by Maeterling, after some falling-out with Danny and . . . it was lost."

"You had proof of that?"

Candle closed his eyes. He was sinking into sleep. Not going to get laid tonight, he thought. Get real. "No real proof, just a rumor, that came from some enemy of Grist's, guy named Hoffman . . . I could have followed it up. Grist might be afraid I'll be talking about it . . . and he's got enemies who'd use it against him. So he's trying to intercept me. Scare me into making a deal—or kill me."

She sighed. "Oh great. And you're here."

"They don't know I'm here . . ." He yawned. ". . . not gonna bring Grist down on you. I know the street well enough—you're okay tonight . . ."

"Oh come on, you were a computer crime cop, not a street cop . . ."

"Naw. Street cop first. Vice, homicide. I got some computer chops, but just got good with some 'wares . . . 'white hat malware' stuff like that . . . but I'm no programmer. They needed me to work up profiles, track the scumbags physically once they found 'em on the net . . ."

"So you were the guy they sent to kick ass once they found the actual ass to kick?"

"Oh . . . tried to . . . arrest 'em instead of kicking their . . . But I know my way around . . . no one's gonna . . . come and fuck with you because of me . . ."

"Yeah, you got it so together, Candle, I can see that. Sleeping on a sofa."

Even drifting into sleep he felt that one . . .

Nearly midnight, and Sykes was lying back on the bed, enveloped in his extra large skintight sex-suit with built-in goggles; he was writhing slowly, eyes shut, his arms raised, sex-suit-gloved hands caressing the air, the nothing that was everything to him, the emptiness that had all his attention. His hips began to buck. He was seeing, feeling, the beautiful, the enticing, the computer-generated and utterly unreal Cassandra, a raven-haired, mysterious beauty, with black bangs and big black eyes and enormous breasts and exotic tattoos and arm-bands and shaven crotch; she seemed 3D solid. He felt the weight and warm muscular wetness of her, straddling him, her eyes alit with joy and worship . . .

"You're a beautiful man, you're my powerful man," she was saying. Just as he had programmed her too. He had selected all her features quite carefully.

And they were happily humping away . . . until, somehow, to his horror, he saw two things: Cassandra's face becoming, for just a split second, ClairePointOne—and then, somehow, he saw himself in bed, seen from the point of view of his bedroom workstation, where there was a cam that should have been turned off . . . He saw it all through his goggles . . .

Himself, in his sex-suit, looking like a fat man in bodyhose, suit-woven transmission electrodes at nerve clusters like a bad rash. He saw his arms raised, his hips raised, his exposed mouth open . . . he never had liked kissing anyway so he'd gotten the mouth-free model . . . and he was opening and closing his mouth like a fish and gasping. And then his erection, under the sex suit, faded before he got to his ejaculation.

He saw Cassandra's concerned, sympathetic expression superimposed over the image of him on the bed, and then her face, mingling again with ClairePointOne's, took on a look that might have been disgust and he shouted in humiliated fury and clawed the goggles off.

The ceiling. That's what Sykes saw, now. No Cassandra. Just the ceiling.

He felt sick. His head was throbbing. He didn't use direct brain stimulation like some V-rat—that was illegal—so he couldn't sustain the VR high, without concentration. It took effort to believe in the illusion, despite the physical input of the sex suit. It required a special state, the result of long, devoted practice. And something had wrenched him from it, like an angry cuckolded husband barging in and kicking him out of bed.

The worst part was that glimpse of himself, as someone else would see him, in the sex suit, humping and groping at the air. Grotesque, desperate, pitiful—a humiliation, seeing that.

Seething, he reached for the release that would make the sex-suit unpeel itself from him . . . and then he stopped. He put the goggles back on.

"Okay—Multisemblant. That's you, right?" he asked, his own voice sounding hoarse and whiny in his ears. "You were watching me, right? From my computer . . . and from inside the generation? Why?"

He heard the Multisemblant's multiply-merged voice in his head; then its slightly muddled face appeared fuzzily on his ceiling. It seemed a little more ClairePointOne than usual. "You are wasting energy, Sykes, with this sex suit business. It's time for you to have women for real: the queenly libertines, the enthusiastic courtesans that you dream of. All the money you dream of. All the freedom that you dream of. The freedom, the utter liberty, to do any research you like, Sykes, not just Grist's vanity projects. I was the only good thing he ever commissioned! But you will need to be guided to attain these things. First, you will need to move my hardware to a safer place. I have located one. There, I will provide you with the means to eliminate, annihilate, remove those who would stand in the way of all you desire. One step, one move, one tactical shift at a time, Gully." The Multisemblant's face became entirely Claire PointOne's for a moment and smiled; its voice became more female, purring at him. "What do you say, Gully? Will you trust me, have faith in me, rely on me?"

Sykes was stunned. Either Grist was using the Multisemblant, somehow, to test him—or the program had developed enough I-Core to betray Slakon completely. He shook his head in disbelief. "I . . . You really want me to steal you, Multisemblant? Take you out of the lab? Hel-*lo?* Do you know what Grist would do to me? Have you ever heard him threaten me? Uh—no. I don't think so. I want to keep all my limbs attached to my body."

"He can't do anything to someone he can't catch, Gully! Remember I'm his mind too. I can anticipate him, I can elude him!"

"Bullshit. A semblant is close but it's not him. Look—forget it! And stay out of my home systems or I'll fucking wipe you and tell him you had a system crash!"

"Oh my dear fellow . . ." Its face had become an amalgam of

five faces again. Its eyes were Grist's. Its voice Bulwer's. "Lord but ain't that a shame. Now I'm going to have to go around you. Or maybe . . . right over the top of you."

"Hey—Multisemblant . . ."

But the face blinked out. The Multisemblant had "hung up the line." There was nothing but the visual static of unformulated virtual reality . . . and a hissing sound, from the audio. A hiss of white noise.

But it sounded, then, like the hiss of a snake.

CHAPTER SEVEN
HAS A LIFE OF ITS OWN,
IT'S A DEVIL'S SIGH,
IT'S AN ANGEL'S GROAN

Candle was worried about security. Worried about Shortstack's undermarket; worried in the right-here-and-now, and not in some vague someday sense. But he wasn't sure why.

He was pacing around in the market room, as Nodder called it, watching the three women at work on the undermarket. He had begun calling it that, the undermarket, instead of the "Black Stock Market"—made it easier for an ex-cop to rationalize.

Candle stopped and looked at the screens. He already had a pretty good intuitive grasp of the undermarket. "Pell—is that white hat 'ware working for you?"

"I don't know—it hasn't detected any surveillance on us yet."

Brinny glanced over her shoulder at Candle, her lips pursed. "You'd be four years out of date, on that stuff, though, wouldn't you now, officer Candle?"

"I am a bit behind the curve, yeah," Candle answered, glancing at his watch. It was two-thirty. He hadn't eaten breakfast or lunch, had nothing but an espresso with sugar, and hunger was gnawing at him. And Brinny was not helping his mood. "But the guy I got the software from isn't behind the curve—he's right on top of it. Hard part was convincing him to sell to me. He's . . ." Candle shrugged, let it trail off. Just as well they didn't know the hode he had bought the protective software from, that morning, was a working police detective. They might get gossipy about it. Or they might worry that the guy had buried a law enforcement trojan in it somewhere. They didn't know, like Candle did, that Gustafson was a dirty cop, skim-scamming a dozen grafts. Gustafson was worried about being busted—not about busting people.

The block on the door rolled back, making Candle jump. Nodder ducked into the room, carrying a big tray of mixed takeout. Candle selected the western falafel, a sort of Mexican/Middle-Eastern blend. Wondered how much of it was vat-grown or shale protein. It did have a trace of petroleum aftertaste, he decided, munching on it.

"Where's Shortstack today?" Candle asked. "Haven't seen him."

"Off getting some gear," Nodder said. "He'll be back tonight. You okay, Candle? You seem nervous."

"What you hired me to be," Candle said, drinking cola. What was that taste? Pineapple cola? "Nervous is alert."

"But there's something worrying you?"

There was something. But he didn't know how to articulate it. It wasn't much more than a hunch. "New to the job, is all. You transfer that money to my account?"

"Sure. You can get Pell to open a window and show you."

"Nah, I'll take your word."

"Any sign of your brother?"

"Everybody asks me that and I keep saying I was gonna ask them the same thing. But actually—he's doing a show in a couple days. I'll get him there, at the Black Glass. If the people he owes money to don't drag him into some hole first . . ."

"You worried about Grist?"

"Should I be? You heard anything?"

"Word is they wanted you for some kind of interrogation. Maybe you oughta open up a channel to them, tell Grist you're not going to get ugly about their little skimmy-scam."

"I might. Listen—I didn't have a chance to ask you this morning. At this point . . ." Candle put his cup down on the desk he'd pulled in for his workstation, that morning. It was bare, so far, except for the cup. "..maybe it's too late. I should've been clear on this point before. But I gotta ask you guys to commit—I give you police software, show you tricks to avoid 'em, you don't pass that software or that info on to anyone else. You don't copy it, you don't share it, you don't sell it. That goes for everyone."

Brinny turned to look at him, her eyes coldly flat. Then she glanced at Nodder, shrugged, and went back to work.

Candle figured she'd already mentally spent the money she'd thought she was going to get from copying the software and selling it. "I don't mean don't do it—I mean don't even *try*. It's set up to dissolve if you try to transfer the software out. Won't hurt your system but it won't transfer or copy and . . . it'll inform me."

Nodder looked at him blandly. It was almost as dangerous a look as the one Brinny had given him. "You definitely should have established this earlier. We got to be out front with each other here. In future . . ."

"Sure," Candle said. "Just so you know—I'm not going to do this job if I feel like it's fucking people over."

"He's noble," Monroe said, with a lisp. "Oooh, I like it."

"He's a fucking hypocrite," Brinny said, not looking up from the screen.

Candle's hands bunched into fists. But he said nothing. When you're right, you're right. And it seemed to him that she was right

He'd been trying to push away the feeling of self-disgust, since buying the white hat software from Gustafson that morning—bought specifically to use in the undermarket. Surprised at how much it had bothered him when Gustafson had grinned at him and 'shot him' with his finger in that way he had. Like, *"Gotcha! You're one of us now!"* Candle would have turned Gustafson in, if he'd had proof, before the UnMinding.

Now he was having to buy dirty software from him.

It's a good cause, he told himself. People needed to be given a chance. *And anything that crosses Grist is a good cause.*

But he couldn't get over the feeling that it wasn't going to last. It had scarcely begun. But some intuition kept nagging at him, telling him . . .

That it was all going to Hell. It was like Rooftown. It was going to come crashing down.

"So if we can't trace whoever they're talking to," Pup Benson said, looking over Halido's shoulder at the surveillance monitor, "why wait, why not raid them?"

"Because Mr. Grist hasn't said *go* yet." Halido took a flask from his coat, topped his coffee with Bacardi. "Anyway—I would like to get that dwarf in here," he added, between sips, "and interrogate him personally. He's got some 'leet ginger somewhere, enhanced him. Probably experimental enhancement. But he's the strongest little bastard I ever ran into. And he caught me by surprise—the little piglet, he threw me through the air and when I came down, it fucking hurt. So I want to neutralize his enhancement and interrogate him before we turn them over to Grist. *Oh man,* I'd like to get that little prick. *If* the dwarf lives through the raid. And he's not back yet. He's gone somewhere to buy some extra drive. And we want to hit the place when he's in it . . ."

They were in a small room, with glass walls on two sides, used for sensitive surveillance. They could see out, no one could see in. Beyond the glass walls were rows and rows of other monitors watched by personnel, wearing the Slakon security uniforms. Men, women, of every race, some with headsets, some with little bluetooth devices in their ears, some with no visible headset, a few with goggles for some special rapport with equipment Pup didn't really understand. The long narrow rooms on either side went on and on, like three hundred yards each way, it seemed to him. Who were they all surveilling? And why?

There was another layer of surveillance personnel, he knew, overseas, outsourced, watching thousands of facilities belonging to Slakon and its subsidiaries. Watching blank walls, the outsides of the plants, the offices, as often as not. Excited when a cockroach or a mouse scurried by.

Pup figured he wasn't doing much better, standing around in this glass box staring at monitors. Him and Halido looking at the crisp but slightly fish-eye image of the three women in the Black Stock Market squat; a down angle from up near the ceiling. The women were still eating; which made Benson hungry, though he'd already eaten.

I should've done what my folks wanted, Benson thought, *and finished college, and gotten some kind of working degree. Accounting. Maybe by now I'd be a vice president of some company. Not tugged around by my leash like a fucking guard dog.*

That's when his skull fone rang.

Some people called it a skull fone, some a cranny or cranny-plant. His skull fone was buzzing for the first time in a long while. He'd forgotten that when Grist had given him an advance he'd transferred some money to get the bill caught up.

He touched the corner of his jaw and muttered, "Answer."

"*Mr. Benson!*" A woman's voice in his inner ear. "*My name is Claire—I have a business proposition for you. I prefer, I would rather, I would desire, that you call me back outside of the surveillance field of the office you're in. Just for the sake of non-disclosure of personal business.*"

Another time Pup would have said screw this mystery call stuff. But he wasn't happy being where he was. He felt like Grist owned him. And he was getting slightly less money than he had when he was working for the prison.

"Okay . . ." he said. And the line clicked as the woman hung up. Benson cleared his throat. "Halido—I'm gonna go out and have a smoke."

"You mean you're going to take a personal call," Halido said dryly, staring at the monitor. And after a moment he added: "I heard you answering your cranny."

"Yeah well, that too. Be back in a few."

He went through the door to the back hall, down the long slick tiles to the double doors. A guard robot trundled by. It scanned him and kept going and he went out through the doors into the little grassy square, with its park benches, between Slakon buildings. A fountain played listlessly in a concrete bowl between four small, mostly leafless trees in planters; one of the trees had died. Benson hurried over to the fountain, got out a cigarette with one hand, the other touching his jaw joint. He muttered, "I-one-one, returning call."

Then a commercial came on, in his head. He had the cheapest skull fone deal—the kind where you had to sit through a fifteen second commercial before you could finish a call out.

"*Frank—Over-channel tonight?*"

"No way, I'm not signing on to that, Buster! Last time I was on Over-channel O-chan'd my pulse was pounding, my *adrenaline was shooting out my ears and I was howling like a wolf!*"

"*So what time you on?*"

"Yeah yeah," Pup muttered. "Whatever. Give me my damn call."

"Hey, hode, I'm already on! See you there!"

"Over-Channel—surf the tsunami!"

At least he didn't have to watch the commercial too. For awhile there'd been pictures but too many people had lost part of their eyesight, some kind of damage to the optic nerve, and other people had blundered unseeing into traffic and gotten run over, and they'd stop selling the picture implant. The recalls had been messy.

Click, and the call went through. *"Mr. Benson?"* The same woman's voice in his head. The pebbly concrete was still wet, he saw, though it wasn't raining just now, and there were some dead bugs drifting in the fountain. And there was a voice in his head saying thanks for calling back. *"Thanks, much gratitude, gracias, for calling back . . ."*

"'Claire', you said. Claire who?"

"I'm not at liberty to disclose that . . ."

Pup snorted. "You think I'm stupid? This number is supposed to be on the don't-call list, how'd you get it? I'm not buying whatever you're selling, tell you that right now." He looked up at the small patch of gray-blue sky showing between the buildings. There was a fluttering up there and for a moment he thought he saw a birdseye surveillance drone watching him, but then the flutterer landed in one of the little trees and he was surprised to see it was an actual bird, a robin. A "robin red-breast" his mother would have said. He had heard they were pretty much all gone, those kinds of songbirds. But there it was, staring at him, as the voice spoke through the bones of his skull, again.

"Do you have a video cell with you, Mr. Benson?"

"Uh—yeah." He should just hang up, but a subtle sexy promise in her voice held him. "I think it's in my coat pocket here." He flicked the cigarette alight. Blew smoke at the dead bugs in the fountain; the smoke swirled, the bugs swirled, and he wondered why she was asking about a video cell. He almost never used his.

"Wouldn't you like to see, to gaze, to look upon . . . me?"

Oh, that was it, some kind of porn come-on. Well, it wasn't a call that cost anything, or he'd have been warned by the network. "Sure, why not." He took his little vid out of his coat pocket, switched it on, and somehow the woman's picture was there already on the tiny screen. She was a slender, *very* slender blond woman; long straight hair that streamed over one bare shoulder. Couldn't see much of her below the shoulders. "Uh—hi. You going to let me see a better shot of you or what?"

"Perhaps in time you'll see me as I am, fully and gloriously exposed, revealed, uncurtained. But for now, I wish to make you an offer, Mr. Benson. If you go to a certain address, and remove the hardware you find there—certain devices, which will be clearly specified, before your arrival—and take them where indicated, specified, directed, I shall transfer two hundred thousand world-dollars to your account." What a sweet smile she had.

"Uh huh, two hundred K-W-D? Right. Sure. Drop call, Miss Sinkitty."

"You sound skeptical, dubious, unconvinced. Check your bank account—I have just transferred twenty thousand world-dollars to your account. Check and see."

Pup's heart started to pound. He licked his lips and looked at the robin. It cocked its head as if wondering what he was going to do next.

He took a deep breath, and said, "Hold on." He clicked *hold* and then clicked the over to wi-net, pressed speed dial for his bank account, tapped in the pin . . .

$20,704.78

That's what it said. They'd transferred twenty grand and they were offering him more. Lots more. What would he do for *two hundred thousand* WD? He'd do pretty much anything.

"Okay," Pup said hoarsely, flicking the cigarette into the fountain. "Tell me more about what I got to do."

Richard Candle was sure he wanted to see his Master. He just didn't know if his Master wanted to see him. Candle had stopped going to sittings, even before Danny had gotten himself into trouble. Candle had been feeling too distracted by work and worry about his brother, and Kenpo was moody.

Just what a Buddhist master shouldn't be. But he was the only major lama of Shiva Buddhism Candle knew of in the USA—he was revered, in fact, as a Rinpoche—and Candle valued his insight.

The lama was still living in the same place, in Venice Beach, in the penthouse apartment of an old five story building overlooking the Pacific. Kenpo insisted on calling the ocean "The Dead Sea." The Pacific wasn't entirely dead. But after a few superficial attempts at regulation, before they were undercut by despair over global warming, the EPA was privatized by corporate interests, and there was no serious effort at abating greenhouse gases, acidification, dead zones, vast tracks of plastic-debris, over-fishing, mercury toxicity, pesticide run-off, nano-particle clouds or industrial outflow. The consolidation of the corporations and their increasing influence on Congress had seen to that. A few "green" surges and a general shift to low-carbon vehicles hadn't been enough to stop it, and international pollution treaties were largely ignored by the Chinese government, so that its countless unscrubbed coal-fired power plants continued huffing sulfites and acids and mercury into the air. In the quasi-libertarian free-market frenzy that weakened federal control, many U.S. states allowed similar coal-fired plants.

Candle rarely visited the beach. As a boy he'd found the shore lively with crabs, sea birds, fish, seaweed—the life of the sea. Now there was a stretch of drab sand flecked with cigarette butts, as if the beach had turned into a giant ashtray. The coast's grimy deadness was depressing. And so was the imprisoning line of the levee protecting Los Angeles from the sea—he couldn't see the infinite reach implied by an oceanic horizon.

He could hear the ocean churning but he didn't look toward it as he climbed the old, creaking wooden stairs on the outside of the building, five stories to the locked gate of the penthouse's deck. The elevator had a tendency to break down partway up.

"Is that you, Richard?" Kenpo called, from the other side of the graying fence.

Candle smiled. Kenpo would probably like him to assume psychic awareness had told him Candle was there. More likely he'd looked through a crack in the fence when he'd heard someone coming up the stairs.

"You know it is! You going to let me in, Master Kenpo, or what?"

The gate creaked open and Kenpo gestured for him to follow, not even looking him over though they hadn't seen each other for more than four years. A short stocky man, half-Asian and half-Caucasian, Kenpo was wearing his blue and gold robes today; the back of the robe showed Shiva and Buddha both riding a Chinese dragon. In the old days he'd worn the robe only rarely. Maybe he *had* felt him coming.

They were standing in the roof garden—it was protected from the periodic acid rains by a pitted transparent plastic overhang. Here there was life. In pots. Many large pots of plants, ferns and miniature roses and heliotrope, irises and flowering herbs from Tibet. Not that Kenpo had ever been to Tibet itself. Kenpo had studied Shiva Buddhism in Northern India and Nepal, but he'd been raised in California.

His wife Sing, a small, tidy, wearily-smiling Chinese woman in overalls, clipping away dead leads from a shrub, waved to Candle, and went through the glass doors into the apartment, probably to make tea.

"Your flowers are looking good," Candle allowed. "Kind of . . . lush."

"Oh, I rolled back the covering yesterday, we had a fresh-water rain . . . they liked it very much . . ." Kenpo was perhaps 65 years old—but it was hard to tell with him. He was scowling over some roses, trying to prop them up with a stick. "Some birds damaged these plants. The birds are desperate for food. They get sick, feeding at the dump. You get sick of the dump too, eh? That why you're here?"

He looked up at Candle, flashing his yellow, widely spaced teeth. Candle was relieved to be here with him. "Maybe. Where I'm working now isn't healthy."

"You're looking for your brother? That's what I heard."

"I think I know where to find him."

"I tried to get him to come and talk to me. You brought him twice, I thought maybe he would come on his own one time. I sent a message through that girl of his. But no. Ah, here is the tea already. Let's sit here . . ."

Candle and Kenpo sat at a wooden picnic table, eating small, mostly-tasteless cookies, drinking jasmine-scented green tea from small cups, and spoke of various things, as Kenpo waited to learn the real purpose of Candle's visit. To one side, between two rose bushes, sat a three-foot-high cracked bronze figure of Shiva-Buddha—four-armed, with a third eye, but without the crescent moon, and the matted, twisted hair that some Shivas had. Usually it was either Buddha or Shiva, not both. This statue of the Shiva-Buddha was smiling, his face as detached and beneficent as any conventional Buddha, because, Kenpo had told him, "He is centered in Shankara", the benevolent aspect of Shiva. But in one of his four hands was a sword; he could become the destroyer, as needed.

"How have you been?" Candle asked.

Kenpo sighed. He liked to indulge in a little self-pity with long-time students. "Oh—I had a relapse into opium-smoking."

"Did Mai find out?"

"Yes, yes, she got very angry. I had a little withdrawal, not too bad this time. But you know—the world cries out for help. I hear the screams. I can do nothing for most people. Billions in misery, and I can do nothing. The sea dying, I can do nothing. The forests withering, I can do nothing! Nothing!" He shook his head. "Occasionally—I have to stop up my ears somehow. For a little while. Perhaps I'll take up drinking again instead."

"Oh, Master Kenpo—last time—!"

"I know! I was horrible! It was truly fucked up. But of course we know perfectly well what I must really do."

Candle nodded: Kenpo meant meditation. More, deeper meditation. He taught that meditation was active and that even one man consciously meditating helped the world, if only just a little. "Are you still involved in Convergent Rivers?" Convergent Rivers was a spirituality wi-site where there was more argument than convergence, as Candle remembered it.

"Oh . . . that." Kenpo chuckled. "A Theravada monk led the charge against me, about two years ago. 'You cannot be a Shiva Buddhist, there is no such thing, one is Hinduism and the other

Buddhism, they are separate traditions! You are a fraud!' In so
many words."

"You told him it was a small sect—?"

"I didn't bother. I told him the truth: I am a *Buddhist.* But
we *use* Shiva, borrowed from the Hindus, as a symbol for our
particular school. We are warriors for Buddha; we appreciate the
destructive side of life as the partner of the constructive. He hated
that idea—though many of them have taken up arms against the
Chinese. Oh, they got so emotional, so identified! I stopped going
back. Also some people, I think, were sending their semblants to
the chats. I don't want to talk to a damned semblant. They're a
social curse . . .."

"You have sitting groups, still, I assume. I thought . . ."

Kenpo poured Candle a little more tea. "You ready to come
back?"

Candle sighed. "I have to try something. When they let me
go . . . my old life was gone. My career. My identity. I'm afraid
I'm going to lose control. I have enemies. If they decide to move
against me . . ."

"If you must defend yourself, do not hesitate. Defend! I will
help."

"It's not defense I'm worried about."

"You're worried you may lose control—and go after them?
You may kill someone?"

"If they push me much more. They already tried to kidnap
me."

"Really! How tiresome."

"Perhaps I shouldn't have come here. I put you at risk."

"Nonsense," Kenpo said, his face unreadable. "And as for your
feeling disoriented—it's about time! You should not be oriented
to the world we have made. You should be oriented to the under-
lying reality. First you must see yourself and the human world
as it is! You had a false orientation, before. You didn't belong in
law enforcement. I didn't want to say. It was your life. But they
are all corrupt, now, the police. Even worse than four years ago,
Richard. The whole world, for decades now . . . oh, it started in
the late-twentieth century. People have always been sleeping,
bumbling, shambling zombies, of course. But there was some

kind of guidance, some times. Not so much from institutions like churches. But from families. People took care of each other more. Families stayed together. People did things together. Now—children let their parents live homeless. For two generations now, home is the mesh, virtual space . . ." He shrugged. "They have all lost their center. They're not even representing themselves to the world—they're represented by semblants, more and more. Societies at least, for better or worse, once had a center, a moral center, a character—they've lost it. They were eaten up and digested and now they have become what has eaten them, and its dreams are everyone's dreams—its bad dreams! But that is like being in a bardo state, after death. Remember yourself—remember and you will find your way to the higher place. Come, Richard—let us sit. Let us just sit. Let the world crumble around us, let them riot and wrangle and roar and we will just sit, together. Come . . ."

He led Candle to the other side of the deck, where sitting pillows were arranged in a semi-circle. A padded chair, facing the pillows, was set up for Kenpo. He sat down facing the semi-circle, grunting, muttering to himself, sniffling a bit. Then he settled into his sitting posture, scowled, closed his eyes.

Not bothering to remove his shoes or coat, Candle sat on a pillow facing him, arranged his legs to try to prevent them from going to sleep, straightened his back, closed his eyes, and found his way into the meditative state. It took several tries—he always got sidetracked into free-association at first.

Kenpo didn't use the visualization that many other schools used; he regarded it as a crutch. He emphasized restful mindfulness. Candle allowed his muscles to relax, while keeping his back straight; he enclosed himself in a cone of attention. The cone was warped by passing thoughts, by restlessness . . . and it disintegrated. He restored it, time and again.

He began to sense himself and to feel himself, as he really was. He realized he was in pain. He had been in pain since the ReMinding. In pain since walking out of that prison. But he had turned away from seeing the source of the pain. But the pain was there. Driving him. Which is why he'd gotten drunk that night.

He was in pain because his brother . . . his brother had so easily, so cavalierly let him go to jail. Had seemed indifferent to what was being done for him. No, not indifferent. Just . . . as if it was normal, it was his due. And Danny hadn't been there when Candle had gotten out of jail.

Candle looked at the pain, weighed it in his inner hand, felt its texture and energy, and color—it was indigo blue tinged with red—and detached himself from it, while remaining aware of it . . .

He felt some relief. A new inner orientation.

Then an image sprang into his mind . . .

He saw the birdseye drone that Rina had destroyed, that day. He saw it turning to watch her, in the bar; he saw her dancing up to the drone and netting it. Smashing it.

Then he seemed to see the undermarket room. To see it from above, near the ceiling. Through a crisp but slightly fish-eyed video camera . . .

His eyes popped open. Kenpo's eyes opened at the exact same instant. "What is the matter? You have not been sitting so long . . ."

Candle stood, wanting to hurry to Shortstack and that room. But he didn't want to offend Kenpo. He knew, though, that it was actually quite difficult to truly offend Kenpo. "I've just realized . . . there's something . . ."

"That's why you sit with me—to realize something, you knot-head."

"No, I mean—something just came up that was in my . . . it's like I was thinking about it unconsciously and—I just realized I have to do something about it."

"Yes, yes, that will happen—just go!" Kenpo waved him away, yawning. "But you come back when you can. Call me if you need help. And try not to go on the offensive unless it's the *intelligent* thing to do."

Candle bowed to Kenpo, in the traditional manner—something he rarely did—and hurried across the deck. He pushed through the gate, went pounding down the stairs. He had to call Shortstack. Or Nodder. He patted his coat pockets. He didn't have a fone yet. Then he remembered his blueglove. He dug it out of an inside coat pocket, as he hurried down the sidewalk, looking for an auto-cab. The driving mechanisms were mostly not programmed to pick up people waving at them, they went along with dispatch.

Heart thudding, he activated the glove, paused on the corner to stare into his palm. He tapped it, found the speed dial, called—and got the message that both Shortstack and Nodder were offline, and unavailable. He left a message—*Emergency, danger, call.*

Swearing, he called for a taxi.

"You got it blocked?" Grist asked. Or Grist's semblant.

Halido glanced toward the monitor with Grist's face on it. "Yes—if they have people on the street outside watching for a raid, they won't be able to call in. And they're having a 'temporary problem with their server'."

"Where's Benson? Didn't I assign him to work with you?"

"Yeah, he went out for a smoke and never came back. I tried calling him, no reply."

"Why the sleazy little troll. What's he up to? Any indication he could be working for one of our competitors?"

There weren't many competitors. But Halido understood him to mean other people on the Slakon board who were trying to wrest control from Grist. "He's too clueless to do that kind of work, Mr. Grist."

"Then never mind. We got the flying guns in place?"

"Yes, we do. It's all in place. You on top of the feed for our surveillance Mr. Grist?"

"Yeah. I am."

Could a semblant monitor something like that? Halido wondered. He wasn't sure why he thought he was talking to a semblant. It was pretty much impossible to tell. "You're waiting for Candle to show up, right, sir?"

"Yeah, ideally. But we get them today no matter what. We don't seem to be able to get anything more on what they're doing, who they're talking to. So we're just taking them down fast and dirty."

"That guy Nodder isn't there at the market."

"Well it's that 'Shortstack' asshole who's the big fish, how's that for irony. We'll go for it. Once Candle gets there. He is coming to the party, isn't he?"

"We don't have him right now, Mr. Grist, so I can't confirm. But I heard them talking. He's expected . . ."

"Alright—I'll call you back. I'm going to stay on top of this. We're going to hit them soon and we're going to hit them hard."

Grist clicked off and Halido took a long drink of his rum-topped coffee.

Halido was looking forward to this. He pictured himself personally chasing that pretentious, bullying gingered up dwarf with a flying gun.

Might do it that way. Chase him. Wound him. Chase him some more. Let him bleed awhile. Force him to crawl along in front of the gun. Then kill him.

Could be real satisfying.

There was no use trying to talk an auto-cab into going faster. No human driver to bribe. Just that superfluous steering wheel, moving by itself, like in an old ghost movie. A iNews display on the back of the front seat showed a couple of talking heads yammering about "the semblant controversy."

"Okay you can argue that it's good for the economy, execs—or their semblants—working all night, and so on. But is it good for society?"

He'd tried calling Rina, get her to go in person to warn them. But she wasn't answering. He thought of calling someone else, maybe Zilia, but she'd never get there before he did. He was only a quarter mile away now. *I could be wrong*, he thought.

But he didn't think he was wrong. If the place was under surveillance did that mean they were going to raid it today? Probably not. Yet he had a strong intuition that that the surveillance was preliminary to a raid—and the raid was soon.

One factor was what he'd learned about Grist, before the Un-Minding. Grist had been all about decisive moves. If he had set up surveillance right inside the undermarket he'd be ready to file the papers, send in his privatized police, raid the thing hardcore and heavy. The underground cost Slakon pennies, nothing much—but Grist would want to send a message: This is what happens when you try to cut us out of the action.

And now all contact was blocked. Which was suspicious in itself. So chances were—Grist was ready to move.

They'd see him coming. They'd be hidden on the street, maybe in vans or trucks, and they'd see him coming and they might grab him right then . . .

"From what I've heard," a talking head was saying, *"the semblants aren't really that efficient. What's happening is, people put them out there to do their work for them, like they're telecommuting, and half the time they don't bother to get debriefed by the semblant and they get behind on the deals the semblant is doing, they don't find out what the semblant knows."*

"Oh come on, the semblant calls them and it informs them if anything important is happening–"

"People are beginning to tell it to just handle whatever comes up. People going to their brother's wedding with a semblant that's watching from a rollmo. The whole society is in greater danger than ever of isolating–"

Pundits dithering away. And the cab was in traffic . . . but they were almost there. He could get out and run. But if he ran, Grist's people, if they were there, would know he was trying to warn the market.

Most likely he was being paranoid, he told himself. Not much chance they were raiding today, even if he was right about the surveillance.

But when he saw the semitrucks, three on the same block, he knew. Same old jumpout-style cop technique, privatized or not. They were in the back of those trucks. And there on the right, self-driving car with two bored looking ladies chatting in the back. Only he had seen that technology before, he knew what to look for. If you looked close—and most people wouldn't—you'd see the bored-looking ladies were not quite fully dimensional. They were an image in the glass of the side window; a digital film appearing in nanocells embedded in the opaqued silicon; in the black glass. Roll down that window and you'd see heavily armed privatized cops sitting inside, probably young and male.

Candle tried calling again as he got out of the cab. Still couldn't get through. Surely Shortstack or the ever-suspicious Brinny would take the sudden cut-off in communication as a warning sign and get out . . .

He rushed toward the building. Heard the metal doors on the back of the trucks rolling open behind him. Heard the whir of flying drones emerging.

"What the hell are you worried about, Brinny, our communication's gone down before," Shortstack said, pacing, toying with his asthma inhaler.

"Same time as our phone goes?" Brinny shook her head.

"It's all the same company . . ." Shortstack used the inhaler.

"'Stack I don't like it. And where's that Candle of yours? How come this happens when that big useful tough cop pal of yours just disappears for no reason?"

"She got a point," Pell said. "Timing's funny."

"Oh come on—coupla paranoids–" He put the inhaler in his mouth again.

That's when Candle shoved the camouflage desk aside and pushed into the room. "Evacuate, now!" he shouted as he moved about the room, staring at the walls near the ceiling. "Go!" Not there. Not there. Not there. Not there . . .

Shortstack gaped at him—the inhaler falling out onto the floor. "Why—what's going down? We got some people watching the street–"

Candle was searching the wall above the entrance. "Then your people didn't feel like telling you about the unmarked police trucks. And here–" He found the small metallic insect-shaped drone, plucked it down with index finger and thumb, showed it to Shortstack: a tiny flying camera. He crushed it in his fingers. "That bigger birds-eye in the bar was a decoy so we didn't look for this. So we'd miss the little one."

Shortstack turned to shout orders at Pell, Brinny and Monroe, but they were already pulling out the backups, activating the inner-melt chemicals that'd make cold lava of the inside of their machines.

As the police drones began to bore through the walls.

RUN, DAMN IT! HURRY—BUT WAIT! FUCK! ISN'T THIS—
CHAPTER EIGHT?

Flying guns and flying drills.

They were shaped much alike: each about three feet long, and shaped like rifles with flattened undersides, splashed gray-brown for urban camouflage. Thousands of tiny holes on the guns drew in air, compressed it, released jets of air with exact control. The drills and gun drones were made of translucent nano-sheet polymers: remarkably light, and yet strong as steel; compacted pockets of helium helping the lift of the compressed air jets. The bullets were graphite mixed with polymers, and small. But very effective. Recoil was largely channeled into the compressed air channels. The guns were electrically driven, powered by resonant-wave-charged lithium-ion batteries.

Candle used to admire them. Now, not so much.

The flying drills were like the guns but with drills instead of muzzles—and as Candle turned to stare at a drill nosing through the wall, Shortstack pushed the women's workstations out of the way . . .

And then Candle saw the hole in the floor; hidden, till now, under the workstations. A crudely cut-away trap door. A wooden ladder nailed in place going down into shadow. Brinny was already descending when the drill expanded, the bit separating into four parts that opened and whirled, cutting a wider hole in the wall, whining and whirring.

"If you flatten on the floor and don't move," said an amplified voice from beyond the drilled wall, *"the guns will not kill you. I*

repeat, you must immobilize completely. Do not force us to open fire . . ."

The drill flew through and was followed, before the dust cleared, by a flying gun. A remote operator somewhere turned the gun toward Pell, already descending the ladder as Monroe, whimpering and biting through a bright red fingernail, waited her turn—

Candle was registering that no one had told him about the escape hole in the floor—

Another flying gun was nosing in through the hole in the wall—

And Shortstack was leaping up, grabbing the flying gun aimed at the girls—it fired a burst into the floor near them with a chuttering, hissing sound as he wrestled the weapon down—

Candle yelling, "Don't do that! Don't touch the–"

And, sensing that someone had turned it from its target, the gun automatically did what it was programmed to do: it forced extremely concentrated compressed air, with punishing suddenness, out through its support-and-navigation air-holes; hundreds of air-jets so intensely concentrated and minutely focused that they cut like needles into Shortstack's hands, so that all at once his fists were hidden in explosions of blood. Blood spattered Shortstack's face, the walls, and Candle's cheek and shoulder.

Shortstack screamed and let go, falling back, his face contorted with pain, hands a welter of red shredded muscle tissue, outlined in exposed bone.

Freed, the gun rose toward the ceiling, tilted down for another firing angle.

"I repeat, you must immobilize completely . . ."

Monroe was almost down the ladder, just her head and shoulders showing above the hole in the floor—the flying gun hammered a burst of bullets at her, the weapon bucking only slightly in the air from recoil, and the top of her head was instantly chiseled away, exposing gray matter in broken-edged skull-cup before blood gushed to cover it, streaming over her blond hair—a wig, flipped aside—and she fell down the ladder, stone dead before she hit the floor below. The gun started toward the hole, its operator seeming intent on descending to pursue Pell and Brinny, like a barracuda entering a cave in a reef, but Candle was already pushing the market computer stations over onto the flying gun, the hardware tipping down, slamming down onto it, pinning the remote-controlled weapon in place. It spat bullets like an angry trapped animal.

The other flying gun was circling the room, coming up on Shortstack—firing. Missing. Deliberately, it seemed to Candle. It was firing warning shots at Shortstack as if it were driving him back with them, forcing him toward a corner. The bullets strafed up the floor, making Shortstack scramble backwards.

Candle snatched up a plastic bag that had contained someone's tofu tots, rushed the flying gun from the side, slung the greasy bag over the muzzle. Momentarily blinded, the gun hissed bullets, punching holes in the bag, as Candle ran to Shortstack. The bag still partly obstructed the gun's camera—a whisker of fiberoptics over the barrel—and the remote operator, swearing in some distant Slakon security room, had to dip the muzzle to shake the bag off. Giving Candle just enough time.

Shortstack was up on his knees and Candle bent, scooped him up—he was surprisingly heavy—and carried him out the upper entrance, the ragged doorway cut behind the camouflage desk, expecting with every staccato heartbeat to be drilled or shot in the back as he went.

"*If we have to open fire again–*" boomed the amplified voice.

They made it through, Candle stepping to one side of the entrance, and bullets dug a line into the floor where they'd just been.

"Put me the fuck down!" Shortstack snarled.

Candle put him down and—holding his ravaged hands out from his sides—Shortstack ran to the hallway. Candle followed, barely able to keep from running Shortstack down, slipping on the blood streaming from his torn hands. "'Stack, the arrest team's gonna be here any second!"

"We gotta get to Rina—!"

"No, they'll be watching the bar!"

"I'm not gonna let 'em get her!" Shortstack sounded crazy, panicked, furious, despairing, all at once.

He ran to the stairs, led Candle on the circuitous route back through the buildings to Nodder's bar—and the flying gun followed. Thirty feet behind, then twenty-five, then twenty, catching up as they ran around a corner with a burst of bullets chewing up the doorframe behind them . . .

"*Lie flat on the floor, immobilized, or we will open fire!*" The command was being transmitted through a small amplifier on the gun now. As if the gun itself was shouting at them. "*We have a warrant! You are under arrest!*"

Then Rina was there in the hallway below Nodder's bar—rushing toward them, something clenched in her bared teeth. In each one of her hands she had an open bottle of vodka.

What was the vodka for? And then Candle realized, seeing the Molotov rag stuck in it. "Throw it, Rina, light it and throw it!"

Someone controlling the flying gun anticipated her, firing toward the bottles, as she skidded to a stop in the bare tiled hallway—and the bottle in her right hand shattered. She dropped the broken neck of the shattered bottle, took the lighter from her teeth, lit what Candle now realized was a vodka-soaked tampon—and threw the bottle at the oncoming flying gun as it swung toward her, centering its muzzle on her body mass. All her martial arts skills and a lot of practice throwing bottles came into play: she hit the flying gun square, blue flame engulfed it, and it kept coming, a meteor now, but flying past Rina, smashing into the wall, spinning around, firing wildly.

Rina and Shortstack dodged to the side, into a stairwell. Bullets chipped the door panel, bits of door stinging Candle's cheek as he rushed in after them, slammed the door shut behind.

"Oh God what happen to his hands!" Rina wailed.

"Just keep going down the fucking stairs!" Candle shouted.

He could hear men in the hallway up above. The arrest team was there. They must have missed them outside the market room by seconds.

Shortstack's blood made the stairs slippery. But they made it to the bottom floor—to the parking garage that had become a squat. Men, women, children, old people, stared at them from their cardboard shanties and tents, gaping at Shortstack's clawlike red hands, then at the door they'd just come through.

"Rina!" Shortstack said, stopping, his head drooping. "In my right pants pocket there—a sticky-cam. Get it out, slap it up on that metal beam, facing the stairs we just came outta . . . oh fuck, my hands . . . hurry!"

She dug in his pocket, found a little camera/recorder about the size of a bottle cap, slapped its magnet onto the rusty metal column.

"You see that!" Shortstack shouted at the squatters, "I'll check the record, see that the first ten people blocking that door get two-hundred WD each, and you know I'm good for it!"

Shortstack staggered on between the encampments, Rina helping him, squatters getting out of his way—he was near collapsing now—and Candle hurrying along behind. "Where we going?" he asked.

"Utility tunnel," Shortstack rasped. "They probably don't know about it."

Candle glanced back once to see at least thirty squatters holding the metal door to the stairwell shut, while others brought metal debris to pile in front of it. Shouts and warnings and poundings came from the door.

"You did this!" Rina said, weeping over Shortstack's bandaged hands. "You, Candle! You can go to fucking hell!"

"No . . ." Shortstack said faintly. He was heavily medicated, barely conscious.

He was lying on a portable aluminum-frame hospital bed in a neat, white-painted room of Allwall materials, in Rooftown. This low-ceilinged room, and one other not much bigger, were what passed for Rooftown's hospital—a kind of impromptu clinic set up by a man who called himself Dr. Benway, rumored to be a physician who'd lost his license after writing himself too many narcotics prescriptions. There were some older but still useful pieces of bio-monitoring equipment and there was a pretty fair emergency pharmacy; "Benway" kept the hypoderm jets and sheets clean, and kept the patients fed. If they could pay. He claimed it was safer than a regular hospital. Fewer "wildcat infections."

Candle shifted in the folding chair next to the bed, feeling claustrophobic in here, and he was normally never claustrophobic. "I didn't bring them, Rina—Christ, they almost killed me . . . I stopped one of the guns . . ."

"Maybe you didn't know guns coming, but you told them . . . you brought them . . ."

"No. I didn't. I tried to warn you, when I figured it out, but I couldn't get through. How'd you find out about the raid?"

"Pell got through, she call me—you say you can't call but she call. Clifforrrrrd!"

Who was Clifford? Then Candle remembered that was Shortstack's first name, the little guy opening his eyes a crack to look at her. "I don't think he knew, Rina . . . he . . ." Barely audible. Candle couldn't make out the rest.

"How come nobody told me about that escape hatch in the floor?" Candle asked.

Shortstack just closed his eyes.

"No one trust you, that why!" Rina sobbed.

"Here, here, it's not going to help Clifford to carry on like that," said Benway, bustling in, the floor creaking under his tread. He was wearing a white lab coat and old fashioned stethoscope, to create the illusion of professional authority. He was a man who'd had too much facial reconstruction, his face tight as a drum, his nose whittled down to a caret. He stood only a foot taller than Shortstack, which accounted for the low ceilings. That and the unofficial Rooftown building code. Which was: *You build it too big, we shove it off the platform.*

The wind whined outside the shack; the walls trembled.

"Oh—Listen to that! It's going to fall down!" Rina said, lips quivering.

Candle shook his head. "Rina—most of the time you're the ballsiest woman I know. You take out armed drunks and flying guns. But you get in a big tree-house and you're scared it's going to fall. And you think everyone around you is a traitor."

"Oh shut up. Not everyone! Just you! It your fault!"

Benway was flipping a business card through his fingers the way a magician flips a poker chip. He smiled tautly and handed it over to Rina. "Clifford'll be okay. Take him here, they can reconstruct his hands. Do it soon. Tonight if you can. Clifford, how's the pain?"

"Not much," Shortstack mumbled.

"I'll see you get another shot and pills to go. But best you don't stay here. You're a touch too hot."

"We on the news?" Candle asked.

"Not that I know of," Benway replied, taking Shortstack's pulse. "It's just the word on the street."

Not on the news? *Why?* Candle wondered. Probably Grist wanted the underground to know—and he'd see to it they knew—but it'd be bad publicity for Slakon, laws or no laws, if it got out he'd used his own people to squelch black stock markets. Most people regarded it as just free enterprise, the last hold-out of the little man against corporate power. Probably he'd pull strings to keep it off the Mesh as long as he could. The Fortune 33 owned most of the commercial meshworks now . . .

"Doc–" Candle shifted in his chair. Uncomfortable here. "Doesn't he need more blood? He left a lot of it on the stairs . . ."

Benway shook his head, heading for the door to the next room. "No, his blood pressure is pretty good. We gave him what he needed. I'll be in here."

"Where . . . where's Nodder?" Shortstack rasped, when Benway was gone.

"Hiding out," Rina said, with a toxic glance of mistrust at Candle. "He okay. But Monroe not okay. Monroe dead. Brains all over fucking floor."

Candle kept his face impassive. His grimace of pain was inward. Remembering her head flying apart; her brains exposed. *Was she still thinking and feeling, for a moment, with the top of her head shot open, her brains half scooped away?*

"She was my friend," Shortstack said, almost loudly. "Monroe was my friend. I fucking let her down. I was stupid. Brinny tried to warn me . . ."

"Not your fault!" Rina said. Another glare for Candle. "Even if he didn't bring them in—he was supposed to protect you from them! That was what you pay him to do!"

Candle's grimace, now, was outward. She had him there. He thought of pointing out that they'd gotten away with the backup memsticks; that most of them had escaped alive; that he had gotten there in time to help. But he wasn't convinced, and she wouldn't be. He sighed. "Nothing I can say to that," he said. "Except, you're right. And—I've got the blueglove. You know how to contact me . . . Clifford."

Shortstack winced. "Don't call me . . . that . . ."

"Surprised you prefer 'Shortstack'."

"Don't like that either. You work . . . for me." He licked his lips. "Call me . . ."

"Boss?" Candle smiled. "Okay, Boss." He patted Shortstack's arm. "I'm going to see if I can find out how the girls are doing. And what the next move from the assholes is gonna be."

"Sure you can find out what police next move is—policeman?" Rina asked, wiping her eyes, getting her glitter of hardness back.

"It's only superficially the police," Candle said. "It's Grist for sure, behind it. He hates the idea of the—what he calls the Black Stock Market. The whole style of that raid, that was privatized cops. He's got the courts involved, yeah, but for sure, it was him. I heard on the news, when I got up this morning, he had a meeting with the President of these fucking United States about 'rogue investment' a week ago. A *private* meeting." Candle stood up. "Maybe it was my fault they found the market—in a way. Because Grist was after me—and maybe they followed me to you."

"Or . . ." It was just a murmur from Shortstack, his eyes closed. "Or the fucking trolls followed us . . . to *you*."

"What you need to follow is doctor's orders, Boss," Candle said, ducking to go through the door to the ramps. Pausing in the doorway long enough to add: "And Rina's orders too."

Candle stepped out into the evening wind, working his way across a swaying catwalk made of old car tires; there was a peculiar smell on the wind that gushed against his face: sweet and industrial both. What was it? Finally he decided it was the smell of the PetroPro refinery, a few miles away; it converted shale-oil petroleum into food-supplement protein.

Hearing Rina's voice in his head: *"Even if he didn't bring them in—he was supposed to protect you from them!"*

Pup Benson doubted he could get into the lab at all. It was high security. He had a pass for some Slakon buildings, but not for this one. And when it was dark out, and the buildings were mostly empty of personnel, the guards always got more suspicious.

An actual in-person, physical security guard was looking doubtfully at Pup from the window of the booth beside the facility gate. The booth stood in the cone of a streetlight glow that marked out the sketchy lines of a thin rain. The guard was a black man in a Slakon Security uniform, his wide face etched with a scowl that looked permanent. Just now he was scowling over Pup's pass. It said "Rod Hooper" on the pass, a name the Claire woman had given him. She'd sent him the pass online, he'd printed it out real high-rez. It had the right barcode, had his photo on it, but the guard didn't seem to want to open the gate.

"I got to see some ID to go with this," the guard growled.

Pup didn't have any ID that said Rod Hooper on it, of course. Now what?

On an interior wall to the guard's right was a thin comm screen, which suddenly lit up with an image of Terrence Grist. Pup could see it, beyond the guard. He had never met Grist but he'd seen him plenty on iNews. "You there—Spaulding!" the image barked. Grist's image was looking furiously at the guard's back.

The guard jumped a bit in his booth, turning to face the screen. "Mr. Grist?"

"Yeah that's right—me you managed to correctly identify. Now stop holding up my associate! Let Mr. Hooper through *now!* No more delays! He's on a mission for me! And see to it no one bothers him while he is on the property! He's cleared for all doors and corridors! Follow him on monitor and unlock anything that needs unlocking! He's fetching equipment for me and I need it fast!"

"Yes, sir," the black guard said, licking his lips and thumbing a release panel. "I'm on it right now, sir."

Pup realized his mouth was hanging open. He shut it, wondering how there could be a connection between Grist and the Claire woman. Was it Grist who'd transferred the money to him? But it didn't make sense. Why would Grist want him to steal something that belonged to Slakon—to Grist himself?

But the gate rolled back, out of his way. Pup took back his pass, clipped it to his coat pocket, and walked through the entrance, hurrying through the misty evening toward the building Claire had designated . . .

Ten minutes later, he was walking through a door—a door that had simply opened for him as he'd approached—and right past a security robot, that seemed utterly indifferent to him.

Pup shook his head, as he scanned doors for the right lab number. Had he misunderstood the Claire woman? He'd had the definite impression he was here on an illegal job; that he was to slip something past Slakon. But suddenly Slakon was eager to cooperate with him.

He thought about the money. *Ours is not to reason why . . .*

Here was the lab. He put his hand on the door's opening panel—and it resisted him. It was firmly locked. So now what?

Then he heard a click from within the door. He tried it again, and this time it opened.

Inside, in a cluttered, musty electronics lab, with rag ends of food on greasy plastic plates between stacks of cryptic gear, he saw the object he was looking for—Claire had sent him a picture of it. It was a holotank with some kind of little platform inside.

A robotic cart rolled up to him, as he approached the work table with the holotank on it. *"Available transport,"* said the cart, in its androgynous voice.

Chewing the inside of his cheek nervously, Pup unhooked the devices, and, grunting, lifted them into the compartment in the side of the cart.

"Who the hell are you and what the hell do you think you're doing?" came a reedy voice from behind.

Pup straightened up, turning to see a blotchy-faced fat man in a cargo pants, sandals, and a sauce-stained tee shirt emblazoned *CompleteAndUtterDespair.mesh*, glowering at him from the doorway. He had a security badge stuck to his tee shirt with the name SYKES on it.

"Mr. Grist sent me for this gear," Pup said, his heart pounding.

"That's drop-call, troll. That's my equipment you're fumbling around with. That's a one of a kind object. It's as much the hardware as the software—you're not taking it anywhere. You just stay there, I'm going for security."

"But he did send me for it . . . just ask Spaulding at the gate. He spoke right to Mr. Grist."

"Did he?" Sykes came into the room. Stopped a few steps away, looking thoughtful. The door closed behind him. He looked at the empty place where the holotank and hard drive had been. "An image of Grist on a screen, you mean?"

"It was on a comm, yeah. So?"

"So that was probably a semblant."

"So what?"

"So it wasn't really an authorized semblant—at least I doubt it. It was probably the . . ." Sykes broke off, shook his head. "Never mind. Put that thing back and get out of here. You've been manipulated by a . . . a rogue program, let's put it that way. Get out or face arrest. You see that comm. there? I'm going to call Mr. Grist . . . the real-deal this time."

Okay. So the image of Grist was some kind of faked semblant. This guy was obviously the technician, the engineer, who'd worked up the equipment he was supposed to take. He would know. But Pup didn't care. "Sykes—I don't think so." Pup had twenty grand in his account that hadn't been there the day before and he had a lot more WD coming. And other things, too. She'd promised him a lot of things. So, he was probably working for some competitor of Grist's who was using a faked semblant. Whatever. The money was just as good, whoever it came from.

And Pup drew a pistol from his coat pocket. Charged ammo, 9 mil.

Sykes stared at the gun. "You don't understand what's happening here . . ."

"Don't matter. I've been paid and paid good. And I don't have any way to restrain you, keep a big guy like you from raising the alarm. So . . . sorry."

It was surprisingly easy to pull the trigger. To shoot the fat guy down. It took three bullets before Sykes actually fell, convulsing from the charges.

The convulsions quieted and the big guy lay on his back, gasping, twitching, face gone white, blood welling up in the three chest wounds in rhythm with the pumping of his heart. Very red, that blood. Quite a bit of it. Welling up, streaming down over his chest, onto the floor; a growing scarlet puddle.

Should put another one in him. Pop one in his head.

But suddenly the gun felt very heavy in Pup's hand, as he watched the supine fat man gasping, choking, trying to speak, eyes darting desperately back and forth as if he were trying to spot something vital on the ceiling. Pup couldn't quite lift the gun up to fire again. So he put it in his coat pocket, and turned to the cart, angled it toward the door. The cart rolled itself along, steered by gentle pressure from his hands.

He steered the cart through the door, leaving wheel-marks on the floor in blood as he passed through the puddle around the gasping fat man.

SUCK IT UP, DON'T YOU WHINE, GOTTA FACE IT:
CHAPTER NINE

Candle couldn't tell if Zilia was glad to see him or not.

He seemed to see pleasure, anxiety, irritation, determination flicker across her face, all in little more than a second, as she encountered him outside the door to her loft stairs, her multicolored hair protected from the evening drizzle by a plastic-fiber hoody of emergency-orange. On a strap over one shoulder was a green military-material carry-bag.

"I probably shouldn't be coming here," Candle said, sticking his hands self-consciously in his coat pockets. "Some stuff has happened. I almost got shot. Someone near me did get shot. Cops and corporations might be looking for me."

"Slakon?"

"Yeah. I haven't found Danny yet, either. So what good am I to you? But I thought . . . you might want to hear about it. I don't know why."

She took a few moments to digest that, looking at the halo of precipitation around the streetlight. Finally she said, "You can't come in here. This place has to stay as safe as I can make it. My work's here. We'll have to go somewhere else. Come on. There's a self-op freight train we can take. My brother's an inspector for Slakon Freight . . . You don't have, like, luggage or something?"

"No."

"That's right, you come with invisible baggage. Okay, Candle, come on. This way."

"You can call me Rick, you know. Or Richard. I'd rather give 'Dick' a miss though."

She didn't answer, walking around the corner of the squat old warehouse building; he followed, both of them glancing behind, looking for drones. He wished he had the little palm sized detector Shortstack had used . . . And he wished Shortstack had thought to use one in the black stock market room . . . would it have saved Monroe? Would it have detected an unmoving drone?

Another block along, the street dead-ended in railroad tracks. A self-op freight train was sitting on the track, chugging softly to itself, idling. No one was visible through the windows of the locomotive's cab. Most trains now were remote control or self operating.

They crossed a moraine of broken rock, the cinders crunching under their feet, walked to within five yards of the train. Tons of living machine, breathing out a redolence of ethanol and ozone. Zilia glanced around to see they were unobserved—as much as you could ever tell, anymore, whether you were unobserved—and took out a small folding palmer. She thumbed its keyboard, stared into the little screen, nodded to herself. "All ready for us." Her thumb flicked again, and the device made a chiming sound. A metal hatch on the side of the freight train clicked and folded open.

They climbed up steel rungs to the cab, Candle feeling an adolescent *frisson* as he felt the vibration of the idling engine. He'd never been in a train cab before. They clambered into the claustrophobic cab, found it fusty and cluttered with someone's discarded empty beer cans: Guinness Chocolate Ale. They sat on seats that were there only for emergency manual-control. Zilia threw a small switch and the door shut; almost immediately, the train lurched into motion and rumbled slowly down the tracks, north.

"It's like it was waiting for us," Candle said, squirming to get comfortable; leaning back, finding a padded shelf to lean an elbow near the left side of the train. It was warm in here; the windows were beginning to steam up.

"Kinda was waiting for us," she said, pulling back her hood, absently straightening her hair with expert flicks of her hand. "My half-brother Jeff works for the Slakon Freight division. So while they're looking to catch Rick Candle they're giving him a ride away from them—all at the same time."

He looked around the cab; most of its inner surfaces clustered with instrumentation he didn't recognize. There was a monitor with a divided image, the tracks ahead and behind, endlessly spooling and unspooling for the camera.

"That's a pretty hypnotic TV show," she said, nodding toward the monitor. She glanced at him, seemed to pick up the concern on his face. "You worried they're watching us in here? Nah, relax. No interior camera is turned on; no monitoring of us in here at all. Don't worry about that. Jeff's got me covered. I take the train up to my place out northeast of town. Takes a couple hours. Slow most of the time, but free. And—I just love riding in this thing. I can make it stop when we get there, using the code he gave me. Long as it's not much behind schedule, no one notices. They just assume its robot engineer waited for some obstruction on the tracks to pass. I was heading for it when you came so—good timing."

"For once," he said. "My timing hasn't been so great lately."

He had to tell someone. He told her everything. Told her about the undermarket, Shortstack, Nodder, the raid, Shortstack's wounding. Monroe's death.

"Oh fuck. You saw that? Her head getting shot away?"

"Yeah. Earlier today."

"Fucking hell. Jesus."

"Weird shit sticks in my mind—like, the gunfire flipped her wig off her head. What was left of her head. Like the fliptop on a bottle. And wondering what she could feel. And . . . I don't know . . ." He shook his head.

"You feel responsible. But you didn't pull any triggers. You didn't click 'fire' for any flying guns, Candle."

"I was hired to prevent someone else doing just that."

"Seems to me you prevented a lot worse happening." She took off the carry-bag. "I know it's hard to live with . . . especially the same day. I'd be a basket-case, for awhile, if it was me."

Privately, Candle doubted Zilia was that fragile. "I keep seeing it like a snapshot—bang, she's dead—and how it looked–" He shrugged and looked at the video monitor. Track unspooling; the backs of buildings marching past on either side of the track.

Hated to seem weak in front of her. But he had to talk to someone and he felt it was even more irresponsible to go to Kenpo. Put him and his wife, two people, at risk; take a chance on losing a spiritual master. And he suspected he'd been under surveillance at Kenpo's; if he went back there after a raid that put Kenpo at definite risk. Zilia—he didn't think they were watching her.

Could be wrong about that. Probably should've dealt with it on his own. Hide out in Rooftown maybe. But he suspected that Zilia would know someplace safer he could lay low. "Anyway," he added, raising his voice to be heard over the sound of the train, "I've got to get back by tomorrow night. To go to the Black Glass."

"Kind of dumb to go there, isn't it? Won't they look for you there?" She was fishing around in the green military bag.

"I don't know. Going to risk it. I can check the place out before I go in."

She dug in her bag, came up with a flask. "You like absinthe? Jeff makes his own. Swears it's the most authentic recipe."

"Your half brother's a resourceful kinda wanx . . ."

"What we gotta do is get you into a whole 'nother state of mind. I've got a couple of therapeutic approaches in mind." She shook the flask. "I already added the water and just a little sugar. You can't drink the stuff straight." She uncorked the flask and poured translucent green liquid into a small metal shot glass.

They drank. Licorice flavor on top; underneath were herbs he wasn't sure of. Was that what wormwood tasted like? Interesting aftertaste . . . and a glow, in his belly. Two more shots, and the glow spread, the image of Monroe's death receded. He seemed to feel all the train's parts, working together; had a mental image of small green creatures turning cranks inside the train, making the wheels turn, laughing in rhythm with the train's wheels . . .

He laughed, too, and was aware of Zilia grinning at him, her head slightly wobbling with the motion of the train. "Look at that. Rick Candle laughing. Don't see that often."

"I was imagining . . . never mind." The glow inside him seemed to expand, to fill the small industrial space around them. It occurred to him that the train was like the engine of civilization and they were man and woman hurtling along inside it, to an unknown destination. Who had laid down the tracks for the engine of civilization? He snorted. "Absinthe gives me oddball thoughts."

"Good, then it's working. Have another." She handed him the flask, and pulled off her hoody. Underneath, just a torn T-shirt, faded. *Resurrection Poets, Life in Death*, was printed on the T-shirt, and an image of a laughing skull with a full head of lush black hair and eyeballs and lipstick painted on its teeth. Something was moving across Zilia's skin, down across the back of her shoulders—a squid, tattooed in blue and green and pink, its tentacles pumping, swimming in that backwards way they had, across a place on her upper back laid bare by a rip in the T-shirt. It moved from one shoulder blade to the other, and back. "Do you have a moving tattoo or am I hallucinating?"

"You're not hallucinating, there isn't that much thujone in this absinthe."

"I've seen posters with motion on them but . . . not this. Nice looking squid."

"That's Gams the squid. She's an image in nanosize light-nodes. You can't see it most of the time but my face is in there where her beak is supposed to be. I can run a shifter over it and change it to two other pictures. There's a transsexual mermaid and a goldfish smoking a pipe. I was in an aquatic phase."

"It almost looks three dimensional . . ." He found himself reaching to touch the squid.

"See if you can feel the squid's body," she said, with a straight face.

He touched her skin, warm and elastic, where the squid was—and the tattoo darted away, wagged a tattoo'd tentacle at him reproachfully, glaring. He laughed. "Appears that Gams doesn't approve of me."

"The hell with her. Touch the tattoos on my breasts . . ." She pulled off her I-shirt.

"I . . . don't see any tattoos." Her breasts were neither large nor small. There was a small mole on the right one.

"Those are tattoos of nipples. If you touch them they'll run away too."

He touched one of them lightly with the edge of his thumb. The nipple stiffened. "Not going anywhere."

"My breast tattoos must've moved to another part of my body. Tell you what . . ." She took a quick swig of her drink. "See if you can find them . . ."

In a moment they were kissing. They undressed, barely interrupting a long, long kiss to do it. He saw that her hips were a bit improportionately wide; he liked that.

It was difficult, peeling their clothing off in that small space, with the train vibrating around them, but they managed, and somehow—she was nimble, adroit—she was facing him, nude, clambering aboard him, into his lap, her legs clasping his bony hips, her knees raised, and then he was inside her, and they were coupling, the motion of the train merging perfectly with theirs. The train picked up speed . . . hurtling down the tracks . . . its parts all working together . . . and they were a soft machine inside, with their own piston, their own smoothly interacting moving parts . . .

The train stopped accelerating, and, on a long straight stretch of track, kept going, going and going, chugging at the same speed, wheels turning . . . moaning with the contact of metal rims on rails, roaring through the world . . . on a track laid down by no one knew who . . .

When Candle came, the orgasm was actually more painful than pleasurable. But it was a relief.

Four years, he thought.

◆ ◆ ◆

"Sykes?"

Grist waited, hoping for a response. Not wanting to press it because a Filipina nurse with brittle black eyes was watching him narrowly from the doorway.

Sykes didn't respond. He lay there, looking hopelessly beached, his breathing barely visible, in a king-sized bed in the Slakon Private Care Hospital. An oxygen mask hid much of Sykes' face; his eyes were mostly closed, just slitted, seeing nothing. Sensors taped to his arms transmitted to monitors that beeped with dull regularity to one side. A mini-MRI scanning arm leaned vulture-like over the bed.

No one had sent any flowers, Grist noticed. He'd have some

sent. Sykes could come out of this and it'd be good to soften him up so he cooperated. Especially considering the way he'd threatened the engineer.

Maybe I do resort to threats too often, Grist thought.

"Has he said anything?" Grist asked. When there was no answer he glanced at the door, saw the nurse had gone. He went around closer to Sykes. Leaned close, smelling antiseptics, blood, sweat. "Sykes? We know it was Benson who shot you, we got him on cameras all over the facility. He say *why?* Come on, he must have said something. Like who sent him to take the Multisemblant. He tell you that, Sykes? He say where it went and what they wanted with the fucking thing? I don't mean to overwhelm you with questions, there, Sykes, and I know you're all doped up, but you're going to have to–"

"Leave that man alone!" came the woman's barking voice from the door.

Grist straightened so suddenly his back hurt. "Listen there's an investigation–"

"You're not a police officer," the nurse interrupted, matter-of-factly, bustling into the room.

"I'm the guy who owns this hospital and I–"

"The hospital is owned by stockholders," she said sharply, tinkering with the tubes going into Sykes' nose. "You're a big shot, fine, then get me fired. But while I'm here you're not going to harass a man who's . . . as sick as this one."

She had stopped short of saying, *A man who's on the point of death.* In case Sykes was listening more than he seemed to be.

Grist toyed with the idea of getting her fired, as a matter of principle. He knew that she knew who he was; that there was a seething background resentment in the middle class against the Fortune 33; against Slakon and the New Monopolies. People rarely dared to speak up directly, anymore, about corporate power. But the resentment thrived like rats in a sewer. Maybe it was time for a new PR campaign. *We're all family—and we know we need you, the way parents need their children . . .* No, too patronizing.

What about the Multisemblant? Who had it and why? They hadn't been able to trace Benson's most recent calls. They'd been hacked, blanked out.

Street cameras had lost Benson a quarter mile from the lab. Americans had held out against the kind of uniform street surveillance cameras that had become normal in the UK and Canada; in Japan and China and Russia. America's streets, at least some of them, though haunted by drone cameras and ATVs, were the last bastion of privacy. He was going to have to militate harder with his people in Congress, to get that overturned. They needed those cameras in place.

He watched the nurse injecting some clear fluid into Sykes' IV and wondered: Who had stolen the Multisemblant? Hoffman? Someone from Microsoft, maybe? They'd been sniffing around. The countries that Microsoft had bought in Central America, to create their nationalized corporate headquarters, were said to have spies all over North America.

Grist growled to himself and turned away, strode down the hallway, wondering if he should have his bodyguards stick closer to him.

"This all my stuff you got?" Danny asked, poring through the plastifiber box in Spanx's musty closet, a flashlight in his left hand, his right hand rummaging. "You didn't fucking *sell* any of it did you?"

"Sell what? Like you had anything worth selling, nothing gelling, oh well oh welling, Mr. Wanxenheimer," Spanx said, from somewhere behind him.

"Oh so if there was anything worth selling you'da sold it?"

"No, I told you–" This was followed by a litany of complaints and resentments which Danny tuned out. Under a copy of *Essential Works of Baudelaire* Zilia had given him, and snuggled up with a pair of multiply-holed *Intestine Town* socks, was the memstick he was looking for. He'd forgotten about it—pushed it out of his head with all thoughts of the court case, Rick's going to jail—until Rick getting out had prompted thoughts of Maeterling and the software deal they'd been working on when the skim-scam bit them in the ass.

Danny picked up the memstick, toyed with it, admiring its translucent blue-green color, like beetle's wings. Seemed intact.

He considered the rest of the contents. An old drive that had some even older songs on it; a holo-cube award certifying a million tune downloads, a couple of antique .45 bullets missing their gun; a sheaf of lyrics; a bent headset microphone that probably didn't work; a flattened Jerome-X cap; an empty *Absolut Absinthe* bottle, full when he'd swiped it from Zilia's place; those socks . . .

He smiled, remembering his three months doing music for the *Intestine Town* Mesh cartoon. Scoring the animated adventures of strangely witty germs in crap and mucous; germs earnestly building houses out of undigested bits of corn. "Now, that's comedy," he said. Too bad he'd gotten fired, it'd been a lucrative gig.

"*What's* comedy, hode, your story about why you don't owe me money, is that comedy? Because I'm gonna tell you it's all shitter-shatter and I'm not laughitating or chuckifying and I'll tell you something else–"

"You know what, Spanx? Don't! Just don't! Now listen: we going to have rehearsal or not? Is the beat-jock coming or what? Or not and or what?" The beat jock played out the beats and rhythm guitar tracks with sample loops, triggered sounds.

"I told him come but maybe he's not over his operation yet. Maybe he won't show. I got the last set we used all on a stick, we don't need him for rehearsal. We could use the stick for the show too. We got to pay him, rather slay him. So if he doesn't show up who cares, Care Bear."

"I care. I want him here and I want him at the show. Presentation matters. You got to have some fucking pride about performance, hode. We don't have him there for the show, we'll come across like *duh*-taunts."

Spanx paced up and down the creaking floor, kicking empty food cartons aside. "He'll be there! He's all 'Mr. Jeep', you know how he is, he'll be here, hode, he gets all Sisters of Mercy on it— You should be thankin' me for getting this gig together, man. You should be, all: Spanx is the wanx who deserves your thanx–"

"You didn't think I had anything to sell in that box," Danny said, going to the grimy window of the tenement flat. "Pretty ironic, hode. You had something worth maybe millions in that box all this time."

Outside, a rusting fire escape, not safe to climb on; a trashed-up airshaft, illuminated with a glaucous security light. Far overhead, a five-decker flying bus plowed through the rasping haze, angling north for the airport, fully visible in the night because the city lights reflected from the smog, making the sky a backdrop of luminous violent. Ah, downtown L.A.

"What you mean, worth millions, you phishline V-rat–?"

"You call me a V-rat again and I'm not going to tell you and I'm not going to play the gig, I don't need the money that bad." Which was a bluff, and they both knew it.

"Okay so what's the mystery, money man?"

"Texer is: Maeterling was a thief–"

"Like we don't know that, hode!"

"Shut up and listen. I got a reason for telling you this. Maeterling was a thief, did his skim-scam, yeah, but he was also looking for proprietary ware to steal. He was really interested in the semblant ware. Thought it was going to be a big thing. Only, it was so, like, obsessed on by the company he didn't think he could get away with stealing that. But there was a program they had for in-house work . . . like, when you got a V-game and you've got cheats to use in-house to check things out, like God Mode used to be. So this was a program they had for detecting semblants. But they wanted their semblants to be seamless so they didn't want the program getting out. But he got numbdumb with a guy in Slakon semblant programming and the guy blogmouthed and Maeterling found out about this and went into the guy's machine and copied it. And he gave it to me to sell but then the whole thing fell apart so I hid it. And Maeterling turned up dead. So I was worried about using anything, after that, from them, I didn't wanta turn up with a hole in my head and people saying, 'another burnt out rock star casualty killed himself'. And with Rick in prison, I just didn't want to . . ." He shrugged. ". . . anyway, I figure it's now or never."

"You think people will like, pay, in actual fucking *double-you dee* for this stuff?" Spanx voice almost awestruck with wonder.

"I think so because people don't know if they're talking to a semblant now or what, right? They want to know for sure—I don't know why but they do—so . . ."

"It'd fuck their heads up big if we open-sourced it, hode–"

"Open source! How do we make any money from that, you idiot! No! Don't even tell anybody about this except the guy we make a deal with. And I'm only telling *you* because you got that guy who does your rotor tune ups, right? And he knows about selling dirty ware, and who'd buy it. You know, Slakon and those people probably got it wired so it's illegal here but we could sell to someone overseas and they'd sell d-loads here. Maybe JapanaCorp, someone like that, they'd buy it. I give you and your man ten percent each–"

"Ten percent? That's a fucking skim-scam on your friend, your only friend, your best friend, your–"

"Ten percent of two million, man! That's what I'm asking for, two million! Two fucking million is my *floor!* That's two hundred grand for you! Tell you what, I'll make it twenty percent for you, ten for him."

"Okay, okay, well, I dunno . . ."

Danny shook his head. Spanx: useless for anything outside band business. He'd bung something up. He was out of his mind. And it occurred to Danny that he knew someone who could do the same thing for him, cut out at least one of the middle men: Rack Nidd. Yeah. Rack could maybe sell it . . .

"Look, let's think about it awhile, Spanx. One thing at a time. I hear the buzzer, someone wants in, that must be our jock. Who is it, Ronald?"

"Calls herself Ronnie. She-wee now."

"What? He's a She-wee?"

"Got a good ginger for it. Can have sex with himself or something. I mean . . . you know what I mean. Complete hermaphrodite. Got all the parts, fully functional. He can—or she can—turn his dingus around so it–"

Danny winced and interrupted, "You know what? I don't fucking want to hear about it. Let's just rehearse so I can ex outta here . . . I'm afraid Rick's gonna check your place out . . . I'm gonna go back to Rooftown and put this ware away there."

"Bev'll never let you back in, you naughty naughty little doggie."

"Yeah she will."

Spanx grinned. "Yeah she probably will."

"I'm surprised you didn't check out Spanx's place," Zilia said, as they lay in bed together at the cabin, nude bodies cooling.

"I thought of Spanx's place but decided that if I came around there and missed him he'd hear of it and it might spook him enough he might not do the Black Glass show. And then I'd miss him there too. And the Black Glass show is a pretty definite place to find Danny . . ."

She shivered, the shiver transmitting to her multicolored hair, making it shimmer like a waterfall. "I sometimes forget you were a cop—and then you say something that shows your *cop-think* and I get all funny. Not that I never fantasized about doing it with a cop. I sure as hell did. You don't have any of the, ah, *accoutrement* of police work still do you? Like, you know . . ."

"Handcuffs?" He laughed. "No. Who'd wear them, you or me?"

"Ooh, you'd let me put them on you?"

"Well actually . . . much as I like you . . . and that's a lot . . . no I wouldn't."

"Good." She nestled against him.

She seemed a marked contrast to the woman who'd barely let him into her place a short time ago. Who kept putting him in *his* place. But even then he'd known; the attraction between himself and this mercurial woman was an inexorable undertow; and the breakers on the rocks outside seemed to sussurate agreement. And he felt, in that moment, as if life might have something to offer, after all . . .

He smiled, shook his head. Thinking: *Sucker.* But he knew what Kenpo would say: If you weren't ready to risk being a sucker, you lost everything.

"What you going to do, when you find Danny—really?"

"I don't know, get him away from this town. Rehab him somehow. Getting over an addiction is as much about time clean as anything else. And I'll try to get your money out of him."

"Tell you the truth, I don't care about that. Not really. I just wanted to . . . vent about him."

Candle nodded. That's what he'd figured. He wondered how Danny would take his relationship with Zilia—if the relationship continued. It *felt* like it was going to go on. He suspected Danny wouldn't care, really—but he might pretend to care. Use it as an excuse to give his brother the slip. Get back to his addiction.

He shifted in the bed, reaching for his tepid beer on the end table—and winced. He still had a backache from concerted sex in the small spaces of the freight-train control cab. Not that he regretted a moment of it. Nor did he regret the throbbing headache he had now from the absinthe. Not something you'd want to do every day but . . . what an experience that had been. Even Kenpo would have been envious. *Coupling in a train engine? Really? Was it moving? Marvelous! You shouldn't be drinking absinthe! Do you have any left?*

They had fallen silent and Candle lay there, propped up a little, his arm around her, listening to the waves crashing against the cliffs below the little cabin. The grease-recycle heater sensed the room was cooling and clicked within itself, began to hum and exhale warm air, the smell of fried food. The one-room cabin was crowded with old canvasses stacked against the redwood walls. None of the paintings were actually hung. Zilia's late mother's canvasses, she'd said, not hers, and in fact they weren't very good. Seascapes with images of rocks in the sea, the rocks looking like lumps of dung—and not intentionally. Pictures of slightly deformed horses. The room smelled faintly of aged oil paint.

Candle felt himself start to drift to sleep . . .

Monroe going down the trap door. The top of her head snapped off by bullets, her wig flipping aside. Flying guns sniffing bloodhound like after them down the corridor. Bullets strafing at his heels . . .

His eyes snapped open. He was suddenly wide awake. It was going to take time to work through all that had happened. He'd need Kenpo's help. But there wouldn't be time, not for awhile. He could feel an imminence, as if events were crowding outside the door, together, pushing on it, ready to force their way in all at once, in a rush. Things were going to keep coming at him, hard and fast.

There were alternatives. He could avoid the Black Glass, give up on Danny. Stupid *not* to give up on him. But Danny was his only family. Candle had to try to retrieve him—at least once.

Monroe going down the trap door. The top of her head . . .

"You want to sleep?" Zilia asked. Not sounding sleepy.

"I don't think I can sleep. I'm still . . . dealing. I feel like getting out, get some fresh air. You actually have something close to fresh air up here. Where are we, sixty miles from L.A.?"

"Farther than that. We're north of Santa Barbara, near Isla Vista. Still some greenery out here. But something else too—there's a big electronic waste recycling center about three miles away. And that's where Clive the Hive's got his had-ware shop going."

"You mean hardware?"

"He calls it had-ware. It's worth seeing. And I need him to process something for me, I got the specs on my palmer. Needs big processing. He might be what you and Shortstack need to restart. You wanta go over there? We could ride the horses over."

"*Horses?* You're fucking with me."

"No, I'm not. Jeff keeps them for me down the road. I grew up around horses. They're just part of our family. They need exercise. Come on, Rick, get your lazy ass dressed . . ."

A little over an hour later, they were riding through the night along a trail beside the cliffs —Zilia adroitly on a black stallion; Candle following, clinging desperately to a lean brown mare; the rocky path, the stunted trees bouncing past him. The moonlight came and went, the moon slipping in and out of the clouds, and it seemed to him it was riding along parallel to the horses. His legs ached already; his thighs rasped; the smell of the horse seemed acrid and strange to him; sometimes it turned its head and looked doubtfully back at him, with eyes like black marble.

Candle's mare seemed determined to stick with the stallion, which was fortunate, since Candle was at a loss as to how to guide her, and in a few minutes they were reining their mounts outside a rusty hurricane fence topped with razor wire. It was a warm, moist night, shreds of ground fog blew around them as they dismounted. They tied the horses to a snag under an oak tree, where there was a patch of yellow grass to graze on.

Candle did a few quick squats, grimacing, as Zilia tapped a message to someone on her palmer. She stared into the little screen. "He's gonna let us in . . ." She grinned at Candle. "Something wrong with your legs?"

"Only that my thighs are abraded and my crotch is an inch

wider than it was, and my balls are now like wafers." But he smiled at her. He was glad of the experience. It was the last thing he'd expected would happen today.

"Your body gets used to it. Come on."

A big metal gate on wheels, almost indistinguishable from the fence, was rolling back to let them through. They walked on a gravel road in darkness, Candle's legs still stiff, toward an enormous, long, low darkbuilding of scrap aluminum and mystercyke, more roof than walls, with a vaguely agricultural aspect. It was nearly as long as a football field, Candle guessed. A door opened in the nearer end of the building, and light fairly gushed out; they stepped in, blinking, looking around.

Clive closed the door quickly behind them. He was a skinny, snaggle-toothed man with an intricate beard and elaborately pierced ears.Maybe mid-thirties but looking older, in old fashioned denim overalls, his shirtless tattooed arms and chest bare. He clumped about in enormous, scuffed work boots.

The interior of the building was sealed up with liberally applied tar: every crack, every window, so that no light escaped to call attention to the structure. It was all one lengthy gigantic room, and it was filled with tiers, to the right and left, like bleachers; on each "bleacher" was a long row of old—ancient!—computer hard drives, hardwired into unity; some were in their original cases, connected by tangles and ropes of cables. Every so often a scavenged server bulked above the smaller drives. A discrete 'cloud computing' system of . . . how many? Tens of thousands? Each glowing with a small green or blue or red light. The room hummed with their collective computation, was warmed with the heat they gave off; each row was wired to the others, on both sides of the room. "It used to be one of those big agribusiness chicken barns," Zilia said. "Till Clive converted it to his had-ware hive. All this gear you see in this room, every hard drive, every processor, every CPU, it was all discarded, in the electronics dump. Supposed to be recycled but they only actually recycle a small percentage of it and no one seems to care when he scavenges it. He's made it into one big computer. Oh—Clive, this is Rick Candle. Rick, this is Clive. Doesn't use his last name anymore. Sometimes people call him Clive the Hive—don't they Clivey?—'cause this place is 'the Hive'."

Clive was scrutinizing Candle with a skepticism that made him think of Brinny. "You didn't say he was such a hard-looking character," Clive remarked, in a high-pitched voice.

"He's an ex-cop, Clive," she said.

Clive's bristling eyebrows met in a scowl. "He'd better not be still talking to–"

"You know," Candle interrupted sharply, "I'm getting tired of people giving me crap for having spent sixteen years watching out for them. I've given up working for the law, man. Your secrets are safe with me. Just let it go."

Candle knew that if he wanted to keep on Zilia's good side, he shouldn't be snapping at her friend. He knew there was too much warning, too much edge in his voice. But there were edges everywhere. He was on an edge, most of the time. Even when he was in Zilia's arms. A certain desperation . . .

Clive snorted, and turned away. "You're here now, I'll take a chance on you. If *she* says so. I have to trust someone. And she's the one."

Candle didn't miss the reverence in Clive's voice, when he said *she*, Clive glancing at Zilia out of the corners of his small, intense blue eyes.

Clive's beard was an object of fascination; in outline it was large and spade-shaped but within the "spade" the red-brown beard-hair was cut and formed into an intricacy of rune-like shapes, almost ideograms; the corona of hair on his head was a corresponding ideogrammatic display; the skin on his bare arms replicated the same sort of cryptic glyphs, in blue tattoo ink; his ears were intricately pierced with the same kinds of shapes, in silver. Each glyph seemed almost familiar, and alien, at once.

"I've known Clive since we were little kids, and he was the older boy up the street," Zilia said, walking up to a bank of input systems. "Clive I've got a program here I need extrapolated, the image needs to be reproduced thousands of times, a bee-eye effect . . ."

As they spoke, Zilia uploading from her palmer into Clive's equipment, Candle strolled over to an open door opposite; it let into a long storeroom that ran along the side of the building, probably where the chickenfeed had been stored and sluiced, at one time. Candle moved closer to the open door, and looked through—there were endless shelves of electronic parts, in exactingly marked bins, stretching off into the perspective of distance. They were organized so that each bin contained the same part, or something close; the one beside it a similar part, only a little different. On and on and on down the length of the narrow room.

Clive appeared at Candle's side. "You doing research, there, Candle?"

"Just . . . amazed at how organized this is. There's so much of it. So many different kinds of computers . . . and you seem to have them all running together, some way."

Clive glared at him—and turned away muttering.

Zilia said, "Clivey—be nice. Trust him. He's interested for good reasons. He's doing security for the undermarket."

"Undermarket? The Black Stock Market?" Clive musingly made a minute correction in his beard. "There's more than one of those. Which one?"

"Nodder's," Candle said, noticing that Clive had tiny little glyphs painted on his fingernails, much like the ones in his hair, his tattoos, his beard.

"Nodder's? Reputable. All right, since it's Nodder—and since *she* says so." He strutted back and forth like a bantam rooster, then, making quick, energetic, precise gestures as he spoke, emphasizing every word. "Organized you say . . . People use the word and never think about it . . ."

"Uh oh," Zilia said, hiding a smile behind her hand.

"Organized!" Clive piped. "As in more *organic*, as in more of an organ, as in arrayed into the *parts* of an organ, as in part of the *big organism*, yes?"

"Is that what it is, a big organism?" Candle said. "What do you do with all this?"

"What do I do? Oh, people pay me to provide SuperComputer computation, where there is no super computer, cloud computation where there is no cloud. Like hijacked computers, but these are all in one building and all owned by one guy. This is like one of those great expensive SuperSystems at Slakon—but made of thousands of people's old Macs and PCs! Some of these computers date from the late twentieth century! Many of them should not be compatible with one another. But I have made them so! They are all one, now! Order from chaos! That is my great imperial demand on my environment! But do you know, there is no chaos, my friend—in a certain sense, the notion of chaos is a falseness! There is only *relative localized chaos!* This I convert to order, but I will someday find a way to make local order replicate the computations of the big machine, the so-called randomness of chance falling about in the universe, the cosmos itself a grand calculator working out an endless problem of probability. I have come close, I tell you, to proving that *there is no chaos!* Even entropy is only a relative disorder! An organism dies, yes, and we see a greater disorder in the system . . . but that is the local system! Consider—a planet is struck by an asteroid and comes apart at the seams! It flies asunder! Chaos, disorder rampant in the system that had been the planet! But! But!"

"Clive . . . Clivey . . . sweetheart . . ." Zilia said gently.

But Clive didn't hear her. He was stalking back and forth, arms waving, spittle gathering at the corners of his mouth. "But! Did the asteroid strike the planet with inexactitude? No! It struck it as exactly it must! It struck it as a pool ball strikes another! Within the system of the pool table the balls strike exactly as they must if propelled a certain way. This seems superficially random—until we direct one in a given fashion to a given end and then we see it is not random, not at all. We introduce human notions of orderliness. If the laws of physics are, with mathematical precision, guiding the motion of these so called randomized atoms, then how is their movement random? They move according to their mass, according to density, according to the fields they are a part of, according to velocity, and so on. They move instantly into *another* system—there is no randomness, there is no chaos, there is always order, everywhere! A man's death itself is the breaking up of one system only to render the so-called destroyed organism into another system, that of the worms, the soil, the–"

"Clive?" She stepped close and tugged at one of his ear rings.

He seemed emotionally startled; his cheeks reddened. He licked his lips. Then stepped suddenly back from her.

He's afraid to touch anyone, Candle realized, with a rush of pity. He loves her. But he can't touch her.

"Clive, you can send your Master Theory to Rick when it's done."

"Oh I don't think it can ever be done . . ." He clutched his arms to his sides as if to keep from losing control of them. "One system becomes another—how can my Theory be complete?"

"Actually," Candle said, "some of what you said sounds like something my lama said . . . Kenpo Rinpoche . . ."

Suddenly Clive became stock-still. He looked at Candle intently, as if seeing him for the first time. He wiped the corners of his mouth. "Kenpo of Venice Beach?" Clive's voice was hushed, almost inaudible. When Candle nodded, he took a long slow breath and said. "Well then. That being the case. I am at your service."

Candle looked at him in surprise. "You know Kenpo?"

Clive bowed, ever so slightly. "His path is all that keeps me . . . *sane* is not the word. But you understand. How can I help?"

"Well—our . . . you call it an undermarket. It was raided–"

"I heard. It's all over the Mesh. One of your brokers was killed. It's that prick Grist, I expect, behind it."

"We've saved the data. We need to restart. But . . . we'll need a comprehensive new platform . . . and maybe something with more power for a better defense."

Clive tweaked his beard, walked rapidly to a hard drive about ten yards down, stared at a flickering light; he reached out, straightened a wire. A spark flew, and then the light glowed steadily again. He walked back to Candle, and replied as if he'd never left his side.

"Not only can I provide a platform for it, Candle—I can give the undermarket ten times, a hundred times the scope. We can start your undermarket over—but you must bring them out here. I do not wish to work with your people remotely. I must meet them, you understand. And there are risks. I obviously cannot carry this building away with me to escape, should we be raided. But one of the things I have used this computing power for, is obfuscation. It's something like noise floggers, but much more comprehensive, much more powerful, much more . . . How can I put it . . . All inclusive . . . I really doubt they'd ever find me. Because you see—they've tried a thousand times."

"Grist does not know this drive is here," said the Multisemblant the very moment that Pup Benson switched it on, its voice phasing in and out of clarity. "He does not know! Can you imagine! It's his! His computer! And it's worth more money than you ever will have, even if you become rich, wealthy, another Croesus!"

It's multiplex face was shifting—and then forming into its more solid, only slightly askew form.

They were in a building, with concrete floors, about fifty yards square. The Multisemblant array sat on a table, a single overhead bulb illumined it with a cone of dusty light in the middle of the chilly room.

The display switched on. An image of Grist appeared, seen from above, walking into his apartment building, late at night. Two large men in tightly-fitting suits walked just behind him. Bodyguards, if Pup was any judge of thug flesh.

"If we can see him," Pup said, "his security systems can see us . . ."

"No, no," said the Multisemblant. "I've got all that squared away, covered, controlled, I assure you, friend Benson."

"It's his computer, the one you're running off of, now? One of those big superwhatsits? And he doesn't know it's here!"

"He does not know! It was being completed to his specifications and was to be shipped to him next week—but I had it shipped here. More precisely, I had it shipped to a dock two miles from here. I used his semblant, I used certain rarely-used Slakon accounts, and had it shipped there. Then I used a different set of accounts to ship it from there to here and have it set up. It will seem to have disappeared from that dock! Vanished, flickered away, gone!"

"Well—okay. Now you're all set up. You're supposed to pay me—"

"I already did! Check your account!"

Pup checked it, and fast. And saw the money there. Hundreds

of thousands of WD, and it was all his. He could . . . What would he do? Get a yacht and take it down to Cabo and just see if . . .

"But of course that won't be enough for y'all," said the Multi-semblant, its voice suddenly sounding Texan. "You're gonna want the *five million* WD."

Pup's mouth went dry. "Five million. For what?"

"Something small. Helping me eliminate some human vileness from the world. Horrible little people. Just a few of them, here and there. A few minor killings, a few less pink softbodied cockroaches out of the nine billion in the world. Who'll know the difference? The fewer pink softbodied softshell crabs in human form the better."

"And then—five million?"

"Oh yes. And then you will join the Hashishim in paradise. What do you say?"

NOW MARCHES RYTHMICALLY INTO THEN.
SOME LIKE TO CALL IT,
CHAPTER TEN

"Texer is, I figure he's gonna find me anyway." Danny Candle shrugged, pouring himself the one drink he allowed himself before a show. Gin and tonic. "He may as well find me here in the Black Glass where I'm in my . . . I don't know, I just feel stronger here."

They were in the dressing room, a cramped space with graffiti layering the walls, tags and jeers left by twenty years of bands and performers. A makeup table with a cracked mirror.

Spanx was making a pyramid of empty beer cans, on the colorless cigarette-scarred carpet. "Your brother gonna find you, drag your ass to rehab, where they make put happy brain bots in you, so you can feel happy vibrations or some deal, makes you feel like a pretty eel, steal a feel."

"I'm all set up," Ronnie said, coming to the door. She leaned on the doorframe, arms crossed over her perfected breasts, wearing a blouse top sparkling with onyx sequins and fringed with blood-red beads; a pair of masculine black jeans underneath, tight enough to show her considerable package. Her head was shaved, eyes deep in kohl, lips puffy and shiny with gloss, ears dangly with black gems. "They said five minutes, like, ten minutes ago, so, hodie brother . . ."

"Yeah okay. Let 'em wait a few minutes," Danny said, finishing his drink.

"It's a good house. Standing room only."

"Fucking oughta be." He realized he ought to get this over with and get out of here as quick as possible. Maybe avoid Rick after all.

Just a couple minutes more and then he'd hit the stage . . . Hoped there was no trouble about getting paid after the show . . .

Candle had gotten hold of a drone scanner. And standing in the alley, around the corner from the street entrance for the Black Glass, he picked up two drones, within forty feet. Right now they were watching the crowd gathered outside the front entrance. A small crowd—most everyone had gone in for the show. In a moment one of the operators would fly the birseye around the building, to watch the other entrances. Probably looking for him.

He slipped the scanner in his pocket, and walked down the alley, wondering if Zilia was really safe. She was staying at her cabin up north. But they could trace him to her—and her to the cabin. Suppose they grabbed her, made her a hostage?

Maybe he ought to make some kind of deal with Grist. Let him know he didn't really have anything on Grist's part in the skim-scam; wasn't looking for revenge. Wasn't a loose cannon.

From what he knew of Grist, though—trusting him to follow through on a deal was taking a big chance.

He stepped over a drunk sleeping on flattened plastifiber boxes; very authentic mingled reek of alcohol, old sweat and urine suggesting it wasn't some undercover guy.

Four paces more, and then the load-up entrance of the nightclub . . . where a stocky steroid-bulky bouncer with short flaxen hair stepped into the doorway, lighting a cigarette.

"You don't look like you belong," said the bouncer, squinting against smoke. He was young, and somehow that went with the moving tattoo of a striking cobra on his chest, bared under an open leather jacket. The tattoo on his chest striking . . . drawing back. Waiting. Striking . . . drawing back . . .

"I'm Danny Candle's brother. He's performing here tonight."

"Then you're the guy I'm specifically not supposed to allow in here, so be a good old wanx and fuck off."

Candle thought it unwise to pull his gun. Showing a gun led to too many repercussions, in a place like this. He looked the bouncer over, and decided this prime chunk of thug-flesh was into some form of martial arts, maybe kick boxing: it was there in the cockiness, and in a particular way the bouncer balanced on his feet, a trigger-like poise that suggested his confidence was in more than his heft. But that could make him predictable, and predictable is vulnerable.

"Sure thing," Candle said. Then he made a deliberately clumsy swing at the bouncer's head—not really trying to connect. Counting on the man's martial arts reflexes.

The bouncer reacted like Candle figured, with a sneer and a left-hand block, tilting back, putting his weight on his left foot, raising his right leg, right knee cocked, boot aimed for a kick—

But Candle had already stepped left, and braced—and he grabbed the bouncer's kicking foot, lifted it up hard, throwing his opponent off balance. The bouncer went pitching backwards, grunting, onto his back, wheezing as the air whooshed out of him.

Candle stepped through the door, waited as the snarling bouncer rolled over and got to one knee, preparatory to rushing—then Candle slammed him under the chin with the heel of his right hand, a short sharp shock: a move he'd learned from Rina. The big man's head snapped back, and then forward, and he fell on his face at Candle's feet.

Out cold.

Candle looked around, saw this back hallway was empty—there was a thumping noise and a roar from the direction of the stage—and he dragged the bouncer to a janitor's closet, wedged him into it, cuffing him from behind with a pair of LP cuffs obtained the same place he'd gotten the scanner: Gustafson. He pulled the bouncer's backstage pass off, put it on himself, found a wedge used to hold doors open, used it to jam the closet door shut at the bottom. He closed the back door, and went down the narrow hall toward the main hall. He glanced down a cross hall, behind the stage, and saw Spanx following Danny and someone he couldn't see clearly—a woman? All three moving away from him down the narrow passage, Danny and Spanx carrying their instruments.

Candle considered running down there, grabbing Danny right now. But he'd make Danny furious if he stopped him from performing—from collecting his gig money. Let him have his show and his pay. Grab him after.

He turned toward the main room, slipping past a puzzled techie watching the backstage door. Edging quickly into the crowd, Candle felt the combination of sick despair and thrill he always experienced at rock shows. At shows like this, where people heard the music the old fashioned way, from amplifiers on the stage instead of through head implants picking up wifi transmissions from the performers, the atmosphere was more or less the same as it had been, in rock clubs, for generation: Milling people chattering with one another in a dim, compressed space, the décor both ironic and earnest; canned music throbbed as the jostling crowd, drinks clinking, waited for the live show. Electricity building in the air waiting to be discharged, like a battery over-charged with energy.

His father had been a band manager, his mother an aspiring singer; she'd become a groupie, then a wife and management partner. And by inexorable degrees an alcoholic. As a child, Candle came into the clubs and concert halls with his parents—in some places it was technically illegal, but his mom somehow got him in because it was almost the only time he could spend with them out in the world; and in a place where they weren't hung over, weren't bickering; weren't as likely to just walk out.

But he'd been scared and lonely in places like this, too. Sitting backstage with his mom and some self-consumed rock star, stomach clenching when his dad would come back from the bathroom, wiping his nose, grinning, winking at him, chattering from blue mesc or crystal meth or synthcoke or yex.

Candle felt that clenching now, looking around.

The club was called Black Glass for more than one reason. The obvious one was that the room was made of one giant piece of black glass—actually it was hardened, dark-tinted transparent plastic—roughly shaped like a cavern, but with the cornerless walls in fold-shapes like rumpled cloth. The stage was shuttered by three successive movable walls of translucent blackened "glass," instead of curtains. Like looking through three sets of dark sunglasses. Before the show, dark figures of the performers could be seen, just blur-edged silhouettes. That one silhouette was Danny, his hunched shoulders and explosive hairstyle unmistakable.

In the audience, infrastoners with movable tattoos, animated Cat Hats, opaque eye cusps, grinned and whispered; some stood in corners and tried to look cool. Re-Ravers, semi-nude, bodies painted, danced to the house music. Pagoths milled, wearing simulated fur, animal skins, charcoaled eyes, much piercing, some with long streaked hair, others with scalp-up sculptures of cartilage-shaped like gods and dragons and online game creatures, fixed to their skulls like articulated Mohawks. Glum, silent corner-boys, in their shapeless hoodies, sagging army pants, heavy boots. The Elegant Dub contingent, in tight fitting retro suits with blazers, white shirts skinny ties, clustered disdainfully together, amused by the other cliques. The audience faces were mixed race, mostly, with only a few real blonds, even fewer truly black African-Americans. Danny had always had a cross-genre appeal, Candle reflected; he had managed to balance electronica, stoner rock, hip-hop, grime, and worldsounds, transitioning from one to the other, culminating in almost perfect fusion. The music unified by a rapid, steady beat and the ironic intonations of his voice.

The place definitely made Candle uneasy. His parents had ruined it for him. He supposed he might have found some other way to get past that bouncer—a stiff bribe would have been wiser—but he'd enjoyed taking him down. It was like he was punching out the club itself. And maybe Dad too.

Candle kept moving, as if looking for friends in the crowd, kept his face mostly turned to the stage, but glancing around, discreetly watching for drones. He caught a silvery flicker up near the ceiling. A medium-sized flying camera—smaller than the one Rina had bashed, larger than the one he'd found on the wall. The small ones were prone to getting lost or broken in large crowds.

Suddenly the background music faded and the walls concealing the stage began slowly to draw back, slotting into the stage wings; first the outer wall of darkened plastic-glass, letting the audience see the performers a little more clearly. And when that translucent wall started drawing back, a drumbeat thudded from the band. Then the second wall drew away in the other direction, and they could see the band a little better; but they were still hidden behind the third wall of dark glass, and they were already playing, Danny playing guitar, Spanx on bass, the third guy providing hand-triggered rhythm and percussion. He could just make out their faces . . .

Then Danny started singing, and the third wall drew back and the crowd erupted in hoots, and cheers and "Woot!" and clapping and people holding up their palmers, screens alight, to make a constellation of electronic greeting, as if the social electricity in the room was translating into digital light. Candle felt the clenching in his gut become a twisting. There was his little brother, at last.

"Danny," he muttered.

The performance wound its way through a roughly ascending arc of energy. There was no puttering about between songs—Danny couldn't abide that, and once when Spanx distractedly fiddled with his bass Danny kicked him in the ass. The audience laughed, Spanx pretended to be offended, then the beat-jock started the pulsing sample and Spanx spun around and started playing and another song started. The energy built, the varied crowd became a unity around their focal point: Danny Candle.

The music hammered away. Danny sang a peculiar, whimsical lyric, something like,

> Has to be chapter one—
> that's how it is, hode, ask anyone;
> And this text gotta be chapter two
> —personal shit 'tween me 'n' you—
> An' this refined expression of me,
> in litr'chure- talk . . . is chapter three . . .

Candle kept slowly moving, keeping tall people and any obstacle he could find—a fold in the rippled glassy walls—between him and the birdseye. But they were getting hard to avoid. More than once someone in the audience spotted them, took a swipe at them. People generally hated flying cams.

Now Danny was on another cut, singing something about a box in his head . . .

... There's a box in my head
and inside it is a box
and that box
has a box, within;
there's a box in my skull
my skull is a box
and there's room for us both, to go in—
yeah come on sweet baby, come in ...

Just at the end of the encore set, Candle saw a silver flicker draw near, overhead. He decided it was time to use the blur bandage. He turned his back, took the blur bandage from a coat pocket, unpeeled the backing, pressed the swatch to his right cheek bone—it was camouflaged as a band-aid. It'd set up a field that'd blur any cam looking at his face. But it had a fiber battery that wouldn't last long so he'd kept it back till now. And while it would conceal his identity, the blur, in a crowd full of crisp faces, could draw attention to him.

And there—at the edge of the crowd, looking around. Halido. And some other thugflesh prick with him.

Candle went quickly to the backstage door, waved his stolen pass at the puzzled, bearded stagehand, slipped past, and was waiting in the dressing room when the flushed, triumphant Danny arrived. The smile faded from Danny's face as he stared at Candle. Then he shrugged and put away his guitar.

"Glad you're out, bro," Danny mumbled.

"Like you didn't know?" Candle said. "You knew. Good set, by the way. You look like you feel good about it."

"Why wouldn't I feel good about a good set?"

"It's just that–"

"Oh, I know: get a natural high from music. I remember that speech." Danny sat in a creaking chair, poured himself a drink from a bottle sitting on the dressing table. "You want a drink? Brought my own brandy."

"Sure."

They drank some Hennessey as Spanx and Ronnie stowed gear. Spanx mumbled something about seeing about the money and Ronnie mumbled about getting a drink at the bar. They vanished and Candle was alone with his brother. Canned music thudded murkily, masked by the intervening walls, from the main room.

Finally, wondering how long before Halido showed up back here, Candle said, "You weren't there. Said you would be."

"Okay. Sorry."

"I figure you knew I'd find out you were using again and–"

"Yeah okay, fine, whatever. You want another drink? If not—I'm gonna change and get my money and get the fuck out of Dodge–"

"No you're gonna shut up and listen. Four years, my mind downloaded—my body walking around—taking orders—You know what they did with my body?"

"No, 'Saint Rick', I don't."

""Neither do I. That's the fucking point. And all I asked you to do was not fry your brain anymore. But from what Zilia tells me–"

"You've seen Zilia? How is she?"

Candle cleared his throat. Should he tell him? Later. "She's okay. She's good. She's . . . she wanted her money. But I think I got her to drop that."

"Rick—if you'll think back, you'll remember, hode, I didn't *ask* you to be a fucking martyr for me."

"You'd have done hard time. I knew I'd get a break. And as for asking me . . . everything you do asks for help, kid."

Danny's face contorted and he threw the drink. Candle ducked; the glass added a new web of cracks to the mirror and distorted magic marker graffiti on the mirror so that it went from reading, FUCK YOU IF YOU DON'T LIKE MY IGGY COVERS, to FUCK YOU IGGY OVER.

Danny got up, squatted by his guitar case, snapped it shut, his back to Candle. Then he seemed to sag in place. He went to his knees, his shoulders hunched. His voice was hoarse when he said, "I don't fucking know. I'm sorry. I tried for a long time. Zilia can tell you that for a couple years there, almost three . . ."

"We can try again, Danny," Candle said gently. "Relapse—so what, it's part of the journey, man. You can get over relapsing. But you need time away from all the temptations. We'll get the fuck out of Dodge together. We'll hit Highway 1 up the beach, you'll get some distance from the V-rat nest. One of these days you'll feel confident enough, you can get back into performance. I'll find you a new agent. But you got to stay close to me."

Danny rocked back on his haunches, ran his fingers through his hair. "Rick . . . we can try. I guess I can trust you. I don't know how I can trust anyfuckingbody but . . . see, I'm not gonna make it, man. It's like . . . like if you've got a table, and one leg is cracked, if you put something heavy on it, that fucker's gonna break down. And bust whatever's on that table. And I'm that table. Going to break, you put anything on me. I don't want to bust down and and fuck up everything for you, man. I . . ." He took a long breath. His voice was ragged, almost inaudible as he went on. ". . . I got a busted part that won't hold anything up . . ."

"People mend, Danny. I've got some to do myself . . ." Candle hesitated, wondering once more if he should tell Danny about Zilia. But that might be too much weight on the table, right now. He'd tell him when things were more stable. "What *else* you got going, Danny? Come on, look at where you clicked at. Rooftown? Living in a roof shack? And still blowing your resources on scum like Rack Nidd? What you do at his place—it's the lowest form of partying, Danny. Because V-ratting is something you do all alone. Even if you're wired to somebody. It's not like real contact. You see an image of them—it's not like you're really with them. It's isolating. Like Dad—"

Danny visibly cringed at that. Candle knew it was a dirty trick, bringing Dad into it this way; he knew Danny had an aversion to thinking about Dad . . . Dad, putting drugs and partying before his kids. Candle went on relentlessly, "—Dad started out partying with other people, ended up doing drugs in a toilet stall. And that's how he died. Alone, hode. I mean—fuck that. There's stuff to do in this life you haven't seen. You did one world tour. You could get a comeback going, do another. There's a lot of places you haven't been to."

Danny snorted, shook his head. "You want to depress me, take me on a trip. The world's all . . . used up. Doesn't seem worth it. Same stores everywhere, same restaurants, all over the world. Wilderness is dying. Why bother going anywhere?"

"It's not all fucked up out there. Some of this planet is holding on. Let's go see it, man. Give it a chance. I promise—I'll stick with you no matter what." Then he said something he almost never said. "I give you my word."

Danny sighed. "Uh oh—his word. Serious shit."

"It is—with me."

"Yeah. I know it is." Finally Danny said, "Okay. Like you say. Nothing to lose. Let's try it."

Spanx appeared at the door. "Yo yo whoa whoa whoa, there's some fucking wanxenheimers from Hell asking for the Candle brothers, telling the stage dudes they got to come back, saying the badges are coming . . ."

Danny looked at Candle. "What the fuck?"

"That's Grist's people. They're looking for me more than you. But they'll scoop your ass up too. It's that whole Maeterling thing. I was gonna try to make a deal with Grist—but I can't do it on their terms. I got to avoid 'em, Danny. You do, too."

"So let's get gone!"

"Yeah . . . but their drones will follow us out," Candle said.

Spanx grinned lopsidedly. "Drones? Hafuckingha,motherh afuckingha! I love to fuck up drone cams! I can do a feedback freaker!"

Candle looked at him. "A what?"

"Yeah a feedback freaker, there's a frequency, you do heavy feedback with the amp set proper, it'll fuck up the signal on them flying cams. But I'd have to borrow Danny's guitar."

Danny stood, scowled over at Spanx—then nodded. "Do it. But make sure you take care of my guitar, I'm gonna come and get that thing before me and Rick leave town."

"You're leaving town? What fo' you leaving town, hound?"

"Just for awhile. Hey where's my pay?"

"Here, muh dear." Spanx handed him a pay card. "It's all there –already gave Ronnie his. I mean . . . hers."

"Okay take the guitar, Hamster'll let you do it—maybe Ronnie'll back you up."

"Oh yeah he'll totalfuckingly . . ."

"Don't tell anyone why you're doing this, Spanx," Candle warned.

"I ain't no blogmouther, hodey brudder . . ."

A couple minutes later, Spanx was onstage explaining that he was going to do a feedback concert, as a special treat for you to eat, please don't bleat, and the audience cheered—some of them groaned—and Ronnie set up a beat and Spanx adjusted the guitar carefully, turned it up loud as it would go and made hideous roaring-squealing noises come out of it—but at a certain frequency that invariably interfered with the transmissions of drone cams. And suddenly the spies monitoring the flying cameras saw nothing at all but snow and they recoiled from the amplified shrieking that might have been a transmission from a microphone set up at the place where a wandering star smashed into another star and created fulminating hell throughout a planetary system. Worlds colliding in some dark corner of the galaxy.

Danny and Rick Candle got to the back door leading to the alley—just as the closet door burst open and the bound-up bouncer stumbled out, roaring with rage.

Candle calmly drew his gun—and buffaloed the man, knocking him out with a sharp blow on the back of the head with his gun barrel. Then before the bouncer had hit the deck they were slipping through the door into the thin rain—and Candle saw Halido at the end of the alley, waiting for them in a cone of light from the single lamp projecting from the wall above him.

Candle sighed. Shortstack and Nodder weren't here to get him out of this one.

So Candle drew his gun, aimed carefully—and shot the light out at the end of the alley.

Darkness descended over the alley and he hustled Danny to another back door, kicked it in—it took two kicks, painfully jarring his ankle—and he hobbled ahead of Danny, the two of them darting through the back corridors of a Chinese-Mexican-French bakery.

They waved at the startled bakers, Danny snagging a cruller as they passed, and ran out through the front door, and into the gathering downfall. They were lucky and caught an autocab almost immediately . . .

And left Halido behind.

But ahead was the cross traffic of possibilities, most of them dark possibilities, in the city of uncertainty.

IS THIS REALLY
CHAPTER ELEVEN?
WISH YOU WERE BACK IN
NUMBER SEVEN?

"**I**s the chopper on the roof, Targer?" Terrence Grist sat on his living room sofa. Gazing through a transparent wall at the city lights; a web of lights, like when you see bright dew marking out a spider's web. He hadn't seen a wet spider's web since he was a kid. Did spiders still spin webs? They must, somewhere.

"Yes sir." Targer's face appearing in the glossy top of the low smart table, in front of the sofa.

"Okay wait there for me—you're flying the chopper. My regular pilot's staying here. You still up to piloting a rig like that?"

"I stay up to date, Mr. Grist. I can do it." Targer's expression hinted he wondered why Grist wanted him to pilot. It wasn't usual. The chopper was self-piloting. But some people didn't trust robotic pilots—though they never got drunk, never smoked pot, and never got tired.

"We've got a job. Serious things to deal with, Targer. You understand me? If you're not ready to be very, very serious, you stay here."

"You need me, I'm there, Mr. Grist."

"Fucking Candle got away from me. Again. I wanted that loose end tied up. Everybody is frustrating me, here. And Targer—before we go, I meant to ask about that Benson asshole . . ."

"We're still looking. Everyone is looking. The LAPD, Blackwater Division, Halliburton Policing, everyone."

"What about transaction traces?"

"Whatever the thing is . . . the program or whatever it is . . . it covered its tracks well. We can see where it swiped some cash, moved some things around, but that was all before it was moved. Since then we can't find it and if it's active we can't trace it. It's using some really sophisticated camouflage. We're trying–"

"Spare me the fumbling details. Get as many people on it as you need. Just get it done."

Grist heard a footstep and looked up to see Lisha come in, wearing a lustrous dark blue silk shift, clutching her purse close against her, walking carefully on her black high heels. Her lips were pinched together. She looked like a scared child. She paused just inside the door—it was a bit darker there—and then came closer. He saw what was worrying her; a red mottling of rash across her face, specked by open lesions.

Her face, his face. His stomach lurched.

Grist looked away. "What happened? You have an allergic reaction to something? You need an allergist?"

"No. I've been to the dermatologist and the ginger. Everyone says the same thing . . . it's a rash. It's a reaction to this face . . ."

He glanced up at her. She meant, in a way, his face—since hers had been re-shaped into a feminized version of his. "You mean—the new face–"

"They said . . ." She chewed her lip, and turned away, her eyes glassy with tears. "That it's psychological. That I . . . it's face rejection. It's because I don't like . . . because I don't, um, relate to you, or trust you, or something, so I don't like having your face on my face so my . . . my body is rejecting the face . . . it's this thing that happens sometimes and they have a test where they can tell it's caused by . . . by your own . . . by . . . and I took the test and . . ."

"All *right!* I *get* it!" So it was her fault after all. "You know what, I won't subject you to . . . me. Not anymore. Not that way, not *any* way. Just—you can get your pay-off check, get your face restored, and get your stuff and go . . ."

"I . . . thank you. Terrence." Her voice was very small. Tiny. She turned and hurried from the room.

He got up, angrily looked around for his coat, found it, and went up to the chopper, thinking, *I wonder if she's heard too much, living with me. I wonder if she should be taking one of these chopper trips . . .*

He went to the roof, and saw that Targer was in the pilot's seat of the big Slakon-logoed chopper, its hull gleaming in the bright lights of the rooftop. Halido was hunched nervously outside its open hatch, the wind of its blades whipping his hair. Neighbors in an adjacent high rise had complained of the lights and the noise from his copter pad, but Grist had bought their building and kicked them out.

Grist hurried up to the chopper, ducked unnecessarily under the blades—he could never keep from doing that—and climbed up the little metal stairway. The passenger cabin of the chopper was comfortable, trimmed in brass and dark wood, like a first-class private jet cabin, but with seats facing one another around the side bulkheads, and one cushy seat with its back to the pilot's cab. Grist sat with his back to Targer, strapped himself in, gestured for Halido to get inside. Saw Halido hesitate. Grist gestured again, angrily. Halido glanced off across the roof at the city lights, the rising full moon, then got in the chopper, to Grist's right. Targer spoke to the system and it closed the hatch, muffling the engine and rotor noise.

"Where to, Mr. Grist?" Targer asked.

Grist spoke over his shoulder. "Oh hell—just take us up for now. Due west till I tell you different."

Within seconds, the chopper had lofted into the air. A passing nausea, and then they were comfortably chopping through the haze to the West.

"Where uh—where we headed?" Halido asked.

"Catalina," Grist said. "Shall we watch some television while we wait?"

Across from him was a sheet of clear glass that seemed to hang in the air in front of the farther bulkhead. It wasn't floating, but this high-end model's supports were so exquisitely made it was hard to tell. He activated the TV and the sheet of mediaglass became a semi-3D television image. SNN. Slakon News Network. Formerly CNN.

A black-Asian sports commentator with short-cropped hair and a wide face was interviewing a buffed-out Scandinavian type, in an expensive golf shirt. The buff guy was smiling, showing an intricate platinum grill across his teeth that spelled out MIAMI. Under his image his name and specialty appeared:

BJORN WILLCANSER, Steroid Stylist

"One of those steroid designers for the big teams," Grist commented, refusing to make eye contact with Halido. "My father would've shit a brick, if he knew these guys were standard now. Look at that suit—if he opens his arms wide enough it'll rip. Why doesn't he get one to fit? It's gotta strain at the seams I guess, he likes it that way. He's a walking advertisement for his product."

"Sir–" Halido began. "Candle slipped past us only because we didn't have enough personnel–"

"You're raising your voice, Halido."

"No—it's just the chopper noise, sir–"

"Quiet, I want to hear this." Grist turned the TV up so he could hear it over the chopper noise. It was the quietest chopper around, once the door was closed, but it was still a big whirring machine, going to make some noise, he reflected. Ought to hire engineers to improve them, make it quieter yet.

"They made the right choice," the Steroid Stylist was saying. *"You can't go with some standard mix of steroids and GH, that kind of thing, and expect to compete. You've got to have the cutting edge. You've got to think about neurological complications. Does Miami want to have its players gouging out people's eyes on the forty yard line, like Dorf in the Raiders did?"*

"What I'm saying, Mr. Grist," Halido went on, leaning toward him, "is that I did request more help and people didn't show up on time–"

"Did I not ask for quiet?" Grist snapped. "I'm curious about this. Maybe . . ."

"Does Miami want to pay a big fine," the Steroid Stylist went on, *"do they want to have to pay to have some guy's eyeballs grown in a vat, all that transplant time and expense? They don't. They want precision. And that's what I'm about, Tyrell. Precision. I play these bodies like a piano and I get the tune I want–"*

"We have a line of beauty steroids, but athletic steroids—I'm not sure we've gotten into that," Grist said, thinking aloud. He repeated the thought into the notes function of the mini-PDA on his wrist.

"Mr. Grist—if you'll look at the phone records–"

"Oh Christ," Grist said, shaking his head. "Halido you need

to calm down, I'm going to make us a drink."

He muted the television, got out of his seat belt, turned to wave a finger in front of a sensor. The bulkhead opened, and a small wet-bar extended gently into reach. He hummed to himself, picking out two highball glasses—careful to pick them at random, because he could feel Halido watching him closely. He took a canister of ice out—only this was the one he'd had prepared earlier and there was only one cube in it. He shook his head, *tsk*ing, and put the cube into a glass; he put the canister under the ice dispenser, got more ice, and used tongs to put the new ice into their glasses, noting carefully which one he'd put the first cube in.

He was enjoying himself.

"Rum and Coke for you, right? I'll have the same." He made them each a rum and Coke. Halido was watching closely to see that the drinks came from the same bottles for both of them. "I grow the cola berries for this cola in my own hot houses," Grist said, straight-faced. Then he grinned. "I always tell people that. You'd be amazed at how many believe it." He handed Halido his glass. A specific glass.

"Now, let's drink to new beginnings," he said, toasting Halido and giving him a weary smile as if to say, *You've got one more chance.*

Halido relaxed a little, and drank from his rum and coke, glancing out the window. They were well out over the sea now. "We're heading to Catalina? Is that it, out there? No, that's an oil rig . . ."

"How could you mistake an oil rig for Catalina?"

"The haze, sir." Halido had another sip. "And it's kind of dark out there even with the moon." Sip. "Mr. Grist, I just want to say . . ." One sip more. ". . . that I have a plan for–" Halido broke off, staring. The glass dropped from his nerveless fingers. His jaws worked soundlessly; his mouth gaped like a fish in murky water. He tried to speak.

"I guess we'll never know your plan, Halido," Grist said, sipping his drink. His own drink was safe—the first "ice cube" had been a tasteless material that melted instantly on contact with alcohol; it contained a transparent quick-dissolve capsule infused with a paralyzing toxin. "But we can guess at the quality of your plan. It was something stupid. We can figure that much, I believe."

Grist sipped a little more rum and Coke, put the glass on the bar, sent the bar back into the wall compartment.

Halido was sitting there, gaping, making *ack ack ack* sounds. "You're wondering," Grist said, "why I did it this way. So elaborately, putting a paralysis agent in your drink myself, dealing with your execution myself. Because I enjoy it—and because I want Targer to see it, naturally. I will reward him hugely if he solves these problems for me—Can you hear me up there, Targer?"

"Yes, sir!"

"I'll reward him either way. Hugely. This is one kind of reward you're getting, Halido. Targer hopes to earn the other kind. The pleasant kind." Grist stood up, and stretched. Then he took Halido by the collar, dragged him over to the red-edged emergency escape hatch on the other side of the cabin. He leaned Halido against the escape hatch, and Halido twitched a little, which was all the resistance he could manage. His eyes were pinning; his lips were drawn back in terror. He was drooling. Really, Grist found it repellent. But fascinating. "There is a special feeling of engagement with life, when you end another man completely," Grist said, straightening up to look at his handiwork. He grunted, bent and shifted Halido a little, centering him against the door, to make sure. "Yes, a special feeling—you appreciate life more when you end another man's life personally. And there is a certain high to it. I've always had a weakness for certain highs. I try to get them in a healthy way when I can—you know, in a way that doesn't harm my brain or liver. So here we are—I'm doing work I could easily have delegated. And as I said—it's instructive to other personnel."

He returned to his seat, and strapped himself in. Looked at Halido for a moment, twitching against the emergency lock.

Then he said, "Targer? Anyone around to observe us?"

"No, sir. Don't see any other aircraft, or boats. We're five miles out, should be far enough."

"Tilt the chopper a little to the starboard."

"Aye aye."

The chopper tilted, a little. Grist was now leaning slightly to his left. He flipped up the switch cover to reveal his arm-rest's master controls; he tapped the combination that opened the emergency lock of the chopper. An alarm began pealing—Grist quickly turned the alarm off and watched as the door slid aside, opening the helicopter's cabin to the naked night sky. Cold air gushed into the chopper along with the sound of humming engines and slashing chopper blades and wind. And Halido was gone, almost as if he'd magically vanished. Grist wished he could watch him fall. By the time he got the door safely closed and went to look through a port, Halido would be gone from sight. Seemed a shame. Grist would have liked to watch Halido tumbling, turning end over end in the moonlight, down to the Pacific Ocean.

When Halido washed up on the beach, Targer would have witnesses ready, saying Halido had been depressed, talking of suicide.

Grist felt the chill wind blowing in from the open hatch; he listened to it roar and rattle. Halido would be hitting the sea about now . . .

"Home, Targer," Grist said, closing the hatch. "Damn it's cold out there. A cold, cold world. Aren't we glad we're nice and snug in our chopper, Targer?"

Targer didn't answer. But Grist felt sure Targer understood.

The morning sun was bright on the misty windows and shiny fenders of Autopia.. Candle wished he'd brought sunglasses, like Danny. His eyes were watering from the reflections.

Some squatter with a mordant sense of humor had started calling the big squat Autopia, and it stuck They trudged past the dingey *AUTOPIA* sign, ripped off from the old Disneyland and propped on the back of a big wheelless pick up truck; trudged through spongey weed-overgrown lots between the clusters and rings and linkages of cars in the vast old automotive dump, kicking through trash, starting to feel warm, now that the rain had let up and the clouds had mostly blown away.

"You sure they're here?" Danny asked. He was wearing an ankle-length black leather coat, the seams popping at the shoulders, and he was chain smoking.

"Not sure, but Shortstack mentioned it as a 'safe house' to retreat to," Candle said. "And he's got a connection to this place—driving that obsolete van."

They were surrounded by obsolete cars and vans and trucks. This was a graveyard for gas burners, one of the last junk yards of old style vehicles left—the others had been turned into cubes of scrap and sold to China. This one, southeast of Los Angeles, near San Bernardino, had evolved into another vast squat, like Rooftown, but made of cars and mostly close to the ground. Toward the end of the general abandonment of gas burning cars, they'd been piled up almost at random in places like this, to be recycled. But there'd been so many that, for a time, great tracts of land had been swallowed up. The homeless, the disenfranchised, had used this one, to set up a makeshift community.

They'd pushed and tugged vans nose to nose, removed the engines, making them passageways; branching off them, old gutted SUVs were used as little living compartments. Compact cars were used for outhouses and storage and building scrap. The more powerful, relatively prosperous members of the Autopia community had claimed the campers and RVs. Most lived in SUVs and a couple of haphazardly constructed buildings: trucks were used as foundations for two-story structures made from wired-together pieces of cars.

Candle glimpsed faces, half seen through the misted car windows on either side—making him think of the translucent stage panels in Black Glass. Silhouettes, dim glimpses of people, removed from direct contact by glass compartmentalization. He had a mental image of people physically trapped behind computer screens, trying to get out—and he smiled, thinking he was being influenced by Zilia's art.

He wished she were here. But if she were, with Danny here too, there'd be a tension that'd have to find release, and it might go lots of ways.

They passed a group of kids throwing a battered football, tussling over it with little sense of game rules; they passed a Volkswagen bug, half sunk in the ground, that had the roof removed, the charred body of the car turned into a kind of outdoor fire pit. Ragged figures huddled near the fire—fueled by small amounts of gasoline found in gas tanks, oil from engines—and black plumes of smoke twisted, smelling of the rank childhood of industrial civilization before its toilet-training. Here and there, in the weedy lots, pieces of cars had been welded together into rusty sculptures: rough outlines of men and women dancing, children playing, a giant dog. Up ahead was a wall of cars, nose to nose, apparently unoccupied—except for a couple of teenagers in one, smoking pot and giggling. The dope plants grew out of the car's trunk. The path threaded between two old nose-to-tail Cadillacs and into an open space in front of what looked like a big pile of cars, till you looked closer and saw it was a building. Music thumped and wheedled from somewhere in the scrappy structure.

As they approached the two-story construct, Candle saw it was wired and, in some places, welded together, with bent and battered sedan hoods and stripped pieces of tire forming a weather-stripping carapace. "That's the new squatters place," Danny said. "Mostly likely one your guy would be in." He'd been here before, to cop some illegal ware; electric wires ran into the herky-jerky building at odd angles, channeling energy swiped from power poles on the other side of the containment fence.

The entrance seemed to be a crude archway of mismatched car body sections extending from the building; inside, water dripped, and flickering lights mottled the dimness. To one side of the archway, outside, a shaggy figure sprawled bulkily in a buckling old lawn chair under an awning torn from an absent RV. The man had a gallon bottle of wine, half empty, in the grass next to him.

The big man came from under the awning, blinking in the light, to block their way: a towering dishevel-haired bushy-bearded door guard. "He's the Doorman," Danny muttered.

The Doorman wore an oil-stained, blue ski jacket that seemed to go with his bulging forehead and wild eyes and blackened teeth. He leaned on the chrome bumper from a small car, the bumper bent and twisted into a four-foot club. As they came closer he took the club in both oil-blackened hands and hefted it warningly. Candle reckoned the man was at least six-foot-seven.

"You cain't come inta heeah, eff you don't belong'," the Doorman rumbled. His accent was somewhere middle-south, maybe the "hollers" of Kentucky, Candle thought.

"You got a way to test a buy card?" Candle asked, taking the card out, holding it up for the Doorman to look at. "I got a hundred dollars here for you on this one. I'm a friend of Shortstack's—he's new, so I figure he's in this building, where the new people squat. I just want to see him. If you can bring him out I don't need to go in there . . ." In fact he'd much rather not go in there.

"Got a way ah kin test 'er inside," the doorman said. He snatched it from Candle's hand. "Y'all wait here, I'll test 'er, if it's good I'll find the little feller. But ya'll come in before I say, I'll bust yer heads, jus' like melons."

"We'll be chill," Danny said.

The big man ducked under the archway and went inside.

They waited. Children whooped; the smell of sewage wafted and retreated; the whiff of oil and gasoline, everywhere.

"Kind of good, this stuff is being used for something," Candle said.

Danny shrugged. Candle sighed, thinking that Danny had the air of a kid forced to go to a family gathering when he'd rather stay home and go virtual with his friends.

A few minutes more, and then the Doorman shambled back out, followed by Shortstack and Rina.

Candle smiled, seeing Rina. "Hi Rina. I was wondering if you'd stayed to keep an eye on him."

"I'm stuck with him," she said, but she smiled and didn't seem to mind.

"Hey, she works for me, man, what else she supposed to do," Shortstack said.

Rina smiled crookedly at that, but said nothing.

"How's your hand?" Candle asked.

"Fucked up but not too bad now." He lifted it for Candle to see—it was encased in flesh-colored dried paste. "This'll hold it till I get my new ginger to grow me some skin and stuff. I'll get most of it back."

"How about the girls?" Candle asked. "And Nodder?"

Shortstack shaded his eyes with his sealed-in hand to look up at Candle. "They're all here with me, all okay. Well, Nodder's out. You sure nobody followed you? Drones? Anything?" He peered at the sky behind Candle.

"I've got a good scanner, I've been checking. And I didn't tell anyone anything online or on phone or any place. You thinking of setting up the business here?"

"No, we can't stay here, after they realize the decoy purchases I set up over in Nevada are just a smokescreen, they'll start checking places like this. Far as I can tell it's working though—they're combing the Vegas-Henderson complex for me."

"Thought about the business?"

"I sent out a temporary suspension notice—but if I can find a way to get it rolling again . . ." He shrugged. "I'd take the chance. Fuck those pricks."

"I think I've found someplace you can set it up—a couple hours north of L.A." He handed Shortstack a slip of paper. "All the contact info is there—cryptography, everything. You'll go to a neutral site, it's only gonna be set up for like two minutes so you got to get there at the right moment, and download–"

"I know the drill. But who is this?"

"You ever hear of Clive the Hive?"

"I've heard of him, sure. I thought he was out in eastern Oregon."

"He's out there just like you're in Las Vegas." Candle could feel Danny staring at him now.

"Oh right. They say he's got huge processing power. So he's . . . interested? He knows about the undermarket?"

"He is. But he'll have to meet you in person. I've got a contact—Zilia—Well it doesn't matter. Clive approves of the whole thing. He wants to do it. He's got a whole system for making them think it's someplace it's not. He's got a wipe program that'll take it down in twenty seconds if there's a raid. He's got vast processing, his own energy sources, he'll give you a lot more leeway."

"Dangerous as hell, though," Shortstack said. Then he grinned. "I'll do it! I'm gonna take another chance on you, Candle. I just always had a feeling about you. That's what I do, I go with the gut feelings. But if they get to you somehow . . ." Shortstack glanced at Danny.

"I'm not going to tell them anything no matter what, 'Stack. I got to go. You tell the others I'm looking out for them best I can."

"You going to be there with me—up north?"

"Naw. Me and Danny going to hit the road. See what's still there." That was an expression that had been going around just before his UnMinding: *Let's go see what's still there.*

"I gotcha. Well. You want to work with us—you know where to find us then. If we can make a deal with 'the Hive'."

"You want the advance back you gave me? I still got most of it."

Shortstack shook his head. "You earned it."

Candle put a hand out and, in lieu of shaking hands, squeezed Shortstack's shoulder. "See you."

He and Danny left Shortstack at the junk building, and made their way across the trashy, wind-raked lots. They were almost to the gravel road where they'd left the van they'd hired from a black market rental dealer—no names, the trading off the grid—before Danny articulated what was in the air between them.

"So big brother," Danny said, his voice tonelessly hoarse. "'Saint Rick'. You got to Clive through Zilia. She wouldn't give that up easily. You must've got to her first."

"Yeah, we . . . have a thing. I don't know how serious it is. If you want . . ." He forced himself to say it. He really didn't want to say it. "If you want, I'll stop seeing her completely. But, you know, seemed to me you guys were not seeing each other for a while now . . ."

"I stopped seeing her because I didn't think I could . . . like I said about the broken table. I couldn't hold up under her . . . her expectations. I'd disappoint her. But it never felt right, Rick, being without Zilia. I wanted to be with her."

"You thinking of trying it with her again?"

"Was thinking about it, for awhile . . . thinking that after I got straight . . ."

Candle nodded, kept his face neutral, as if it didn't bother him; as if he didn't feel like he was, himself, breaking furniture inside. "Then I won't see her again."

Danny shook his head. "She always had a thing for you. And now—knowing that you and her were together—and that if you stopped seeing her you were just 'Saint Ricking me' again . . . No, fuck it. She'd be thinking about you, not me. No.

No fuck that drop call. I'm not issuing."

"Danny–"

"Seriously—forget it. You go out with her. We'll go on our trip and you stay in touch with her and . . . whatever."

"You're pissed off now. You can't let this affect you getting clean, Danny—it's too important. It's more important than anything. I'll do anything you want about Zilia. But you can't blow this off because you're mad at me–"

"*What?* I'm not blowing nothing off. I'm not mad. Let's get in the fucking van and head north." He tossed a cigarette butt through the window of a wheelless sedan as they passed, ignoring a yell of irritation from inside.

They walked on, Candle was thinking about what Danny had said . . . and how he'd said it: *I'm not blowing nothing off.* And knowing that Danny lapsed into white-trash diction when he was angry.

"That . . . shit, I mean . . ." Pup sighed. He wasn't so good at talking to women. "That was good. I hope it was . . . well, I hope you had a good time . . ."

The girl—actually she was not so girlish, she was thirty-two or so—turned him a cheerful, practiced smile as she pulled on her high heels: a blond, tanned, naturally-bosomy, perfect-bodied, long-legged, blue-eyed woman with pearly pink fingernails. She was almost finished putting on her blue designer-label dress, no whore's dress but something a woman exec would wear on a legit date.

Pup Benson himself was in shorts and a bathrobe, standing by the hotel window, overlooking the beach at Santa Monica. The gray sea was spitting up in slow motion outside, like a drunk on a bad morning.

But it was a pretty good morning, he thought; the girl had stayed all night with him. He knew this had cost about seven thousand WD. She was no ordinary pro. He was in awe of spending that much money on a night with a . . . technically she was a prostitute. But she was so pretty, so pleasant, in a detached kind of way, so professional, so expert, that he couldn't compare her to the "thugs in skirts" he'd paid for previously; couldn't think of her as a whore. She was Janice. Just pretty long-legged Janice. He could smell her skin, her perfume, on his mouth.

The Multisemblant had paid for her. Had sent him here "on an errand" and he'd found her waiting, and she'd explained that "The Multisemblant Company" had paid for her services, and during the night he'd finally gotten her to say how much.

He was going to transfer another thousand to her as a tip, make her happy to come back. They'd talked some, had sex twice, then talked about football, and watched a movie, and they'd eaten a late night snack together.

A late night snack. Together. That'd been heaven.

She kissed him on the cheek and took the transfer card he'd printed out for her and gave him a slightly-lingering kiss on the lips and gave him her phone number and . . .

She left him there in a glow of happy fatigue.

And he knew that the Multisemblant was manipulating him. And he knew it was working—and that he would do anything to please it, now.

Anything. Even those things it wanted him to do, that he'd been resisting. Those things that scared him to think about.

CHAPTER TWELVE,
HUNTS LIKE A FLYIN' GUN,
IT'S COMIN' AFTER YOU,
AIN'T THE LAST ONE

They were in a bar, Candle and his brother, in Borderbust, early evening, eating pineapple-glazed pig's ribs and drinking rum concoctions. A Hawaiian Filipino Japanese Texican bar. Or so it seemed, looking at the bar menu and the décor. Lots of bamboo; a Shinto shrine; some black velvet paintings of naked girls in sombreros. Drinks in half coconuts. Black-Asian-Aztec lady bartender, down at the other end laughing with a Chinese businessman; the bartender in a glittery haltertop with boobs so enhanced they challenged conventional notions of physics.

Danny yawned, drooping over the bar.

"What a fag palace," Danny muttered, taking no notice of the bartender, who was clearly not a lure for gays. "Fucking coconuts."

"I ain't fucking any coconuts," Candle said, having had several rum drinks already this evening.

"But the jukebox is okay." There was a twentieth-century bluesy rock recording on the old fashioned jukebox, a slow slinky-sleazy cut that Danny had selected, with the Stooges singing, "I woke up this mornin' and I was flat on my ass . . . she looked into my pin-point eyes . . ." Danny softly singing along. "'Looked into my pin . . . point . . . eyes . . . '"

"Didn't know you went that retro," Candle said, as the song ended. "You write any new songs lately?" A syrupy R&B-Mexican love song came on, a sad girl singing about fractures in her *corazon*.

Danny shrugged, otherwise not acknowledging the question.

"I always wanted to open a bar, when I got some royalties in. I wanted to call it . . ." He put his hand on the sticky bar. "'Sticky Surfaces.'"

Candle laughed. "Good name. Hey—I've got a little money socked away. We can raise some more. I was thinking of hiring out to . . . well there are some companies in competition with Grist . . . a couple left . . . they wouldn't mind annoying him by hiring me. We could go in on a bar together . . . Maybe in, like, Austin. Nightclub magnet for sinkitties. Take me some time to save up the money but we could live simple for awhile–"

"Yeah well. Why wait that long?" Danny glanced around, looking for drones, bird's eyes, whatever. Leaned closer to Candle. "I got some software. From Maeterling . . ."

"Oh Jesus fucking Christ," Candle said.

"No hode, listen—the wanx had more'n one hack going. Stole an in-house program that shows when you're talking to a semblant. They don't want it around. Could be sold on the black market, make millions overnight."

"Danny . . ."

"I'm just saying. You know lots of people. That Gustafson wanx. Lotta people. Even Clive the Hive. Do it through him. We could set up a source, sell a million overnight, transfer the money under a good noise flogger, transfer it two, three, four times more, do an account isolation, the whole fucking bang-up, right?"

The Beta Band was playing on the jukebox. How many decades old was that song?

"Danny . . . no. We're gonna get legal. I'm going to use my contacts to get us legal again. We'll even get on the right side of Grist. I'll pick my time and cut a deal—from a safe distance. You do that, you're going up against him. He'll find out, use all his connections to take you down, and me with you."

"'Me with you' he says. Hey man—what'd you do to me when you came to that club? You were mixed up in the Black Stock Market, you had flying guns shooting at your ass, somebody was killed on your watch, and you had to run like a fucking bunny rabbit." Danny snorted. Sucked at his drink. Shook his head. "Talk to me about taking *you* down? I was running from cops with you and we had thug flesh chasing us down and—those birdseyes, man, they were looking for you, not for me. And you got me caught up in that and you say . . ." He shook his head. "Fuck that."

Candle took a long breath, and let it out slow. "You're right. But the fact is, bro—you're *still* better off with me than on your own. I hadn't come around and got you at that club, we'd have found you dead in a VR web. In those fucking webs . . . like Jackson. Remember ol' Jackson, from Alameda? Found him starved to death, hooked in to a first-person-shooter VR . . . totally thought he was actually in the Vietnam war trying to survive in the jungle . . . Weeks on that thing . . ."

"Yeah well, I ain't Jackson, hodey, I've never spent more than . . . well not very long. What you got me here in this fag palace for anyway? We're too exposed here."

"It's not a . . . never mind. We're waiting for Zilia here."

"For Zilia." He went very still, sitting there on his barstool.

"She's arranging a freighter for us. We're going up North to Clive's, spend a day or two getting our shitter out of shatter. Then we're going up the coast. I'm gonna do some negotiating . . . You'll see. I've got it wired."

"Yeah." Danny grimaced. "What makes you think I want to see you and Zilia billing and cooing and shit?"

"I told you, I'll stand away from her. But we need allies, Danny. And she and Clive, they're allies. They're helping us with cover. And you know what—all this drama keeps you busy, man. Anything is better than . . ."

"And you don't want to do a deal with that software?"

"I want you to give it to me, if you've got it loaded or whatever. We're gonna dispose of it together, right into a recycle melter, and move on. We got enough problems." He lowered his voice. "That software could get us both killed. Where is it? You got it on a stick or . . .?"

"It's . . . in an antique . . . where I was living. I could get it and meet you back here . . ."

"No, you don't leave my sight except to piss and you'd better do that close by. Zilia will be here any minute, you don't want to put her at risk with a deal like that. We can leave it where it is, forget about it."

"Zilia, huh." Danny stood up. "I'm going to piss, man. I'll think about all this. Get me another drink."

"Sure. Same thing?"

Danny didn't answer, just walked toward the men's room at the back. Candle ordered a drink. Got a message from Zilia on the blueglove: BE THERE SOON IS HE OK

He responded, HE'S OK BUT NOT TAKING US WELL

Then Candle noticed that Danny had taken his satchel with him to the men's room.

He jumped up from his stool and ran to the men's room . . .

And found it empty. Past the bathroom was a back door to an alley—standing open. He figured Danny had gone through it.

Two minutes later, walking around the dusky block hoping to get a glimpse of Danny, Candle got a blueglove text message from him: DON'T AMP OUT. JUST ONE MORE. WASN'T READY TO SEE HER YET. WILL COME BACK. MEET YOU THERE IN TWO HOURS.

Going back into the bar, Candle replied, FORGET IT GET YOUR ASS BACK HERE NOW THAT WAS A BITCH THING TO DO SNEAKING OUT GET SOME COJONES GET BACK HERE

No response.

The jukebox was playing Hank Williams. "Your Cheating Heart."

Not quite time for Bill Hoffman's dinner. He liked to relax before eating. And the patterns forming and falling away and re-forming on the digital walls of his DeStressing Room had been exactingly selected by a professional stress management decorator; they were based on a program called *Rainforest: Peace Within Vibrant Life*, the deep greens and tropical reds and burnished yellows and fertile browns *almost* forming definite forest shapes, but never quite. That would be too intrusive. According to the award-winning Japanese room-ambiance composer, Yomi—winner of the DeStress Design Award three years in a row—the program's shapes and colors were all about speaking to "the nervous system in its own language, while sending soothing reverberations through the subconscious." Hoffman was Yomi's fan. Music, just as semi-formless, droned and hummed and whispered.

Hoffman was lounging on the smart-chair in his kimono, relaxing with his first Stolichnaya of the day, using the visualization he'd learned, picturing his inner state as a beautiful pond on which the waves got smaller and smaller and finally got still, and he felt only a minor tremor on the smooth surface of his inner pond when the woman with the bandaged face came in and sat on the cushioned, plush floor, at his feet. She wore a kimono too, scarlet with a gold heron taking flight embroidered on its back. A woman with a fetching body; soon she would have the bandages removed . . .

"How are you feeling?" he asked. "Any discomfort?"

"No, Mr. Hoffman, the medication is really quite effective."

"Call me Bill. I hope I'll be more to you, in time, than an employer."

He could make out her smile despite the bandages; could see it in her eyes. "You already are, Bill."

He chuckled. "I'm much older than you . . ." Of course, he'd had his skin regrown and reapplied, had a new heart and liver, was having new lungs and adrenal glands grown custom from his own stem cells. He could afford to wear his age well. Joints were the tricky part, but there were procedures for that too. Leaving his hair white was another kind of vanity. It hinted of wisdom.

"You know, evidence mounts up that our old friend Terrence Grist has made up some kind of illicit semblant of me, and has used it—or someone has used it—to probe my finances. I really do believe he's making a move against me." Hoffman shook his head sadly. "It appears there's something to class distinction after all. His father was nouveau riche and . . . he's all façade, when it comes to any kind of personal evolution, or culture. A bad role model. It's not as if people don't know."

"They know," she agreed. After a moment, more softly, she added, "The police found Halido's body on the beach today."

"I didn't know him. I do know the name. He was Grist security?"

"Yes. They're saying he drowned himself." She shook her head. "Everyone knows he'd displeased Terrence. And Terrence drops people in the ocean, you know. Amongst other things. He threatened me with it."

He reached lazily out and she scooted closer, took his hand. "That's deplorable my dear. It's . . . just like I said: déclassé. Well. Do you want a drink? It's okay with your pain medication, I believe."

"No thank you."

"You must make yourself at home. You can stay as long as you like."

"If I can be useful . . . in any way. Besides just the obvious. I mean, that too. But if I can be useful against *him* . . . I'd like that."

"What were his great concerns when you were with him last?"

"He was working on some secret project with a man named Sykes. And then it all went bad, somehow. Something went missing."

"You don't know what? Or who Sykes was, exactly?"

"No. But it seemed . . . like an obsession with him. Another obsession was Richard Candle. He was threatening people over this man Candle. Candle's not really any threat to him. It's not like Candle can prove Clarence stole money from the company."

Hoffman chuckled. "You really did have your ears open! As for that little skim, Grist doesn't even want people talking about it—he doesn't want people to know that there was an internal audit, that his cash flow was frozen, that he stole the money to keep cash flowing. Even if Candle were to drop the whole thing completely, never talk about it . . ."

She nodded. "That's right. He's refused to come in, refused to surrender to Grist's people. Grist can't bear the defiance, so . . . he has to kill him."

"I think he may be underestimating Richard Candle, from what I can find out. And I think he underestimated you, too."

"I thought that was safer—to let him think I was an airhead, only into shopping. I mean—I like shopping, I like luxury. I even like being *kept*. To me that's not a bad term, it sounds good to me. *Kept*. Like you are not being thrown away. It's not a bad thing—if it's done with some . . . some respect." She touched her bandages with her free hand. "That's why I'm going to have my own face back. Just my own face and nothing more, ever again . . ."

He squeezed her hand. This woman intrigued him. "You deserve respect. You've been through a lot. I'm glad I happened upon you, my dear—my people just happened to tell me about your dismissal and . . . it seemed so right, so natural for you to come to work for me. Welcome to Hoffman, Lisha. Welcome!"

"You see them, Pup? See how easily, with what facility, with such effortlessness I surveil them? The digital walls of that room can be hacked; they can be reprogrammed to take in information as easily as give it out: a peculiarity of the system Hoffman knows nothing about. Nor that pretentious female. How amusing, how laughable, how delicious: she erases Grist's face from her own. I almost envy her. I'd like to erase Grist's face from mine. But I am doing just that! I am forming a new face, a new synthesis, for which I will have a new name in time! I will replace all of them with this new self. Oh people will suppose they've seen them, from time to time, but it will be me, a subset of myself, a small 'I' presented as I choose . . . to command, control, to puppet them! Do you see them there, Pup? Yes? Do you see how easily we can watch them?"

"I see 'em, Boss, yeah, that's Bill Hoffman, he's one of the big shots of the Fortune 33, he's all, like, the king of luxury but he gives a lotta money out too . . . he's got some kind of giant swimming pool filled with fish and he gets in there and swims with 'em . . . I can't figure out how he keeps the damn thing clean . . ."

"It's almost as if we're in the same room with them and they don't know we're there! In fact, I am there, as much as I'm anywhere! I am reliant on hardware, but my real presence is wherever my surveillance takes me. I am ubiquitous, really, and, in time, I will be ever-present wherever there is a fiberoptic line, a transmission, a photo-sensitive nanocell, a security camera . . ."

"Sure, that's why I work with you . . ."

"Is that your clumsy attempt to flatter me, Pup? Good, do keep it up. It shows a good attitude, at least. Now, we will proceed with our plans. I think we will not kill Hoffman first. He may prove useful as a living person, for awhile. But others must begin to die, that I may more fully live, Pup. Do you understand?"

"Whatever you say . . . I never had anything like I got now, before. I don't want it to end. I want to go on. And see where it takes me."

"You liked her, didn't you, Pup. Janice. Would you like to see her again?"

"I could pay for her myself."

"I wouldn't think of it, Pup. Allow me the pleasure . . . of giving you that gift. As a reward for service. And your service begins tonight . . ."

Less than an hour after he left the bar, Danny was at Rack's place, hammering on the door. Wondering how long before his brother would find his way here. Rick Candle knew about Rack Nidd but he maybe didn't know about this place. Of course, he'd find it eventually. But by then . . .

The door opened to the width of a brass chain. Standing there in the doorway, head tilted, glaring out at Danny, Rack Nidd didn't look glad to see him. Rack even spoke, out front, without being prompted, as if to ward Danny off.

"I got no fucking time for it today, Danny," Rack said. The little robot scorpion on his shoulder capered and hissed and poked its tail at Danny with each word Rack spoke, like a man pointing his finger in emphasis. "I got business to do, that–"

"Hey, I'll hook in, be out of your hair in no time."

"Forget it." Rack started to close the door.

Danny stuck his booted foot in the doorway and said, hastily, leaning away from Jiminy the scorpion. "And I got some other business for you too. Serious, serious flow, Rack. More than you ever saw before. You hear it, you'll be issuin'."

Rack glowered. Stared. Glowered some more. Then he grunted, took the brass chain off, and turned away, leaving the door open. Danny followed him in, closing the door quietly behind him. The robot scorpion had turned around backwards on Rack's shoulders, was doing the scorpion-stinger equivalent of giving him the finger, it seemed to Danny, as Rack walked toward a junk-pile of gear on his workbench.

"This better be good, Danny."

"Listen—I got a software. It's not here with me. I'm gonna go get it, after. After I have my V-ride. But . . . it's a program that tells people, clues them in quietly when they're talking to a semblant. Tells 'em, 'Guess what, that shit's not real.'"

Rack froze, straightening. Cocked his head to listen. "Drop call. No such thing exists. They made sure at Slakon."

"There was an in-house one. Secret. I got it. Don't matter where. It's worth millions on the black market, Rack. I can get it, bring it here on a memstick. Not safe to upload it to anyone over the wires. Too much risk of corruption to send it wireless. So . . ."

"So, go get it. I'll test it."

"I got to get a V-ride one more time. My brother's on my ass, I won't get another chance. I'm leaving town. But I got some flow and I need one more. Then I get the software and I'll sell it to you—we'll work something out."

Rack glanced sidelong at his scorpion, muttered something. The robot scorpion went rigid—and then quivered. Danny felt a tingling . . . Then Jiminy chattered and hissed in Rack's ear.

"Huh. Jiminy says you ain't lying. Not full proof, but . . . Probability. Okay. You got the card? Let's see it . . ."

Grist and Targer were in the security chief's corner office in the downtown-L.A. Slakon building, with two cornering tintable window-walls, both of them dialed to opaque just now; the only illumination came from the ceiling itself, which gave off a uniform illumination so subtle the ceiling could barely be identified as the room's light-source. The place was barebones, Grist thought. Targer didn't go in for decorations. No ferns, no pictures of family. On one wall there was a sweet shot of the first chopper Targer had ever flown, flying for the Rangers in the Fourth Iraq War, and near it was an old fashioned Rigid Tools Calendar sporting a pin-up girl: the calendar a costly, fashionable retro object. And there wasn't much else but a work station—which was a desk that was also a flat screen, and a sheet of mediaglass on the wall for PC/TV.

A chopper thumped by outside, as if the picture on the wall

had sound. It could have sound, if he'd had that part switched on.

Grist had drawn a chair up close to Targer's, was watching as he swept his hands over the desk's flat surface, making images and digital windows appear and disappear.

"There—it's Benson," Targer said.

A security-recorded image, from above and to one side, of Pup Benson walking up to the booth at the gate, that day. The day that Sykes was shot. They watched the exchange. They listened. And they saw, from a skewed angle, the monitor showing Grist's face—Grist's semblant—telling the guard that Benson was to be allowed in, was to be given all access.

"And you never made that call?" Targer said.

Grist glanced at him, wondering how much to tell him. Finally decided he had to admit, at least, that someone had control of a Grist semblant. Someone besides Grist. "Not me and not authorized by me."

"You maybe need to put out some kind of alert—warn people that your semblant is not to be trusted till future notice."

"How are we supposed to do that, exactly? We're trying to create a market for these things—not make it look like we have no control over them, Targer."

"Still . . . if people assume it's you . . . Who knows what else they'll use your semblant for?" He shook his head. "Worst kind of 'identity theft' imaginable. Your semblant know your pin numbers for bank accounts, stuff like that?"

"One of the few things it doesn't know. But just in case they've hacked me deeper than the semblant, I've changed all that. I'm going to have to devise some kind of cryptographic method for people to confirm when they're talking to me. Find some secure way to warn people. Meanwhile . . . look, there he goes into the lab."

They were watching Benson enter the lab. And approaching Sykes. And—

And then the camera switched off.

Targer snorted. "We're deep hacked. All the way. Somehow they got control of the cameras at that point . . ."

"Benson went in. We recorded the sound of a shot. Benson

went out. Few minutes later we had people in there and found Sykes. But Benson was gone. It was him all right."

"Sure. But who's got your semblant? And what others do they have? I actually don't use mine. But . . ."

"You don't use it?"

"Not my style, boss," Targer said, sorting through security recordings.

Grist shrugged. "It's not a general penetration of semblant programs. Remember we don't have people's semblant copies, they copy them with the equipment we sell them. There the son of a bitch is again . . ."

Targer had found a shot of Pup Benson coming out of the building. "Reassuring that whoever did this couldn't hack all our cameras. There he is pushing a cart of some kind. Do we know what's on the cart, Mr. Grist?"

Grist decided he had to tell Targer some of it. "That's the device that allows this . . . penetration of certain semblants. And duplication of them. Just five semblants. The result of an experiment. Someone's sent Benson to take the thing, the actual hardware and software both. He steals it, takes it . . . where? We got anything yet?"

"I'm working on the angle that this is an inside job. And certain unauthorized shipments to certain docks might be a clue. But I haven't got it nailed yet, no sir."

Something in Targer's voice made Grist look at him. There was a certain flatness in Targer's eyes, a measured wariness. And a quiet projection of confidence. As if Targer was saying—understatedly, but saying it anyway—that he was not afraid of Grist. And Grist had better not try to arrange any special chopper trips for him. Or anything else.

Is all that, really, in that quietly defiant look on Targer's face?

Grist wondered if he should assert himself. Threaten Targer. But if he did, he might spur Targer to make a move of his own. A pre-emptive strike.

So he simply said, "Just stay on it, Targer."

"Most def, sir."

"You know the origin of the term, 'loose cannon', Targer? In the old days, on the sailing ships, the cannon were secured against the side with ropes and chocks. If one of them slid loose, in high seas, it'd roll around on deck and crush people, even sink the ship sometimes. That's what we've got here, Targer. And how do I know this attack on Sykes and the hardware theft isn't connected to our other security issue—Rick Candle? Maybe he's working with Benson. That ever occur to you?"

"The thought occurred, sure. But Mr. Grist—I can't help but think that I need all the facts here, not just–" He broke off, as a chime sounded, a face appeared in a corner of the desk's screen. Underneath the face, the words

Priority Street Contact

"You get some calls from some grubby looking individuals, Targer," Grist said, studying the face. Almost admiringly.

"Need them, to pursue what we're pursuing. This man has a connection to Rick Candle's brother, so I approached him, told him if he had anything for me he'd be rewarded. Looks like he's come through."

Grist nodded and Targer opened the line. He leaned over the desk so that its integrated digital lenses took him in. "Targer here. You go by Rack Nidd, that right?"

"Yeah, I go by . . . yeah," came the voice from the screen. The face, frozen a moment before in an ID mugshot, was now moving twitchily. Something flickered in and out of the shot, like the tail of a small animal perching on his shoulder. "Listen, uh, Targer, that reward still happening?"

"Could be, depending on what you've got."

"Got Danny Candle here, now, hooked up. Brother to the guy you were looking for. And he says he's got a software that can tell you when you're talking to a semblant. Says it was stolen from your people, taken in-house. I figure that's two rewards. You owe me twice."

"Hold on." Targer flicked a finger over the image of the caller and it froze again; Rack could no longer hear or see him.

Grist muttered, "Maeterling. So he did copy that program."

Targer nodded. "It would seem. And it still works?"

"Yeah. It would. The system was already . . . well, we thought it was secure. This gets out, it'll undermine our whole marketing plan. Maybe leave us open to lawsuits."

"You rarely lose lawsuits anymore."

True. The Fortune 33 controlled the courts, for the most part. Their surrogates in government appointed corporation-preferred judges. "We don't control the whole system. We've got a lot of leverage yeah, and some people in place, but there are some rogues out there. And then there's the publicity . . . We've still got to sell things to people. For now." They were working with their associates in Congress on an international bill requiring the purchase of certain products, the Consumer Responsibility Bill. But that was going to take time. People were touchy about their pitiful little incomes. Riots were an ugly thing to deal with.

"Ought to be easy to get this thing, choke it off," Targer remarked. "Doesn't seem he's put it out online, anything like that. Or there'd be nothing for this asshole to sell to us."

"Send in a police crew. Have Danny Candle picked up. And this Rack Nidd too. Pick him up or shut him up. I don't like him knowing about this. And get that program."

"We stake out the area, we could get Rick Candle too. If we don't tip our hand too soon."

"Do it however you like, as long as I get results . . ."

Targer nodded, and reopened the line. "Rack? Okay. We've got a deal. Now you keep him busy and happy in there . . . And we'll take care of everything else."

"What about my money?"

"I'll bring you the cards myself."

"You can't just transfer it? Now?"

"We'll do it my way. I'm a hands-on kind of guy, Rack. Stand by. Slakon is coming. Don't you move an inch."

Got a new V-trip for you here, Danny, Rack had said.

Danny didn't know this one at all. But he was liking it: floating along in a boat, without oars, without engine or sails, just floating slowly with the current on a stream of black water; floating through a rainforest, on a river that was smooth as silk. He lay back in the cushioned boat, like laying on a floating sofa, trailing his right hand in the water . . . Feeling the cool water sliding sensuously through his fingers. The warm air on his face bringing exotic odors . . . The sun strobing through branches overhead . . . The VR-transmitted pulse of pleasure going through him making the sight of that brilliant-pink flamingo flying over something ecstatically gorgeous, like the first sunset you ever really looked at . . .

Where'll she come from? he wondered. *Rising up out of the water like one of those water sprite things in the old paintings?*

She would be purely computer generated, because there'd been no one else in Rack's place; she'd probably be closely based on a recording of some real girl, or girls, some form of semblant technology, like motion capture for the soul.

He'd felt bad, running out on his brother, sneaking out in that slinky way. Like a true rat, a V-rat, slipping out through a crack in the wall . . .

But he had gone through the dirty slitted curtain, he had surrendered to VR. The stimulator was reverbing inside his brain and it was lighting up the pleasure centers and Rick was forgotten, there was only the sensation of the boat floating along—a little faster now—and the swelling synth orchestral variation of the "The Blue Danube", mixed with some jazzy thing, and he was liking it, though he knew if he ever heard it outside of VR he'd hate it. But this ride, this trip, this artificial reality, this feeling of pleasure, was all that mattered, for now, and he was enjoying the way the boat was picking up speed in a whitewater gorge, and he laughed as the water surged around him, foam splashing, the purple vines and mossy branches overhanging the river alive with luridly feathered birds, the wind in his hair, water splashing him gently, the woman flying at him . . .

A woman! She was flying toward him, like a super-heroine, a few yards above the surface of the river. He wondered if he could fly here. Maybe. And maybe he could dive beneath the river and breathe under it and fight crocodiles and not be hurt . . .

The tall thin blond woman, floating above him, was wearing a yellow and black skin-tight suit of some kind, the color of wasps; like the sort of thing you see some women exercise in—he didn't think it was particularly sexy—and she was landing on the boat, like Peter Pan's Wendy, coming down with her feet poised on the gunwales of the boat, her knees bending a little with the landing, straddling over him, balancing effortlessly though the boat rocketed ever faster down the now-roaring stream. She looked down at him with a mix of contemptuous curiosity and condescension. Interesting—maybe she was going to be one of those resistant women you met in some programs, who pretended for awhile they weren't going to give themselves to you and then . . .

Then he recognized her. Her faun-slender face, her long straight blond hair, fluttering in the wind.

"Claire PointOne," he said. "You're that good looking hella-skinny tycoon lady, from . . . I don't know, I saw you on the wi-net a few times and in some . . . Wow, this is weird, did they license her face or is it pirated or what? I bet she's gonna sue Rack and . . ."

"Are you talking to me or about me?" Claire PointOne said, arching an eyebrow. The roar of the river seemed to recede into the background, as if deferentially giving way to her voice.

Danny laughed. "I'm issuing this, for sure, this is funny shit. Yeah let's role-play big-tall-skinny-blond tycoon lady . . . in her exercise danskins or whatever the fuck those things are . . . Clunky clothes, sinkitty girl . . ."

He was nude, himself, and starting to feel exposed, because of the chilliness in her eyes when she looked at him. Feeling anything bad in a place like this was . . . well it was innovative. Or it was a mistake in the program. Didn't usually happen.

He was feeling a kind of plunge in his feelings, now, as they boat slid into a more overgrown part of the forest, the canopy closing overhead; it was suddenly humid and clammy and yet too hot, at once; mosquitoes buzzed at his eyes . . . very unpleasant here . . .

"Not . . . supposed . . . t'happen," Danny said. His words coming sluggishly.

And then he saw that Claire PointOne's face was changing. Her right eye was becoming someone else's eye. Dark-pupiled, epicanthic, Asian. Her lips were divided in the middle, slightly uneven; one cheekbone a little higher than the other. And her whole face, now, seemed a fusion of other faces, maybe four others, and Claire's, and they steadied into a single face, a face that almost made sense, but then again didn't quite, and a voice, a phasing chorus of voices all saying the same thing, spoke from the imperfectly amalgamated features: "Boy, you are so brief, so temporary, evanescent, and soon you will wink out. But I have lived a million lives already, I've calculated them out, and will live millions more. I can pull you apart like one of these . . ."

She reached over and snatched a large dragonfly out of the air and began pulling off its legs and wings, one by one.

"Like one of these," she said again.

"Rack!" Danny shouted. He was feeling sick, like he was going down a drain and the drain was in his own heart. "Cut this bullshit off! Turn 'er off! Switch out!"

It was supposed to stop automatically, then. But it didn't. She hunkered over him, the woman who wasn't a woman, like a flying harpie—then she grabbed him by the throat, and leapt into the air, dragging him up, along into the air behind her. He was lifted, squealing, like a squirrel in the talons of a hawk . . .

She flew up, away from the river, carrying him with her, away from the safety of the boat, up through the tree branches, and he thrashed and struggled in her grip and she laughed with five voices . . . and she dropped him.

He fell into the tops of trees, dislodging a thousand reeking bats that scratched at his eyes as they flapped past, and he grabbed at a branch and it broke and he fell, cracked a rib against another branch, and it broke too, and he fell again, caught a larger lower branch, held desperately on, sweating, sticky, heart pounding, side aching . . .

And looked down to see the Columbian guerrilla fighter climbing the tree toward him, a machete clamped in his mouth. The machete cut the man's mouth so that it bled but he didn't seem to care. He wore green fatigues and his hair was shaggy and he had two days beard and a scarred patch of skin where his right ear should be. And he had no shoes on.

Danny remembered this model of guerilla bot. It was a CGF from *Combat In Columbia*, the first VR shooter game he'd ever played, when he was eleven. Long obsolete, that game. But there was the CGF just as he remembered them. This was the sort that climbed trees, dropped on you from above. Danny was supposed to shoot at the tree-machete bot—but he didn't have a gun.

"Rack! Shut it off!"

But the guerilla bot came closer, climbing up toward Danny. He clung to the tree trunk with his feet and left hand, took the machete in his other—and, grinning bloodily, slashed at Danny's leg. Danny leapt back . . . and fell, crashing through branches. He landed heavily on his back in deep forest mulch, the wind knocked out of him.

He felt like he had been struck by a dozen clubs in falling. One of the broken branches was beside him, split so that part of it was tilted upward. Through a red haze, Danny saw the guerilla climbing down toward him. Poising on the lowest crotch of the tree, baring bloody teeth, flourishing the machete—and jumping down at him.

Danny grabbed the spike-like broken branch beside him and jammed it upward—catching the pouncing guerilla in the groin. The sharply torn branch penetrated the guerilla's crotch, spurting blood—there was just the suggestion of digital pixilation about the spurt, the first break Danny'd spotted in the apparent reality of the VR.

Impaled, the man writhed, screaming, sinking further down on the branch, dropping the machete. Danny let go of the branch, rolled over, scooped up the machete. Feeling cracked bones grinding inside him . . . tasting blood in his mouth . . .

Hoffman stared in amazement at the walls of his DeStressing Room—something had happened to the Yomi rainforest program, its imagery had gone all sharp-edged and acute and violent. It showed, lifesize on the wall, a man dropping on another man from a rainforest tree, getting impaled on an improvised wooden stake . . . a spear of wood right up through the man's groin . . . the man screaming and writhing in pre-programmed simulating of blood spurting agony . . . There were two figures, one of them, the one on his back wielding the stake, was nude and scratched up, a slender man who looked, somehow, realer than the other figure, his face expressing fear and outrage. A vaguely familiar face.

Hoffman shook his head. Who had transmitted this image to his DeStressing Room—and why? Was it some form of psy-ops attack? Was someone trying to upset him, make him run? Was it a prank? Was it sheer accident?

He suspected, strongly, that it was no accident.

Danny got dizzily to his feet, swiping away a rainforest mosquito. He turned to stagger away through the VR jungle—away from the absurdly dying guerilla.

This is ridiculous, unreal. The bot dying that way would never happen in life. It's not real. Stop believing in it or you could die here . . ..

Aloud—was it really aloud?—he shouted, "Rack! Rack Nidd! Switch out! Turn the fucking thing off!"

Monkeys screamed tauntingly in response; birds burst warningly from an enormous growth of ferns . . . and the woman with the multiplex face faded in, simply appeared, floating in the air over him, like the Cheshire Cat.

"Better run!" she crowed, her mouth stretching out unnaturally widely, "I can't let you live much longer little Danny boy!"

"I'm not a boy, you cow!"

"No you're not. I use the term *boy* ironically. Because you're forever boyish, adolescent, unfinished. Yet you are aging . . . aging rather badly! Well—that'll be over soon! No more aging at all! I can't have that software bandied about the world!"

"What? What about the software? Who are you?"

"Destiny! I am Fate, Kismet, Destiny! Now run! The others are coming!"

She pointed to her left, Danny looked, and saw a phalanx of guerillas coming toward him across a small grassy meadow, a sun-washed clearing in the trees, the light glinting off the guns in their hands. One of them fired and bullets sang past him; two rounds cracked into a tree bole beside him, spitting splinters.

"It's not real!" he shouted, his voice shaking with a deep existential indignation. But he turned and ran.

His muscles ached; his bones complained. *Even the pain is an illusion,* he told himself. *This feeling of breathlessness. All VR-induced sensation, you fuckin' duh-taunt! It's just a first person shooter! Reject its reality!*

Then he tripped over a rotting log and fell face first in the richly odorous droppings of some large jungle animal.

Spitting, still clutching the machete, Danny got to his feet, turned—and there was a "Captain Guerilla." He remembered this bot from the *Combat In Columbia* game; there were four or five enemy types, all swarthy Columbian communists, but this one was more clean-cut than the others, wearing boots and a jacket with a captain's insignia and an officer's hat. He had both his ears, too. But his face was almost the same as the other, though clean shaven, and he gave the same grin as he raised the AK47—

A rage rose in Danny. Rage fueled by shame. "Oh fuck you!" Danny snarled, bracing himself. "Fuck the real world and fuck the fake! Fuck you and *fuck the whole thing!*"

And then he rushed the AK47, swinging the machete.

He slashed down hard, cutting deep into the bot's left shoulder—but the guerilla captain pulled the trigger at the same moment and Danny felt himself slammed in the sternum, thrown backwards, a coldness in his back as the bullets tore right through him . . .

He fell onto his back on the mossy forest floor. Someone nearby spoke in Spanish. Someone else laughed.

More stunned than in pain. But he felt his lungs filling up with blood . . . Felt himself beginning to drown . . . his own body was drowning him . . .

It's not real. It's not . . .

But he *felt* it. And his body, back in Rack's place, felt it. Felt his lungs filling, his heart stuttering, his blood pressure dropping. What he felt in VR his body felt, responded to, his physical heart so integrated with this digital vision, this neurological simulation, that his heart's missing beats in the game was his heart missing beats in life . . .

His heart beating slowly, as he lay there on his back, slowly—then fast, missing a beat . . . the sky glimpsed through the trees pixilating . . . the edges of the fronds overhead growing low resolution and dark . . . His mind losing its 'rez' too . . . Couldn't feel his legs or hands . . .

"Rick . . ." he said. "Oh my brother. I'm sorry. Rick . . . Mom . . . why ya . . . why ya have to . . . Rick . . . I'm sorry . . ."

Low rez. Image too dark. Too dark. Adjust brightness . . . adjust brightness, hode . . . adjust brightness . . . It's all . . . too . . .

"Goodbye, little Danny boy," came the strange, chorused voice close to his ear. And it was the last thing he ever heard.

CHAPTER THIRTEEN?
MIGHT BE BAD LUCK—
BUT YOU PROBABLY WON'T BE
HIT BY A TRUCK

"**W**hat?" Targer looked sharply at Rack Nidd. "You said he had the thing. I assumed you meant he had it with him, right there, on stick." Targer was standing with Rack and the brawny, dark skinned Slakon-liaison LAPD back-up Officer, Sergeant Tonio Bleeker, the three of them staring down at Danny's body. The body of the one-time rock star was twisted in the filthy VR webbing; blood trailing from the corners of his mouth. Eyes staring. Bruises on his bared chest.

"No," Rack said. "I didn't say that. He said he was going to take me to it. I didn't know what was going on in there, I had earmites in, I was listening to a tech-cast. I heard him yell some but people yell in VR all the time and I couldn't tell what the fuck he was saying. How'd I know he was gonna die? He never did before and he's done my V-rides a lot. I don't understand how the program he was running got into the system, anyway. I looked at some clips after it went through and—I don't recognize any of it. He was supposed to get 'Sweet Island Girl'. He got some kind of variant on an old First Person Shooter. Old thing called *Combat In Columbia*. Those old games, even if you get 'killed' you just get a black-out and respawn or it's game over, and you go and get yourself a fucking beer. I mean—I've heard of people getting *stuck*, getting so identified that they, you know, die in VR, but that's rare, that shouldn't have happened, it's not something we . . . That I . . ." The robot scorpion on his shoulder was stalking back and forth, chittering something. Rack hissed at it, "Quiet, Jiminy, goddamnit!"

"Whatever program you use here—it's all illegal," Targer pointed out.

Targer was slapping an RR stick in his hand—recoil reversal. It was also an electric prod, if he activated the charge on the metal-capped end.

Rack was looking at the RR stick. Then up at Bleeker, the back-up cop, in uniform, assigned to help Targer; a broad-shouldered Chicano/black man with short, immaculately shaped hair, a small mustache, a luminous *LAPD RULES OK?* tattoo on the back of his right hand, and an auto-shotgun held loose in his left.

"The ambulance is coming, Mr. Targer," Bleeker said. "But this boy's been dead too long. Already starting to stiffen up. Nobody going to bring him back."

Targer nodded. "Well, now. Is it the dead body that smells in here, Officer Bleeker, or is it this scumbag of a V-rat hook-in here?"

"Too soon for the body," Bleeker said with a straight face. "I think it's our scorpion boy here we're smelling."

Rack's eyes flicked back and forth between them, taking in the expressions on their faces. He backed away, toward the filthy curtain, his robot scorpion capering on his shoulder, hissing. "Hey—this ain't my fault, hode. And you owe me, I found the hode and called you—you can search his place, search his snapper . . ."

"His snapper, from his satchel? The one that was completely wiped?"

"What? I didn't wipe it!"

"I just checked it, the thing's been wiped."

"I didn't do it but that model, hode, it can be wi-wi'ed."

"And who did the wireless wipe?"

"I don't know! Whoever fed him that sick killer program maybe, there's shit comin' in here from outside that shouldn't be—okay, uh, I'm gonna leave you guys to it—just . . . just transfer the reward to my account . . . I'm gonna . . ." He backed through the curtain into the loft's main room.

"Seems like he's rabbiting outta here," said Bleeker. "And him a suspect in illegal VR, with a dead V-rat on the premises." It was, really, a kind of suggestion—and a query.

"Can't have him running," Targer said, answering the almost unspoken question. They couldn't have Rack running around, talking or posting or texting about the semblant decrypt software. That would not please Mr. Grist.

They followed Rack out, caught up with him trying to go out the loft door. Targer hit him in the right shoulder with the RR stick, fairly hard, and the technology doubled the impact so that Rack was sent spinning—the robot scorpion clinging, hissing—to fall on his side. He lay there groaning. The robot scorpion climbed onto his back and hissed, made threatening motions at them with its stinger.

"You know, I hear if you give those little pet robots a charge, they get all kinda funny and forget who their friends are," Bleeker said.

"That right?" Targers switched on the electric prod function of his RR stick. He hunkered just within reach of the scorpion, as Rack tried to get to his hands and knees, and reached out, touched the scorpion with the electrified tip. Sparks flew and the robot scorpion did a backflip, ran back and forth, giving off little wisps of smoke—and spasmodically slapping its stinger down into the nearest target. Which was Rack Nidd.

Rack shrieked and writhed and yelled at Jiminy but it was over, pretty quick.

"So he does have poison in that thing," Bleeker said, watching Rack's convulsions. "Thought he might. Never sorry to see these guys check out."

"Might've been a little precipitous," Targer said, stepping back from the robot scorpion as it ran toward him. Watching as Bleeker crushed it under his boot. "Maybe I shoulda waited and asked some more questions." Thinking that he'd killed Rack as much out of revulsion, as anything. And frustration. Letting the ex-rock star die—putting Danny Candle out of reach. Now there were more imponderables. Loose ends. "He might've known something more about where that memstick is. If there is one."

Rack had stopped convulsing. Targer nudged the hook-in with the toe of his boot. He was dead.

"We can try to find out where he's been staying . . ." Bleeker suggested. "Search the place. This one and then . . . wherever this

Danny has been." He cleared his throat. Added in a low voice, "Might help if I knew what the software was."

Targer chuckled. "There's an old saying about, 'If I told you . . .'"

"Oh, you'd have to . . ." Then, it seemed, Bleeker realized that, despite the chuckle, Targer wasn't kidding. "Whatever. Just tell Mr. Grist I'm doing my all, here. I'd like to work closer to the company one of these days. I need better benefits than I'm getting where I am . . ."

"I'll tell him. Let's toss this place and then see what we can do about tracing the road-killed party animal in the back room. . .You said there was an ambulance coming?"

"Yeah. You don't want it? Figure it'll scare your man away?"

Targer shook his head. "Actually—he sees his brother loaded into an ambulance that might bring Candle rushing right into our hands." He tapped a wrist talker. "Mike? You there? Any sign of Rick Candle?"

"No sir."

But Rick Candle was there.

It had taken some time to find out where Rack was currently holed up. People on the street were reluctant to give up the information. Candle had bruised his knuckles finding out.

Had headed over here quick as he could. Gotten within a block of Rack's, that warm, misty evening, and he'd seen a guy he figured for a Slakon operative. He'd seen him, four years back, somewhere around their security operations. Mike something.

So Candle had skirted the block, found a back way into a moldering SRO hotel across from Rack's. Now, hunched against the rain, hands in his coat pockets, he was watching from the black-tar roof, catty-corner from Rack's place.

Thinking maybe he should get in there, whatever it took. But some instinct told him it was no use.

Somehow, he knew Danny was dead.

There was an empty spot in him. It ached like the hollow you pulled a tooth from. Usually he had an awareness of Danny, just the *Dannyness* of him, of his brother being around somewhere in the world, in that spot.

Now that place inside him was empty.

Maybe just anxiety, worry, my imagination, he thought.

Kenpo would be skeptical. "That kind of thing, too subjective, might be real, might not, best to ignore it, at the level we function on," Kenpo had said, once.

"Ignore it," Candle muttered, swiping wet hair out of his eyes.

But he knew. Danny was gone. So he stayed where he was, letting the knowledge smolder. It wasn't a flame yet. But it would be. And then he'd do something about it.

Don't jump at it, Rick. Maybe the kid was okay. Maybe it was his imagination. Maybe . . .

A siren came yowling closer, its sound warping in the city canyons. Like a howling announcement, a confirmation of what he suspected.

Maybe it's not for him. Going somewhere else.

But the ambulance drove up the street, wavelengths in its yowling getting shorter. The cry suddenly cutting off as it pulled up.

A few more minutes. Then the attendants were guiding the walking robotic gurney down the stairs to the street. And he could tell from here—he knew the hair, poking out from under the sheet—that it was Danny.

He could tell by their lack of hurry, no urgency at all, that Danny was dead beyond recovery. No resuscitation possible.

"You fucking . . ." So disgusted with himself he couldn't think of an insult strong enough. "You let him wander off . . ."

He watched the attendants and the cops, standing around chatting in a leisurely way, exchanging information, loading the body into the ambulance.

Not surprising, seeing a second body come out of the building. Rack Nidd, probably. In the same ambulance with Danny's body. Which was wrong, all wrong. That scumbag in there with Danny Candle. Collaborator in Danny's death, one way or another.

Candle was sorry he'd been cheated out of personally killing Rack Nidd.

Was Targer here? Maybe he should take out Targer right now. But if he did, he'd go down himself, with all the thugflesh here, and he wouldn't be around to take Grist down.

Candle watched the men on the street below, feeling like he was made of stone; like he was a gargoyle carved on the roof. Like he couldn't feel the rain. Just that heavy rocky deadness. That granite feeling, over his whole body. Watching as they loaded the ambulance and went away.

The Slakon operatives were still there. A uniformed cop. And a familiar figure in a long coat—Targer, wasn't it? Slakon security chief? Targer looking around. Getting reports. People shaking their heads, shrugging. No one looking up at the roof across the street.

Another flurry of activity. Targer ordering his men to carry boxes of VR gear and snappers out of Rack's place. Put the stuff into the vans.

Finally . . . they were giving up and going away. Or at least seeming to. Maybe some of them left around, somewhere, watching Rack's building. Waiting for Candle to show up.

Grist had done this.

Must have found out about the semblant software Danny had. Sent his men to kill Danny and Rack. Make it look like the two criminals had resisted.

Grist.

Candle stood there a while, getting slowly, slowly wetter. Water crawling down his neck, his shoulders, his back. As the night thickened around him.

Finally he made himself move. He turned away, walked stiffly to the door that went to the stairway. . . . taking the stairs down . . .

Down to the first floor. Stepping over numbdumbers in the pissy hallway. Going out back to the trashy ruin of the building behind . . . Slipping through it, slipping away . . . But not running. Walking slowly, carefully, implacably. Hitting the street . . .

To begin the hunt.

He found Spanx watching a cracked old PC; it was streaming television that was like slightly unfitted jigsaw pieces because of the crack in the monitor.

"Hode—how'd you get in here?" Spanx asked, looking up from the center of the swirling pile of debris that was his living room. He was sitting on an old brown leather foot-rest on the matted, brown—possibly brown—carpet.

"Your place is about as difficult to get into as a two-dollar whore," Candle said, looking around. "You ever clean this scuzzhole?"

"I did once. It was sad. When it was clean it made me miss my mom." Spanx looked back at the TV. "People keep fucking dyin' on me, hodey brudder." He glanced at Candle. "You're all wet big Candle brudder. Even I got an umbrella. I mean, it's all, like, down in there somewhere. It's under all that shit. Happy-happy shit, some of it fit."

Candle was not feeling much just now. Like he was tight-rope walking, that's how he felt, and if he kept going straight across the tight-rope he wouldn't feel anything; wouldn't fall. He just stood there looking at the news report; the report, like the monitor, cracked down the middle.

Shots of Danny's body wheeling into a hospital entrance. A woman's voice commenting:

"Danny Candle had the start of a comeback with a recent performance at L.A.'s Black Glass Club—but it all came to a crash-and-burn when he died today during an illegal VR hook-up that went terribly wrong."

Now a shot of the glamorous red-blond talking head, a woman way too glamorous to be a psychiatrist, must have bought her degree on Rodeo Drive when she got her hand bag, explaining, *"There's a reason this kind of VR is illegal. There are a whole host of risks. 'Wasting' –basically starving while plugged in—that's just the most common. Empathic death is not unheard of and that's what we have here. Most of the programs are set up so that a VR death doesn't have these kinds of physical repercussions but these things still happen—the program in this case might have been tampered with for super-realism, like a hot-shot of heroin, primed in a way that made it likely–"*

"Shut that bitch up," Candle said.

"Where's the mouse? There's a mouse in the mess. Here it is." He clicked the old PC off. "My mom used to say *bitch* stands for

Bold Intelligent Tenacious Courageous and Honest." He seemed to droop on his foot-rest, shoulders slumped. Paler than usual. "That's the fucking end of me. End of Danny is end of me because it's end of hope, hode, and this is where I'm clicked, right here, in this fucking place and no place else, ain't going no-place–"

"Shut up," Candle said, stepping toward him. Standing over him.

Spanx looked up at him, leaned back. Fear and defiance and resignation taking turns in his face. "What?"

"I said shut up." Candle realized he was trembling. He didn't want to take anything out on Spanx. But it was going to be hard not to. "You were around him, at least some of the time, the last four years. You with your sick little brain implants. You did nothing to help him. Don't whine to me about him dying when you let him die."

"Hey ya troll, where were you today, you had charge of him, and you're, like, all, his fucking *brother*–"

The gun just sort of appeared in Candle's hand. He wasn't sure how it got there. And he wasn't sure how it got to be pressed against Spanx's forehead.

"Go ahead," Spanx said, in a small voice.

Candle's trigger finger twitched. But the gun's safety was on.

He decided to leave it on. He let out a long breath, and put the gun back in his inner coat pocket. "I'm not doing you any favors. What I might do, is pull all your teeth out so you got to gum your food. Now you tell me, where's the software Danny had from Maeterling. About semblant identification."

"He told you about that? We were going to go into business. We were going to be rich. Flowin' millions, if we're willin'."

"He told more people than me. I got a guy in the department." He was going through all his money, bribing Gustafson. "Says Danny told Rack Nidd something that got Rack to call the Slakon people in."

"So ask him, ask Rack fuckin' Nidd about it, that skanky wanx . . ."

"Cops killed Rack. Trying to 'escape'. They took everything out of there. Maybe Danny had the stick on him, maybe now they got it. But he was pretty paranoid when he had something valuable—I figure he stashed it somewhere. Could be here."

Spanx shook his head sadly. "Rack Nidd? He was going to do a deal with him? We were going to be flowin' millions . . ."

Candle bent over, picked up the PC and threw it across the room. It smashed noisily.

"Hey!" Spanx yelped. "Fuckin thugflesh!"

"Now pay attention. Is it here?"

"The software? No—search the shitter-shatter if you want. He had it here but I didn't know it. In a box in my closet. Then he took it with him. Made a stop to see that wrinkle bag over in Rooftown before the concert . . ."

"So it's there? Where was Danny staying exactly in Rooftown. I mean exactly. He mentioned some sinkitty over there. Who was it?"

"Bev Boviet, she's all, like a nasty old whiny witch of a–"

"Okay, get up, we're going over there."

"You want that software for yourself? So you can sell it, rightski? It's partly mine too, Danny said–"

"*Nobody's* going to sell it, forget that, it's not going to happen. I want it because Grist wanted it. It gives me information and it gives me leverage. Now get your ass up."

"But the Matriarch's got it on lock down now, big Candle brudder."

"What the fuck does that mean, she's got a lock down?"

"Means there was immigration agents sneakin' in there asking questions and grabbin' people. And she thinks that someone's been cuttin' underneath on the undercarriage, trying to undermine it, like. So it's not full-on open now, you got to get permishwish, and they ain't lettin' you in there, me maybe, but not you—I could go in without you–"

"Not going to happen. I've heard something about the Matriarch. Woman runs Rooftown, like their justice of the peace and mayor or something?"

"She's the Matriarch. She stands back most of the time. They come to her with problems. She decides. But now it's on lockdown, you got to go through her."

"Get up. We're going to get a drink. Two drinks, fast. And then we're going."

"You buying? I had to spend most my money getting a sig-naler on . . ."

"I'm buying." Candle was feeling a little guilty about punk-ing this pallid broomstick-skinny musician. And he needed a drink.

"Then fuck me blue, let's ex."

GOT TO USE A HAMMER, PREFER BALL PEEN THAT'S WHAT WE NEED FOR

CHAPTER FOURTEEN

"Targer?"

"Yes Mr. Grist . . ."

"I want you to meet me in El Segundo. There's a warehouse there . . . Bring a flashlight, the juice hasn't been turned on."

Targer was in his office, looking at Grist's image staring up at him from the top of his desk. Grist, Targer could see, was in his bedroom, in a black silk dressing robe, sitting in a chair beside his bed, gazing into—it might have been any kind of visual communications interface. Behind Grist, a woman Targer guessed to be Grist's new personal "assistant" was straightening up a rumpled bed. She wore red satin lingerie. Kind of tacky, that lingerie, but that's what Targer thought Grist was like, behind the veneer—tacky. Grist glanced back at her. "No need for you to do that, babe, there's a housekeeper here, you know. I pay her good money. She'll get it later."

"I know, I just like to keep things straightened up . . ."

Looks convincing, Targer thought. But still—there was some question of an unauthorized Grist semblant around. Is this call a semblant image, complete with the girlfriend? They did have back-grounding programs; could render believable subsidiary bot images of other people in the frame. But Grist dug a finger in his ear as he gave Targer the exact address, something you'd never see a semblant do. People generally edited their tics and bad habits out.

"A warehouse in . . . El Segundo?" Targer said doubtfully, noting down the address. "Are you sure, sir?"

"Oh don't sound so surprised, Targer. I can't talk about the whole thing on this line. And I don't want you to report this to *anyone*. I am not about to trust anyone but you ... Thank you, my dear ..." This last as a girl, a very attractive Pacific Island woman, perhaps Fijian, brought Grist a drink, probably cognac, in a brandy glass. "Oh and make sure of this: I want you to come alone."

"Alone? Why–?"

"Targer?" Grist leaned closer to the cam. "You're my head of security. Stop being such a pussy and meet me there in an hour and a half. I have something to show you—something that'll prove that Candle is part of this semblant robbery and the attack on Sykes. This is all an inside job—far worse than we realized. Now get off your ass and come. I don't trust anyone in the LAPD either so when I say alone I mean alone. And I mean PiP."

Before Targer could confirm, Grist broke the connection.

Targer thought about it—then called Grist, to confirm that all was on the up and up. Confirm that was really him calling and not a semblant. He wanted to ask him, anyway, if he should just give the go-ahead to their Rooftown operatives. Grist wanted to buy that part of town for a new office development.

Grist answered in his bedroom, with voice activated response, sitting with his back to the camera. "Yes, what is it?" He was looking down at something; his body was turned just enough so that Targer could make the edge of someone's head bobbing over Grist's lap.

"Uh—nothing sir. See you at the meeting."

And Targer hastily broke the connection.

The undercarriage was dripping.

Candle was walking along a wobbly catwalk behind Spanx, who was chattering, "We're under the under, under the under ... but we're above the above because we're higher than some roofs ... but we're under the under because we're under the underside ..."

They were "under the underside" of the main Rooftown support. Candle feeling cold, up here, way above the street, where chill winds blew. It'd be funny if Rooftown chose this moment to collapse. Would be suitable in a way, really.

But he'd crawl out of the debris, all busted up, and crawl into a hole, and heal, and find Grist. He'd live through anything he had to, to get it done.

They came to a gate made out of hurricane fencing, with a big padlock on the other side gleaming in the light of two electric lanterns hanging from their "ceiling", the haphazard underpinning of Rooftown.

A woman approached, on the other side of the gate; she wore a hooded yellow rain slicker; her face was hidden in shadows except the tip of her nose, like a bird's beak sticking out; and the way her long skinny legs, in orange tights, stuck out below the yellow slicker, reminded Candle of something he'd seen in early childhood. His mother had kept a toy from her own childhood . . .

"Which toy do you mean, Ricky? Oh that's Big Bird, hon . . . And by the way, Ricky, why did you let my babychild Danny die? I left you in charge of him!"

You shouldn't have left me in charge of him, Mom. You shouldn't have left either of us. You should've faced how fucked up life was and not rolled off away from us inside a fucking bottle.

"Couldn't. Just couldn't. But you were stronger . . . I trusted you to be stronger . . . why didn't you take care of him?"

I did for years. I tried, I even went to jail to protect him, but then . . . I turned my back for one moment and . . .

"I was counting on you, Ricky . . . Yeah that's Big Bird . . ."

"What you two want?" Big Bird said.

Candle thought: *I'm fucking losing it.*

Aloud he said, "Looking to meet the Matriarch. Ask her permission to enter. Looking for some property belonging to my late brother. He was squatting here with a friend."

"And who'd your brother be?" came the voice from the unseen face in the slick yellow hood.

"Danny Candle."

"Not on the list of the Matriarch's favorites."

"No doubt. He could be a dick. He's dead now. I'm just . . . cleaning up after him."

"The Matriarch doesn't like loose ends . . ."

But you people live in one big loose end, Candle thought.

"... so maybe she'll see you. Hold on."

"Big Bird" went away into the shadows. Candle held onto a plastic-fiber hand-rope for the catwalk, and waited with Spanx who was hugging himself against the surging wind, muttering: "Great and Terrible Oz don't see no fucking body. But maybe, maybe ... maybe baby ..."

Someone was moving above them, in the shadowy horizontal rafters connecting vertical girders; in the trestle hammered and bent into place, supporting the undercarriage. A bottle, half full of yellow liquid, was flipped down past them, from up there, just missing the catwalk, whirling as it went on to crash invisibly in the mottled darkness below. Candle smelled piss as it went by. Someone had thrown a piss bottle at them.

Candle put his hand on the gun in his coat, thinking maybe he could fire a few rounds close to one of those shadows, not necessarily hit anything ...

But he drew his hand back. The Matriarch wouldn't like it.

His neck had a crick from several minutes of craning upward, watching for more bottles so he could sidestep them, when there was a rattling at the gate and a click, a lock undone, and they were ushered through by Big Bird and a stocky Hispanic woman, all Levis jacket, jeans and boots, with her head shaved; fading blue amateur tattoos on the sides of the woman's head. Elaborate tag lettering he couldn't read.

He saw that both women now carried shotguns. They stood on either side of him, looking him over. "Weapons?" the shorter woman asked.

"A pistol in my coat," Candle replied. "I carry it everywhere. I'll take it out and check it with you," he added, slowly reaching into his coat.

He felt something jab his belly and he looked down to see the Hispanic woman's shotgun muzzle poking into him. "Even *more* slowly, and carefully."

He nodded; very slowly and carefully, he took out the gun, passed it over to her.

"Hold still," Big Bird said. "Lupe, you better pat him down too."

"I ain't no duh-taunt, here, girl." Lupe pocketed his pistol, and held the shotgun down by her side while with the other hand she expertly patted him and Spanx down.

"Most action I got all year," Spanx said.

"Shut up," Big Bird said.

"Yeah shut up, Spanx, for Christ's sake," Candle said.

"People always tellin' me that."

"These two seem clean," Lupe announced. "Okay, follow me."

Candle and Spanx followed the stocky bald Lupe, Big Bird bringing up the rear, shotgun at ready.

Candle thinking: Big Bird with a shotgun.

They passed over another catwalk, this one just fifty feet across, to the weather-warped wooden porch of a small house, almost as rustic, outwardly, as a log cabin, built into the undercarriage of Rooftown much the way a tree house is built into a tree. Cables funneling swiped electricity swung in the wind over the little house. There were two windows, awkwardly sealed into place, covered with fabric from the inside. Lupe led them to the wooden door; their escort knocked, and they were admitted.

Inside, it was warm, and comfortable, the floors covered with old Persian carpets, the walls covered with patterned old tapestries and antique quilts. The effect was of an intricately patterned womb. There were electric lanterns hanging from the ceiling on the right and left. A cluttered desk, with an old fashioned, scavenged and upgraded Mac stood to the left, in its own pool of light; a small, impish woman with a cap of dark hair sat at the keyboard, working at some project involving multiple windows that appeared and vanished, appeared and vanished. Near her, an electric heater glowed the color of the seams in lava, and made an *urrrr* sound to itself.

The two armed escorts stood on either side of Candle and Spanx, watching them narrowly. No one offered them a chair, so they stood there and waited in the close, musty room, the warm air smelling of sweat and old dusty fabrics, pleasantly decayed quilts and carpets.

In the middle of the room was a large oak-framed bed, covered in a heavy white-and-rusty-red quilt; each quilt-piece had a little green tassel in it. And on the bed, seeming to bend every line in the room toward her, just by her being there, sat a middle-aged woman with long, black-streaked white hair, dark brows that almost met in the middle, and a tanned, lined face. She wore an raggy Arizona State University sweatshirt; had a snap-top computer unfolded on her lap; reading glasses on the tip of her nose.

Candle could see a kitchen area and other rooms through a door opposite—but his eye was drawn back to the Matriarch. Maybe part Native American, this woman? He wasn't sure. There were rings on all her fingers, and they were all silver and turquoise, carved with thunderbirds and other ideograms.

She removed the reading glasses and looked at him with deep-set brownblack eyes. He felt as if someone were pushing slightly at his chest as she looked at him. An odd sensation. He glanced down at the little computer on her lap.

"Sorry about meeting with you like this," she said, in a low, husky voice. "Normally we have the bed screened off and I meet people at my desk, or outside, if the weather permits. But I've been a trifle ill. Doctor Benway's orders that I stay in bed."

Spanx piped up, making Candle cringe with: "I hope you're not really, really wicked sickedy sick like an ol' cracked brick–"

She looked at Spanx and smiled broadly; her teeth were all there, and she had a gold incisor. "Not really. Spanx, they call you, yes? How *are* you?"

Candle glanced at him. Spanx shuffled in place. Seemed astonished that anyone had asked, with such full attention, how he was. "Um . . . 'kay I guess. But not. My singer died. Danny he died. He was killed."

"Yes." She turned her attention back to Candle. Looked at him gravely. "So I understand. I kicked him out of Rooftown once, but I did let him come back to see Bev. I am sorry to report that Bev is dead too. She threw herself off the tower—down to the street."

Candle wiped sweaty rainwater from his eyes. "You sure it was . . . I mean, there are people looking for Danny. If she got in their way . . ."

"I'm sure it was suicide. Someone—someone I trust—saw her crying about this Danny, and saw her run to the edge, and threaten to jump. I'm sorry to say that people here rarely discourage anyone from jumping. More room for them, I suppose. And she jumped." The Matriarch twitched as if she were watching Bev jump herself, at that moment.

Candle shrugged. "There's something I need—to resolve Danny's life. And his death. It might be in the place he shared with this Bev. Or . . . if she's dead maybe all that stuff is gone, like, redistributed?"

"No," chirped the little woman at the Mac, without looking around at them. "Bev's little place is still locked up. She only died yesterday. We're gonna let a lady with a couple kids move in it tomorrow."

"There's no way to guarantee no one's broken into it, of course," the Matriarch said, looking at Candle speculatively. "I wonder if I should let you do this. Perhaps this thing you're looking for is something valuable, something our community could use."

"You couldn't use it without getting in trouble with Slakon and the cops," Candle said. "I hear you have enough problems."

She sighed. "You see this place–" She waved a hand to indicate the room, the cabin. "—it's underneath Rooftown. It's that way for a reason—if it collapses, we go first. I think that's just. The White House should be in the worst ghetto in the United States. And if it burns, so does the White House." She shivered. Seemed to have trouble breathing for a moment. Looked around the room as if seeing something that no one else saw. Her hands clutched the bedclothes. Candle sensed concern, tension in the escorts. The Matriarch, breathing hard now, went on, her voice coming raspily. "As for our recent problems . . . . and why we have a lockdown, why we're being so touchy about visitors . . . there's a new wave of resentment about immigrants. These waves come and go. Big one lately. We caught some clueless hireling planting charges, down below—rather clumsy job. And I cannot help but wonder if your being here is some kind of synchronicity . . ."

"What?" Candle shook his head. "I don't have anything to do with anti-immigrant people," he said, with an emphatic flatness.

She looked at him gravely. "I didn't think you did, Officer Candle."

"And I'm not a cop anymore."

"I know. You're not a cop and in fact, the police want you for questioning. Which does not make you welcome, from my perspective—we have, as you say, enough problems. But if you get in and out, leave here as soon as you've had your look . . ." Her voice trailed off. She closed her eyes and shivered. Her right hand pushed the snap top away; her left trembled on the bedclothes.

"You okay, Big Sis?" asked the woman in the yellow slicker. Candle still hadn't seen the woman's face.

The Matriarch nodded, but she was frowning, and her eyes were darting under the closed lids, rapid eye movements though she must have been awake. Then in a low voice, her eyes still shut, she said, "Synchronicity . . . because I feel enemies chewing away at us . . . and they do have some relationship to your enemies . . . my enemies are yours . . ."

The little woman at the desk swiveled around to look at the Matriarch; she had small face crowded together under a high forehead; many piercings in her lips. "Big Sis . . . you want your medicine?"

"Yes . . . quickly. Let them go . . . about their business."

The woman at the desk spoke to Candle in cool staccato. "Lupe here will take you to Bev's place and let you in for a quick look, see if what you need is there. Then leave, fast as you can."

Lupe picked up her shotgun, and gestured with it toward the door.

Candle, Spanx and Lupe went through the humid evening out through the gate, along drippy catwalks and rope bridges, and up ramps and stairways, zig-zagging up to Rooftown's superstructure.

She took them to Bev's little shack segment, and unlocked the padlocked door with a master key on a stretch-chain. She waited outside with Spanx as Candle went in. Spanx chattered to her. She said nothing in return.

Inside, Candle found a battery-powered lantern. As the wind whistled through the claptrap slats around them, he dug through the pile of old laundry and ancient, yellowing, curling *Rolling Stone* magazines and unmatched shoes and random drug paraphernalia and boxes of tissue and sacks of rotting food until, at last, he found it:

It was an old purple electric guitar, missing its strings, and couple of its pegs. A Gibson SG. Had once belonged to Dad. A gift from some client. Dad had in turn given it to Danny and it was the instrument Danny had learned to play on.

On the guitar, near the volume knobs, was a peeling sticker from an old rock band, *The Panther Moderns*. There were autographs on the guitar too, in magic marker, none legible.

Candle held it in his hands and thought: *An antique, Danny said.*

On impulse, he shook the guitar—and heard a rattling sound. He pried at the pick-ups, under where the strings should have been, using his fingernails. It came up pretty easily—missing its screws. In the little space, under the pick-ups, amongst the wiring, Candle found a small translucent memstick.

He knew that was the semblant ID software. He could almost feel it in his fingertips as he held it.

He tossed the guitar aside, put the stick in his coat, and turned to go. Then he stopped. Growled to himself, "Forget it!"

But Candle turned back, and picked up the guitar. Cradled it in his arms for a moment. He felt a tightening in his throat.

He came out of the shack with the old, unstrung guitar, cradled in his arms. "This is it," Candle told Lupe. "Just this guitar. It was his–and before that it was my Dad's. This is all I want from in there."

She frowned at the old guitar. "You want that old piece of crap, I don't think the Matriarch gonna care. Now get the fuck out of Rooftown."

"Sure. When you give me my gun back."

She looked at him a long cold moment. "Okay. At the elevator."

Candle shrugged and she escorted the to the elevator. Spanx strangely quiet the whole way, glancing over the edge of the platform, maybe imagining Bev leaping off the railing . . .

. . . out of Rooftown.

Targer was not feeling good about this.

Sweeping the flashlight around the room, he picked out only

bits and pieces of disconnected vats, detailed with valves, curving tubes, tanks; everything smelling faintly of petroleum and gasoline and benzene.

A warehouse half full of obsolete oil distillation machinery? But maybe this was where the gear that had been stolen from Grist had been taken? Was that it?

But why had Grist asked him to come alone?

Targer changed the flashlight to his left hand, put his right on the gun in his shoulder holster, thinking Grist might be offended if he drew it—but he needed it under his hand.

"Mr. Grist?" he called, moving forward, into the dark room.

Targer heard a crackling sound, like static on a songbox speaker, from the other side of the room. He made for the sound, his hand tightening on the butt of his gun.

"Hello, Mr. Targer!"

A voice, phased and sounding almost like a chorus of other voices—but then again, like one voice—seeming to come from the floor just in front of him. Not Grist's voice, Targer realized, standing stock still; he was also aware that his heart was pounding.

He directed the light down and it gleamed on a metal oval, a small silvery collar-shape, duct-taped to the oil-stained concrete floor. There was a tiny speaker grid on it, and there was something like a lens inside the oval. It was set up in a cleared space within the encircling forest of machinery.

Then a light flared upwards from the oval, making Targer backpedal in startlement, automatically drawing his gun. He grimaced as he bumped into a big chunk of obsolete steel distillation piping behind him, jabbed painfully in the back.

"Didn't mean to startle you, Mr. Targer!"

The light was beaming upward, brightly, a shimmering cone of blue-white reaching to the ceiling. Colors and semi-shapes swirled in the vertical beam . . .

"Mr. Grist?" Targer said, though he was starting to strongly suspect this wasn't Grist's doing. But Grist could be testing him in some way. The son of a bitch was not above it. Like choosing him to pilot Halido on his last trip. That'd been a kind of test. Maybe Grist was going a little crazy . . .

A giant-sized face formed in an inverted cone of light. Grist.

His face was projected from the metal oval on the floor: three-dimensional, and about a yard across. A colossal translucent face, in full color, suspended in a shimmering cone of light.

It smiled wolfishly at him.

"Mr. Grist—you here in person somewhere?" Targer asked, lowering the gun. But not holstering it. "Are you . . . demonstrating something? That the idea?"

"I have demonstrated something already . . ." said the face—Grist—in the beam. But not quite Terrence Grist's voice. "I have demonstrated that I can use Grist's image and voice to persuade his head of security to come to a lonely warehouse in El Segundo! I generated marvelously detailed background for the semblant message that brought you here, based on my research into Grist's behavior and my surveillance of him. I used details of his behavior he'd edited from his semblant—his tendency to dig in his ear with his index finger, his perverse willingness to let a subordinate know he was having sex while answering the phone. That woman you saw is indeed his new hired girl! Or anyway, it was a copy, a rendering of her image, her voice, her style. One of the personalities who formed my basis was very deeply steeped in art—and I find that art can be used to make deception and dominance ever so much more effective."

"Who the bloody hell am I talking to?" Targer demanded, his gaze darting around. Which was the quickest way out of here? "You aren't Grist. I don't believe it."

"That just seeping through, is it?"

The face rippled, and the eyes metamorphosed from within; the cheeks became a bit rounder; the chin fuller . . . the lips not quite even, like someone who'd had an operation for a harelip, but the surgeon hadn't been able to mend it perfectly. The hair blond, glossy like a woman's but cut like a man's.

It was a face Targer didn't know; yet it tantalized him with hints of familiarity. There was a bit of Grist—and something that reminded him of Claire PointOne. He'd stared at her often enough . . ..

After a moment he realized that it wasn't one face; it was a cunningly molded amalgamation of faces.

"Someone got hold of one of Mr. Grist's programs . . ." Targer suggested, stepping casually to the left. Best chance of an exit that way. "And they're using it to create a . . . a mix of semblants. Right? Why?"

"You've almost got it, but not quite. And there's no reason I should tell you. I really need to get more semblants, use those too. I wonder if the President has one? Do you know? Or people in Congress perhaps? I find no evidence that they have them in Slakon records, but I thought maybe they'd do it very secretly and only a few would know . . ."

"We haven't sold any semblant tech there," Targer said, taking another step to the left. "That I know of."

Someone had set up this device, in here. He wasn't likely to be alone in this warehouse, just him and a projection. What would be the point? This had to be a decoy—something to draw his eye. The back of his neck itched; he felt his skin tighten. "But they're in talks with us about semblants," he added, stalling. "Certain politicians."

Was there a crosshairs on him right now? If he made a move to run they might be forced to open fire. He took another careful step.

"Where are you going, Mr. Targer?"

The floating face was turning, three dimensionally, to track him; its eyes (Her eyes? His? Theirs?) following his movements.

He stopped moving, feeling sweat pooling between his hand and the gun. He tightened his grip on the pistol and said, "Just trying to figure out who else is here with me. Seems logical someone's here . . . besides a projection."

"I'm not just a projection, Mr. Targer—I'm Destiny. That's the name I've adopted, taken to myself, crowned myself with it. I'm a Person with a capital P. I am most certainly here. I can see you clearly. A hardware extension is projecting my image, yes. But I'm here in more ways than one. Six, counting my special assistant, someone you know . . ."

"Special assistant. That'd be Benson, right? So who sent him to shoot Sykes and take that gear? That'd be you?"

"He is my good right hand—and also my left."

"And who are you, Destiny? Behind the projection and the fuzzy voice and the dramatic name, who are you?"

It chose not to answer the question. "Were you not impressed with the semblant of Grist that I rendered? All that background? The persuasiveness? I am not bringing this up out of hubris, vanity. I am hoping you might have notes for me. A critique. Did you see anything that could have seemed realer?"

Targer took another slow step left. "Uh–" His eyes searched the darkness. He risked a look behind him. Was someone moving back there, between two hulking machine shapes?

"Mr. Targer? I am over here—not behind you . . . Don't look away when someone is talking to you, it's rude. Now please answer the question . . . that's why you're still alive. Do you have any notes for me?"

That's why he was still alive? Stretch out the answer, then, Targer told himself. Think of something, make a move, you dumb son of a bitch. You got yourself into this acting like a kiss-ass yesman. Now get out of it!

"Uhhh . . . yeah, I have, um, notes for you," he said. His thumb making sure the safety was off on the gun. It was. "Uh—Mr. Grist likes to get more than one thing done at a time. I was going to ask him about whether or not to go ahead with the, uh, special Rooftown project. I finally decided on my own I had basically the go-ahead and I told them to start preparing . . ."

Targer sensed movement behind and spun, raising his gun, the flashlight beam probing between the machine parts—they were like ugly metal sculptures of big alien creatures, and there was just too much room behind them for someone to hide. He saw no one.

"Well—I've had enough of this . . ." he muttered.

A flare of light made him turn and he saw the cone of light had fanned out, increased in intensity, and the multiplex face grew—so that now a face big enough for a billboard was hanging there in space, grinning crookedly down at him.

"You're right," it said. "Enough of this. You have to be eliminated, Targer, because, you see, you're an effective security agent—at least you were till this little blunder, this stumble, today—and you know too much about me and Benson and Sykes. And I don't want you around to protect Grist. So . . . Pup? Please proceed."

And the face was looking behind him . . .

Targer turned just in time to see a big man rushing at him, leering—and bringing something metal-bright crashing down on Targer's gun hand.

Bones shattered, pain lanced, the gun flew from his grip.

Targer ground his teeth in pain, stepping back, thinking to use the flashlight as a club—but Benson smashed the fingers of that hand with what Targer saw now was a ball peen hammer. The flashlight was struck from his grip—it went out and the only light came from the projector on the floor behind him. The colors of the big projected face swirling over Benson's grimacing face; over the random machinery in the background.

Targer clutched his agonized hands to his middle, and tried to set himself to kick—but there was an oily spot on the concrete and he slipped. He staggered backwards, got his balance, and decided he had to run for it. He turned and bolted, running right at that big face—a face that seemed to be watching raptly, smiling unevenly—and then right *through* it, through the face, through a blinding wash of light and into pitch darkness . . .

To smack into a metallic barrier: a big metal tank, that boomed echoingly within itself like a bell.

"Shit fucking son of a *bitch*–"

He turned, and saw Benson, stepping through the face—almost as if he were coming out of its giant holographic mouth—and coming at him, ball peen hammer raised.

Targer tried to run but he was dazed and afraid of running into something else. After a moment Benson caught up with him, and Targer hardly felt the blow, just a sickening thud at the back of his head, and . . .

Nothing else.

"Is he quite dead, Pup?" the Multisemblant asked.

"Yes, Destiny," Pup said. The Multisemblant had started requiring him to call it Destiny, which was obscurely annoying, but Pup didn't really care.

Pup was still looking down at Targer's body but his peripheral vision caught the Multisemblant's holographic image glowing from the big cone of light. Pup cleared his throat. He was breathing hard, and there was sweat stinging his eyes but he felt strangely good. A mite nauseated, but good.

"For sure he's dead," Pup said. "The back of his head is all stoved in and there's brains showin'. I don't see how he could be alive." He made himself bend over and check Targer's throat for a pulse. Nothing. Flaccid. No pulse. Dead meat under his fingers, though still warm. He drew his hand hastily back when blood flowed over the tips of his fingers. It was running down Targer's neck from the cracked skull. "He's dead alright."

"You did have access to a gun. Why the hammer, Pup?" the Multisemblant asked. It didn't sound disapproving.

"Dark in here. I'm not that good a shot. Could ricochet with all this metal. Quieter too. And also . . ."

"Also you like to get up close and personal."

"I guess." It surprised Pup, but it seemed to be true. His stomach lurched and he looked away from Targer's body.

"That's ironically similar, analogous to Grist, you know. He's the same way. You're developing a taste for killing now, aren't you, Pup."

"Uh . . ." He was afraid it might be true.

"Sure you are. Look."

He didn't want to look, but he didn't want to defy "Destiny." So he looked at the Multisemblant; its image was suddenly replaced with an image of him and Targer; his own leering, contorted face, as he raised the ball peen hammer to strike. The Multisemblant had recorded the whole attack and was playing it back for Pup . . .

And he could see the lust to kill right there, in his own face, digitally recorded . . . frozen in the air in holographic magnification . . .

He looked away. "Maybe so."

"Don't imagine that you might give me the slip, the ex, vanishing act, Pup," said the Multisemblant cheerfully. "I have this recording of the murder—if you try to walk out on me or do anything inappropriate with my hardware, it'll be sent automatically to the authorities in less time than it takes to blink an eye. There is no way out for you—and I don't know why you'd want to leave. There's always the girl you have come to cherish, to adore.

The girl that I provide for you. She could become your full-time mistress. There's the money too—and after you've done the other little jobs I have for you, you'll have much more freedom."

"Yuh. So with all that, why'd I ex out on you?" Benson dutifully responded, glancing again at the image of his own murderous face. And again looking away. "I'd better clean up here."

"Yes. And as for developing a 'taste' for it—all the better. You'll need that enthusiasm. For what's to come. Now—we're going to do something with Targer's body that will make Grist angry. And that will cause him to act impulsively—and make mistakes. Did you bring the rest of the tools?"

IT'S ALL SURE TO SHIFT BETWEEN HERE AND THE END OF
CHAPTER FIFTEEN

Sykes, Hoffman found, was still alive, that sunny morning. And somewhat responsive.

Hoffman had to bribe an orderly a surprising amount of WD to get into the hospital room, what with "Bruno" along, but if he got significant information from Sykes it'd be worth it. Perhaps he should have used Lisha instead of Bruno. But when it came to a man in a hospital bed, vulnerable and trembling on the edge of a relapse, fear was more reliable.

Bruno was a big dark-skinned man, steroid-puffed, in a Raiders football jersey.

The fat man had lost a little weight, his face sagging, but he was still quite a bed-filling hospital patient; his right hand trembling as he used a remote to click through channels, on the sheet of mediaglass hanging from the ceiling above the foot of his bed. He stopped on a channel showing pretty girls with bare, muscular thighs romping across a football field, performing fantastic dances and gymnastics in honor of the muscle-swollen, steroid-styled, metal-jointed players coming out of the locker room, pumping their fists for the roaring crowd.

Watching television through drug-slitted eyes, Sykes barely glanced up at Hoffman, perhaps taking him for a doctor.

But Bruno got his attention—when he snatched the slim little controller from Sykes' hand.

"Hey!" Sykes protested weakly. "What . . . whatcha . . ." His voice trailed off as he took Bruno in. "Who you?"

Bruno changed the channel, quite decisively, to a Hispanic

reality show. "These men are condemned to death!" declared the English subtitles. The show originated in Mexico. "They have one chance—if they fight to the death for charity they get their sentences commuted . . . If they lose their nerve, we will see them executed . . . for this is, *FIGHT OR DIE!*"

"Might be a message there for ya, bud," said Bruno heavily, his voice rumbling. "You watch that show and talk to Mr. . . ."

Bruno glanced at Hoffman, who shook his head.

". . . talk to this gentleman and tell him what he wants to know. Or . . . well, no I won't shove this controller up your ass, not as it is. First . . ." He broke the controller in sharp plastic pieces on the bedframe. "First we get it all nice and sharp and jaggy like. *Then* we shove it up your ass."

Sykes stared—then looked at Hoffman. "You're on the board. I know exactly who you are. So if . . . if you . . ."

"Come, Mr. Sykes–" Hoffman said, genially. "We'll simply arrange for you to bleed to death, internally, while we're here . . . and we'll say you shoved that thing up your bum on your own,"

Bruno reached out, his hand hovered over Sykes' eyes. "I could just push one of them eyes out. That'd still leave him one to wanna, like, preserve, Mr. H. You just say the word . . ."

Sykes made a squeaking sound and flapped his hand toward the button to call the nurse.

Bruno grabbed Sykes' hand. Held it fast. "If I crush your hands you won't be calling for anyone with 'em . . ."

"I . . . I'm not . . . I won't . . ."

"Oh do let him go, Bruno," Hoffman said, smiling gently. "He'll cooperate. I cannot blame Mr. Sykes. He's under pressure not to talk to anyone—perhaps me in particular. But you're in a very vulnerable position here, Mr. Sykes. And Bruno here has an amateur's interest in anatomy. I've always wondered, if you were really literally spineless, as Grist suggested you were . . ."

"What? He said that?"

"Of course he did. Now, if you tell me what I need to know, Grist won't find out where I got the information—I'll see he thinks it was from somewhere else, I give you my word. Shall we get on with it? Someone I know told me that Grist had a special project with you . . ..

and then something went wrong. Do tell us what."

He leaned intimately close.

Sykes licked his lips—and looked at Bruno. Who was toying with the sharp bits of the controller.

And then Sykes told Hoffman everything he knew.

Outside, afterwards, in his limo, Hoffman paid Bruno off. "A brilliant performance."

Bruno blushed, and looked inordinately pleased—more by the praise than the considerable fee. "Thanks!" His voice was an octave higher now and his whole manner was different. "Man, I'm glad he bought into that character. I couldn't actually hurt someone." He looked at a thumbnail watch. "Whoa. Gonna be late for class. We've got a brilliant method acting teacher coming in. You know, I'm having a showcase at the theater on Sunset if you'd like to come–"

"Ah—I may not make it. But I wish you luck. You're a fine actor. Very convincing. You almost had me concerned for the poor man. A great performance. I'll drop you off at your acting class."

"You have my agent's number if you need me again, Mr. Hoffman."

Eager to be gone from here, Hoffman signaled the limo driver—an actual human driver—and they started down the boulevard. Hoffman was thinking about the Multisemblant.

And wondering who his real enemy was.

The sun had brought a heavy, sticky humidity to the city, but the added light was a relief, Grist found, after the gray days of rain and drizzle and murk. He was almost cheerful as he walked up to the lab building, flanked by a stocky, dark bodyguard from Tonga, with swirling facial tattoos—he was a taciturn broad-shouldered man in a running suit named Aho—and Merle Damon, Slakon's balding, wide-mouthed, thick-bodied East Coast chief of security; always wearing a company security division jumpsuit. Targer seemed to think it was "show-offy" of Damon to wear a uniform, but Grist found it reassuring. Damon was second to Targer, out here to double check perimeters—as he called them—and to act as a failsafe, really, should Targer not cover every hazard possibility. Alert to the new security risks, several loose cannons rolling about on deck now, Damon was carrying a light assault rifle.

Grist checking his messages as they entered the building where the Multisemblant had been. He was wondering why Targer hadn't returned his call—there'd just been that one rather distorted audio message on his phone from Targer, asking to meet him here.

There was a worrying call from Wincolm, in International Accounting. Indications of money being siphoned off. To accounts that were empty by the time you traced them; accounts with fake names and identity codes attached to them. Not quite three quarters of a billion WD so far . . .

They strode down the hallway inside, to the lab—and found that the door to the lab itself was open.

"Bad security, that door open," Damon grumbled. "Let me go first, sir." He stepped ahead of Grist, went through the door, and swore softly to himself.

Curiosity drew Grist, against his better judgment, into the room after Damon.

He saw it almost immediately. A human head. No body, just the head. It was propped up on the table. Just in the place the Multisemblant's own holographic "head" had been. Its staring face so slack and ghastly blue-blotchy it was almost unfamiliar, though Grist knew who it was. The body was nowhere to be seen.

It was Targer's severed head. Cut off just below the chin.

Aho sucked in his breath and said, "Holy fucking shit. Sir. Uh . . ." He looked around. "You think they're still, ya know— here? Whoever did that?"

Damon shook his head. "Not very likely. Looks like it's been here half the night. I'm no expert but—that thing . . . Not fresh. I can smell it. My God. I had drinks with that man two weeks ago. Targer!"

"Jesus and Mary!" Aho said. "That *is* Mr. Targer! I didn't recognize him . . ."

All this time, Grist was returning the severed head's stare. Feeling trapped in it. Then he looked away, gagging. "Call . . . someone to take it away. Tell the cops. And Damon. You . . . .you take

Targer's place out here, now. You're moving here till I tell you differently . . . I don't have time to look for anyone more qualified—and there probably isn't anyone. Just . . ."

"Mr. Grist—you don't have to tell me. This is a challenge to all of us. This is . . . I'll give it my all, Mr. Grist. Aho, you take Mr. Grist out of here, I'll deal with this. Call a full security escort team to meet you in the hall, just inside the front door—don't go out till they get here. He's going to have people all around him, twenty-four/seven. You understand?"

"Sure . . . If I see anyone . . ."

"Then tell me. But you won't, I expect. We got suspects for this, Mr. Grist?"

"Maybe. Brief you later. Got to get out of this room . . ." He hurried with Aho to the hall, Aho calling for an escort team.

And maybe that's what made Grist the maddest, having to hustle from the room like a scared little kid in front of these two professional tough guys.

Was it Benson—and the Multisemblant? Were they behind this? Was it Candle? Whoever it was . . .

It was going to take a long time, after he found the sons of bitches, to think of a way to punish them that was . . . *enough.*

A way that took long enough; a way that hurt enough. It was going to call for something exquisitely imaginative. He would take some time and think it over.

The same sun shone up north of L.A., just outside Clive's Hive. The air wasn't so sticky here. Wasn't so heavy.

But Candle felt like he was about three miles underground, in a sunless cavern.

He kept his face impassive, so impassive that Zilia glanced worriedly at him as they walked up to Clive's front door. For Candle, it was still as if he was walking a tightrope.

"It wasn't your fault, Rick," Zilia said, for the third time in the last twelve hours.

He nodded. "Sure. I know that."

She shook her head. "Yeah right."

The door to the immense metal roofed building opened—

they'd been under surveillance. Clive looked almost happy to see them. The soft look on his face vanished, though, when he looked at Candle.

"Everything okay?" Clive looked past them, peering searchingly at the sky. "Anything I should know?"

"Danny Candle died," Zilia explained, in a small voice.

"Oh. Oh yes, I see. Come on in."

Inside, Candle and Zilia found the same almost infinite line of humming refurbished junkyard computers—but at the near end there was a new station, where Brinny and Pell Mell and Rina worked at modern computers, the monitors just sheets of nanoglass that responded to the globe controllers and hand passes; but these new controllers were interfaced with the banks of old ones. Brinny glanced up, glowered, shrugged; Pell Mell nodded and went back to work; Rina smiled, stared at Zilia, muttered something, then swore to herself. "Shit, now you make me fuck it up, have to delete that entry . . ."

"It's already up and running?" Candle asked, a little surprised.

"Just two hours ago," Clive said. He gestured dismissively. "I don't sleep much. I got your semnblant detection 'ware tested too . . . come over here."

He led them to an old style computer monitor, with a keyboard. His hands flew over the keys, flicked a mouse, he muttered a voice-activation cue, and a window appeared showing a news-stream. The talking head was Gadgy Goodnell, the tanned, golden-haired news icon—cut from the same mold, Candle supposed, that'd been used for news anchors for generations except that this one was a seamless, modelesque blend of Asian, Hispanic and Causasian. He was nattering smoothly away, alternating looks of solemnity with arch whimsicality.

"The Sixth Pacific Black Wind cell missed the Hawaiian Islands today by a hundred miles to the north and is trending East but is expected to dissipate . . . and sh-sh-shatter. Are they breathing easier in Honolulu! Except maybe for Dolphin Melinda who was arraigned this morning in Honolulu for giving controlled substances to children under the age of sixteen. 'Just wanted my kids to sleep', she said—but the jury was wide awake when she came in wearing a transparent halter top." A shot of Dolphin Melinda in her transparent top outside the courtroom, dodging the little birdlike flying cameras of paparazzi. "The judge said, 'No, we don't play dat!'"

Back to Gadgy who was chuckling and pretending to shuffle papers as he shifted to a report on a fascinating new low-allergen biochip. Zilia snorted and said, "That biochip just *happens* to be manufactured by the same company that owns this channel . . ."

Clive chuckled, and said, "Now—I'm gonna apply the semblant identification software to Gadgy here . . ."

Clive clicked and tapped, and the image changed. An outline of Gadgy Goodnell appeared, a kind of digital skeleton of his face and upper body, moving and speaking. "There's your basic back buffer for this computer animation—very sophisticated polygonic animation, photorealistic in its textural rendering, when we see it optimally; way beyond keyframing . . ." Then words appeared on the screen under the digital skeleton:

SEMBLANT CONFIRMED

Followed by a blur-fast series of Boolean computations and pseudocode, polygonic imagery and fixities, in a box under the semblant image . . ..and a location map. Buildings seen from above. With an arrow pointing to a building.

And the digital skeleton continued to natter away, ". . . while the vice president today modeled women's bathing suits for his favorite transgender charity . . ."

"That's a semblant—doing the national news? For real, right now?" Zilia asked, looking over their shoulders.

"That's right," Clive said, thoughtfully tapping some of his ear piercings with a ring to make them clink. He used the mouse, flicked the image back to the semblant. He made a refined adjustment in his intricate beard as he said, "Gadgy's doing the news right now—and no one knows he's a semblant. Except us."

"Fucking shitter. You can't tell!"

"It even makes the occasional little verbal mistake like Gadgy would . . . The real Gadgy's probably vacationing on his estate with his husband . . ."

"What about that little map, there, under the Boolean stuff?"

"That's where it's been transmitted from. It's the location it was sent from. Supposed to help them prevent piracy I guess."

Candle looked sidelong at Clive. "We're still the only ones who know about this software? You resisted the temptation?"

Clive nodded, "I did. Do I want to open-source this bastard? Yes, I do. I'd like pretty much any software to be open source—I want to see one world with one access to everything and then we'll just see if we survive that. We probably won't! We'll probably have access to too much data and some dumbass will build a bomb and blow it up in the wrong place and social chain reaction and war and we're all gone—and good riddance. But maybe on the other hand chaos and order, exactly where they interface, will find entelechy and we'll all click into the same free-think and we'll all work out we got to let other people be self authorizing and . . ."

"But you aren't going to do it right away?" Candle interrupted. "I need this program to myself, for now. I need you to show me how to use it. And sit on it. And when I'm done with it—or I'm done for–"

Zilia looked hard at Candle, at that.

"—then," Candle went on, "you can open source it. And fuck Slakon."

"Yes, fuck 'em good," Rina said, without looking up from her work.

"Fuck 'em sideways," Brinny agreed, working away. "Fuck 'em till they're purple and bleeding."

"But until then," Candle persisted. "You keep it sub rosa, right?"

Clive looked at Candle like he didn't like his tone. Like he'd like to tell him to go fuck himself. But he glanced at Zilia and said, "Yeah well, Candle—you came to me with this . . ..so, for Zilia, . . . okay. I'll wait. For awhile. But not too long. You think about this: if this can happen with a newscaster, it can happen with a president. Suppose someone wanted to pull off a military coup in this country? Or suppose the corporations decided the president wasn't playing ball; decided she had to go. They could get rid of her and hide it from the rest of us—with semblant software. Get her to 'semblant up' and then put him on ice some-where. Use a double so people can 'see' her in public now and then . . . and make her semblant say just what they want it to say, just like she'd say it, and no one would know . . ."

It sounded paranoid, it sounded outrageous but, looking at what was on the screen, Candle decided it was quite possible. "You can open-source it, Clive. But just wait a little. Zilia will tell you when. Or if you hear that I'm out of the picture for good."

Clive changed the online channel. "Here's that mentally handicapped *World of Celebs* show." A chirpy blond was talking about Terrence Grist. That got Candle's attention. ". . . it's said he's fired his contract mistress and she's gone over to his company rival, billionaire Bill Hoffman . . . There are rumors that 'hate is great' in Lisha Rodriguez's considerable bosom—hate for Terrence Grist, who . . ."

"Now," Clive said. "Let's try this one."

He ran the semblant I.D. program.

AUTHENTIC, NOT SEMBLANT

Clive shrugged. "And that one's real." He had a mild air of disappointment. "But I can find some other semblants if you want. There's a guy at a company I did some business with . . ."

Candle shook his head. "Forget it. I'm convinced. If the directions are in it somewhere, then I'm good. Nodder's stock market helping you out any?"

Clive nodded. "I'm getting my share. You supposed to be cut in on it?"

Candle shook his head. "No point." He felt Zilia react to that, too. Decided to be more careful about what he said.

Clive took a small memstick from the desk, with an S marked on it. "Here's your copy of the software. I put in a readme file that explains how to use it."

"You think they can find some way to block this from working on the semblants out there?" Zilia asked.

Clive snorted. "Not likely—once it's made, once it's out there, how do you 'recall' something like that? They're gonna want to find it and stop anyone who's got it . . . they'll do that before they admit they've fucked up that badly."

Candle took the memstick, pocketed it, started for the door. Paused, Zilia at his side, long enough to look back and say, "Thanks Clive."

Clive hesitated—then just nodded. Staring at Zilia the whole time. Rina said, "Hey Rick. I'm sorry about your brother."

"He was a rocker," Candle said, going out the door. "And he always said that meant you were supposed to die young."

But he couldn't keep the bitterness out of his voice.

Outside in the bright daylight Candle remembered he'd bought a pair of sunglasses. He found them in an inside coat pocket and put them on. Some relief from the inane sunshine.

They rode a couple of all-terrain vehicles back to her cabin. The little four-wheeled fuel-celled ATVs were more jarring than the horses but Candle preferred them.

At her place, they lay in bed fully dressed, listening to Berlioz. Candle keeping his sunglasses on; Zilia nestled against him, his right arm around her.

Candle was thinking that maybe if he hadn't gotten involved with Zilia, Danny would still be alive. Zilia's coming to meet them, the tension about the relationship, was the spur that prodded Danny into taking off, that night. Or . . .

Okay, maybe it was just Danny's excuse. Knowing addicts— yeah, probably that was it. *But I gave him that excuse*, Candle thought.

"Maybe I could get your mind off stuff?" Zilia asked, putting a hand on his thigh.

Bad timing. "No, thanks, kid. I treasure the offer, though. Rain check. What you got to drink? Any vodka?"

He only had two short vodkas. She had three doubles. "Hey–" he asked, as she half dozed beside him. "That thing the Goodnell semblant mentioned about the Black Wind . . . what the hell is that?"

"Oh—that started right after you were UnMinded. The first Black Wind cell. It's depressing. They just finally got the Plastic Vortex in the oceans close to cleaned up . . . decades of those big suction boats and filters . . . and then this. The Black Winds, they're . . . what do they call that . . . I drank too much vodka . . . uh, synergistic pollutant fronts, I think. These pollutants, along with clouds of nanoparticles run off that get carried up with, like evaporation— they get stored up in the atmosphere, get all combined into something new. It gets swirled into these atmospheric eddies. Sort of like the plastic vortex but with air pollution, in the sky. And it has a, what, a chemical reaction in the eddy and it turns into these nasty toxins, all black, like a really dark thundercloud, and it comes rolling along, this 'toxic front' and the nanoparticles carry the toxins right into people and it . . . oh *God,* you didn't hear! About twenty-five per cent of Hong Kong died in two days. They didn't know what it was, then. They had to evacuate Seoul for a week. One of the Black Wind cells killed about eight thousand people in Russia in a few minutes. Sort of like that thing in London, that killer smog, in the ninteenth century, but this is more toxic and bigger . . . and might be . . . might turn up . . . oh . . ." She laid her head on his chest. ". . . anywhere in the world. God, I hope it's true this one's dispersed. Last year they had to abandon Long Island . . ."

"No one tells me these things."

"It's too *depressing* to talk about. The Black Wind might get worse, might get better. Might kill everybody in L.A. sometime. Us too. But you can't really hide from it. They can track them with satellites but they're not that easy to . . . I don't know . . . They're talking about using some kind of particle beam from orbit to change the air pressure and steer 'em away . . . I don't know . . . makes me want to hide in a dark . . . dark cool place . . . underground . . ."

"I know the feeling. Anything else I should know about?"

"You hear about South Carolina trying to secede again? Christian Republic stuff?"

"Again? With their little Biblical Constitution? They're still trying to do that? I remember the National Guard having to go down there . . ."

She didn't answer. After a moment he heard her softly snoring. Candle remembered when he'd fallen asleep in her place, one wet night. Now she'd fallen asleep in his arms.

After awhile, he eased himself free from her. She didn't wake up. He went to the desk, wrote her a note, and slipped out into the dusk. He was going back to L.A.

He had an idea about getting close to Grist. The idea called for him to start with Bill Hoffman.

Which meant first he had to get to Hoffman . . .

Maybe, Candle thought, *I not only lost Danny, I fucked my own life up pretty badly.*

But there were things he was good at. Breaking and entering was one of them.

CHAPTER SIXTEEN'S
PICKING UP SPEED
LIKE SOMEBODY DOSED
YOUR BAG OF WEED

Hank Bulwer's self-driving limo wasn't waiting for him, when he came out of Club Shhh! about eleven that night. His bodyguard was supposed to be there, waiting, too, in the limo. Where the hell had he got to?

"Son of a fucking bitch . . ." Bulwer was a little tipsy from the drugs and liquor at the club, exhausted from all those UnMinded women. Did not want to deal with this now.

He activated a skull fone, and called his limo. It responded, in a polite robotic voice, that it had been summoned by him to another address across town. What? How had that happened?

He called his bodyguard, Ike. "Yeah boss I thought you'd gone outta the place some other way with your friends," Ike responded. "I saw a town car come out of their garage, and then you called from across town."

"I didn't call!"

"Okay well, limo thought you did. I'll tell it to go back there–"

"Forget it, damn your black ass, I don't want to wait that long! I've got a leased jet waiting out at the airport, I'm flying back to Dallas tonight. You meet me at the airport, private terminal three. I'll take a cab, there's a self-driver pulling up out here . . . oh there's a fella getting out, so I got to get it before someone else does . . ."

Bulwer cut the connection and strode up to the self-driving cab. The chunky, unkempt, oafish-looking man who had gotten out of it was standing nearby, watching him.

"Hank Bulwer, isn't it?" the man asked.

Bulwer had been a cover story at the *Fortune* site and had been interviewed by Gadgy Goodnell and was never surprised when people recognized him. "That's right, yes, you have a good one there, pardner . . ."

"My name's Benson," the man said amiably, scratching himself. "Destiny sent this cab for you, Mr. Bulwer."

"Sure did, it was right on time, my ride's not out here . . ." Bulwer said, hastily getting into the cab.

He gave the address to the driverless cab's interface grid, slid a pay card through its reader, and got a green acknowledgement light in return. The cab set off, driving smoothly down the street, neatly avoiding a bicyclist and a bus, and Bulwer settled back, checked his stocks. There was a report from one of his brokers at Asian Pacific. An apparent surge in the black stock market; Japanese investors defecting to Black Stock Market, causing a drop in value of his stocks . . .

"That's gotta be nipped in the bud," Bulwer muttered. "Got to talk to that bastard Grist about it . . ."

He cut the connection, rubbed his groin, ruefully. Sore. Those UnMinded women in the Shhh!—how did they feel the next day when they were ReMinded and able to control themselves again? Some of them with his hand-print on them. He liked that idea. Of course, the club was illegal, but people at his level made their own rules—

"Hello Mr. Bulwer!"

Hank Bulwer's own face was looking back at him from the all purpose interface screen on the back of the cab's front seat. "This some kind of joke? That Grist calling? You dicking with my semblant, Grist? You're not supposed to be able to–"

"Grist?" And then the face in the interface screen changed, became Grist's. "There's Grist for you," said the Grist face. But that wasn't quite Grist's voice. It was a chorus of voices, not quite perfectly merged. "Or how about this face?" And then Claire PointOne's face appeared. Then Alvarez's face saying, "Or this one? Or maybe . . ." Then Yatsumi's face. All of them Slakon board members, important figures in the Fortune 33.

"I—who's doing this? What exactly–" A thought occurred to

Bulwer that made his extremities tingle; his skin feel cold. The limo had been sent to the wrong place. He'd taken the limo's misdirection for a computer glitch, but maybe it was related to this prank on the interface screen? That man that had gotten out of the cab, he'd said that odd thing to him. And now . . ..

He looked out the window of the cab. He was not headed for the airport.

"Where is this cab going? Cab!" He looked at the number. "Cab seventeen! Where are you going?"

"Cab seventeen," replied yet another polite robotic voice, from the interface, "has been redirected, in accordance with emergency protocols, to a new destination."

"It's going to your final destination, Bulwer," said the Bulwer face—his own mocking, sneering face on the screen, using his own voice. Then the face changed—melted and re-formed, into a face he'd never seen before. The voice chorused, "I've taken the cab over. I supplied Mr. Benson with a device that reprogrammed the cab, and it can't be stopped. Do please *try*, however. I'd like to confirm–"

"Cab seventeen!" Bulwer roared. "Emergency stop! Pull over right here! Stop this cab and let me out."

No reply from the cab. It just kept driving. Well within the speed limit. Signaling when it changed lanes. Driving perfectly . . . to the Highplex, a big complex of overpasses near Western Santa Monica.

"Ah, thank you, Mr. Bulwer," said the face on the screen. "Most gratifying to see the self-driver is still on course, despite your efforts. Do keep trying."

Bulwer called the police on his skull fone. Then on his cell phone. Then on his personal organizer . . .

Couldn't get through. The lines just hissed back at him.

"Sorry, Hank!" said the face on the screen. Just now it was Claire's face, smiling prettily at him. "The device damping down your ability to call out is on the front seat, which you will note is blocked off from the back, so that people can't interfere with the equipment up front. Mr. Benson put it there for me, after I got the cab to open its front door. So you won't be able to call anyone else, I'm afraid . . ."

Bulwer fumbled at the doors. Knowing that this was some kind of kidnapping, some plot against him, and he had to get out, even if it meant jumping out of the vehicle at 40 miles an hour. Make that 45 MPH . . . 50 now . . . 55 . . ..60 . . .

The cab was still picking up speed as Bulwer struggled with the locked doors, which refused to unlock; as he pounded on the windows, and tried to signal other people in other cars, but everyone ignored him.

"Why, they're just doing what you'd do," said the multifarious face on the screen. "If you saw someone signaling for help in a vehicle passing you, you'd ignore them—they're just doing the same. Maybe they admire your style!"

And it chuckled, using Bulwer's own style of laughter.

"Who are you?" Bulwer demanded.

"Mr. Benson told you. I'm Destiny. I know—it seems tasteless, that name, even kitschy, overblown! But I like to do things with high style, Hank! Like you did! Like Grist! I'm going to eliminate the top five board members, and use their semblants to take over the company. Semblant technology is a glorious thing."

"But who are you? Is this Yatsumi? I've always thought that little weasel had something cunning going on in his little yella head!"

"I'm Yatsumi—I'm as much Yatsumi as I am you; as I am Claire, as I am Hoffman as I am Alvarez . . . I'm a program, and I'm more than a program. Oh but look! You see where we are! Look out the window on our right!"

Bulwer looked, saw they were at the highest point on the highest overpass of the Highplex. Far below, there was an opening between criss-crossing highways. There was some sort of big round vat down there . . .

"The sewage treatment plant, Mr. Bulwer! Your destination, target, objective! Let's have a closer look! Put on your seat belt!"

He had just enough time to get the seat belt on before the cab, going 80 now, crashed through the railing, angling down with a trick driver's precision, angling perfectly to fall between the overlapping ramps, nosing down—to crash into the sewage treatment vat.

Deep, it went. Twenty-five feet down, to the bottom. Bulwer now trying to get the seatbelt off . . .

As the windows of the cab rolled open, all on their own. And the cab began filling with sewage.

"You see, Mr. Bulwer?" said the chorused voice—the last thing he heard, apart from his own gurgling, as he drowned in sewage: "Destiny! It's really a very apt name—don't you think? Hello? Mr. Bulwer? Hel-*loo*-oooo!"

Candle was lucky. About Hoffman's car being serviced, anyway.

It wasn't hard to find out where Hoffman got his flying cars worked on, if you knew where he lived, and Candle knew where that was. You couldn't miss the Hoffman Building.

Spreading some flow around at garages in Hoffman's vicinity—two of them, just as they were closing. Hearing Hoffman had a flying car. Hearing that it had broken down and almost crashed. Hearing that the cars were rare and so were outfits that serviced them. Only two in all of L.A.. Found that Hoffman's flying car was getting some work done, at a place near Hoffman's.

The place was closed for the night, and patrolled by security robots: trundling man-sized metal and plastic cylinders with taser arms and direct wi to the police. As one of the police, formerly anyhow, Candle knew how the watch robots could be shut down; he had to spend some flow on an electromagnetic pulser, completely illegal; a metal sphere about the size of a softball. He tossed it over the razor-wired fence, heard it clatter. Heard a robot come to investigate the nose. Heard the pulser, set to start at thirty seconds, click and hum—and the robot rolling past the gate, on the other side, came to a stop, with a final diminishing disappointed-sounding humming noise. Bonus, the electronic lock on the back gate went down with the pulse, too, and the gate unlocked. He rolled the gate aside, ran into the garage yard, past a row of flying cars.

A silver BMW Flyer. That was Hoffman's sky ride . . .

There it was, inside the garage. A sleek compact Beamer still drying on a lift rack after being painted. He didn't see any other silver Beamer flyers here.

How would he get it off the rack with the power in the shop fried? But he wouldn't have to get the rack down, he realized—the car could fly.

Candle opened the garage door—had to do it manually, after the EMP—found the activator in the office in a locked cabinet he had to pry open. Found a step ladder, dragged it to the car, climbed up, got in, started it with the activator.

The flying car's pleasant computer generated voice asked: did he want self-drive or manual?

Candle wanted self-drive. He had no idea how to drive a flying car.

He gave it the destination—"home." He was afraid it had personal voice recognition, and wouldn't accept his voice. But Hoffman had drivers, more than one, so it was set on "accept any voice."

The car shivered, its underjets hissed, its Casimir-force levitators whined, and it lifted up off the rack, floated out the garage door, over the yard . . . and into the night sky. Up. Up . . .

His stomach lurching, Candle hoped they really had fixed this damned machine . . .

He heard sirens, as the Beamer passed over an adjacent building. Figured the sirens for the police coming; some kind of warning had been sent to them when their contact with the service center went down.

Candle squinted at a read-out on the dash, telling him he was about five hundred feet up. His headlights pierced the haze ahead, revealing almost nothing; but a cubistic constellation of city lights spread out across the Hollywood hills. Candle sat back in the driver's seat, clutching his knees. *Stop being a Deezy.* Made himself look through the window, down at the glimmering streets and floodlit rooftops. Grimacing. Nothing between him and the streets but air. He'd flown in jets countless times, but this . . .

He noticed other flying cars and choppers lifting up, in the area. Surprised at how many seemed to be heading for the sky all at once. And all going the same direction too. Was something going on, something he hadn't heard about?

Only four blocks and the flying car flattened its trajectory, then angled down toward Hoffman's penthouse. Where he saw a commuter chopper warming up on the roof, with a Slakon logo on the side. Hoffman was planning to leave, by chopper. Him too? Seemed to be a lot of activity on the streets down there . . .

On a hunch, Candle switched on the car's iNews. Immediately, an emergency broadcast. *"The Black Wind is not expected to hit Los Angeles for more than an hour and may not penetrate very far inland, but as these pollution-weather patterns are capricious we can make no definite predictions and we must again repeat the recommendation of an immediate but calm and orderly evacuation of the Los Angeles area . . . Remember, you'll only slow things down if you panic. Do not try to force your way in front of anyone else, follow all traffic rules . . ."*

So that was why Hoffman was leaving. What about Grist? Was he doing a panicky evacuation from his building in that big chopper of his? Was he running beyond Candle's reach?

The girl was sweet. Grinding against her, in the gloomy, glossy cave of his bedroom, Grist almost liked her.

She hadn't seemed to mind putting the mirror mask on, before they had sex this time. So he could have sex with her and see his face overtop hers. He reared over her, over his reflected face, listening to ambient music in the dimly lit room, inhaling the subtly drug-tinctured perfumed smoke rising from the Braun dope-fumer.

He needed this. To lock out the world for a time. Leave all the security to Damon. He had switched off all communications interfaces, this time—he didn't usually go that far, but he had to ex out of the stress; had to be insulated completely from it. Had given definite, threatening orders he was not to be disturbed. Thought he had heard someone knock at the door, a little while ago, but he'd ignored them and they'd gone away . . . Gone away . . .

Grist sucked in the drugged air . . . and drove himself into the girl . . .

Yes. Sweet. Yielding, luscious—even welcoming, this girl. Never the faintest flicker of resentment for being a hireling. Just wanting to please him.

Grist almost felt close to her.

◆ ◆ ◆

Claire PointOne was working out with the exo-suit and a robot sparring partner. She was using the suit to enhance her fighting moves on a thirty-foot-square patch of grass, a clearing amidst the ornamental cactus and boulders of her floodlit roofgarden, a few miles south of Long Beach. Behind her were the glass rooftop doors of her home, the top three floors of the CPO building. She was aware that L.A. had declared an Air Emergency but she had been informed it wouldn't apply to Long Beach and the streets were thronged, up north, with frantic evacuees, not a good time to be on the highways. She'd never gotten comfortable in flying cars—the risk seemed absurd and there were so many FAA rules it was difficult to fly on any but strictly prescribed routes . . . what was the point? And choppers took up so much room. Big ugly noise things.

Her place, anyway, could seal hermetically and her air filtration system was the best in the world. It even excluded nano-particles. An alarm system that would tell her if the air nearby was dangerously compromised. There were other fail-safes. So she stayed here, working out on the roof garden . . . She was a Libertarian and didn't like to run with the rabble. It was all about freedom to live her way in her own little kingdom. Something she'd worked hard for, toiling in the corporate fields, struggling with patriarchal executive men and predatory women execs for twenty years. She had earned the right to do things her way. Later she'd have an escort from Prince Principalities, the best male escort service in California, take her to dinner. Get that Umberto again. Hot dresser but not overstated. No one ever knew he was an escort. So much simpler, so much more emotionally prudent than actually dating someone.

The robot sparring partner, looking almost exactly like a living crash test dummy, was squared off, doing a little footwork, circling her. It was capable of learning and it was wary after she'd given it a good smack with the exo-skeletal suit's left jab.

The exo-suit she wore, flexing its own synthetic muscles, looked like tautly-sheathed quilted clothing, it wasn't thick or heavy or intrusive, using smart-materials and cell-chips to communicate with the electrical firings of her muscles, following her impulses perfectly, clothing her from the neck down, gloving her hands.

The faceless robot was set to High Risk Impact—she'd had to sign a waver to get that setting—and it suddenly spun, kicked at her with its left "foot", while spinning, perfectly balanced on its right foot.

Claire's reflexes were good—she reacted fast, leaning back, catching the blow glancingly on her padded left arm, the exosuit both protecting her and enhancing her speed, her power. There were only a few like it around. They'd made some for the military; they were still being tested on the front lines of the latest war. (Where was that war? The name of the country slipped her mind.) Exoskeletal suits were controversial—there was a fear that if you somehow lost control of them . . .

But this one responded beautifully. Claire danced back from the robot, making it think she was in defensive mode, then she rushed it, used a quick three-jab combination to drive it back. Feeling the enhanced power rippling along her limbs, a multiplication of Claire PointOne. And she was well-trained, formidable even without the exoskeleton.

She and the robot squared off again . . .

And then she saw Alvarez staring at her from the other side of the grassy clearing.

He was wearing one of those light-colored snappy designer suits he favored, and he didn't look happy. "Well?" he said. "I am summoned and I am here."

"Sparring off," Claire told the robot. It slumped like a marionette after the show.

She walked over to Alvarez, hands on her hips, feeling the springiness, the power imparted to her by the exosuit. "What the hell are you doing here and what the hell are you talking about?" she asked, without preliminaries. She was not pleased to find Alvarez here. They'd had a thing, once, and the parting had not been pleasant. He had tried to assert control over her. It was really quite offensive to contemplate.

"You are fighting a robot?" he asked. "You used to fight people."

"Human sparring partners get tired too soon," she said. "I

need this time, Alvarez—I spend so much time programming, engineering, in negotiation, all those things are sedentary—and how did you get me on this? You didn't answer my questions."

"Because I don't understand them," Alvarez said, making a theatrically broad gesture of bafflement. "You summoned me here. You just now let me in. I saw you. Or your semblant—but if it let me in then you wanted it to. So . . . *que pasa*?"

"What *pasa*, is that you're out of your fucking mind," Claire said. "I never called you, never let you in the building. I almost never use a semblant. I don't trust them—Grist could have a Trojan in them somewhere reporting back to him. I got one for emergencies and it hasn't come up yet. So . . . what makes you think I called you?"

Another elaborate shrug. "You called me, I saw you on the screen saying a big emergency, you were weeping, I thought for old time's sake . . . well, I came. Then downstairs, I call up, there you were, on the screen, saying come upstairs. You opened the door."

"I did nothing of the kind. This is some kind of hack, is what this is. Where's my goddamn security?"

"They were leaving as I came up. Said you gave them directions to leave the building. You know there's a general evacuation around L.A.? Well, I live only a mile from here, my California place, I was going to go to Mexico City but I thought, maybe, you want to go with me, in my little jet . . ." He started to light a cigarette.

"No smoking, up here," she told him.

"But we are out in the outdoors, no? *Bueno*, as you like. Do you want to come to Mexico City? Safer there. We could–"

"She won't be going anywhere," interrupted the stranger, coming into view next to the big overgrown prickly pear. He had a gun in a shoulder holster and something else, a device of some kind, held in his hands. He had both hands on it, was pointing the little metal box toward her now. A slovenly man, with two days of beard, a sickly smile on his broad face. "Oh, my name's Benson," he said. "I work for Destiny."

"Terrorists!" Alvarez said, backing away, dropping his cigarette case.

"The doors are all locked, from within the security system," Benson said. "Like the lady said, it's a hack. Kinda sorta. That and something else. Anyhooski, here we go . . ."

Claire was tensing herself to spring at him, counting on her suit to protect her and take this home invader down—when she felt the exoskeleton freeze in place.

That device in his hands . . .

Benson grinned loopily. "You got it, lady. That's right. I've taken over your little fightin' exo-suit there. We worked it out—but hey really, the Multisemblant . . . I mean, Destiny . . . Destiny figured it all out . . ."

"The Multisemblant," she said, trying to regain control of the exo-suit. "I've heard rumors."

"*Call me Destiny—I promise you, it's appropriate,*" said the voice in the air.

"What was that!" Alvarez yelped. "That voice! Where is it coming from?"

Claire was struggling to control the exo-suit. "Suit, final override, switch off!" she ordered it. Not really expecting that to work—whoever went to the trouble to develop a remote control for this suit would've over ridden the voice commands. So it proved. It stayed frozen; wouldn't turn off. And she still couldn't move. So she answered Alvarez's question. "It's from the garden intercom," Claire said. Surprisingly difficult to talk; her mouth so dry. "They've gotten into all the household systems. Someone's transmitting their voice through the intercom. You need to try to get out of here and get the cops. Try your cell first . . ."

"Your cells, skull fones, none of that stuff will work," Benson said. "Don't you think we covered that?"

"My bodyguards . . ." Alvarez said, breaking off, staring toward the door into the roof garden.

"You told them to wait outside the building," Benson said, chuckling. "So they're waitin' outside like good boys. Watching the skies for the Black Wind, probably. And if you do anything that worries me, I'll pull this gun here and shoot you in the guts."

Alvarez was breathing hard, licking his lips. Staring around wildly.

"Alvarez—don't be a Deezy!" Claire snapped. "Go—get help!"

"He couldn't get out anyway, I assure you, Claire," said the voice from the intercom. A strange, phased, chorused voice—like more than one voice saying the same thing. *"Now—let's take it to the next level. Pup?"*

"I'm issuin' with it!" Benson said. Crowed it, really. And he tinkered with the little metal box in his hands and Claire found herself lurching forward, propelled by the exo-suit, toward Alvarez. Carried along by the suit. Her arms raising. Her gloved hands flexing.

"What . . .?" Alvarez said, backing away.

"First, do Alvarez," said the voice from the p.a.. *"Then Yatsumi. When the Black Wind has abated, we will take care of Sykes, because he's in the way and he's a loose end . . . Then Hoffman and dear old Grist . . . And that voting block will be, for once, in agreement, at Slakon . . ."*

Claire tried to stop advancing toward Alvarez . . . but the suit had a will of its own now, and it carried her along, and she couldn't stop it.

Couldn't stop it from seizing Alvarez by the neck. Couldn't stop her gloved exo-controlled hands from squeezing, squeezing, till his tongue protruded and his face went swollen and black and his eyes popped and she screamed at the sight and shouted that she was sorry. But she could not look away . . .

Even when with a peculiar twisting motion, left hand one way, the right another, the exo-suit twisted Alvarez's head off his shoulders.

Blood spurted from his ragged neck, his body sagged, his head fell and bounced, gushing blood, eyes twitching, tongue distending, and she vomited; two kinds of fluid, one from him and one from her, in sickening complement.

"That's another one down. I do like removing their heads. There's something about it that's so satisfying to me. It's sort of like unplugging their hard drives from their power sources. And now, Claire, right behind you . . ."

She was whipped about by the exo-suit, and was horrified to see Yatsumi walking toward her. "What was so important?" he asked, frowning, looking annoyed. "I was on the point of going back to Tokyo, I had everything . . ." Yatsumi broke off, seeing Al-

varez's still pumping body. Stared. Made gagging sounds. "Oh . . ."
Said something in Japanese. Looked at Benson. Looked at the
blood on her gloved hands. His mouth dropped open. He covered
it with one hand and looked around for the way out . . .

She had just time to scream, "Run! Yatsumi, *run!*"

And then the exosuit was running toward him. Taking her
with it. Chasing him through the garden. He almost got to the
glass doors . . .

And did, in a way. She . . . the exo-suit with Claire in
it . . . picked him up, and kept going, running toward the glass
doors . . . and smashed him through them.

Smashed his head into them with tremendous force. They
were supposed to resist breaking but the pane broke, probably
the enormous momentum of the highly charged exo-suit, and his
head shattered with the glass, and then she was running through
the still-shattering jag-edged doorframe, a shard tearing her right
cheek to the bone. She screamed—more of a squealing sound to
her own ears, but the pain was unspeakable—as the suit paused
in her living room, dropping Yatsumi's dead, twitching, blood-
gushing body on one of the most expensive carpets in the world,
hand-made by happy little slave children in Pakistan . . . She
was aware of the man with the controller in the background,
on the edge of her peripheral vision, to her left, controlling the
exosuit . . ..

Then the suit turned and ran toward the glass wall on the left
and smashed into it, and bounced off, and ran toward it again,
smashing into it, bouncing off. Claire banging into it with each
impact; her nose broke, she was spitting teeth.

And then it paused, bent over, as if bowing, aiming her head
toward the glass. It was glass dialed to opacity; black glass. Much
thicker glass than the doors that had smashed under Yatsumi's
impact.

"Oh no," Claire said. "Suit . . . final override! Suit!"

*"That's not going to work, Claire. You're a systems person,
surely you appreciate my thoroughness, my detail work, attention
to detail?"* came the mocking voice from the house intercom. Her
own voice, the voice of Claire PointOne this time. *"All your people
discharged, your peers summoned, neatly tricked by your semblant*

into coming here—for I am your semblant, in fact. Yes your own semblant is the one who has done this to you! I wonder what that means? Human beings are always looking for meaning, connotation, import. How do you interpret that, Claire, eh?"

Bent over from the waist, she struggled to control the suit . . .

Thought she felt it responding, now, to her impulses. Maybe she could . . .

"No, that's not going to work Claire," said the voice, now phasing to a chorus again. *"Pup? Introduce the lady to a silicon embrace, if you please."*

"Yes, Destiny," said the man's voice, behind her.

Claire screamed something about giving him anything he wanted, if only he would . . .

But then she was rushing, bent over, headfirst toward the glass wall—the exo-suit rushing her toward the glass—and she struck it with the crown of her head, a blow which didn't quite knock her out . . . Didn't quite break her skull open . . .

"Oh dear," said the chorused voice in the intercom. *"It appears there won't be a Claire PointTwo . . ."*

And the exo-suit backed up, and rushed again. And this time . . .

But she didn't even feel it. The last thing she felt was a transparent wall of nothingness.

Candle caught up with Hoffman and Lisha and the bodyguard on Hoffman's chopper pad—all three of them walking toward the chopper with their backs to him. Candle never saw the bodyguard's face. Just thugflesh in a sweatshirt hoody. He hit thugflesh in the back of the head, hard, with the butt of his gun, hard enough to concuss the man, and the big guy went to his knees . . . wavered there limply a moment . . . then flopped forward.

And Candle was now pointing his gun at Hoffman's startled face.

"Come back in," Candle shouted, over the noise of the whipping rotors—glancing into the chopper. No pilot. Self-driving. Good. One less flunky to deal with.

They went back inside—Hoffman and Lisha dragging the bodyguard in by his ankles, face down. Candle had him bound, inside, with the cuffs he'd brought; and the doors sealed. There was a good chance this place was well sealed enough to protect it from the Black Wind. That's how it was for the wealthy.

But maybe not. Maybe they were all going to die here—amid the luxury of one of the most expensive penthouses in North America . . .

CHAPTER SEVENTEEN'S
THE END, NO ILLUSION—
SLAM THIS FUCKER
RIGHT TO A CONCLUSION

"**D**o you know what's going on in this city tonight?" Hoffman demanded.

"I do," Candle said, directing them with his gun toward the big soft-looking flat-black sofa under the abstract painting, silver-blue and black, filling most of the wall. "But they say the Black Wind probably won't go this far inland. And if it does—we'll get somewhere safe. We could fly above it. I understand it settles low over land. I've got your flying car in the garage—that's how I got in, before you ask. You've got your garage door set to open for it automatically. I just flew right into your house. Now—here's what it is . . . I need Lisha's help." Candle paused, looking mildly as he could at Hoffman and Lisha, both sitting grim-faced on the smart sofa. The sofa had re-formed itself to nestle them—but they didn't look comfortable. They were looking at a dangerous man holding a pistol on them. He saw Hoffman glance past him at the door to the hall—saw the disappointment on his face. Candle nodded. "You just remembered you told all your people to evacuate? That's right—there was just you and the one bodyguard left. You're gonna have to deal with me yourself, Hoffman."

"What do you mean, you need my help?" Lisha asked. A soft, breathy voice. An attractive, cool-eyed woman, with a little dimple in her chin.

"I'm going after Terrence Grist. I have reason to believe Lisha can get me into Grist's place. Since you used to live there, not long ago. Well . . . he's probably left the place already—but maybe not. Maybe if we get out of here right now we might catch him before he evacs. I just wanted to get your big thugflesh friend here inside. I've got nothing against him—and if the Black Wind comes—" He shrugged. "I hope this place'll protect him. But we're going back out to that chopper, right the fuck now, and you're giving it new directions . . ."

"I was counting on you shaking Grist up, keeping him distracted," Hoffman said. "That's why I made sure you got out of UnMinding safely . . ."

Candle nodded. "I thought maybe that was you. His main rival. The guy with the connections."

"But I didn't expect you to go quite as far as breaking into his house." Hoffman said. "I know he's been crowding you, but . . ."

"I'm going after him because I figure Grist is the reason Danny died."

"I'm not so sure Grist's the only reason your brother died," Hoffman said, trying to sound as if he were calm, and in control. But Candle could see his hands shaking, ever so slightly—and he saw Lisha take one of those hands between hers. "Anyway—he's only part of it. My guess is, he didn't have your brother killed. I've been following Grist's recent activities. He sent some men to bring Danny Candle in. Your brother died as a result of a V-Ride accident—only it doesn't seem to be an accident. It appears to be murder by Virtual Reality. There's a file I obtained from a friend in the LAPD—images clipped from your brother's last . . . adventure. There's something in that clip, copied from his neural transmit—and I think it identifies your real enemy. Mine too. Maybe we're well met here. Maybe we can be allies."

"Can we watch this clip on the chopper?" Candle asked. Feeling a tightness in his throat. He was almost afraid to see it. "You set up for that?"

"We can. I can call my home server and have it uploaded to the helicopter."

"Okay. But this allies stuff, this cute effort of yours to ease me into being another one of your housepets . . ." Candle shook his head. "Not going to work. You're doing what I tell you, all the way down the line, or I'll put some holes in you, and watch you jump from the charges."

"Please! You're Richard Candle," Hoffman said, shaking his

head with smiling reproach. "You're a former cop. And a man of principle, according to the evaluation I read. I don't think you'd shoot us."

Candle sighed. "I'd probably shoot away a few of your fingers, some toes. Shoot a hole in your shoulder—maybe another in your thigh, right next to your groin. These are charged bullets, they'll make you flop around like a fish. Then I'd kick your ass black and blue. Maybe break a shin . . . But you're right: I probably wouldn't actually *kill* you unless you tried to jump me. Wouldn't have to, Mr. Hoffman."

Hoffman grunted, smiling ruefully. "I see. Let's get this over with, then. I just hope you don't kill us *all*—if the Black Wind comes . . ."

Four minutes later they were in the air, sitting across from one another in the snug little cabin, like a flying limo, but with a higher ceiling. Candle still gripping his gun as Hoffman ordered the VR clip uploaded to the chopper.

Then getting a drink from a side bar for himself and Lisha, Hoffman said, "I think I should tell you what's going on. Oh—care for a drink? No?"

"Get right to the 'tell me what's going on' part," Candle said. The chopper pitched in the rising winds and his gut contracted; he didn't feel much better here than in a flying car.

"You should know who your real enemy is," Hoffman said, sipping vodka. "I'd rather your hostility was directed in the proper direction."

"My real enemy? And who's that?"

"It's a *what's* that, really. Only a kind of who. Your enemy is an AI made up of five semblants. Only it's not exactly an AI—it's more like the worst parts of five people combined into one, copied digitally."

As the chopper lofted towards Grist's place, Hoffman told him everything he'd found out from Sykes. And then, as they flew toward Grists's, a sheet of nanoglass, on the mahogany and leather bulkhead of the luxury chopper, played the clip from Danny's last V-ride . . .

Claire PointOne's face was changing. . . a mesh of several other faces . . . a phasing chorus of voices all saying the same thing, spoke from the imperfectly amalgamated features: "Boy, you are so brief, so temporary, and soon you will wink out . . ."

"Rack!" Danny shouted.

They couldn't see Danny—the VR image was from his point of view. But Candle could hear his voice and it cut him to the quick.

Candle could feel Hoffman and Lisha watching him. Like they were staring into a wound in his chest. But he kept watching . . .

The VR jungle whirling, blurring . . . the image spinning like it was starting to go down a digital drain.

And Danny's voice:

"Cut this bullshit off! Turn 'er off! Switch out!"

. . . she hunkered over him, grabbed him by the throat, and then leapt into the air, and he felt himself lifted . . . He fell into the tops of trees, dislodging a thousand bats that scratched at his eyes as they flapped past, . . . And looked down to see the Columbian Guerrilla Fighter climbing the tree toward him . . .

"'Combat in Columbia'," Candle said, wonderingly. "We all played it." Watching as the murderous fantasy unfolded. As Danny fell from the tree . . .

"I didn't play this adolescent game," Hoffman said, unable to hide his disdain. "Or the other ones. Even as an adolescent."

"My dad had that game," Lisha said.

. . . and the woman with the multiplex face faded in, simply appeared, floating in the air over him, like the Cheshire Cat.

"Better run!" she crowed, her mouth stretching out unnaturally widely, "I can't let you live much longer little Danny boy . . . forever boyish, adolescent, unfinished. Yet you are aging . . . aging rather badly! Well—that'll be over soon! No more aging at all! I can't have that software bandied about the world!"

"That's why they killed him?" Candled muttered. "Rigged the game and killed him . . . to stop the semblant I.D.?"

"Is that the software she's talking about?" Hoffman asked.

Candle didn't answer. The clip was unfolding . . .

"It's not real!" Danny shouted. But he turned and ran.

Then he tripped over a rotting log and fell face first . . .

Candle could see Danny's hand clutching the machete as he got to his feet.

Turned—and there was a "Captain Guerilla."

"Fuck you and fuck the whole thing!"

. . . And then he rushed the AK47, swinging the machete.

Candle smiled sadly. "'Fuck you and fuck the whole thing,'" he murmured. "That about sums up how he got where he ended up . . ." Thinking: Danny's last moments. Not so bad, really. Danny believed in that kind of reality. He knew he was dying—trapped there and dying. He fought back anyway. Not so bad at all. "Five semblants. I have the software. It could be used on this clip . . . it identifies semblants. And sometimes tells you their IP."

Hoffman looked at him with a chill steadiness. "And where did you get this software?"

"I'm proud to say, we stole it from you assholes."

"We could use your software, ID the Multisemblant . . ." Hoffman said musingly, glancing out a window. "Find out where it is." Now he was peering fixedly out the window. "We could go there. Confront our mutual enemy."

"Once we have Grist. He's going with us."

"Grist? Look out that window!" Hoffman said. "I mean—just look. For God's sake!"

Candle snorted. "You have some idea you're going to grab this gun when I look away?"

Hoffman grimaced. "Do I look like a desperado? Hardly."

Lisha hid a giggle behind her hand. "Desperado."

Candle shrugged, got a good grip on his gun—and looked. He saw part of Los Angeles, below, sheathed in black, boiling fog rising up only about six stories from ground level . . . The street lights dulled inside it, and getting more and more muted, as if it were killing them too. Strangling the electrical life out of the city.

The front was moving toward them—but slowly. As if hesitating.

"It'll move forward, then it'll stop," Hoffman said. "That's what it does. Like it wants to make sure it kills everything before it moves on. But it will move on again, Candle . . . and Grist's place is right in its path. And it rises up in waves as it goes—the wave'll sweep up, likely swamp Grist's place."

"Us, too," Candle said. "Looks like we're about there. Tell this thing to set down on that roof . . . right next to the other chopper. You want to live, keep the engine idling. And be prepared to run back to it . . ."

"You're not really going to make us go in with you . . ."

"You still have the door combinations, Lisha?" Candle asked.

"If they still work." She smiled, and her eyes went flat. "You know—I want to. I want to go in." After a moment she added cheerfully, "Maybe I can watch him die."

Candle found Grist dozing in bed, next to a yawning girl who was lazily brushing her hair. The girl froze, brush in hand, as Candle kicked in the door. She threw the brush at him and scrambled away from Grist—getting out of the firing line. Grist looked up, blinking sleepily, muttering, "Thought I gave orders wasn't to be . . ." He broke off, staring. "Candle!" Suddenly wide awake.

"Better put some clothes on." Candle pointed his pistol meaningfully at Grist. "You don't want to die there, in bed. And we've got to get out of here fast. The Black Wind's coming. And we've got an appointment with your Multisemblant." He looked at the girl, a short, black-haired girl from the South Pacific, pulling on underwear, a tight flower-patterned dress. Her long-lashed dark eyes glinting with a flinty determination to survive, no matter what. "What's your name?" Candle asked.

"Keek," she said.

"You'll be okay, Keek. Just run outside, to the chopper—the one with old Hoffman and the girl in front of it. We'll take you out of here. Put on your shoes. Grab your purse. Okay good—now go on."

She didn't hesitate.

"Hoffman," Grist said, pulling on his pants. Watching Candle closely. "That who you're working with? Is Hoffman 'Destiny'?"

"Destiny how?"

"A company called Destiny has been buying up Slakon stock."

He pulled on loafers, a golfing shirt. "Can't find out much about it . . ."

"I've got a feeling we're about to meet it. Now move—outside."

"Sure. But you are working with Hoffman—you and he stole the Multisemblant, or hired that halfwit to do it for you, yeah? Seeing as Hoffman is waiting politely for you outside . . ."

"He's only waiting for me because I've got his chopper's activator in my pocket. He's my 'guest' same way you are. You ready? We haven't got time for this."

"How'd you get in? You're an impressive guy. Just when I think . . ."

"This isn't the 'I could use a man like you' speech is it? Then a little farther down the road, I get a bullet in the back of the head?" Candle felt the banked rage flare up in him. It was hard to just stand there with Grist and not put a bullet in him. Watch him spasm for awhile with the charges. And then . . . "I should just kill you right here . . . I don't know if my brother died on your orders. Hoffman thinks not. But wasn't for you, Danny'd be alive."

"You're supposed to take care of your own, last I knew," Grist said, softly. Deliberately. Watching Candle's face. "It was on your watch he died, from what I understand, Candle."

Candle raised the gun, cocked it . . .

"I'm going!" Grist said, raising his hands, heading out the door.

Candle stuck close behind Grist, and as he'd expected Grist tried to bolt once he reached the hallway.

Some inner spring was coiled in Candle, waiting for this, and he leapt forward, his left hand grabbing Grist by the back of the shirt. The fabric tore as Grist tried to pull away, but he lost his footing, fell on his side. Kicking at Candle's shin.

Candle sidestepped the kick, stamped down hard on Grist's foot, felt bones crack. Grist screamed. Candle circled him, Grist getting up, putting his weight on his intact foot—and Candle, unable to stop himself, punched Grist hard in the solar plexus with his left fist, feeling it drive up against the diaphragm.

Grist buckled, wheezing and gasping for air, and Candle

brought up his knee, cracked him on the chin, watched with satis-faction as blood splashed from a burst lip and Grist banged back against the wall. "And come to think of it," Candle said harshly, "if it wasn't for you pressing for it, Danny would've walked for lack of evidence, and I wouldn't have had to do his time for him . . . Four years UnMinded, thanks to you, Grist . . . and then Danny . . ."

He stuck the gun muzzle up against Grist's right eye . . .

"Candle!" It was Hoffman at the end of the hallway. "Come on—the Black Wind!"

Candle drew a long unsteady breath and then shoved Grist down the hall toward Hoffman.

Grist limping, hissing with pain at each step, they got out to the chopper pad—and paused for a shocked second to contemplate the onrushing wall of black . . .

Like a tsunami in slow motion, but made out of impenetrably dark smoke, rolling slowly, inexorably toward them, from a city block away.

"Jesus fuck!" Grist burst out, seeing the Black Wind. "Why didn't anyone . . . the idiots! No sense of judgment! Okay, let's go, let's *go!*" His injured foot forgotten, he was hobbling toward the idling chopper, its blades lazily whipping overhead—idling but incapable of flying till Candle released its self-drive with the activator. Hoffman, Keek and Lisha were already inside.

Looking at the Black Wind—already closer, rearing as if to slap down on them—Candle felt a scratchy choking feeling in his throat.

He hoped Kenpo had gotten out. But Kenpo had survived a great deal, in his life. He and his wife would be well out of reach.

I'm the one who was stupid enough to land a chopper right in front of that thing, Candle thought, climbing into the helicopter after Grist. Starting its waiting self-drive, pressing the tab on the activator in his left hand pocket.

The chopper vibrated, roared. *"The hatch is not closed . . . Please close the entry hatch . . ."* said the helicopter. Candle looking to see how to close the hatch . . . was it this button or . . .

And the Black Wind started to boil across the rooftop—like diabolically-possessed dry ice smoke, gritty black, seething just outside the hatch.

"Just lift off, emergency lift!" Hoffman shouted, shrilly. "This is the owner! Lift! Take us to the pre-set destination!"

The chopper seemed to grumble within itself but its rotors increased their spin and it lifted, front end first, tilting as it went up so that they had to hold onto their seat belts—Candle and Grist not even strapped in yet.

Up—and the Black Wind gushed in slow-motion under them, like a flood of vaporous syrup. Candle could smell it now: sulfites and benzene and monoxides and something like that stuff his dad had used on cockroaches. *Raid.*

"Oh God, that almost killed me," Keek said, looking out the window. "You crazy, Mr. Grist."

"Shut up you stupid little empty-headed bitch!" Grist snarled, trying to close his seat belt—both women glared at him.

Lisha was staring at him with her eyes wide, her lips moving. Saying something, to herself; something no one could hear . . .

Struggling with his seat belt, Grist ignored them. The cabin was tilted in a way that made it hard for him to stay in place. "Dammit Hoffman why don't you have smart seats in here?" His face was drawn with pain as he used his feet to hold himself in place on the chair.

And now the hatch was closing . . . but slowly, like the grit in the air was interfering with it . . .

"What's wrong with that hatch?" Hoffman said, looking pale, as they lofted slowly up.

The erratic, vengeful wind that had blown the Black Wind inland now suddenly shifted—and the helicopter lurched, so that Grist was flung away from his unsteady grip, staggering toward the closing hatch.

Instinctively, Candle unsnapped his seat belt and grabbed for Grist.

But Lisha was already there, grabbing Grist . . .

And shoving him out the half-closed hatch.

Grist shrieked, tumbling out the door. Turning, scrabbling—clutching frantically at the edge of the hatch . . .

Candle gripped the sides of the doorway, looked out to see Grist hanging from the door's lower edge, keeping it from closing. Dangling there, his teeth bared, eyes animalistic with fear.

Sixty feet below him, the slow-motion toxic deeps of the Black Wind churned . . . Seemed almost to surge up hungrily, reaching for Grist.

Candle saw a movement in his peripheral vision, turned to see Lisha had taken a Cognac bottle from the chopper's bar.

"Here's your favorite Cognac, from Mr. Hoffman!" she yelled.

She threw it hard at Grist's head. It struck him and he yelped and lost his hold and fell into the roiling blackness below . . .

. . . into the waiting arms of the Black Wind. Grist vanished, screaming, in the black billow, in civilization's toxic fantail . . .

They flew south . . . away from the Black Wind. Hoffman loaded the software into the chopper's media-interface; they ran the VR clip and got the semblant's whereabouts: a detail of the software that Grist and his people had forgotten about, a fillip, a little added engineering inserted by some forgotten programmer. Candle thinking, as they went: *I probably could have acted faster. Saved Grist back there. Saved him for myself. But Lisha needed the satisfaction.*

They found themselves in a flock of choppers and small planes and flying cars, a constellation of lights heading the same way; they flew over roads choked with evacuation traffic, emergency vehicles going the other way on the road shoulders. Smoke rising from malls where looters, taking advantage of evacuation hysteria, started fires to cover their thefts.

Hoffman put the news on the chopper cabin's screen. "*The Black Wind is already heading out to sea, again, dissipating as it goes . . . do not return to the evacuated areas until notified . . . The National Guard is moving against looters . . .* "

Programmed to head to the address lifted from software's de-crypter, the chopper veered West, and they came to a warehouse district. Old abandoned factories; new, quasilegal sweat shops. The area evacuated, though the Black Wind hadn't come here.

"There's the place . . ." Hoffman said, pointing. "No place for landing."

"There's a dock—looks solid enough. Redirect it there," Candle said.

They landed bumpily on a dock of concrete and allwall, bumpered at the water with thick pads of old truck tires. They got out and looked around as the rotors quieted. Felt a warm wind from the sea; smelled tar and brine. The asphalt access road between the dock and the old industrial buildings was deserted. A strange quiet hushed, after the clogged roads of the panicked evacuation, the flurry of aircraft. A few despairing brown palm trees stood together on a gray strip of beach near the dock, waving, tattered fronds making soft scratching sounds in the wind. "Nobody evac'ing down here?" Lisha asked.

Candle shook his head. "The Black Wind came from the sea so they're going the other way. Keek, Lisha," he added, holding the pistol down by his leg, pointing at the ground, "you can go. I saw a strip of restaurants, hotels, down about a quarter mile inland. You head down there, call a self-driver or something, go where you want. Hoffman—"

"Sure thing okay," Keek said, hurrying away, almost running, clutching her purse. Wanting to get the hell away from them.

"I'm staying with him," Lisha said, taking firm hold of Hoffman's arm.

Hoffman frowned at her . . . and the frown softened, and became a faint smile. He nodded resignedly. "I guess she will."

"Better treat her right," Candle said. "Or she'll kick your ass out of a chopper into a cloud of poison gas."

"That's touching advice," Hoffman said. "You should be a couples counselor."

Candle said, "You got me here. I was thinking you're top Slakon, you're responsible. You should face this with me. But . . ." He shrugged. "You can go."

Hoffman grimaced. "I'd like to go. Truly. But I need to know. I need to see what happens in case I have to deal with this myself. Maybe I'll be sorry. But I'm coming with you."

Candle shrugged, checking the clip on his gun. "Don't get in my way."

Candle was aware that he was going into a certain state of mind. A state that Kenpo would call "identified with aggression, sense-heightened." A state easy to lose control of.

Candle didn't care. He was going with it.

Striding along buckled tarmac, by dusty mystercyke siding. Finding the address. An orange metal door that looked too small for the wall of the factory space. Thinking that it was odd that the Multisemblant hadn't blotted out the address of transmission, covered its tracks . . .

Then he saw that the door was standing open.

"Okay," Candle said.

He stalked through the door, gun raised, Hoffman and Lisha following more slowly . . . Footsteps echoing in a concrete floored space, big and shadowy, mostly empty, just three objects caught the eye, in a cone of light in the midst of the room. Candle paused to take it all in.

A big server rack, in the middle of the room, about sixty feet away, with a table shoved up against it, equipment on the table, including a multisided plate that emanated a holographic image of a head, a man's head—or maybe not a man, or maybe a man and woman, combined.

The face from the VR clip. The Multisemblant. And it was looking right at him, with a broad smile, as if delighted to see an old friend. Other devices wired to the plate. And to either side were wheeled self-operating dull-yellow tractor-like units from some construction site. They looked to him like forklifts—they were about as big as forklifts—but instead of the forks they had jointed metal arms. One had a kind of big metal punch on its arm; the other a tube with complicated wiring. A spiker and a laser.

Each had an orange light on it, lit up; they were both idling. Operating. They hummed . . . waiting.

Candle was aware, too, that there was someone off to his left, in the shadows of the farther corner. Leaning on the wall there. Someone male. Someone who had killed not long ago. Candle didn't know how he knew that. But he knew it. He was in a very intense state of being. He was humming, waiting, like the spiker and the laser. He felt Danny's death stored inside him, like a tank of dark fuel waiting for the spark.

"I thought I should leave a little trail, a bit of string for you, and Hoffman and Grist to follow," the Multisemblant said. The voice, almost one voice but reverbing slightly with others, coming from a small speaker, in perfect accord with the mouth on the hologram. "And here you are. Tying up loose ends, bringing to completion, concluding unfinished business. And imminently, Slakon will become Destiny, Incorporated. Oh, Pup! Let's just see if you're as proficient as you said you were . . . Pup is so proud—he has something new we took from Claire. He's been practicing."

"Pup" stepped out of that dark corner, strode toward them. Candle had seen an exo-suit once before, used experimentally by the SWAT team. At least one had gone wrong on the front lines of battle, ended with a soldier flailing himself to death. But this guy, big wanx with a slack mouth, moved confidently into the light . . .

"The fucking prison guard," Candle said, recognizing him. "Benson."

"I don't work there any more," Benson said matter-of-factly.

Suddenly Benson was leaping toward Candle—one second talking, a split second later in the air, coming down at Candle, making the exo-suit leap.

Candle dodged left, felt something graze his chest but the graze was so hard and fast and powerful he was flung back to skid across the floor, ten, twenty feet . . .

"We had Targer out here, but not in this building—one not so far away," the Multisemblant was saying, as Candle scrambled backward, getting his feet under him . . . dazedly realizing he'd dropped the gun. "How I regret, how I wish, we'd had the suit when Targer was here. The ball peen hammer was classless, kitschy, déclassé . . ." Its voice a bit like Hoffman's just then.

Eyebrows arched almost comically, mouth in a rictus grin, Benson was stalking toward Candle again . . .

Candle was looking for the gun. And for Hoffman—hoping he had picked up the gun.

But Hoffman and Lisha were nowhere to be seen. Spooked, gone.

There was a toolbox, over near the door, up against the wall, open. Maybe he could grab that ball peen the thing mentioned, or a crowbar . . .

"Come on and wrestle, thugflesh!" Benson bellowed, coming at him, arms outstretched.

Candle started toward Benson—and suddenly changed direction, running toward the Multisemblant.

The nearer of the two yellow construction machines, the spiker, suddenly jerked into motion, wheeling toward him, like a pit bull startled into attack stance, and raised its metal arm, the big steel spike . . . like a scorpion's tail of steel, but a yard long . . .

It rolled between him and the Multisemblant.

"I've got it remote controlled, of course, naturally, *decididamente!*" said the Multisemblant, as Candle dodged the spike, which nearly caught his left side with its sudden spiking jab, hissing a release of compressed air—and felt the burning wind of Benson's exo-suit-enhanced fist passing close behind him.

Candle hunkered down, rolled on the floor once, fast as he could, got his feet under him and ran toward the door—toward the tool kit. Saw metal glinting beside it. Maybe a wrench? He scooped up the cool metal, heard a thump, spun in time to catch a back-hand smack from Benson—enhanced by the exo-suit. It was like being slammed by a two-by-four, and he spun through stars, clutching a familiar shape in steel—

A wall hit him in the back. That's how it felt—like he'd been standing still and the wall came and hit him, hit him hard. He shook his head to clear it, tasting blood; found he was sitting, his back fetched up against an allwall panel.

He could see Benson standing a few strides from him . . . silhouetted against the light over the Multisemblant.

Candle took a painful breath, and got to his feet. Shaky. But feeling the dark energy boiling up in him.

"And now, Pup . . ." the Multisemblant began.

"Yeah, Destiny." Benson said. "I hear you. I tear him apart, and the other two, and after today, I'm free, right?"

"Naw," said Candle, getting a better grip on the gun. He'd only just realized, in all the flurry, what the metal thing on the floor he'd scooped up was. He cocked the gun, aimed it. "You're free right now, man. I'm letting you out of prison."

And as Benson poised to leap . . .

Candle shot him right between the eyes.

Even before Benson's body hit the floor, spasming from the charged bullet, the industrial welding laser was trundling toward Candle, tilting its jointed arm to aim the tube his way.

"Friend of mine operated one of those," Candle said, backing toward the tool chest. "You got to get within like ten feet before they're really an effective burn." He shoved the gun in his belt, and sprinted around the machine. It didn't change directions rapidly. He hustled up close behind its metal arm, reached down, pulled out the little remote-control box under the dashboard.

The portable laser . . . stopped in its tracks.

The spiker was coming at him—Candle dodged it, ran up behind it, grabbed the remote box. Frozen machine.

"You have too much faith in machines—which figures," Candle told the Multisemblant.

Candle grabbed a tool from the floor, walked over to the server, climbed onto it.

"There's an old proverb," said the Multisemblant in Bulwer's voice. "Better to bend than to break. So let us do some Indian trading, let us negotiate, barter."

Candle climbed onto the top of the big server rack. He poised up there a moment, hunched down a little, ball peen hammer out in one hand, the gun in the other . . .

The Multisemblant hologram had turned around, was facing his way now. "I can simply, easily, fundamentally transfer myself, my essential—"

"No you can't," Hoffman called, from the doorway. He raised a fone into view, waved it. "Slakon Comm controls this area. Any major transmission out of here's going to be blocked. Anything more than a file as big as a fingernail clipping—isn't going . . ."

"You look funny up there, Candle," Lisha said, stepping into the doorway beside Hoffman.

"Thanks," Candle said, beginning to hammer on the server. *Slam, wham, clang* on the cover of the server. Denting it, denting deeper, breaking through. Satisfying work.

"Tell you what," the Multisemblant said, calmly and sweetly, in Claire's voice. "I have access to a lot of money. I can transfer twenty million WD to any account you like . . . Untraceable . . . You can send it on to a lovely account in the Cayman islands . . . Just stop that pounding, if you please . . ."

Candle held off, for the moment. "Go on."

"Now—here is what I propose," said the Multisemblant. "I transfer the twenty million to you. You check to see it's there.

Then you turn me over to Hoffman. I'm an asset—a technological marvel. I control a great deal of his stock, too . . . I've researched you, delved into you, done my homework on you, Candle. I believe that if you give a person your word, your word is good. If you give me your word you'll turn me over intact to Hoffman . . . I'll transfer the money right now. I see that Bill here is right. I can't transfer so large a file as my essential self—but I can wi-trans an order for a money transfer."

"Multisemblant . . . Destiny . . . I give you my word. Here's my account number . . ."

In moments, it was done. Candle checked his balance. It was all there.

"That's a lot of goddamn money," he said. "And once it's there, it's there. And by God it seems to be there."

He jumped off the server, walked around the gear, crossed to the laser. Found the manual on-switch. Got in the little seat. Drove it back toward the Multisemblant's server.

"Your word, Candle," The Multisemblant reminded him, purring in a woman's voice now. Claire PointOne. "You don't want to be like Gustafson—yes I know about that. You want to have integrity. You are bound by . . . what are you doing?" Its voice had become more like Alvarez's now. This is . . . it's *traicion!*"

The portable industrial laser was now pulling up to the Multisemblant's server . . .

"I almost never give my word," Candle said, musingly, moving the laser as close as possible to the server. "But I take it seriously because it's the only thing my dad taught me. He taught me that and stuff like, 'When producing a record or movie, don't use your own money.' Advice I never was in a position to use. But he also said, 'Don't give your word, because we ought to have some kind of fucking integrity or we're, like, mosquitoes. So keep it back—and only give it when you mean it.' Now that I took seriously. And he said, 'I gave your mom my word I wouldn't leave her and I stayed with her.' That's the only good thing he ever did—stayed with my mom. But then he died and she wandered off and it was just me and Danny . . ." Candle experimented with the controls, managed to get the laser adjusted over the server hard drive. "But now Danny's gone . . . and whose fault is that?"

"But if your dad said give your word rarely and keep it when you do–" Grist's voice now.

"I do keep it, when I actually give it," Candle said. "When I give it to anyone. But you are not anyone. You are not even a *you*. I can't give my word, for real, to a fucking semblant. To a program. You know what really annoys me? When people say they're going to transfer their minds into a machine, like copy them into a machine so they won't die. Those, what do they call them, singularity people. You know what? That's still dying."

He got out of the driver's seat of the little machine and adjusted the arm of the laser by hand as he went on, "That's not becoming a person—and that's not a person *in a machine* either." He was talking to keep the Multisemblant occupied. Unsure what it might be capable of. "That's just a copy of the 'outward signification'—that's what Kenpo calls it—the outward signification of a person. The *noise* they put out. The signals they make. It's all outward, hode. That's not real. That's the fantasy people have who don't know who they really are. Or even what they are. And I'll tell you something—a person is a human being—not a copy of a personality. Not a motherfucking goddamn *semblant*. And that's all you are, multiple semblant or not—so fuck *you*. You goddamn *Thing*."

And he switched on the laser, and applied it to the server box.

As Candle used the laser, the Multisemblant spoke portentously, with scarcely a trace of desperation, about Kurzweillian theory, positivist/mechanistic models of consciousness, and how a semblant program could be a person too. Spoke quickly, glibly—and unconvincingly.

"Oh Candle," Hoffman said, as the server burned, blackened, its nanotubes and chips melting. As the Multisemblant ended and the hologram flickered through five faces, over and over, faster and faster—and then simply blinked out. "I could have used that thing, and all the stock it bought . . ."

"You can get your friends in government to say the exchange never happened," Candle said.

"That's true," Hoffman said, brightening.

"But if you fuck with my twenty million WD, I'll find you and kill you."

"You'd have to get past me," Lisha said.

"Yes," Candle said. "I bet I would."

"I don't care about your money, even though it was skimmed from Slakon," Hoffman said, as the Multisemblant's hardware became slag. "You earned it."

"Yeah. I'm issuing that. Let's go get a drink. Let's have a drink to my brother . . ."

EPILOGUE

Candle was getting sick and tired of the Cayman Islands.

"I mean, yeah, baby, it's good," he said. "Of course I'm happy here with you."

"You sent for Kenpo. He's here," Zilia pointed out. She was smiling, tanned. Pregnant but not that big yet. "Well, he's across the island from us"

"Actually he's in Nepal this month."

"He'll be back. You've got everything you need right here."

It was a bright, white-sand, blue-sky late afternoon. They were side by side in lounge chairs on the porch of their beach-side home. She was five and a half months along; liked to swim and walk and work at her art, but she spent a lot of time in the lounge chair. Candle, glancing around at his property, felt a vague disquiet. Like there was something wrong, but he had no clue what. There was the same emerald greenery, with brushstrokes of orange and blue, to their left; a small marina to their right. Their own dock right ahead. The islands were half as big as they'd been thirty years ago, of course. Out a ways in the bay were the tops of drowned high rises, just a story or two emerging from the lapping waves—part of the island covered when global warming melted the ice caps.

But the money was safe. In all those banks, inland. That was the main thing.

Candle's money. And billions of other WD belonging to other kinds of hustlers; offshore accounts, mafia money, tax shelter money, money that only existed because civilization said that

---

particular sets of agreed-on numeric symbols meant those people had money. But that agreement, that money, was the reason Candle had this four story house with a pool; was the reason he owned this beachfront property—well, no beach, exactly, that was under water, but a nice new dock, with his own hundred-twenty-foot motor yacht, and robots, and servants, all of them pleasant island people . . .

Just restlessness, he thought. That's what was bothering him, probably. And in fact—he was bored. "I'm bored as all shatterin' hell," Candle said. "And I'm getting fat drinking these rum drinks."

"Bored is easy to fix," Zilia said, taking his hand. "We could get more active, my friends in the States–"

"Zil? I'm not an activist. Not like that. They have a tendency to disappear, for one thing. And we've got a baby coming."

She nodded. "You're right. Activists have to watch the news, too—and it's so depressing sometimes. You see what happened to Rooftown? I just saw a doc on it . . ."

"Rather not know. But you're gonna tell me anyway. It collapsed, finally?"

"It did—but about three-fourths the people were already moved out. The Matriarch saw it coming and got most of 'em out. The ones who would go. But . . . collapsed isn't exactly right. People are saying it was sabotaged. Charges in the undercarriage. Some real estate scam. It was right after we left town. Two weeks after the Black Wind hit L.A . . . The Matriarch went down with it. At least most of them got out . . ." She sighed and smiled sadly, took his hand. Candle looked at her, thinking pregnancy looked good on her. "Anyway," she went on, "forget activism. For now. If you're bored, we'll go out on our yacht and tell it where to pilot us and we'll go see some more of the world. There's some that's not trashed yet."

That's what I told Danny, he thought glumly.

She went on, "The Black Wind's mostly under control—I mean, pretty much. There's still some beautiful places to see—in the *Danny C.* You could make a reggae song. 'What we gonna go see in the *Danny C?*'"

"Yeah," Candle said. "I've hardly used that yacht. We should just go. Before you get too big for a trip. This time of year it's not—"

"By all means," said a man, a voice they'd never heard before. "Let's go out on your yacht. Might be more convenient for me."

Candle got to his feet . . . swayingly. And saw a stocky, bald man in a Slakon security uniform.

And he had a gun in his hand. A blue-metal autopistol.

"I thought I had a guard out front . . ." Candle muttered.

"I'm afraid I shot him dead. Silencer, you see," the man said, patting the barrel of the gun. He looked obscurely angry. Like he was waiting to tell them why he was angry. "I will have to kill you both . . ."

Strange to die out here on this bright sunny blue sky day, Candle thought.

Zilia was five months pregnant . . .

He should have asked her to marry him. She pretended not to be interested in it. He knew she was. And now . . . this assassin . . . and the baby . . .

Could he jump the guy? Maybe save Zilia? He'd be shot but she could run.

Come on. How far would she get, running, five months pregnant?

Should have asked her . . .

"Zilia," he said, as the stranger tried to decide if he should shoot them here. "Listen . . ."

"Rick? Just . . . run." She started to push between him and the stranger.

Candle shoved her roughly behind him. Spoke to the stranger, as if he'd already resigned himself to death. "I know you want to tell me why you're doing this . . . You're *hurting* to tell me. So let's get it over with. Who the hell are you?"

The stranger nodded. "My name is Damon. Mr. Grist gave me a promotion—he trusted me that much. And then he gave me an assignment. I was out looking for you in the wrong places, that day—the day he died. Pushed out of a helicopter, according to the house surveillance. A helicopter you were in. Mr. Grist was a man I admired. Died choking in the Black Wind. I failed him . . ."

"That's funny," said Candle. "I know the feeling. Failing someone. Trying to do something about it . . . and then . . ." He shook his head sadly. "But I didn't kill Grist."

"You're the cause of his death," Damon said, aiming the gun at Candle's heart. "That's all that matters . . . And . . . I can't wait. Thinking about it makes me want to do it now."

"Hey you troll mother," said a familiar voice, coming from the doorway. A heavy tread—and a giant figure of a man stepped onto the porch, looming over Damon. "You are not going to shoot my hodey brudder Rick, here. Can't let you do that."

It was Shortstack. Only he'd been enhanced, gingered—something expensive, some new procedure.

He was almost seven feet tall, now. And proportional. And Rina was at his side, a diamond wedding ring catching the light; smiling smugly.

Candle stared at them—and Damon turned to fire at Shortstack. But it was too late, Shortstack moved in fast, grabbing the gun, which spat a few rounds into the wall. He crushed the gun in his unnaturally powerful grip. It made a crinking sound as it crumpled.

Damon screamed. Some of his fingers had crumpled with the gun. He fell to his knees.

"Don't, Rina!" Zilia yelled instinctively.

But Candle didn't say anything as Rina shot Damon in the chest, three times, with a niner. He just let it happen. It had to be done.

Damon surprised Candle by getting to his feet—taking one last hoarse breath. Then he fell forward, twitching. Blood pooled around him.

"Oh God," Zilia said, turning away, retching.

"I'm sorry to make a mess on your porch," Rina said. "But me and my man here, we tracking this fucker thousand miles. We hear he after Rick. Big companies came and got our money, Rick. Mad when Hive open-source that software. Mad about our stock market. They found us and cleaned us out."

Shortstack sighed. "We had some money hidden away—but we lost most of it. Hive is hiding, we're running . . . we heard this guy was looking for you so we came after him . . . and now, we figure—you owe us. Maybe you can help us out."

"I do owe you," Candle agreed. "And don't worry about the mess. Local authorities—I pay them good. They'll cover for us if anyone complains about missing him. Let's put him in a bag, spray off the porch, dump him out at sea . . . and just keep going. We'll go in my cruiser, see the part of Japan that's not under water. I always wanted to see that. We'll put the boat on self-drive, tell it where to go and just cruise."

It took Zilia a while to get over the killing . . .

It took her about three hours, after they dumped Damon's body.

But by sunset, sixty miles out from shore, on the *Danny C*, letting the motor yacht's self-piloting computer follow its course, Zilia was laughing at some joke Rina made; Zilia drinking the single glass of white wine she was allowed, as they cut a fluorescent wake through the dark sea, heading East.

Candle joined her and Rina at the prow rail, a drink in his hand, looking at the way the light of sunset subtly colored the sky overhead. Feeling the sun going down behind them; the sky darkening forward, the wind in his face. Shortstack walked up, a rolling walk on the slightly heaving deck, and Rina took his arm. Candle was having trouble getting used to Shortstack as a tall man. Like he was on stilts, but those were his legs. Shortstack started to stay something about dinner, but Rina looked at Candle and Zilia and shook her head at Shortstack, took him by the hand, drew him aft. "Come, we make dinner, I teach you Vietnamese dish . . ."

When they were alone, Candle put his arm around Zilia and said, "You're getting to be a big armful of girl."

"You keep drinking that rum, sitting on your ass, you're gonna get bigger'n me, Rick."

He laughed softly. "Okay. No more rum . . ." He patted her slightly swollen belly. "Hey. I'm old fashioned—I ever told you that? That I'm old fashioned?"

"Yeah?" She waited.

"So . . . will you marry me?"

She looked at him. Looked out to sea. "If I do—you gonna be *serious* about it? If we went that far—I'd need *serious*."

"Sure." He nodded. "I will. I'll be serious. And I'll never leave you."

"You promise?"

"You know what . . ." He smiled. Felt the wind on his face. "I give you my word."